ALSO BY TATE JAMES

HATE

TATE JAMES

Bloom *books*

Copyright © 2020, 2024 by Tate James
Cover and internal design © 2024 by Sourcebooks
Cover design by Antoaneta Georgieva/Sourcebooks
Cover images © Getty Images, PepeLaguarda/Getty Images, allanswart/
Getty Images, Michael Dunning/Getty Images

Published by Bloom Books, an imprint of Sourcebooks
P.O. Box 4410, Naperville, Illinois 60567-4410
(630) 961-3900
sourcebooks.com

Originally self-published in 2020 by Tate James.

Cataloging-in-Publication data is on file with the Library of Congress.

Printed and bound in the United States of America.
PAH 10 9 8 7 6 5 4 3 2

For Megan D'Ath and her beautiful baby, Archer.

CHAPTER 1

I shouldn't be here.

If my father knew…

But I would take those risks to witness this fight. This *fighter*.

Music boomed from the speaker beside me, and the crowd got louder. More frenzied and impatient. Adrenaline pulsed through my veins, pushing my own excitement to such a level that I could barely stay still. I started bouncing lightly on the balls of my feet just to keep from screaming or fainting or something.

A grin curled my lips, and I nodded my head to the familiar tune. "Clichéd choice but could have been worse," I muttered under my breath. "Bodies" by Drowning Pool continued to rage, and I pushed up on my toes, trying to catch a glimpse of one of the reasons we'd skipped out on our shitty Halloween party.

"MK, I don't get it," my best friend, Bree, whined from beside me. Her hands covered her ears, and her delicate face was screwed up like she was in physical pain. "Why are we even here? This is so far from our side of town, it's scary. Like, legit scary. Can we *go* already?"

"What?" I exclaimed, frowning at her and thinking I'd surely just heard her wrong. "We can't leave now; the fight hasn't even started yet!" I needed to yell for her to hear me, and she cringed again. She had reason to. In a crowd dominated mostly by men—big men—Bree and I stood zero chance of even seeing the octagon, let alone the fighters. Or if I was honest, one fighter in particular. So we'd climbed up onto one of the massive industrial generators to get a better view.

The one we'd picked just happened to also have a speaker sitting on it, and the volume of the music was just this side of deafening.

"Babe, we've been here for over an hour," Bree complained. "I'm tired and sober, my feet hurt, and I'm sweating like a bitch. Can we *please* go?" She tried to glare at me, but the whole effect was ruined by the fact that she still had a cat nose and whiskers drawn on her face—not to mention a fluffy tail strapped to her ass.

Not that I could judge. My costume was "sexy witch," but at least I'd been able to ditch my pointed hat. Now I was just wearing a skanky, black lace minidress and patent leather stiletto boots.

It was after midnight on October 31, and we were *supposed* to be at our friend Veronica's annual Halloween party. Yet Bree and I had decided that sneaking out of the party to attend a highly illegal mixed martial arts fight night would be a better idea. Even better still, it was being held in the big top of a long-abandoned amusement park called The Laughing Clown.

Like that wasn't an infinitely better way to spend the night than being hit on by a boy with a Rolex and then spending all of three minutes with him in the backseat of his Bentley.

Yeah, Veronica's parties all sort of ended the same way, and I, for one, was over it.

"Bree, I didn't force you to come with me," I replied, annoyed at her badgering. "You *wanted* to come. Remember?"

Her mouth dropped open in indignation. "Uh, yeah, so you wouldn't get robbed or murdered or something trying to hitchhike your way over the divide! MK, I saved your perky ass, and you know it."

I rolled my eyes at her dramatics. "I was going to Uber, not hitchhike. And West Shadow Grove is not exactly the seventh circle of hell."

Her eyes rounded as she looked out over the crowd gathered to watch the fights. "It may as well be. You know how many people get killed in West Shadow Grove *every day?*"

I narrowed my eyes and called her factual bluff. "I don't, actually. How many?"

"I don't know either," she admitted, "but it's a lot." She nodded at me like that made her statement more convincing, and I laughed.

Whatever else she'd planned to say to convince me to leave was drowned out by the fight commentator. My attention left Bree in a flash, and I strained to see the octagon. Even standing on the generator box for height, we were still far enough away that the view was shitty.

My excitement piqued, bubbling through me like champagne as I twisted my sweaty hands in the stretchy fabric of my dress. The commentator was listing his stats now.

Six foot four, two hundred and two pounds, twenty-three wins, zero draws, zero losses.

Zero losses. This guy was freaking born for MMA.

It wasn't an official fight—quite the opposite. So they didn't elaborate any more than that. There was no mention of his age, his hometown, his training gym…nothing. Not even his name. Only…

"Please give it up for"—the commentator gave a dramatic pause, whipping the crowd into a frenzy—"the mysterious, the undefeated, *The Archer!*" He bellowed the fighter's nickname, and the crowd freaking lost it. Myself included.

"Paranoid" by I Prevail poured from the speaker beside us, and by the time the tall, hooded figure had made his way through the crowd with his team tight around him, my throat was dry and scratchy from yelling. Even from this distance, I trembled with

3

anticipation and randomly pictured what it'd be like to climb him like a tree. Except naked.

"I'm going to guess this is why we came?" Bree asked in a dry voice, wrinkling her nose and making her kitty whiskers twitch. Her costume wasn't as absurd as it could be, since most members of the crowd were in some form of Halloween costume. Even the fighters tonight wore full face masks, and the commentator was dressed as the Grim Reaper.

"You know it is," I shot back, not taking my gaze from the octagon for even a second. I hardly dared blink for fear of missing something.

One of his support team—a guy only a fraction shorter with a similar fighter's physique and a ball cap pulled low over his face—took the robe from his shoulders, and my breath caught in my throat. His back was to us, but every hard surface was decorated with ink. We were too far away to see details, but I knew—from my borderline obsessive stalking—that the biggest tattoo on his back was of a geometric stag shot with arrows. It was how he'd gotten his nickname. The stag represented his star sign: Sagittarius, the Archer.

"Ho-ly shit," Bree gasped, and I knew without looking at her she had suddenly discovered a love for MMA.

"They say he's being scouted for the UFC," I babbled to her, "except they said he has to stop all underground cage matches, and apparently he told them to shove it."

Bree made a sound of acknowledgment, but knowing her, she didn't even know what the UFC was, let alone understand what an incredible achievement that was for a young fighter.

"Shh," I said, even though she hadn't spoken. "It's starting."

In the makeshift octagon, the Archer and his opponent—both wearing nothing but shorts and a plain mask—tapped gloves, and the fight was officially on.

Totally enthralled by the potential of the main event fight, I waited eagerly to see how it was all going to pan out. Would it be an even match of skills and strength, spanning all five rounds? Or would it be a total domination by one fighter? I could only cross my fingers and hope The Archer hadn't grown cocky with his recent successes and ended up KO'd in thirty seconds like Ronda Rousey.

The other guy struck first, impatient and impetuous. Watching the way The Archer blocked his attack, then struck back with a vicious jab to the face and knee to the side, I could already tell it would be over before the end of the first round.

"Damn, he's quick," I commented, while my fighter of choice dodged and weaved, not allowing any contact from his opponent. Each strike he blocked or evaded, he returned threefold, until eventually he had the other guy down on the bloodstained mat.

"Is it over?" Bree asked, gripping my arm.

I shook my head. "Not until one of them taps out or you know"—I shrugged—"gets knocked out."

"Brutal," she breathed, but there was a spark in her eyes that said she was having fun.

The Archer's opponent thrashed around like a fish on a hook, just barely holding back the arm threatening to get under his chin. Once the bigger, tattooed fighter got his forearm under there, it'd be all over for the guy whose nickname I hadn't even listened to.

"Come on, come on," I urged, bouncing slightly in my stupidly high heels. "Come on, Archer. Finish him!"

The struggle continued for a few more moments, and then some huge-headed asshole moved into my line of sight. Something happened, and the crowd roared. I could only imagine Archer had locked down his choke hold.

"Yes!" I exclaimed, craning my neck to try and to see. "Oh come on, *move!*" This was aimed at the guy blocking my view. Not that he could hear me.

The commentator started counting. It would all be over in ten seconds if the other guy didn't tap out before that.

"…three…four…five…"

Frustration clawed at me that I couldn't *see*.

"…six…seven…"

Bang!

Startled and confused, I jerked my attention to Bree at the loud noise. Had a car just backfired? Inside the big top? How the hell was that even possible?

"What was that?" I tried to ask but couldn't hear my own voice. My ears were ringing with a high-pitched sound, and everything else was on mute.

Bree was saying something and tugging on my arm, but I couldn't hear her.

What the fuck is going on?

"MK, come *on!*" Her words finally penetrated the ringing in my ears, and I stumbled as she dragged me down from our elevated position and into the chaos below.

I shook my head, still confused as fuck, until Bree's panicked yell sank in.

"Someone just got shot," she told me. "We need to get the hell out of here. Now."

Several more shots—because holy shit, she was right—rang out in the crowded space, and people scattered like bowling pins.

Bree and I clutched each other's hand as we crouched low and made our way as fast as possible to the exit, but we soon realized there was a whole lot more going on than a lone shooter. Between us and the door, an all-out brawl was happening, with at least thirty people swinging punches and kicks. Blood and fuck knew what else flew everywhere, I just barely dragged Bree out of the way when a burly guy in a leather jacket stumbled back from a punch to his face and would have knocked her over.

"We need to find another way out," I told her, stating the obvious as I searched around for another exit. It was a freaking big top, and there must been almost five hundred people spectating the illegal MMA fight night. The venue had to have loads of other exits. "This way!" I shouted, dragging her behind me as I ducked and weaved through the violent mob.

"MK," my friend exclaimed, tugging on my hand. "Look!"

I followed her shaking finger and saw a puddle of red across the polished concrete floor. A spill of pale-blond hair—the same color mine would be if I hadn't just dyed it hot pink for this costume—and a lifeless hand with chipped nail polish.

"Don't look," I snapped to Bree, yanking on her hand again to get her moving. One girl was already dead, and I sure as shit didn't want to join her.

It only took a few more minutes to get clear of the violent mess inside the big top. The night air held frost, and my teeth chattered as Bree and I hurried away through the dark amusement park.

"Th-that was..." Bree stammered over her words, and I slowed just enough to check that she was okay. Her eyes were wide and haunted, her face pale. She hadn't broken down into hysterical crying yet, so maybe shock was working on our side for once.

If nothing else, it'd hopefully keep her from mentioning why I was so seemingly unaffected by seeing a dead body and all that violence. All that bloodshed.

I locked down the memories of the last dead body I'd seen, stuffing them back into the tiny mental box they'd been in for exactly six years. Halloween was the anniversary of my mom's murder.

"Stay quiet," I whispered to her, my attention on the shadows around us. "We need to get back to your car and away from here."

My best friend, for all her amazing qualities, had zero clue how much danger we were in.

"What's going on, MK?" she demanded, her voice pitched way too loud for my liking.

"Shh!" I placed a hand over her mouth to emphasize my point. We were tucked into the shadows beside a dilapidated sideshow booth, and I frantically searched around us to check that we were alone. "Bree, you need to trust me. That was no random act of violence. Didn't you see the tattoos on those guys brawling? The patches on their jackets?" Her eyes grew even wider above my hand, and her breath came in jerky, panicked gasps. I nodded, confirming what she'd just guessed. "Yeah. Exactly. We're neck deep in the middle of a gang war, and if we don't get the fuck out of here soon…" I trailed off. She knew what I meant. If either gang—the Wraiths or the Reapers—caught us, the consequences didn't bear thinking about. Let's say death would be the easy way out. Bree would probably get ransomed back to her filthy-rich family, but I wouldn't be so lucky. Not because my father couldn't pay but because he'd somehow made an enemy of the Reapers' leader.

Voices came from nearby, laughing guys, and I pulled Bree farther into the shadows until they'd passed us.

"Let's go," I said softly when their chatter faded away.

Bree was right behind me as I started hurrying back toward where we'd parked. More and more people were spilling out of the big top now, so we kept our heads down and tried to blend with a group in costumes. It helped that Bree was still in her sexy-cat outfit and my waist-length hair was hot pink. We just looked like regular girls out for a Halloween party.

I almost let the tension drop from my shoulders around the time we made it halfway through the park, but we couldn't hide with the crowd forever. We'd parked Bree's car in a shed behind the south gate, and everyone else was flowing toward the west one.

Silently, I tugged her hand, and the two of us broke away from the crowd, immediately picking up our pace and hurrying past the broken-down bumper cars.

"This was a bad idea," Bree mumbled, but she stuck close behind me as we jogged—in heels—through the scary-as-fuck park. Why had it all seemed so damn exciting when we'd arrived?

Suddenly it was like we were stuck inside a horror movie and any minute now someone would jump out with a knife or chainsaw or something.

Adrenaline pumping through my veins, I rounded a corner without checking first and ran straight into the back of a guy in a full Beetlejuice costume.

"Shit, sorry," I exclaimed, catching my balance on my stripper-esque stiletto heels.

I made to move past him, but a huge hand circled my upper arm. He stopped me in my tracks at the same time as I saw the guy he'd been talking to…and the large, open bag of cash on the ground between them.

"Uh…" I licked my lips and flicked a look from Beetlejuice to the other man. "Sorry, we'll get out of your way."

I tugged on Bree's hand, ignoring Beetlejuice's grip on my arm as I urged her past me on the outside, away from Beetlejuice's leather jacket–wearing friend. It was dark enough that I couldn't make out what patch he wore, but it didn't really matter. They were both bad fucking news.

"What did you hear?" Beetlejuice demanded, shaking me a bit and getting up in my face. His friend just watched. Uncaring.

"Nothing," I snapped back at him. "We were just getting out of here. Some bad shit is going on in the big top."

Beetlejuice sneered, and the leather-jacketed dude snickered. Like they already knew and were happy about it.

"Let me go," I said, my voice firm. "We didn't see or hear anything, and we honestly don't care. There's already one dead girl in this park, and a whole ton of witnesses. This place will be crawling with cops any second now."

Beetlejuice narrowed his eyes at me, his gaze suspicious before jerking a nod. "You saw *nothing*," he snarled, the warning clear as he released me with a shove. "Dumb bitches." This was muttered to his friend as he dismissed us from his presence.

I walked a few paces, not wanting to run while they could see me, but gave Bree a look that practically screamed *hurry your ass up!*

"Wait." That one word hit me like a lightning bolt, and my whole body tensed, my foot frozen in the air. "Don't I know you?"

It was the other guy speaking, and his deep, *familiar* voice sent chills down my spine. He was closer now; I could feel his intimidating presence looming behind me. He was near enough that I could smell the leather of his jacket. He could simply reach out and break my neck if he wanted to.

Panicked, I made a snap decision.

"Bree, whatever you do, don't stop until you get to the car. I'll meet you there." I said this under my breath, but the glare I gave her silenced any protests she might have. "I mean it," I assured her. "Fucking *run.*"

She gave me a tight nod, her eyes brimming with fear and determination, then kicked off her heels and disappeared into the night.

"Fuck this," Beetlejuice snapped, and his footsteps quickly faded in the opposite direction. But only his. My creepy shadow hadn't budged an inch.

"Yeah," he murmured, his breath stirring the hot-pink strands of my hair. "I thought I recognized that ass. Now what is a girl like you doing in West Shadow Grove, Madison Kate Danvers?"

I didn't run after Bree because I wasn't a fucking idiot. There was no way I'd outrun this guy in what I was wearing. And now that he knew who I was, he wouldn't just stand back while I took off either.

Instead, I did the only thing that came to my mind.

I spun around and punched him right in the face.

CHAPTER 2

Pain exploded in my hand, and I stifled a scream as the guy fell backward with a dumbstruck look on his face. I wouldn't get another opportunity like that, so I'd damn well better not waste it.

"What the fuck!" the guy roared, but he was shouting at shadows because I was long gone.

My heels clicked against the pavement as I ran, and I cursed my choice of footwear for the thousandth time inside my head. Bree had been smart to kick hers off, but my boots would require me losing precious seconds to unzip them and wiggle my feet free.

Footsteps pounded somewhere behind me, and I held my breath, ducking inside the fun house, and then froze. I was safer staying hidden, staying silent, than randomly sprinting through the park.

"Give it up, Little Princess," my pursuer shouted from somewhere way too close. "You're not getting away that easily."

Fury underscored his voice, and fear sank into my bones. I'd escaped because I'd had the element of surprise, but I wouldn't be so lucky a second time.

"Madison Kate," he called out again, closer. "Don't make this harder than it needs to be."

I stayed silent, frozen dead still.

His boots crunched on dead leaves, and I held my breath. He was so close. So freaking close.

Any second now, he would find me. He'd find me and drag me back to the Reapers' clubhouse and…

Panic flooded my system, and I made a dumb decision.

My brain screamed at me not to move, not to give away my hiding place, and to hope that the leader of the Shadow Grove Reapers didn't find me.

But my body reacted like a startled rabbit, so I ran.

A shouted curse came from behind me, but I didn't spare a second to look. I knew who it was, I knew he was chasing me, so why the fuck should I need to look?

Deeper into the fun house I ran, ducking and weaving between obstacles and grotesquely aged mannequins, but still those heavy boots followed.

Something moved ahead in the shadows, and I swallowed the scream of terror clawing at my throat when a spring-loaded clown popped out in my face. I ducked under it and kept going, desperate to locate somewhere to hide, somewhere that Zane D'Ath couldn't find me.

Strong hands grabbed me from the shadows, and a blood-curdling scream spilled out of my throat, only to be muffled by the hand clamped over my mouth.

Instincts kicked in, and I slammed my elbow backward as hard as I could, making my captor grunt with pain, but his grip didn't falter as he dragged me into the shadows. I thrashed, fighting against him but pausing when I heard *his* voice again. Zane.

"I don't have the time or patience for this, Madison Kate," he shouted, his voice echoing but…not coming from behind me. Who the fuck was holding me captive?

My terror kicked up a notch as I realized there was more than one person lurking inside this fun house, and I stomped hard on my captor's instep, attempting to break free. When it didn't work, I tried to slam my heel up into his groin—only to have him trap my ankle between his legs instead.

"What the fuck?" His curse was a muffled whisper, and instead of loosening, his grip around my waist and over my mouth tightened.

"Shut it," someone else whispered, and I damn near leapt out of my skin. Even though the sound was soft, it'd clearly come from a man. So that was three. Three men, all undoubtedly a whole lot bigger and meaner than me.

I was so fucked.

"Keep her silent," the second man breathed, his breath warm on my cheek from how fucking close he stood. They'd dragged me into an area of the fun house that was pitch-black. I couldn't see a fucking thing, and it was taking every inch of my self-control to hold back the bone-shaking fear running through me.

What kind of idiot hides in a fun house when they're terrified of small, dark spaces?

"Easier said than done," the guy holding me whispered back, his voice pitched equally quiet. There was no way Zane would hear them, and I wasn't sure I wanted him to. So far these two hadn't *hurt* me. The same couldn't be said for Zane D'Ath. "Fucking bitch just tried to nail my balls."

Boots scraped over hollow wooden floors farther into the fun house, and I jerked against my captor's grip. Whatever they wanted, it wasn't to safely escort me to Bree's car. I'd take my chances with the demented, moth-eaten clowns and shit.

"Quit it," the guy in front of me growled, and I got the distinct impression he was towering over me. I fucking hated when guys did that. Like their height automatically made them so intimidating.

"Fuck you," I tried to snarl, but it just came out as a few muffled noises, which only served to enrage me. That was good. Anger was good. So much more useful than fear.

"Madison Kate," Zane called out again, clearly not giving up so easily. "I know you're still here. I can practically smell your fear. Where are you hiding, little mouse?"

My anger drained out in an instant, and I practically cowered into the guy holding me. I'd changed my mind. Anyone had to be better than Zane D'Ath. It was no coincidence his surname was literally pronounced *death*.

"Gag her or something," the bossy guy in front of me said, his voice still pitched softly enough that no one but me, my captor, and the skeletons could hear him. "Just do whatever it takes to keep her quiet and out of fucking sight."

A sudden displacement of air and a cool breeze told me he'd moved away from us. Seconds later, a little door opened, illuminating the tiny space we were in, and a broad-shouldered guy in a hoodie squeezed out, back into the main fun house.

He didn't fully close the door behind him, and the light was enough for me to gain my bearings. Grabby hands had pulled me into an area that must have been used by staff and actors and the little door a false panel in the mirror maze.

For a moment, everything was still. The guy holding me seemed to sense I wasn't going for his balls again, and his grip loosened just a fraction, allowing me to put my foot back on the floor for balance.

"You're not going to scream, right?" he asked me, whispering the words directly into my ear. "If you scream, we can't help you. You're on your own."

My spine stiffened, bristling at the implication I needed their help. But…I did. And he'd just said they were trying to help me…

A shadow passed in front of the cracked door, and I sucked in a gasp, swallowing the sound even before my companion tightened his hand over my mouth.

"Just fucking chill, Madison Kate," he said, sounding annoyed as all fuck.

Who the hell was he? Did he know me? Or was he just repeating my name from Zane's taunting?

Inside the mirror maze, shadows seemed to swarm the room, even though I knew they were just reflections of that first one. Or were there two now? Fucking fun house. Why had I decided to hide in a fucking fun house?

"What the fuck are you doing in here?" Zane snarled, addressing shadow one. Or two. Or…fuck, I had no idea. As freaked out as I was, I kept my focus on the maze room. It was either that or acknowledge the tiny space I was being held in. And if I did that…

"Whoa, calm the fuck down," my captor hissed in my ear. I hadn't even noticed that my breathing had spiked to just this side of hyperventilation. But that was what small, dark spaces did to me. *Fuck.*

I tried to focus on that small crack of light, the small promise that I wasn't *stuck*, despite the tall, strong guy holding me. But it wasn't enough. Without the distraction of running for my fucking life, the walls closed in on me and terror clawed at my throat. My airways started to constrict, and my breath came in ragged gasps through my nostrils.

"Shit," my captor cursed. "Hey, hey, stop that; you're going to give us away. Seriously, babe, calm the fuck down." Something in his slightly frantic tone took the sharpest edge off my panic. There was something more going on here.

Turning my head to the side, I tucked my chin against my shoulder and peeled his hand away just enough that I could utter two words.

"I'm claustrophobic," I whispered, my hushed voice drenched in fear and pleading.

With those two words, his hand dropped away from my face so fast it was like I'd imagined the whole thing. Except his muscular forearm was still firm across my middle with his fingers of that hand tight around both my wrists pinned together. There was no mistaking the fact that I was still his captive.

"Fuck, I'm sorry," he told me, sounding genuinely apologetic. "Just stay quiet a few more moments. Just until Zane is gone." His voice was still so quiet, his lips brushing my ear as he spoke. "Trust me, you don't want him catching up with you. Not tonight."

I gave a jerky nod. "I know. Why do you think I was fucking running?"

For all the steely sass in my voice, I was physically shaking. Tremors quaked my whole body, and although I'd been able to calm my breathing since my face was free…I was still in a small-as-fuck closet.

Deep voices rumbled from within the mirror maze, too muffled and quiet to make out their words, but it was Zane and the other guy. Bossy dickhead. They almost sounded…friendly? Familiar at very least.

"Who are you?" I whispered to the guy behind me, trying to distract myself while we waited. "Do we know each other?"

The guy huffed a small laugh, his breath warming my cheek. He shifted his grip on me, and although I was still firmly restrained, I could almost pretend it was an embrace. In fact, I leaned back into him a fraction, seeking some strength where my own was failing.

"Everyone knows you, Madison Kate," he told me, sounding amused and only half answering my question. "I like the new hair by the way. Very eye-catching. Edgy."

I rolled my eyes in the darkness but wasn't surprised by his answer. *Everyone knows you, Madison Kate.* Story of my fucking life, thanks to my father. A major investor and land developer in Shadow Grove and totally pretentious asshole, Samuel Danvers the Fourth had forced me to stand beside him at countless events, parties, and ground breakings—the perfect, dutiful daughter filling in for her tragically deceased mother. What a crock of shit.

"It's temporary," I muttered, referring to my hot-pink hair. I'd planned on wearing a wig for my sexy witch costume, but it'd been itchy, so I'd used a drugstore wash-out hair color instead.

The guy holding me made a small sound of amusement. "Of course it is."

That condescending comment irritated me, but I said nothing. Getting into an argument with this random dude in the back of a fun house while an actual, honest-to-fuck *murderer* was hunting me…just didn't sound like a good idea.

"Are you okay now?" he whispered after a few moments of silence. The sounds from Zane and the other guy had faded away, and I allowed myself a small amount of hope that I'd make it out alive.

I shook my head, clenching my teeth. Just by asking if I was okay, he'd reminded me where we were. With Zane D'Ath somewhere out there on the other side of the door too…it was as close to my nightmares as it came.

The guy holding me shifted his grip again, this time only holding me against him with one arm.

"It won't be much longer," he assured me, his voice soft. With his other hand, the one no longer pinning my wrists together, he trailed his fingers down my bare upper arm. "Just focus on something else." My skin pebbled under his featherlight touch, such a stark contrast to the way he'd held my wrists. He reached my elbow, then started again from my shoulder.

I shivered, but this time it wasn't from fear. "This is your idea of a distraction?" I whispered back, trying and failing not to react. My voice was breathy, and I didn't think it was entirely from my near panic attack. So yeah, it was working.

He didn't reply immediately as his fingers started at my shoulder again, this time toying with a strand of my long, pink hair. His lips touched the side of my neck, ever so lightly, and I damn near jumped out of my stripper boots.

"Shh…" He laughed lightly, then repeated the gesture, kissing my neck more deliberately this time while his fingers continued their teasing path down my arm.

Before I had time to wade through what the actual fuck was happening—or why the hell I was so totally turned on—the little door flew open, and I swallowed a scream.

"What the fuck are you doing?" the tall dude taking up the *entire* door frame snarled. The light was behind him, so he was just one huge shadow.

Somehow I got the feeling that question wasn't aimed at me.

My captor's lips curved into a smile against the side of my neck, but he made no move to create space between us. "What you told me to, bro. Keeping Princess Danvers from screaming." He very deliberately kissed my neck again, then released his tight grip on my waist. "At least not in fear, anyway." His dark chuckle left no mistaking his meaning, and damn if it didn't spark excitement in my belly.

"Fuck's sake," Tall-and-Angry snapped, reaching out and grabbing one of my tender wrists to yank me out of his friend's casual embrace. "Hurry up."

I wobbled on my heels but quickly caught my balance as he dragged me out into the mirror maze. Shadows danced over the reflective surfaces, distorting our multiple reflections in all kinds of scary-ass ways, but he seemed to know exactly where he was going.

"Hold up," the guy behind me called out just as Tall-and-Cranky pushed open a heavy industrial door marked Exit.

"What?" Tall-Dark-and-Shadowed barked, turning back around and giving me the first glimpse of his face. His seriously jaw-droppingly gorgeous face. Black stubble dusted a strong jaw-line, and a fresh bruise decorated one high cheekbone. His ice-blue eyes ran over me with a lightning-fast glance before dismissing me. His attention shifted over my shoulder, and he dropped my wrist.

I turned my head too, taking note of the handsome guy shadowing us. His hair was bleached platinum blond, shaved on the sides and long enough on top to be artfully messy. His green eyes sparkled with mischief, and his lips…those lips that had just been against my skin…

As if reading my thoughts, he reached up and dragged the zipper of his hoodie down, stripping it off to reveal nothing but smooth, tanned skin decorated with detailed ink across his chest and arms.

"Here," he said to me, ignoring his scary, blue-eyed friend. Instead, he draped his hoodie over my shoulders, indicating I should slip my arms in. He then zipped it right up to my chin and pulled the hood up. "That hair is sexy as fuck, but incognito is probably the only way you're making it out of here alive." He shot me a wink, and his friend growled an angry noise.

I bit back a laugh but didn't hesitate when the angry guy pulled me out of the fun house and into the frigid night air. In fact, I was pretty glad for the warm hoodie.

The two guys weren't running, but they were sure as fuck walking fast to get us out of the park. I needed to jog a bit in my cursed stilettos to keep from falling on my face. Blue Eyes had a death grip on my wrist too, so I'd probably just get dragged along like a rag doll.

"Boo!" Someone wearing a bedsheet leapt out into our path, then cackled and ran off to join a handful of other "ghosts" hanging out beside the busted-up old carousel.

The guys with me barely even flinched, but I stumbled and would've damn near kissed the concrete if the angry one hadn't caught me and physically lifted me back onto my feet.

"Watch it," he snapped with a scowl on his sexy face before taking a left and leading us toward the old Ferris wheel.

Anger finally dominated my whirlwind of emotions, and I jerked to a stop, yanking my wrist free of his grip.

"What's your fucking deal?" I snarled back at him. "I didn't ask for your help, and you're acting like I'm some huge burden on you.

Just fuck right off; I can get out of here on my own. Thanks." The last word was shot at the other guy—Green Eyes. I wish I knew their names, but they hadn't even dropped them when speaking to each other.

"You didn't ask for our help?" Blue Eyes growled, getting all up in my personal space and towering over me like a limp-dicked prick. If that was the best he had... "You shouldn't fucking *be* here, Madison Kate. What in the hell were you thinking? Do you have any idea who was just chasing you down? Huh? Do you have any concept of what would happen if the Reapers got their hands on the princess of Shadow Grove? And there wouldn't be a fucking thing your daddy could do about it because you made the dumb-fuck move of coming *here*." His perfect lips twisted in a disgusted scowl, and he ran a hand over his close-cropped, black hair in obvious frustration. His left cheekbone was red and puffy with a shadow of purple welling up underneath. He'd taken a solid punch recently. From Zane?

Green Eyes cleared his throat. "What he means is you didn't ask for our help, but you're damn well getting it. You picked a really crappy night to rebel against your perfect life, Princess." He arched a brow at me, and there was just enough teasing in his voice to stop me from punching him in the teeth.

I shook my head, mentally chastising myself for appreciating how hot these dudes were when I should have been more worried about getting out of the fucking amusement park. And what about Bree? Was she still waiting for me? What if one of Zane's guys had grabbed her?

"I'm going that way," I told the two guys, jerking my thumb in the direction of the south gate. "My friend is waiting."

"No, she's not," a third guy replied, jogging up to us from the way I'd been pointing. He was the same height, maybe an inch shorter than Green Eyes, but still made me feel like a hobbit in comparison. He was also male-model handsome, and I almost swallowed my tongue when he turned his steel-gray eyes on me. "Pretty little brunette chick in a white Merc convertible?" He cocked his head to the side in question, and I nodded. "She's gone."

I frowned. "What? No, Bree wouldn't leave me here without a ride home."

The third guy—I'd call him Gray Eyes just to keep things simple—shrugged and grinned. His long, graceful fingers ruffled his brunette hair, and the moonlight reflected off a piercing in his brow. "I told her you had a ride." His suggestive wink implied a whole different type of ride, and my cheeks flushed. "Besides, cops will be here in about three minutes. Your Bree was smart enough to get the fuck away from the crime scene."

"Huh?" I blinked at him in confusion, but apparently that news was all the other two needed to hear.

Green Eyes dropped a shoulder to my stomach, and before I could utter another protest, my butt was in the air with my head hanging down near his ass. "Sorry, Princess," he said, starting to run with me over his shoulder. "You'll thank us tomorrow when you're back at your preppy, rich-kid school."

"Fuck!" I cursed, resigning myself to what was happening and just wrapping my arms around his bare waist in an attempt to stop my face from bouncing against his butt. His back also had some impressive ink, but I was in altogether the wrong position to appreciate any kind of artistry.

He ran with me through the mess of overgrown paths, stepping effortlessly over debris from fallen-down sideshow booths, and a quick glance showed the other two guys keeping pace on either side of us. Until they weren't.

The distinctive sound of a fight breaking out made me struggle in Green Eyes' grip, but he just smacked my ass and picked up his pace. "Quit it!" he shouted at me. "Don't be a fucking airhead."

His sharp words stilled my struggles, and I raised my head to look back in the direction we'd come. Blue Eyes and the new guy—pretty

21

Gray Eyes—were neck deep in a brutal fistfight with three leather jacket–wearing thugs. Fists flew, blood sprayed, and one of the leather-jacketed assholes pulled a knife from somewhere before Green Eyes abruptly changed directions, cutting them off from view.

"Get on," he ordered, dropping me back to my feet beside a motorcycle. It was a sleek beast, and my stomach flipped with excitement. He swung his leg over, then gave me a look that clearly said to hurry the hell up.

I hesitated a second, but when the other two guys came sprinting toward us, I made a snap decision. They'd kept me safe so far, so...*fuck it.*

My ass hit the seat behind Green Eyes a split second before he revved the engine, and I instinctively wrapped my arms around his waist. Moments later we peeled out of the amusement park and onto the road with the other guys on their own darkly gleaming motorcycles beside us.

I only had a few moments to enjoy the ride, though, before Blue Eyes pulled off the road, indicating we all do the same. He stopped his bike with just his feet on the ground, pulled his phone out of his pocket, and read a message.

Neither of the other guys spoke, just waited patiently while he read the message, then scowled at me.

"What?" I demanded, feeling edgy at being stared at.

His eyes narrowed, and he looked up the road in the direction we'd been heading, clearly thinking.

After a moment, Green Eyes must have felt the awkwardness too. "What do you want to do?" he asked his friend, who swung his attention back to me again.

"Get off," he ordered me. "Wait here; someone will be along to drive you home in a minute."

Anger and indignation flared up in me. "Fuck you," I spat at him. "I'm not a two-year-old. I can sort myself out if you've got better shit to do."

He glared back at me like I was indeed a petulant child. "We do. Now get off the bike; your ride will be here in"—he checked his phone again—"one minute. Let's go."

Furious, I slid off the back of the bike and tugged my minidress back down to cover at least some of my vagina. "I don't need your ride. I can sort one out myself. Thanks for fucking nothing."

Blue Eyes rolled his…uh…blue eyes and revved his bike. "Make smart choices, Madison Kate Danvers." With that, he took off. Back in the direction we'd come. Back toward West Shadow Grove.

"I don't like this," Green Eyes said to Gray Eyes.

The handsome brunette just shrugged, but his frown said he agreed. "He said someone's picking her up; I believe him. Come on, bro; shit must be going down."

Green Eyes just grunted, then gave me a regretful look. "Sorry, Princess. Get home safe, okay?"

I scowled and said nothing, folding my arms over my chest as the two of them followed their dickish friend.

"Fuck their ride," I muttered to myself once they were gone. "I'm perfectly capable of Ubering home."

Ugh. Except Bree had my phone in her bag.

My panic over how to get home was short-lived, though, as right on cue my "ride" turned up. With lights and sirens and everything.

"Hey, I guess you're my ride home?" I asked the police officer who stepped out of the cruiser. I hadn't known what to expect when Blue Eyes said he had it taken care of, but this wasn't it.

The officer's partner exited the vehicle too, and both approached me with a confusing degree of caution.

"Miss, did you just come from The Laughing Clown Amusement Park?" the first officer asked, and I frowned.

"Uh, yeah? I thought…" I trailed off. Saying that I thought they'd been sent to get me by a nameless, beautiful man who'd saved me from a ruthless gang member sounded…stupid.

"Miss, we're going to need you to come with us," the officer stated, and I nodded. "But first, we just need to check your pockets, okay?"

Confused, I nodded. I'd never dealt with police before, not like this, so I had no idea if this was standard procedure. I was at least eighty percent sure they weren't allowed to search me without probable cause, but I was in too much shock to protest.

I raised my arms, allowing the second officer to check my pockets. Or...the pockets of Green Eye's hoodie, seeing as my minidress couldn't hide a Tic Tac it was so tight. His hands lingered longer than they should have, and the wolfish gleam in the first officer's eyes made me all kinds of uneasy.

"Miss, what is this?" the second officer, the handsy one, asked. He held up a single key on a labeled key ring.

I shook my head. "I have no idea. Sorry, it's not my hoodie."

Both officers eyed me with suspicion, and the one holding the key shined his torch on the key ring, then grunted a cold laugh.

"Well, would you look at that," he murmured, handing it to his colleague with a smile. "Seems we've found how they all accessed the park tonight. A Laughing Clown Amusement Park master key."

Blood drained from my face, and dread pooled in my belly. "That's not mine," I quickly told them. "Like I said, this isn't my hoodie."

The first officer smiled a smug grin. "Sure it's not. Don't suppose you have a name before we arrest you?"

I gaped at him. "Arrest—*What?* No, that's not my key; I didn't do anything!" I was panicking now, but the cops looked unimpressed.

"Miss, just tell us your name," the second one suggested, sounding bored even while he unhooked handcuffs from his belt and clipped them over my wrists.

Shock turned me numb. "M-Madison Kate," I said in a hoarse voice. "Madison Kate Danvers."

One cop froze while the other smiled a weird, creepy kind of smile. I had to assume it was because of the power my surname held. Little did I expect the next thing they told me.

"That would be hard," the first cop said, "seeing as Madison Kate Danvers was just murdered inside The Laughing Clown tonight."

CHAPTER 3

Eleven months later...

The luggage carousel chugged and creaked as it rotated in front of me, and I rubbed my tired eyes with a weary hand. I'd been standing there for ages, so my suitcase was probably going to be the last one off. Fantastic.

I reached my arms over my head and stretched, the kinks in my spine protesting. It had been a long flight back to Shadow Grove, and in economy class no less. I shouldn't have been surprised at the low-cost ticket—considering my father had all but disowned me a year earlier—but when I'd found my assigned seat crammed between two large, sweaty, old women, I'd had to swallow a lump of bitterness.

It'd been eight months since I'd left the only home I'd ever known. Eleven months since I'd been charged with a slew of offenses and sentenced for crimes I'd never committed.

Anger curled in my belly, and my lips tightened. Fury had been my constant companion over the time I'd spent living with a distant aunt in a converted Cambodian monastery.

Not that I regretted the time I'd had with her or the work we'd done together for the orphanages there. My father had decided it was better for his public image if I suffered the consequences of my accused actions and had refused to pay my bail. The one grace he'd granted me was that he'd paid off enough officials that my trial was held swiftly and I didn't have to rot in prison for years on end. So after three months in holding at the Shadow Grove county jail while my trial was conducted, it had actually been a welcome relief to be sent halfway across the world and away from the train wreck that was my life.

"Hey," someone said, breaking through my dark thoughts, "you're *her*, aren't you? You're Madison Kate Danvers?" It was a middle-aged woman, her hand resting on a suitcase she'd probably just pulled from the belt. She didn't look angry or accusing, just curious.

I nodded slightly. "That's me." My voice was scratchy and dry from lack of use. I had barely spoken to anyone in weeks. Not since my caregiver, Aunt Marie, had died.

The woman nodded back, pursing her lips thoughtfully. "You got a rough break, kid. Your daddy should be ashamed of how he handled things after Riot Night."

I sucked in a breath, counting to five silently as I controlled the anger that *always* resided inside me. "Yep, he really should."

It wasn't for me to defend my father's actions. He *had* handled things badly. Making an example of his daughter to support his own public relations and business aspirations was the least of his sins. He just hadn't wanted the spotlight on him—again.

The night I'd been arrested—the night of the fight inside The Laughing Clown—the entire town of Shadow Grove had suffered. East *and* West. In the days following, the media had dubbed it Riot Night, thanks to multiple riots, which resulted in millions of dollars of property damage and several deaths. I'd missed most of it, sitting handcuffed in the back of a squad car for the first part of the evening, then locked up in a holding cell for the rest.

That hadn't prevented them labeling me as the "mastermind" behind Shadow Grove's most violent event. It didn't matter how preposterous the charges were; they had intended to make a scapegoat of me.

Apparently the fights between the Reapers and Wraiths at The Laughing Clown had just been the straw that broke the camel's back. They'd been on the brink of war for a long time, and that night, Riot Night, was the detonation point.

"Well, welcome home, girl," the woman said, giving me a sympathetic pat on the shoulder. "You'll barely recognize the shiny new Shadow Grove."

I gave her a tight smile and shifted my attention back to the luggage-claim belt as she walked away. I knew what she meant, of course. In the wake of Riot Night, my father—ever the opportunist—had seen potential to boost his own star even higher by developing the damaged real estate and uniting both sides of the city. Supposedly bridging the class divide that defined Shadow Grove for so long. The new university built on what used to be the border between East and West Shadow Grove was his latest PR stunt. But it was my *only* option if I wanted a higher education now.

Finally my faded suitcase came into view, and I let out a small sigh of relief. It held everything I owned. Everything. All the clothes, shoes, cars here in Shadow Grove were his. My father's. Everything from before Riot Night had burned when our home was set on fire in the various arson attacks of that evening.

Dragging my suitcase behind me, I headed out of the small airport and stopped short when I saw the empty taxi rank. Of course. My luggage had taken so long to arrive, there were no taxis left.

"Is that it?" A deep, melodic voice behind me made me startle, and I swallowed a small scream as I spun around.

"You!" I snarled, eyeing the beautiful guy before me. His hair was shorter than it'd been eleven months ago, and the caramel-brown color of it glittered lighter in the sunlight than in my shadowed memories. But those fucking eyes were the same—pretty, framed by dark lashes, steel-gray eyes.

His grin was wide, pleased, and a flash of metal betrayed a tongue stud.

I wanted to punch him right in the fucking nose.

"Oh good, Kody owes me fifty bucks. He thought you wouldn't remember me." He winked one of those steel-gray eyes like we shared some kind of secret. "Clearly he underestimates the impression I leave on a chick. No matter how briefly we interacted."

I blinked at him, dumbfounded. The last time I'd seen this prick, he was riding away into the night with his two buddies just moments before I was arrested for *their* crimes.

"You've got a lot of fucking nerve," I started to say, but caught myself when that hot, wild anger rose back up in my throat. I'd spent so much time, done so much work to master my own emotions, and here I was about to lose my shit. Not even one hour back in Shadow Grove and the eight months in Cambodia may as well never have happened.

But I hadn't prepared for this. I hadn't prepared to face one of the three who'd *set me up* so soon. I hadn't expected the raw, primal *hate* coursing through my veins.

The guy arched his pierced brow, waiting for me to continue. My memories had dulled his appearance—understandably, seeing as I'd only seen him for a few moments after escaping Zane—but he really was stunning. He wore a short-sleeve shirt, and his left forearm showed some seriously detailed ink.

A small shiver of dread ran through me. If *he* was here…did that mean I was going to run into the other two? Blue Eyes and Green Eyes, the two gorgeous boys who'd saved me from Zane D'Ath and probable painful death on Riot Night, then hand-delivered me to the police for *their* crimes.

Despite how many dirty pockets *must* have been greased to maintain the bullshit charges of me orchestrating Riot Night, the charges had eventually been dismissed due to lack of evidence. And rightly so. But by the time they were, the damage had already been done. My school had expelled me, my Ivy League college had withdrawn their early acceptance, and my father had exiled me to Cambodia. I'd completed my senior year by correspondence, but it'd only afforded me very limited prospects.

It's for your own safety, Madison Kate.

Not that he'd cared about my safety while I was in lockup for three months.

Still, he'd stuck to that one excuse over and over and over until I was packed up and shipped off to the other side of the world without a second glance. The girl who'd died inside The Laughing Clown, the blond one whose body Bree and I had tripped over, had been using *my* ID. She'd stolen my wallet from Bree's car earlier in the night, and when paramedics arrived at the scene, they'd assumed she was me.

Why shouldn't they? After her lifeless form had been trampled by hundreds of panicked, drunk spectators, it would have been impossible to make a clear facial identification. She *still* hadn't been identified and had been buried a Jane Doe.

Of course, this had led my father to think I was the target. Someone had deliberately tried to murder *his* daughter...so I'd been sent away. *For my own safety.*

"What do you want?" I snapped, folding my arms under my breasts. I was dressed in loose linen pants, a baby-blue tank top, and a sloppy, hand-knitted cardigan. I looked *nothing* like the Madison Kate of a year earlier...except for my hair. When Aunt Marie had died and my father had *summoned* me home, I'd been furious. Determined to remind him of the last time he'd laid eyes on me, I'd dyed my hair back to the dusky rose color it'd been when I left Shadow Grove. After the hot-pink dye had faded a bit from shitty, holding-cell shampoos, it'd actually turned a really pretty shade.

More fool me, my father hadn't even bothered to pick me up.

The pretty, tattooed, and pierced boy with steel-gray eyes just grinned again. What was his fucking problem anyway? No one smiled that much.

"I'm your lift home," he told me, jerking his head toward the sleek, silver muscle car parked in the zone clearly marked Taxis Only. "Your father...uh...couldn't make it."

I snorted a bitter laugh. "No shit," I replied. "Too busy fucking my new mommy?" Gray Eyes wrinkled his nose, and I sighed. "Whatever. Do you work for him or something?" As badly as I wanted to castrate this asshole and his two friends...I wanted a shower more. There was something about sitting on a plane for the better part of an entire day that made a shower seem like the holy grail.

The guy shook his head slightly, then nodded to the car again. "Why don't I explain on the way? You must be pretty wrecked. How long was the flight from Singapore anyway?"

My lips pursed. "Siem Reap." I corrected him on where I'd flown from. "Fucking long." I wasn't in the mood for idle chitchat with this prick.

"Okay, so..." He took a step forward, reaching out for my case.

"So, nothing." I snatched my luggage out of his reach and backed up a few steps. A taxi was approaching from behind Gray Eyes, and I much preferred that mode of transport. I stuck my hand out, waving it down.

"Seriously?" he asked, his brow creased with confusion. "I literally came here just to pick you up."

I shrugged, letting the taxi driver take my suitcase and load it into the trunk. "Well then, for one thing, you should have been here an hour ago when I landed. And for another, you shouldn't have fucking framed me for breaking and entering and manslaughter. So thanks but no thanks, Gray." I grabbed my sunglasses from the strap of my fringed, boho handbag and slid them onto my nose. "Next time I see you, I won't be so nice. Stay out of my fucking way."

I dropped heavily into the backseat of the taxi and slammed the door shut. The window was halfway down, so while the driver slipped back into his seat and shifted the car into drive, I could hear Gray Eyes mutter something.

"What?" I demanded, refusing to let him have the last word, even if I couldn't even hear it.

"I said, *Steele*. My name's Steele, not Gray." His infuriating grin grew wide again, flashing the metal of his tongue stud, and he winked one of those *steel-gray* eyes. "Close, though."

My taxi pulled away from the curb then, sparing me the need to reply, and I dropped my head back onto the seat with a groan.

Steele. What a stupid fucking name. It suited him.

My phone buzzed in my pocket when the taxi's GPS showed us about five minutes from my father's new home.

"Hello?" I answered, barely bothering to glance at the screen. Only two people even had my number, and one was dead.

"Madison Kate," my father's gruff voice sounded on the other end, "I was hoping to see you before we left, but Steele just arrived back without you."

I rolled my eyes, biting my tongue before I snapped at him. He hadn't believed me on Riot Night when I told him about the three boys who'd gotten me out of the amusement park and left me on the side of the road. He hadn't believed me that the stolen master key was only in my pocket because the whole jacket belonged to a gorgeous, flirty, green-eyed boy. So I wasn't going to waste my breath now telling him of Steele's involvement. Nope, I'd just have to get my own revenge for the destruction he and his buddies had rained down on my life.

"I don't accept rides from strangers," I replied with just a tiny hint of sarcasm. "Why didn't you come to pick me up yourself? I'd have thought you wanted to see your only child after exiling me for months."

My father made a vexed sound, and I could hear a woman's voice in the background. Ugh. Cherise. His new girlfriend. I definitely wasn't looking forward to *that* introduction.

"I'm sure I told you, Madison Kate," my father replied, sounding annoyed and distracted. He didn't even acknowledge my comment about what a shitty, neglectful parent he was. "Cherry and I are leaving today for Italy."

It shouldn't hurt. It shouldn't. He hadn't visited me *once* in Cambodia and had only called when he absolutely had to. But still, hearing he'd planned a vacation with his arm candy for the same day I was arriving home? Yeah, it stung.

"Right," I said back, my voice flat and devoid of emotion. "Of course. I guess I forgot." Or he never told me. "How long will you be gone?"

"Eight weeks. But don't worry, your room is all set up for you."

I clenched my jaw to hold back a sigh. My room. I'd never even *seen* his new house. Our old one—the one I'd grown up in and the one I'd seen my mother murdered in—was long gone.

"Okay, sure. See you in two months, I guess." Despite my best efforts, bitterness crept into my voice.

More murmuring in the background of the phone, Cherise saying something to my father, then he spoke again. "Thanks, hon. You won't be too lonely, though. If you need anything, I'm sure the boys can help you out."

Wait, what? The boys? What boys?

"Dad—" I started to say, but he cut me off.

"Got to run. Our car is here. Give me a call on Monday and tell me how your first day at SGU goes. You know how important that project is to me." He didn't even wait for me to reply before he ended the call, and it took all of my willpower not to throw my phone out of the window.

A minute later, a blacked-out Rolls-Royce glided past us, and I knew it was him. He couldn't even wait two more minutes for me to get home.

Bastard.

His words sat like a lump in my gut. What *boys* would be able to help me out? The fact that Gray Eyes—*Steele*—had been sent to pick me up from the airport…I had a seriously bad feeling about what I was going to find at my father's house.

"Is this it?" the driver asked, breaking through my distraction.

I peered out of the window and up at the enormous mansion behind high, ornate gates. Worked into the iron was a fancy monogram of a *D*. For Danvers. Ugh, Samuel Danvers was so arrogant.

"Yep, I guess so," I replied with a sigh. I paid the guy with some crumpled cash from my bag—U.S. currency that had sat untouched the entire time I'd been away—then retrieved my suitcase from his trunk.

"You going to be okay, girl?" the cabbie asked me, giving the monolithic structure behind me a wary look.

My smile was tight. "I'll be fine," I replied, silently praying I wouldn't be proved wrong. "Thanks."

The guy nodded, then climbed back into his car and drove away, leaving me standing there with my bag at my feet. I didn't even have a fucking code to open the front gates; how messed up was that?

"Thanks a lot, Dad," I muttered under my breath, heading over to the intercom. I could just call him and ask, but I was pissed as hell that he hadn't waited to see me. Hopefully one of these "boys" could let me in instead. Failing that, my father always had staff lurking around in the shadows.

I pressed the buzzer heavily, then stood there fidgeting when I heard the security camera click on. No one spoke, and I stifled an annoyed sigh.

Count to five.

Breathe.

"I know you're there, asshole," I snapped. Whoops, maybe I should have counted to ten.

"Can we help you?" a smooth, male voice asked. It wasn't Steele…I didn't think. Maybe a butler? But the kind of hired help my father employed took politeness to all new levels. They were basically invisible for the most part and impeccably mannered when seen.

"Yeah, can you let me in? My dad forgot to give me the gate code." I peered up at the camera, folding my arms and tapping my foot in irritation.

There was another long pause, then: "You're an independent woman, Madison Kate. You got yourself here from the airport all on your own after all. I'm sure you can work it out."

He—whoever *he* was—sounded like he was laughing at me.

Fucker.

After flipping off the security camera, it took me all of two minutes to throw my suitcase over the gate, then climb the damn thing using my father's ostentatious wrought iron monogram for purchase. I dropped to the other side with a puff of breath, then dusted my hands off on my pants. I'd long since ditched my "Danvers" look of designer dresses and high heels *all the time* and had never been more comfortable. Certainly made shit like breaking into your own family estate easier.

It took me a solid five minutes to drag my suitcase up the paved driveway to the main house. Five minutes that I could feel someone watching me and laughing.

Whoever this prick was, he'd chosen the wrong day to mess with me. The wrong fucking *year*.

"You made it back." Steele appeared from the side of the house, giving me a lopsided grin. He was wiping something black off his hands with a dirty rag, and peering past him, I could see a half-open garage door. Inside, his shiny, silver-gray muscle car had its hood propped open.

"That I did," I replied, narrowing my eyes. "Why are you here?"

His grin spread wider and he tucked the greasy rag into the back pocket of his ripped black jeans. "Oh, you didn't know? I live here."

CHAPTER 4

The sound of the front door slamming open echoed through the enormous foyer like a gunshot, and I smothered a grimace. Not quite what I'd been aiming for when I'd shoved it open, but there I was, letting my anger get the better of me. Again.

"Madison Kate, wait up," Steele called from behind me, but I was in no mood.

I whirled around to face him, my waist-length pink hair flying out around me like some kind of superhero cape. "Just show me where my room is," I half demanded, half pleaded. "I'll call my dad after I've showered. I'm sure he has a really great explanation why *you*, of all people, live here."

He ran a hand over his short brown hair, leaving a smudge of grease in its wake. "Or you could just chill the fuck out for two seconds and let me explain it? We really thought you already knew."

"We?" I repeated, then remembered my father's use of the plural *boys*. "Great. There's more of you." I pinched the bridge of my nose, screwing my eyes shut in a pointless effort to hold off my mounting migraine.

"About time you showed up, Princess. We were starting to think you were too scared to return to Shadow Grove after all."

The voice was familiar. So fucking familiar. It was a voice that had replayed over and over in my mind for eleven long months while I dreamed of all the violent and painful ways I'd make him pay for what he'd done to me.

My eyes snapped open and locked on to a pair of unforgettable baby blues. "*You*," I snarled, snapping out my curled fist and punching that gorgeous man right in the fucking nose.

Or it would have landed on his nose if he hadn't dodged with some scary-fast reflexes. As it was, my knuckles glanced off his cheekbone, and I stumbled off balance.

"Fuck!" the stunning, blue-eyed man shouted, clapping a hand to his cheek.

For my part, the only reason I didn't face-plant into the ugly Persian rug we stood on was the fact that a pair of hands had circled my waist and caught me in midfall.

"What's your fucking problem?" Blue Eyes roared, even while I was spun around in my savior's grip and kissed swiftly, *right on the lips*, by the third stooge. Green Eyes.

"Hey, girl." He grinned, his emerald eyes twinkling with mischief. "I thought I'd never see you again. Love the hair." He flipped one of my long, dusky-rose tresses and winked. My lips tingled where he'd just kissed me, and a barrage of conflicting emotions zapped through me.

What. The. Fuck?

I wrenched myself free of his grip and slapped him for the stolen kiss, then took some seriously long steps away from the three of them.

"This isn't happening," I muttered aloud. "One of you had better explain what the *fuck* you're doing in my father's house, or so help me..."

"So help you *what*?" Blue Eyes taunted me. His cheek and right eye were already coming up with a red mark, and I was smugly proud of that. It wasn't what I'd aimed for, but I hoped it hurt nonetheless.

I shook my head slowly, letting all my year-long anger and hate well up in my eyes. "Trust me, you don't want to find out. I already owe you for *framing* me for B&E and nearly sinking me for manslaughter." My voice was scathing, sharp enough to strip paint.

"What?" Green Eyes asked, wrinkling his brow. It only fueled the fire of my anger.

I sneered at him. At them. All of them. "Oh, you're going to pretend you didn't hand deliver me to the Shadow Grove police to take a fall for shit I had *nothing* to do with?"

Green Eyes at least had the decency to look ashamed. Steele just frowned, and Blue Eyes? He looked ready to fight. Bring it on, pretty boy. I had a year of hatred stored up inside me just begging to be let out.

"Well then," Blue Eyes said, and I got the distinct impression he was the leader of this little crew. He wasn't the tallest—Green Eyes had maybe a half inch on him—but he was the most imposing. He had *presence*, like he was used to people ducking and cowering when he walked into a room. "I sure hope you learned to forgive and forget while you were on that meditation retreat, because we're not only attending SGU together when classes start on Monday... we're practically family."

I blinked about sixteen times. "Excuse me?" I spluttered.

A cruel, menacing smile twisted his lips. "You didn't know? My mom is dating your dad. He was kind enough to offer the three of us a place to live while we're attending the shiny new Shadow Grove University."

I shook my head, disbelieving. How could my father not have mentioned this? I'd think three strange men living in his house should have been pretty high up the list of things to mention to his only child. Then again, he hadn't even bothered to hang around and see me.

"This must be a fucking joke," I muttered, scrubbing a hand over my face. "This isn't fucking happening. I'm not this unlucky."

"Not the reaction we usually get," someone muttered. Green Eyes, maybe.

"Shut up, Kody," Steele muttered, and my eyes snapped back open, spearing him with my laser gaze.

"Show me where my room is?" Steele stirred the least amount of fury and disgust from me, and I had no desire to wander the mansion aimlessly for hours. "I need to sleep for about six days, then I'll call my dad and sort this all out. I'm sure he can find the three of you a nice hotel elsewhere."

Blue Eyes snorted a sarcastic laugh and shook his head. "Good luck with that, Princess." He turned to leave, giving Green Eyes—Kody?—a pointed look.

"Run along, pup," I sneered at him when he frowned after his beautiful, angry friend. "Your master has summoned you."

Green Eyes just frowned at me again, looking confused and hurt, before running a hand through the longer top of his messy, platinum hair. He puffed out a resigned sigh and followed his friend out of the foyer, like a good little lapdog.

"Madison—" Steele started to say, but I shook my head with a sharp gesture.

"Literally *nothing* you say will make up for what you three took from me on Riot Night," I told him, my voice glacial. "No pretty words or apologies can fix what *you three* broke. Just show me where my room is, and then stay out of my fucking way."

Steele's brow was furrowed deeply over his gray eyes, but he just sighed and grabbed my suitcase from where I'd dropped it at the base of the massive grand staircase. He was quick enough that I couldn't snatch it back without looking like a petty child, so I just clenched my fists and followed him up the sweeping stairs.

He honored my wishes and didn't speak again until pausing outside a closed door. There was nothing special about it—we'd passed half a dozen identical ones on the way down the hall—but apparently this one was mine.

"Your father asked Cherry to help decorate, so it could be awful," he informed me with a small shrug. "Anyway. We were going to order pizza for dinner because the staff takes Friday nights off. What's your favorite?" I just glared at him, and he gave me a small, teasing grin. "Everyone's gotta eat, Madison Kate."

I just shook my head and opened the door to "my" bedroom. "Oh god," I groaned.

"Yikes," Steele commented, sucking in a breath as he peered into the room behind me. "I had a feeling... Cherry always wanted a daughter."

I turned to him, horrified and speechless. The whole room was pink. No, not just pink. A vibrant, tween girl sort of pink with... "Are the walls painted with *glitter*?"

Steele really seemed to be holding back laughter, but to give him credit, his lips only twitched slightly despite his eyes brimming over with amusement. "Uh, I guess she wanted to match your hair?"

My glare turned murderous, and he lost it a bit, releasing a quick snicker before wiping a hand over his handsome face—almost like he could physically wipe the laughter away. "Look, we can get it fixed. A couple coats of paint will make a world of difference."

I almost accepted his offer of help. Almost. That was how truly awful the cotton-candy-pink bedroom was. No wonder that douchebag downstairs had called me "princess."

But... "I think you three have done enough," I said in a quiet, hate-filled voice. The poison of my own negative emotions seemed to burn through my whole body, pushing me to lash out.

I took my suitcase back from him and dropped it on the floor by the end of the bed, then shrugged off my sloppy, hand-knitted cardigan. I spun around to face Steele with my hands propped on my hips, only to find his gray gaze skimming over my tight blue tank top. The edges of my black bra showed, and I gave zero fucks because it was a bra, not a butt plug.

"Don't be subtle or anything," I snarked, narrowing my eyes. He didn't even seem to feel the slightest bit guilty to be caught checking me out either. Prick.

Steele just shrugged and gave me one of those sexy, lopsided smiles. "Can you blame me? When I met you on Riot Night, you were drowning in that black hoodie. I never realized you were... all *that*." He indicated to my body, and I glowered harder.

"Oh yeah, that hoodie that held the incriminating key in the pocket? That one? The same one that saw me rot in fucking lockup for three months while I was put on trial for crimes I had *nothing* to do with? That hoodie?" Yeah, I was flogging a dead horse, and I didn't care. These fuckers clearly didn't have any appreciation for how badly they'd messed up my life that night, and goddamn I was going to *make* them understand. Somehow.

Steele heaved a huge sigh, like he was annoyed.

Fucking *seriously*?

"Look, Madison Kate, I know you think—"

"I don't *think*," I hissed back at him, cutting off whatever bull-shit excuse he was about to spew at me. "I *know*. I know your buddies downstairs set me the fuck up, and now you're living in my father's house? What the actual fuck, Steele?"

His lips twitched with another one of those half smiles that I wanted to smack clean off his face. Or maybe kiss. But that was just my year of celibacy talking. But damn if I wasn't interested to see what he could do with that pierced tongue.

"All right, well...I'll give you a yell when the pizzas get here. Any preference?"

I blinked at him a couple of times, dumbfounded at his rapid change of subject.

Steele wrinkled his nose and clicked his tongue, his tongue stud making a sound against his teeth. "You look like an all-or-nothing kinda girl. Supreme or plain cheese?"

Furious, I closed the space between us in three long strides and shoved him with a hand to the center of his chest, pushing him back out into the hallway. I tried *really* hard not to think about how firm and defined his chest was, or about the teasing hints of ink peeking out of his collar. Instead, I slammed the door in his face and covered my face with my hands in exasperation.

"Okay, I'll order both!" Steele yelled through the door. "I can already tell we're going to have so much fun living together!" He laughed then, this deep, throaty chuckle that made a curl of fire ignite in my belly as his footsteps faded away. I wanted to yell and scream. Punch something. But that was the total opposite of everything Aunt Marie had been trying to teach me over the last year.

When I'd arrived on her doorstep in Cambodia, she'd seen how angry I was. How totally filled with hate. She'd done her best, I had to hand it to her. But I was a terrible meditation student, and all those feelings inside me had just festered.

"*Fuck!*" I shouted into my hands, smothering the sound of my own voice.

Exhausted, confused, and mad as hell, I flopped down on the frilly pink-and-purple comforter and screamed into the pillows. When I was done, I forced my body still.

One...two...three...four...five...

Calming breaths filled my lungs with each number, but they did little to shift the venom in my heart. I was doomed; I had accepted that months ago. Now, all I wanted was to drag those fuckers down with me. While I was probably willing to accept that Steele had very little to do with my arrest, I couldn't say the same for the other two. Green Eyes—Kody—had given me the hoodie with the key. And Blue Eyes? He'd delivered me right into the cops' hands. He'd known exactly where to leave me at exactly the right time. He'd known what he was doing, and no amount of flirting from Steele would change that fact.

"Motherfuckers," I whispered aloud, blowing out a heavy breath. I was exhausted, my muscles all ached from the long flight, and my eyelids were like sandpaper. I wanted nothing more than to sleep for the next month…but I was shit out of luck on that front.

In just three days, come Monday morning, I'd be starting at Shadow Grove University.

With a groan, I rolled over on the awful comforter and fished my phone out of my bag. I needed to know that the fuck I'd just walked into here, and I knew just the person to fill me in.

If she'd speak to me, that was.

CHAPTER 5

Bree didn't answer, but she also didn't have my new number and was probably call screening. Not that I blamed her; I used to do the same thing.

"Hey, Bree," I said when the voicemail beep sounded. "It's me, MK. I'm…uh…I'm back in Shadow Grove. Can you call me when you get this?" I paused, feeling awkward as fuck and guilty to the point of nausea. "I missed you, girl."

Before I could get all emotional and gushy on her voicemail, I ended the call and stared at my phone. Chances were, she wouldn't call me back. I couldn't say I'd have done anything differently in her shoes either. I'd been such a bitch last time I'd seen her, outside the courthouse when I'd been acquitted of my charges.

She'd refused to testify in my defense. Refused to show up and verify my statement of events. All because she was too scared of her father finding out she'd been at The Laughing Clown on Riot Night. Somehow, she'd made it home before the worst of the looting and damage had started. Somehow, her father still thought she was a perfect little angel and I was finally getting what I deserved for being such a bad influence on his darling girl. And Bree never spoke up.

I'd been so mad at her for so long, but while Aunt Marie had failed to help me let go of my hatred toward the three boys downstairs, she'd succeeded when it came to Bree. I knew now that my friend was only doing what she needed to survive her own life. She'd still been a minor—as had I—so there was no way she could have testified without her parents' consent. And straight up, she was terrified of her father. I couldn't hold that against her.

Still, I'd thrown away my old life the second I stepped off the plane in Cambodia. Now I had to deal with the consequences of that decision.

After several minutes staring at my blank phone, I gave up and took myself for a shower.

"Jesus fucking Christ," I muttered when I saw the princess-pink theme had carried over into the en suite. Pastel, fluffy towels; a glittery bath mat…even pink shampoo with a purple conditioner.

Whatever. It was Dad and Cherry's house; they could decorate however they wanted.

I took my time washing away the grit of my journey, then bundled up in a rose-colored towel to dry my hair. It was naturally wavy, but keeping it so long weighed it down a lot. All it needed was a blow-dry, admittedly a long one, then a quick swipe with straightening irons. Voilà.

It was while I was riffling through my suitcase, hunting for underwear, that my phone lit up and started vibrating on my bed.

My stomach flipped with anxiety, knowing it wouldn't be my dad calling me. He was probably checked into the first-class lounge at the airport already, sipping on a cognac.

"Bree?" I answered, nervous as all hell. She'd been my best friend practically since birth, but it'd been almost a year since we'd properly talked. Way too long.

"MK," she replied, "holy fucking shit. It's actually you."

I bit my lip, at a loss for what to say.

"Sorry," she hurried to continue. "I had a moment there

where I thought someone was pranking me. But holy shit. It's you. You're...back in Shadow Grove?"

"Yeah," I replied, swallowing the lump of awkwardness in my throat. "Hey, I should have called you sooner. I wanted to apologize for—"

"Whoa, no," she cut me off and my mouth turned dry. This was what I'd worried about. The rejection I'd been avoiding by just ignoring the problem. "No way, MK. I need to apologize to *you*. I was a totally self-absorbed bitch back then. You could have seriously gone to jail for shit you had nothing to do with, and I did *nothing* to help you out. Dude. I'm so freaking sorry."

The relief that her words provided was like an iron band being cut away from my heart. "Bree, girl, you have no idea..." I laughed then, a bit delirious in the absence of fear. "Let's call it even? I said some shitty, shitty things to you that day at the courthouse. I'm sorry."

Bree laughed too. "Okay, we're both sorry. Let's put it behind us and pretend that chapter of our lives never happened, agreed?"

"Agreed," I replied, collapsing onto my bed and staring up at the ceiling. At least *that* wasn't pink. "So...what's new?"

My estranged friend started laughing then, so hard I actually worried it held an edge of hysteria. It made me wonder what the fuck had gone on with her in the last year. "Sorry, that's... Yeah, man, lots is new. How about you, though? You're back in Shadow Grove. When did that happen?"

"Uh, about an hour ago, I guess? Just caught a cab from the airport and met my new...housemates. That was a surprise..." I trailed off, waiting for her to fill in the blanks. Because she would. No question about it.

She made a sound like she was sucking in a breath between her teeth. "Yeah, I bet. I'm guessing by your unimpressed tone your dad didn't mention Arch and the boys?"

I frowned, and something curdled in my stomach. "Arch? That's Blue Eyes's name?"

Bree paused a moment. "You're shitting me."

Now I was really getting a bad feeling. "Bree...?"

"Sorry, babe; just wrapping my brain around the fact that your dad never mentioned to you that his new girlfriend's son—and *your* future stepbrother—is Archer D'Ath."

I choked on my own saliva and couldn't speak to reply.

"You remember the fighter we went to see on Riot Night?" She continued talking, not realizing I was having a fucking heart attack on my end of the phone. Bree seriously developed blinders when hot guys were involved. Or maybe she was deliberately acting blasé to spare my fragile feelings around that family. "Bet you never would have guessed he was Zane D'Ath's little brother, huh? Then again, his nickname isn't all that original when you know his real name. Seriously, girl, where have you *been*? Under a rock? He's a legit celebrity now."

"Cambodia," I whispered, my voice hoarse from the panic attack threatening me. "I was in Cambodia."

"Uh, okay," Bree laughed, but it was a forced sound. She was definitely trying to breeze past the whole subject to keep things normal. "I'm sure there's internet there. Anyway, your head must have just exploded. Damn, I wish I'd waited to tell you in person so I could see your face right now. Take a selfie for me?"

"Fuck you," I croaked back at her, and she cackled, sounding a bit more like herself. "My head did just explode. I didn't even know Zane *had* a brother."

"Half brother," Bree explained. "Cherry was Damien's second wife, much younger. Have you met the boys yet? Kody and Steele? I'm not even going to lie here; you're officially the luckiest bitch in Shadow Grove. Probably the world. Those three are thermonuclear hot." *Nice change of subject, Bree. Good save.*

"Met them?" I spluttered, regaining a bit of my brain power after the shock of Blue Eyes's real identity. "Those three are the pricks who framed me on Riot Night."

There was a long pause on the phone, followed by "Oh, shit."

"Yep."

"So...not going to be creating your own reverse harem out of your new living arrangements, then?" There was an edge of laughter in her voice, and I wished we were having this chat in person. So I could smack her.

"I can safely say I'd rather set my pubic hair on fire than join an orgy with those three assholes," I informed Bree, my voice sarcastic and full of disgust. Hate. "I'd rather stick rusty pins under my toenails, then dance in pointe shoes for an hour. I'd rather—"

"Pizza's here," a deep, husky voice interrupted me, and I sat bolt upright on my pretty pink bed.

"Speak of the devil and he shall appear," I snarled. I was still holding the phone to my ear, but my sole focus was on the shirtless, tattoo-covered demon lounging against my open door. "Don't you know how to knock, *Archer*?" I sneered his name with disdain, and the corners of his full lips pulled up in a smug smile.

"Oh shit, did he hear you?" Bree asked in my ear, then dissolved into giggles. I loved her, but fuck, I hated her sometimes.

The blue-eyed bastard just shrugged those perfectly toned shoulders. "Apparently not. You coming down for food, or did you have better things to do? Like sticking pins under your nails, perhaps?"

I glowered at him, refusing to feel embarrassed for being overheard.

"Oh, for the record, Princess Danvers? You can't set your pubic hair on fire when you don't have any." He shot me a knowing wink, then disappeared out of my room again while I dropped my phone and frantically grabbed for the edges of my towel. Yep. Sure enough, when I'd sat up in such a shock, the flaps of my towel had fallen open. While I wasn't exactly sitting there spread eagle with my full vagina on display, he'd definitely seen enough to know I maintained regular laser hair removal appointments. Yes, even while in Cambodia.

Motherfucker.

Retrieving my phone, I found the call still connected, so I put it back to my ear. "I fucking hate him, Bree. I hate that asshole more than anything I've ever hated." My hands were trembling with the adrenaline rush facing Archer had caused, and I fumbled for my underwear.

Bree made a sympathetic sound on her end. "You hate him more than Zane?"

I froze, ice forming in my gut and a chill sweeping over me. "I don't hate Zane, Bree. I'm terrified of him. Big difference."

She blew out a breath, the phone picking up the sound of it. "Yeah, I get that. Kinda a dick move for your dad to date Cherry, huh?"

"No shit." I bit the edge of my lip as way too many thoughts and emotions bumped around my brain, fighting for supremacy. "Zane murdered my mom, and now Dad has invited the devil's own family into his house. Either he has the shortest memory in history, or Cherry's vagina is made of diamonds."

Bree laughed a humorless laugh. She knew what I meant. "Yep, 'cause the only thing your dad loves more than himself is money."

Old grief welled up in my throat at the reminder of my mother's brutal death. It'd taken years of therapy to work through my trauma, and the only lingering effect now was my mild claustrophobia. Not too bad, considering at age eleven I'd been locked in a closet while my mom was murdered just twenty feet away.

"I'm so sorry, girl," she said, her voice soft and sincere. "This is a shitty situation."

I swallowed heavily, pushing aside those seven-year-old emotions and fears.

"What the fuck is he thinking, dating the widow of Damien D'Ath? She probably still has ties to the Reapers, for fuck's sake." I was just thinking out loud, but Bree replied anyway.

"Supposedly not, but like…it sort of plays into your dad's whole marketing bullshit of a clean and shiny Shadow Grove. What better way to prove the gangs are no longer a threat, right?"

She had a pretty valid theory.

"Hey, I better go," I told Bree, hopping on one foot while trying to pull some jeans on. "The guys ordered pizza, and now that I know who *he* is, I refuse to cower in my room like a scared little girl." Because I'd done that enough in my life. Zane had haunted my nightmares for too long, but I was different now. I was stronger.

"Good luck, girl," Bree offered. "When can we catch up? Want me to come by later tonight? We can hit up Cold Stone for ice cream or something."

As badly as I wanted to say yes, a yawn tugged at my jaw. "Rain check. I'm dead in the water after flying today. Do you have plans tomorrow?"

"None that I can't change. I'll pick you up at eight."

I blanched. "Make it ten, girl."

Bree laughed. "'Kay, see you at eight!"

She hung up before I could contradict her again, so I shot her a quick text message.

Me: ten o'clock and not a minute earlier

Her reply came quickly.
Bree: missed you, MK. Followed by kissy-face emojis.

Ugh. I couldn't argue with that. Bree was my long-lost sister.

I tossed my phone onto the bed and finished getting dressed. I'd meant it when I said I refused to be intimidated by these boys. I couldn't afford to get my own place, not until my trust fund hit when I was twenty-one—two and a half years away—and I had lost my acceptance to the various Ivy Leagues who'd once wanted me. My only hope for a future was to attend SGU and live with my father.

There was no way in hell I'd share the house with those three. Not after what they'd done and not knowing who *he* was. Nope. There was only one course of action here.

Archer D'Ath and his boys needed to go.

CHAPTER 6

In the space of time it took for me to wander—slowly—from my room down to the kitchen, I was able to conduct several fruitful Google searches on my phone. In fairness, I did get lost within the enormous house twice, but by the time my nose caught the scent of pizza, I felt like I knew my enemy better.

Archer D'Ath was their ring leader. The clown who bore the worst of my anger over Riot Night. His significantly older brother, Zane, was the leader of the Shadow Grove Reapers—he'd taken over when their father had died several years ago in a shooting. Thanks to gossip sites and social media, I knew that Archer had recently signed a contract with the UFC—Ultimate Fighting Championship—and had already picked up several lucrative sponsors in the form of athletic brands and sports drinks. He'd done several small "introduction" fights, but his big break was coming up after Halloween in the form of a televised title fight. Sure explained his stacked physique and quick reflexes when I'd punched him.

Admittedly, I was a bit smug that my punch had landed at all, now that I knew who he was.

Stooge two: Kodiak Jones, also known inside my poisonous

thoughts as Green Eyes. An MMA fighter like his buddy Archer, but on a promising path as a trainer rather than a star. He was all over Instagram—and I mean *all freaking over it*—as some kind of fitness model, personal trainer, and all-around social media pinup boy. He, Archer, and Steele seemed to have some kind of cult following for their edgy, shirtless, bad boy pictures, which were so painfully staged it was laughable. Posers.

That brought me to number three. Gray Eyes. Max Steele. The first time I'd found his full name, I'd done a double take. Surely his parents hadn't *actually* named him Max Steele? But yep. Sure enough…

"Find anything good?" the gray-eyed hottie in question asked, snatching my phone out of my hand and scrolling. "Oh, ugh. Don't form your opinions based on this shit," he told me, wrinkling his nose in distaste. "These profiles are run by our PR manager."

My brows shot up. "You have a PR manager? For what?"

Steele grinned, handing my phone back. "Ah, I see you didn't get that far into your internet searches yet, huh? Too bad, guess you have to get to know me the *old-fashioned* way."

His eyes sparkled with challenge, and my fingers curled into a fist. If he thought we were going to be engaging in cute banter over pizza, he was dead fucking wrong.

"Lighten up, Madison Kate," he sighed. "Are you always so serious?"

I scowled harder. "When faced with the prospect of sharing a house with the three people I hate more than anyone on this earth? Yeah. I am." Brushing past him, I followed the aroma of pizza sauce and cooked cheese until I found the other two boys sprawled out on the couch in front of an enormous flat-screen TV. Several open boxes of pizza lay on the low table in front of them, half gone already, while the two of them battled it out in some intense car-racing game via PlayStation.

Of course there were no dishes out; they'd probably been eating straight from the box. I started heading past the den to find myself a plate until—

"Pay up," someone said.

I froze, thinking they were talking to me, but an annoyed sigh came from one of the other boys. "Damn. I'll be broke if the pretty, pink princess keeps up this unpredictable bullshit."

Ugh. That was definitely Archer. No mistaking that surly, dick-ish voice.

Still, it made me happy to know he was losing money betting against me.

"Coming to sit with us, Madison Kate?" Green Eyes—Kodiak—asked, slinging an arm over the back of the couch and giving me a curious look. "Steele made sure we didn't eat all the pizza until you got here."

I shot a quick look at the pierced, tattooed guy, but he was ignoring me as he helped himself to the pizza in question, then flopped down on a beanbag.

"Uh, no thanks," I replied, running my tongue over my sud-denly dry lips. Kody's gaze dropped to my mouth, and I was reminded of the fact that he'd *kissed* me when I arrived. What the fuck was that all about anyway? Not that I was any stranger to kissing boys, but it had been a *long* time… "I was just going to grab a plate and head back to my room."

"Told you," Archer commented from the couch, not bothering to turn or even sit up to look at me. "She's a scared little girl. Fifty bucks says we hear her crying into her pillow tonight."

"Damn, Arch, you hate your money or something?" Steele laughed, his mouth still full of pizza. "I'll take that bet. I need new parts for the Ducati, and those fuckers don't come cheap."

My jaw had dropped slightly at the blatant bullshit I was listen-ing to. Were these bastards for fucking real?

Anger burned through me, and my jaw clenched. Kody was

still watching me, and his eyes widened a fraction at what was probably a very obvious shift in my mood.

It pissed me off that they were taking bets on my behavior, but of the two of them—Archer and Steele—I disliked Archer more.

"You know what?" I announced, forcing a bit of fake sunshine into my voice, which otherwise dripped scorn. "I guess I am feeling social after all." Marching my butt over to them, I stepped quite deliberately over Archer's legs. I bent over and scooped up a big slice of supreme pizza, then plonked my ass dead center on the couch between Archer and Kodiak. Blue and Green.

Crap, this might have been a mistake.

"Interesting choice," Steele murmured, almost under his breath. I frowned a moment before seeing he was talking about my choice of pizza. What had he said to me upstairs? I looked like an *all or nothing* kind of girl?

How right he was.

"What are we playing?" I asked, like casual confidence was in my damn bloodstream.

Archer just glared at me, and as we were sitting close enough that our knees brushed, it was kind of intense. Like, scary intense. My stomach flipped, and a little part of my brain challenged me on whether that was nerves or attraction.

"*Beach Buggy Racing,*" Kody replied, drawing my attention to my other side. He was in one of those obnoxiously male sprawls, where he took up way more space than a normal human should. It also meant that his arm was draped along the back of the couch, behind me, while his other hand held the PlayStation controller loosely. "You want a turn?"

His lids were heavy over those gorgeous green eyes, and a telling dark shadow of stubble dusted his jaw. Not that I'd thought his blond was anything but bleached. He looked like he was about to fall asleep any minute now, which only made my stupid, sex-starved mind wander off to what his bed might look like. Or whether he slept in the nude.

That little voice in my head laughed at me, and I wanted to punch the bitch.

"Sure," I replied with a shrug, holding my hand out for the controller. As he passed it to me, our fingers brushed, and it took all my self-control not to jump like I'd been electrocuted.

Kody smirked, like he knew the effect he was having on me, so I scowled back at him. I had to keep reminding myself he wasn't just some hot guy who'd saved me from Zane and his gang. Who'd given me his jacket when I was cold and in shock. He was the one who'd almost seen me locked up for being in the wrong place at the wrong time, and no matter how fucking sexy he and his friends were, I'd never forgive that.

"Hey, if Madison Kate is playing, we can do four player," Steele commented from his beanbag, licking pizza grease from long fingers. Tattoos stretched from the cuff of his shirt and webbed across the back of his hand, and I was crazy curious to get a better look. Pity he couldn't be someone else. *Anyone* else. I'd have been all fucking over him.

"No," Archer snapped, shooting a flat stare at his friend. "You're not allowed to play, and you know it."

Steele rolled his eyes dramatically. "Come on, Arch. One game of *Beach Buggy* won't spark the apocalypse. Don't be such a stick in the mud."

"Besides," Kody added, "it's about sixteen thousand times less dangerous than working in the garage. Yet you don't stop him from doing that."

Archer made an angry sound in his throat, and for the first time since arriving, I wasn't the target of his ire. "Have *you* tried to stop Steele from working in the garage?"

Kody just snickered, and Steele whooped.

"Four-way it is!" the gray-eyed enigma announced, then shot a sly wink at me. "Four *player*, I mean. Unless..." He left the question hanging, and my cheeks flamed with heat. Words failed me. Had he seriously just propositioned me? With a *four*-way? How did that even work? Wait, why the fuck was I thinking about this?

Archer made a snide sound. "Princess Danvers would rather stick rusty pins under her toenails than have a four-way with us," he reported, smug as all fuck. "Or what else was it? You'd rather set your pubic hair on fire?"

The other guys cringed, and I glowered.

"If I had any, as you already pointed out, yes," I snarked back at him. "Now, are we playing this beach cart game or not?"

Archer just laughed softly, shaking his head at me like he'd somehow won that round. He hadn't.

"It's *Beach Buggy Racing*," Kody corrected me, getting up from the couch to fetch two extra controllers. "Do you need me to give you a crash course?"

Not wanting to accept *any* kind of help from these guys, I shook my head. "I'll work it out."

Archer snorted, like he thought I was incompetent or something, which just made me more determined to work it out on my own. Bastard.

———————

As it turned out, the *real* reason why Archer didn't want Steele to play—at least as far as I could tell—was that Steele kicked his ass. He kicked *all* our asses. Not that I put up much fight. I spent the first twenty minutes driving into walls or going backward around the track. Some people had a natural affinity for video games, and I was not one of them.

"You seriously suck at this," Kody commented after my seventh straight loss. By a long shot. I'd tossed my controller back onto the table and declared I was done.

"Shut up," I grumbled, rubbing my hands over my face and

trying to swallow a yawn. "I'm jet-lagged and consumed by rage and resentment. It tends to split one's focus."

Except, those words felt hollow. For the first time in a really long time, I *wasn't* feeling those venomous emotions. I was just straight up exhausted. Maybe too tired for hate?

Then again, the fact that Archer had left the room to take a phone call some half hour earlier and not returned might have played a part in my improved mood.

"It is pretty late," Steele agreed. "Play again tomorrow?"

He was so hopeful, I opened my mouth to agree. Thankfully, Kody cut me off.

"Nice try, asshole," he scolded. "You shouldn't have even played this many games. Jase will murder us if he finds out tomorrow."

Steele huffed and grumbled something about living with jailers, and I wrinkled my nose in confusion. Jet lag was making me all dizzy, like I'd been drinking all night.

"Who's Jase?" I asked them. "And why is everyone stressing over you playing PlayStation? Do you have a gaming addiction or something?"

Kody started to answer me, but Steele cut him off with a shake of his head. As he shifted his attention to me, his smile turned sly. "I thought you'd learned everything you needed to know about us on social media."

I rolled my eyes. "About those two, sure." I jerked my thumb in Kody's direction. "I'd only just started on you when you swiped my phone."

Steele grinned. "Well, come find me tomorrow if you still haven't worked it out. I'll tell you if you can't guess."

I frowned. "What? Why not just tell me?"

Kody laughed sleepily beside me. "'Cause Steele likes games." He yawned heavily. "I'm done. Catch you guys tomorrow?" It was phrased like a question, and his gaze rested on me like he was waiting on a response.

I stood up myself, stretching my arms over my head and flipping my long, pink hair over my shoulder. I'd woven it into a quick braid while we'd been playing, after it kept distracting me. "I live here, so I don't see why not."

Despite the casual comfort of the evening, I needed to snap out of it. This was clearly early onset Stockholm syndrome setting in, where I started humanizing my enemies. I needed to cut it off before it got any worse.

My jaw tightened more and more with every thought, my arms wrapping around my body in an unconsciously defensive pose, and Kody sighed.

"I see. Princess Danvers is back. It was nice while it lasted." Shooting Steele a quick nod, he swaggered out of the den.

For his part, Steele just watched me with those mysterious gray eyes.

"What?" I snapped.

He shrugged. "Wondering what just changed inside your head, pretty girl. You seemed to be enjoying yourself for a minute there. What happened?"

"I remembered where I was," I replied with biting cold. "I remembered who I was with and what you all did to ruin my life."

He drew a deep breath, releasing it slowly as he stood up as well. A couple of steps and we were toe to toe, with his storm-cloud eyes peering far too deeply into my soul.

"Yet here we are, living under the same roof. How do you plan to deal with that conundrum, Madison Kate?" His voice was soft, but the challenge was clear.

I let my lips curl into a cold smile, meeting his eyes unflinchingly and raising my chin with defiance. "Simple, Max Steele," I whispered. "We don't. You three need to find somewhere else to live, or..."

He raised a brow. "Or what, pretty girl?"

"Or I'll make your lives hell here. It's your choice." I smiled sweetly. "Don't say I didn't warn you."

He stared down at me, his face impassive. Steele was an easy eight inches taller than me, and my neck was getting a bit sore at this angle. For a moment, I second-guessed myself. Was I making a mistake, taking on these three? They could destroy me. They already nearly had. Did I seriously have the ovaries to go head-to-head with all three of them?

Steele ran his tongue over his lower lip, showing off that tongue stud I'd glimpsed as he'd smiled, and I found my attention all but fucking *glued* to his mouth.

"Game on, Madison Kate," he laughed, reaching out to tuck a loose strand of hair behind my ear. "I doubt you'll find it as easy to get rid of us as you think." He paused, giving me a smirk. "But it'll be fun to see you try."

Scowling and at a total loss for words—because my heart was thundering and my mind kept focusing on that tongue stud—I brushed past him and skulked back to my room. Thankfully, Archer was still nowhere to be seen, but I still went to sleep with plans for revenge on my mind.

CHAPTER 7

The incessant vibration of my phone was what woke me up early Saturday morning. And when I say early, I mean way too freaking early, considering how late we'd played racing games the night before.

"What the fuck?" I grumbled into the device as I stabbed at the speakerphone button. "What time is it?"

"Uh, like, 10:01?" Bree replied, sounding distinctly like she was full of shit. "What's the gate code, babe? I'm out front."

I groaned like a dying animal and rubbed a hand over my face to try to wake up. "Huh?"

"The gate code, MK," Bree repeated. "So I can get into your Dad's mega-mansion. Dude, this place is *massive*."

Slowly, the fog of sleep was clearing from my brain. "Uh, I don't know it," I told her.

"What?" she replied. "How do you not know your own gate code?"

I sighed. "Long story. Hang on."

Dragging my half-asleep ass out of bed, I staggered out into the hallway and made a beeline for the closest door to mine. It was closed, but I gave less than zero shits about the privacy of my temporary housemates. So I barged in without pausing to knock.

I expected to find the occupant of this room fast asleep. I'd wake him up, get the gate code before he fully comprehended the question, then get out again. I didn't expect to find Kodiak fucking Jones stark freaking naked and dripping wet as he exited the attached bathroom.

"Fuck!" I shouted, clapping my hands over my eyes and smacking myself in the face with my phone. Not before I got a damn good eyeful, though, and ho-oo-ly shit. Wow. If I didn't hate the guy on principle, I'd be probably offering to—

Stop it! Stop sexualizing the enemy!

"Can I help you, gorgeous?" Kody asked, his voice full of mirth.

Biting my lip to keep from saying any of the thousand inappropriate responses on the tip of my tongue, I silently counted to five.

"Sorry," I muttered eventually, keeping my hands over my eyes. Not because I respected his privacy—because fuck him—but because I didn't trust myself not to drool. "I need the gate code."

Kody laughed, and it sounded like he was coming closer. Fuck, I hoped he'd put a towel on or...something. "So you thought you'd bust in here without knocking? Where are your manners, Princess?"

He was mocking me, and it just pissed me off. "I guess I left them in the Shadow Grove lockup last year," I snarled back, dropping my hands from my face. I just felt fucking stupid having this argument with my face hidden like a blushing virgin. That was one thing I most definitely was not.

Ugh, goddamn. I should have known.

Of course he hadn't put any pants on. He hadn't even bothered to cover up with a towel. And I mean, I couldn't blame him with a body like that. Was it even legal for a guy of... I had no idea how old Kody was. Twenty? Twenty-two? Hard to tell. Either way, his body was to fucking die for. Then again, considering his whole profile as an up-and-coming celebrity fitness trainer, it made sense.

"See something you like, Madison Kate?" he teased, reaching

out to brush a long strand of pink hair behind my ear. His fingers followed it the whole way to the ends, brushing lightly down my bare arm, and I couldn't suppress a shiver. He was deliberately reminding me of the night we'd met. The night he'd helped me control my claustrophobia by turning me on...and the night he'd set me up for B&E.

That was like an ice-cold shower over my arousal.

"Hardly," I sneered unconvincingly. "Give me the gate code, Kody. Then you can continue...whatever you were doing awake at this ungodly hour." I waved my hand vaguely in the direction of the bathroom, where steam was still billowing out. Now that I'd torn my eyes off his hard, tanned, tattooed chest—thank God he was now so close it was his chest in my direct line of sight and not his dick—I noticed the work-out clothes dropped haphazardly on the carpet.

Kody just grinned, but no four-digit numbers exited his mouth.

"Kody," I growled. "Give me the damn code."

He tilted his head to the side, giving me a mischievous look as he stroked another long strand of my hair. Ugh, I needed to start tying my hair up around this dickhead.

"Hmm, let's see. You want something from me...I want something from you. So let's make a trade." His deep-emerald-green eyes twinkled with danger, and my anger was only stoking higher.

My hands balled into fists at my sides—or one did; the other still clutched my phone where Bree was probably listening to the whole exchange with a box of popcorn.

"What could you possibly want from me, Kodiak Jones?" I demanded, my voice full of scorn as I used his full name. Partly because it infuriated me when people used my full name. Partly to remind him that he was supposedly some hotshot Instagram superstar and could have anything he wanted.

His full lips pulled up in a smile, like I was playing into his hands. "I want *plenty* of things from you, Madison Kate Danvers," he replied, and I seethed. "But for now, let's keep it simple. Coffee. Come out with me for coffee today."

My brows dropped into a confused scowl. "Huh?" That…was not what I'd expected him to say.

His grin only spread wider. "See, I'm not such an asshole. I could have asked you to blow me."

I glared death at him. "I'd just as soon bite your dick off."

"And I knew that. See, I already get you on a deeper level, babe. We're practically made for each other." There was an edge of sarcasm in his voice but not enough. "So? Gate code for a coffee date. Deal?"

I shook my head, biting the inside of my lip. I should just tell him to fuck himself and call my dad for the code. But…

"I can't right now," my traitorous mouth said instead. "I'm doing shit with Bree."

Confusion creased his brow a moment. "Who's Bree?" Then he shrugged. "Later then."

He was up to something; it was so painfully obvious. But my curiosity was hooked. "Just coffee?"

Kody smiled like a cat with a bowl of cream. "Maybe cake too. Think you can handle that without gagging, Princess?"

His choice of words chilled me, but then there was no way he knew about my brief experimentation with eating disorders as a thirteen-year-old. It was a coincidence.

"Fine," I snapped, and his gorgeous face flashed with victory. "The code?"

"Five-two-eight-three," he told me with a smug smile. "Now, I was about to get dressed, but if you're sticking around I'm happy to stay naked." He paused, pulling an exaggerated thinking face. "But full disclosure, I won't be held responsible for how hard my dick gets around you. He's got a mind of his own and keeps fantasizing about getting you alone in the dark again."

A shiver ran through me at the mention of that dark, confined space where Kody and I'd first met, but a small part of me had to admit that shiver wasn't all fear. Feeling my cheeks heat, I whirled on my heels and left the room, slamming his bedroom door after me.

Still, his laughter followed me as I rushed back into my room and put my phone to my ear with a sigh.

"You still there, girl?" I asked Bree, and the sound of her howling laughter was all I needed to hear. "Whatever," I grumbled. "Five-two-eight-three. I'll meet you in the kitchen; I need to shower."

"Better make it a cold one," Bree cackled. "I'm all turned on just listening to that banter."

I growled and ended the call, not finding the need to respond to that.

It wasn't until I stood underneath an admittedly chilly stream of water that I even realized my father's gate code spelled KATE.

CHAPTER 8

When I got downstairs, Bree was leaning over the kitchen counter with her butt popped out and a coy, girlish giggle falling from her pink lips. Archer was speaking quietly, so much so that I could only hear the low rumble of his voice and not the actual words, but the smile on his lips had me stopping dead in my tracks.

He looked…so *normal*. Relaxed and at ease while he flipped pancakes. He was shirtless—which explained the puddle of drool under Bree's jaw—and his gray sweatpants hung loose on his hips. Fucking hell, I couldn't even blame my friend for acting like a fool over this guy; he really was fucking gorgeous. The tattoo that *supposedly* gave him his nickname stretched across the hard planes of his broad back, and my fingers itched to touch it—just to trace the stunning lines of the Sagittarius.

Uh-huh. Yep. That's totally the reason I wanted to touch him. To appreciate his *art*.

Giving myself a mental eye roll, I cleared my throat as I forced my feet back into motion.

The second Archer saw me, his carefree expression shut down faster than a jail cell door. "Nice of you to keep your friend waiting,

Princess Danvers," he sneered at me, and it immediately got my back up. "Good thing I was here to offer some hospitality."

This time I didn't bother to hide my eye roll. "She wouldn't have needed to wait if some arrogant prick had just given me the gate code yesterday when I arrived instead of playing stupid games."

Archer smiled, but it was a mean smile, totally unlike his easy, relaxed one before he'd seen me. "I happen to like games, Madison Kate," he replied with an edge of mocking. He slapped his spatula against his palm, and my breath hitched. Fuck. I needed to steer clear of these assholes when they were wearing so few clothes.

Bree cleared her throat, and I dragged my gaze away from Archer and his endless expanse of inked skin. "Hey, girl," she drawled, a shit-stirring grin on her face. "Arch was just telling me about his upcoming title fight. You know it's going to be televised on pay-per-view?" Her eyes sparkled with excitement, and I shook my head at her.

"Legitimately couldn't care less," I told her, giving Archer a disgusted sneer and dismissing him from my attention. "Shall we go?"

Bree bit her lip, glancing at Archer from under her lashes. "Oh, uh, Arch was making pancakes for us…" She trailed off as my glare turned murderous. "But you know what? I wasn't that hungry anyway."

"Running scared?" Archer asked oh so casually as I started to leave the kitchen. The challenge was clear, and my shoulders bunched with tension.

Turning slowly, I narrowed my eyes. "Nothing to be scared of here," I replied with a stubborn tilt to my chin. "Unless you're a really shitty pancake cook."

His blue eyes were like fucking magnets, catching and holding my gaze as he moved around the kitchen with practiced ease. "So what's the problem, Princess? Sit down and have breakfast with us."

Bree, the fucking traitor, sank her ass down onto one of the barstools and gave me a small shrug. "It's just breakfast, MK. We'll head out straight after."

I sucked in a deep breath, feeling anger and frustration wash over me like an old, prickly blanket, then tightened my hold on my emotions. "Sure," I said, biting my words off, "just breakfast with the three bastards who would have happily seen me go down for twenty to life."

Bree's face fell, and a twinge of guilt pricked at my heart. She clearly felt some responsibility about that period of my life too, and this wasn't the time or place to hash it all out. So I sighed and brushed past Archer to make myself a proper coffee.

Thankfully, my father's love of barista espresso hadn't changed in the time I'd been gone, and a shiny, chrome-finished machine sat proudly on the counter. I doubted any of the guys knew how to use it—they looked like gross drip-coffee kind of guys—so I cleaned out the old beans and replaced them with fresh before starting the process.

Grind, tamp, brush off the excess. I worked almost on autopilot, since I'd learned to make *real* coffee as a twelve-year-old. The first chef my father had employed—after the massacre that saw my mother die alongside our entire household staff—had been an Australian guy called Steve. He'd come from Melbourne and spent *weeks* instructing me on how to use the espresso machine and how to correctly steam milk to perfect, velvety consistency for a flat white.

Bree's groan was what cut through my coffee-making trance, and I glanced over at her.

"Girl, please tell me you're making one for me too. I swear I haven't had good coffee in over a year, and I'm getting the shakes just smelling it." She'd halfway collapsed on the island counter, being all dramatic and shit, so I grabbed another mug out of the cupboard for her.

"I feel like I'm missing something here," Kody said from somewhere *really* close behind me, and I startled. I hadn't even noticed him come into the kitchen. "It's still coffee, right? Just made with a bit of douchery."

I snorted but didn't answer. All I could picture was his naked, wet body and his huge...uh...biceps? Yeah. Sure. Let's go with that.

"Clearly you have no idea what you're talking about," Bree snickered. "But hey, I'm Bree."

This made me turn my attention back to her, curious. I'd assumed they already knew each other, seeing as Shadow Grove wasn't exactly a huge city.

"'Sup, Bree," Kody replied with one of those cool-guy head nods. "I'm Kody."

Her cheeks flushed with heat. "I know," she responded, her voice practically dripping with lust. "You're on the billboard opposite my mom's office downtown."

Kody grinned, arrogant fucker. "Cool."

I rolled my eyes for what felt like the billionth time since arriving back in Shadow Grove. "You're on a billboard?" I remarked, unable to help myself. "For what? STD awareness?"

He gave a sarcastic laugh, but his gaze was way too freaking heated for my liking as he dragged his eyes down my outfit. "Hot outfit, babe. I preferred that see-through tank you had on earlier, though. It really complemented your black lace panties well."

Instantly, my face flamed. I'd been so half-asleep when I busted into his room—and then so shocked at the sight of him naked—I hadn't even thought about what I'd been wearing. Apparently I wasn't the only one who'd gotten an eyeful this morning.

"What?" Archer snapped, pulling both our attention and breaking the lust-filled stare down we were engaged in. One-sided lust, of course. My hate was stronger than my libido. "When did you see Princess Danvers in her underwear?" A scowl pulled his dark brow low over those beautiful blue eyes, and I tensed against the shiver of desire threatening my body. What was it about angry bad boys that turned me on so hard?

Kody's grin was all trouble. "Wouldn't you like to know?" He

70

smirked at his friend before throwing an arm casually over my shoulders like we'd just fucked or something. "I'll tell you this much, though, Arch. Your future stepsister *did* get to see my newest tattoo." He threw that out with a heavy wink in Archer's direction, and it took me a quick second to connect the dots. Kodiak Jones had a few tattoos—not as many as Archer, not by a long shot—but the one on his right thigh had looked a bit fresher than the rest of his ink. Not that I'd stared at his…uh…*thigh* for long enough to know for sure. But considering what he was implying…

"Fuck off, Kody," I growled, tossing his arm off my shoulders. "Quit stirring up shit. I honestly couldn't dislike the three of you more than I already do, so you're wasting your breath."

He wisely didn't say anything more, and I finished making coffee for myself and Bree in relative peace. Along the counter, Archer had made a pot of drip coffee that smelled so stale I wanted to gag. If I'd been a bigger person, I'd have taken pity on them and made everyone a flat white.

What a shame I was petty as fuck.

While Archer's back was turned, taking the massive stack of pancakes to the huge marble island where Bree waited, I did a quick swap. Moving quickly, I flicked the top off the sugar jar—a fancy sterling silver thing that my mother had purchased forever ago—and dumped the contents down the sink. Keeping an eye on where the guys were, Steele included as he stumbled into the kitchen looking half-asleep, I filled the sugar container back to the brim with salt. It meant the salt dish was left empty, but I seriously doubted anyone would notice that at this time of morning.

Of course, I had no way of knowing whether any of them took sugar in their coffee, but it was worth a shot.

Humming under my breath, I took a sip of my perfect coffee and ran the tap to wash away the evidence of sugar from the sink.

"Didn't expect to see you joining us for breakfast, Madison Kate," Steele commented. He slid into a chair, rubbing a hand over his sleep-creased face. "Who's this?" He squinted at Bree, then frowned. "You look familiar. Have we met?"

Bree—horny bitch—blushed from head to toe and batted her lashes. "Once," she replied, "briefly. On, uh, Riot Night. You told me not to wait for MK after things went to shit at The Clown."

Recognition registered in Steele's sleepy gray eyes, and he nodded. "That's right. I never forget a pretty face for long."

I made an exaggerated gagging sound as I slid into my own seat and reached for the plate of pancakes. "Dial it down, Steele," I sneered. "It's too early to choke on your oozing sex appeal."

His eyes flashed, and his grin brightened. "Oh, so you noticed my sex appeal, then? Good to know."

Goddamn it all to hell, I'd missed the mark on that insult.

Releasing a long-suffering sigh, I decided to fill my mouth with fluffy—admittedly, really tasty—pancakes rather than engaging further.

For a few minutes, everyone ate in silence. Bree picked at her syrup-covered food with her knife and fork, while the boys seemed to be making a sport of who could eat more pancakes in the shortest space of time.

Eventually, Kody reached for his pitch-black coffee and took a big gulp before wrinkling his nose in disgust. "Ugh, maybe I do need to try that fancy coffee, Madison Kate," he muttered, shooting my half-empty mug a longing look. "This crap could strip paint."

I shrugged, keeping my face carefully neutral. "Tough shit," I replied. "Just load it up with sugar, and you won't taste anything."

He grunted an annoyed noise but got up to grab the sugar dish from the counter. Raising my own coffee to my lips, I sipped slowly and watched from under my lashes while he dropped several large spoonfuls into his mug, then stirred.

"So what are you girls up to today?" Steele asked Bree, tugging at my attention. She was probably still batting her lashes at all three of them, but I couldn't take my eyes from Kody for even a second. Not when he was about to—

"What the *fuck*?" Archer shouted as a dark spray of coffee hit him in the side of the face. Kody'd just taken a huge sip of his coffee and promptly spat it right back out...all over his bestie.

Ha, that had worked better than expected.

"Who the fuck switched the sugar for salt?" Kody roared, glaring at his friends. Amazingly, it didn't even seem to have crossed his mind that I was responsible. Steele knew, though, if his narrow-eyed glare was anything to go by.

"Well," I said, dabbing my mouth with a napkin, then pushing my chair back, "I think that's our cue to leave. Bree?"

My friend practically tripped over her own feet as she shot out of her seat and grabbed her handbag. "Yep, sure is. Uh, thanks for breakfast, Archer." She was biting her lip and blushing at him, but he was too busy mopping coffee from his face and glaring daggers at Kody.

"Don't forget our coffee date later, Madison Kate," Kody called out when I was almost out of the kitchen.

I paused, looking over my shoulder and giving him a sly smile.

"I haven't forgotten, Kodiak," I said, "I always keep my word, and I won't even be *salty* about it." I shot him a wink and had the satisfaction of his storm-cloud scowl before I hurried out of the house.

Okay, sure, if I'd put some thought into that plan, I could have come up with a much better punch line. But for a spur-of-the-moment prank, I was pretty pleased with the results. So much so that I was grinning from ear to ear when Bree and I cruised out of the main gates and hit the road.

Maybe being back in Shadow Grove wouldn't suck as much as I'd thought.

CHAPTER 9

"Okay, so what's the plan?" Bree asked me some time later in the day. We'd spent hours lying on the banks of Dogwood Lake—despite the chilly weather—catching up on the past year of friendship we'd both missed.

I didn't answer her straightaway because I didn't know the answer. Everything she'd told me about what'd happened to Shadow Grove since Riot Night had thrown me for a loop. My father was no longer pushing for a political position—when had *that* happened?—and seemed content as the all-powerful developer of Shadow Grove. East and West Shadow Grove had been abolished, with all kinds of new structures going up along the strip that had once denoted the center line of our town—one of which was the university we'd both be starting at come Monday.

"I have no idea," I admitted with a sigh. "Why are they going to SGU anyway? There's no way they're freshmen too."

Bree shrugged. She knew which *they* I was talking about. The three pains in my ass had been our number one subject of conversation. "Your dad is super-determined to make SGU a *thing*," she said. "Almost every student enrolled was bought or blackmailed away from more prestigious schools to fill the halls here. Or their parents were, anyway."

I guessed—based on her grimace—that was the case for her. Last we'd spoken, she had early acceptance to Stanford along with me. But Bree's father had told her she was attending SGU instead? Well then, that's what she did without questioning his motivation.

"But you're right. They're all older. Pretty sure Arch is turning twenty-two in December." Her cheeks heated. "Not that I've Googled him or anything."

I snorted a laugh, shaking my head. "Sure you haven't. You're lucky I did a lot of self-improvement in Cambodia, babe. A lesser woman would be shitty at you flirting with her mortal enemies."

Bree paled slightly, so I gave her a grin to show I really was joking. I didn't blame her for flirting shamelessly with those three douchecanoes, and I didn't expect her to shoulder the burden of my hatred toward them. The score I had to settle was a private one, and I wasn't childish enough to drag Bree down with me.

"Anyway, I guess step one is just getting them out of the house. I can't fucking breathe there without one of them staring at me." I shuddered dramatically and pushed away the whispered thought that maybe I *liked* them watching me.

Bree nodded, her face scrunched up with thought as she sipped her iced chocolate-coconut drink. There was a chocolatier on the outskirts of Dogwood Park that made awesome drinks, and I was so freaking glad to see they'd survived all the changes in Shadow Grove.

"Why don't *you* move out?" she asked, frowning slightly. "You and your dad aren't exactly on the best terms, and it's not like you don't have options. You could stay with me." I arched a brow at her, and she sighed. "Okay, maybe not me. My dad is hardly an upgrade on yours. But, you know, there are other places."

"One," I started, holding up a finger, "because my inheritance from Mom doesn't become available until I turn twenty-one, so

I'm essentially broke without Dad's help. Two, because I can't even get a job to support myself because, oh yeah, I'm a fucking criminal in everyone's eyes around here." I seethed over that because it was fucking unjust. I'd been cleared of all charges, but it didn't matter. The damage was done. My father's lawyer hadn't even requested the records be sealed during my trial—something that *should* have happened, considering I'd been a minor at the time—so my reputation was totally shredded. "And three." I held up a third finger. "Because it's the fucking *principle* of it, Bree. Those bastards set me up, then left me to fall for their fuckups. Now they're living in my house, acting like they belong there? And I'm, what? Supposed to just smile and hug my new brother?" I scoffed a bitter laugh. "Yeah, no. Not happening. I need to make them regret the day they ever fucked with Madison Kate Danvers."

My friend stared back at me for a long moment, her eyes wide, and then she let out a low whistle. "Damn girl," she muttered. "You've always been a bit intense, but you're kinda scary now. I'm almost intimidated myself."

I laughed. "Almost?"

She nodded, sucking on her straw with a loud gurgle. "Almost. Keep working on that death-glare thing; with a bit more effort it could make a grown man piss his pants."

My eyes narrowed, and she cracked up. "That's better! Like that."

The glare melted off my face as I grinned back at her. "Whatever. We better go, anyway. I have to go for coffee with Kody this afternoon." I sighed, like I'd just said I was on my way for a pap smear or Brazilian waxing.

"Uh yeah, what's up with that?" Bree questioned as we dusted off our jeans and wandered back to her car. "Kinda seems at odds with your whole *make them regret the day they were born* thing."

"Oh, trust me, I'm well aware. But those bastards hadn't given me the gate code, and I was too tired to negotiate a better trade. I *told* you not to come so early." I shot her an accusing look, like it was all her fault I was going on a coffee date with one of my worst nightmares.

Bree just laughed. "Okay, so he swapped you the code for a coffee date? Seems…suspicious."

My brows arched. "Right? I thought so too."

"Aha," she replied, nodding with understanding. "Girl, your curiosity is going to get you killed one of these days. Like, for real, this time."

I snorted a laugh at how casually she referenced the brief moment when everyone had thought I was dead. "I don't even doubt that," I agreed. "But it won't be over a coffee date with an infuriating asshole who thinks he's god's gift to women everywhere."

Bree climbed into the driver's seat of her shiny white Audi and gave me a serious look. "I should hope not. But I think you meant to say, an infuriating-*ly gorgeous guy whose dick you still kinda want to suck despite his terrible judgment.*" She ran those words together so quickly I only just caught what she was saying.

Lucky for her, she gunned the engine and accelerated up the street, and I was too cautious to smack her while she was driving. She knew it too, if her peals of laughter were anything to go by.

When she dropped me off at the front door of Danvers Mansion, I flipped her off and she sent it straight back to me as she peeled out of the circular driveway.

I smiled, shaking my head. Some things really didn't change, and if my friendship with Bree could withstand almost a year of silence and hard feelings, then I felt secure in the knowledge we'd be friends for a long time to come.

"Ready to go?" Kody's voice in my ear startled me, and I glared daggers.

"Don't sneak up on people," I growled up at him. Damn, he was tall. "It's rude."

He nodded with a healthy dose of sarcasm shining through

his face. "Unless, of course, you're saving that person from being kidnapped and brutally tortured by a psychotic gang leader. Then it's okay, right?"

My glare turned darker. "You keep reminding me of Riot Night and we're going to have a seriously unpleasant coffee date, Kody."

"Solid point, Madison Kate," he replied with a nod. "Let's go, then."

There was something weird about his whole energy, but I shrugged it off and followed him past the perfectly manicured hedges and into the garage.

"Typical," I muttered under my breath, eyeing the ridiculous line of luxury cars parked inside Samuel Danvers's garage. That was nothing new. Dad had been working on his car collection since before I was even born. What *was* new was the workshop section with a black Challenger propped up on a jack and plenty of well-used tools scattered around. Now that I was looking closer, the motorcycles weren't really Dad's style either.

"You guys sure are making yourselves at home here," I commented as Kody led me over to a royal-blue Maserati and opened the passenger door.

He just gave me a cryptic look, then jerked his head to the car. "Get in, Madison Kate. We're already late."

I grumbled under my breath about being late for a time we'd never set but got in and buckled my seat belt nonetheless.

"So, where are we going?" I asked when we'd left the estate and been driving in silence for some time. We were heading in the direction of what used to be West Shadow Grove, and my muscles tensed out of habit.

Kody flicked a quick look at me, then turned his attention back to the road. "I told you," he said, "for coffee."

His whole demeanor had shifted. Where he'd been joking and playful this morning, now he was brooding and serious. For some reason I'd never understand, I felt the need to lighten the mood.

"And possibly cake," I reminded him. "But *where*?"

He shot me another quick look, and his hands tightened on the steering wheel. "Nadia's Cakes," he responded after a moment. "You wouldn't know it. Not really your scene."

Irritation zipped through me, and I glowered. "How the fuck would you know what my *scene* even is? You don't know me."

This statement earned a sly smirk from Kody, and he held my gaze for a touch longer than was really safe while operating a fast-moving vehicle. "Everyone knows you, Madison Kate," he replied, echoing what he'd said on Riot Night.

Anger and resentment burned through my veins. "Not anymore."

Neither of us spoke again for the rest of the drive, each wrapped up in an invisible bad-mood blanket. When Kody finally stopped the car, I could see what he meant.

Nadia's Cakes was a run-down, decrepit, little bakery-cum-coffeehouse firmly in the middle of what had once been West Shadow Grove. Evidence of my father's integration projects was everywhere, with a fancy shoe store right next door, so new the paint still smelled wet, but Nadia's Cakes looked untouched.

"Come on," Kody said. "I promise her cakes are worth the drive."

Curiosity burned through me so powerfully I was helpless to do anything but follow, and I soon found myself parked on one half of a threadbare love seat while an elderly woman fussed all over Kody.

Her face was split with a smile so wide her eyes almost disappeared, and she gushed words of affection all over the tall, muscled guy like he was a four-year-old.

"Nadia, this is Madison Kate," he finally said, breaking away from her hugs to introduce me. "She's living with me and the guys."

I arched a brow. "He means to say, they're temporarily staying in my father's house until they find something more suitable."

"Well then," Nadia replied, parking her hands on her wide

hips and giving me a small smile. "It's lovely to meet you, Madison Kate. We heard talk that Kodiak had found himself a woman, but no one said how pretty you are. That hair color is just something else."

I bit back a grin because I suspected it was the nicest thing she could say about my pink hair. Then again, who gave a rat's ass? It was just hair.

"Uh…" I started to correct her and say that I was most definitely *not* Kody's "woman," but the fucker cut me off by ordering coffee and cakes for both of us, then sending Nadia off with another tight squeeze.

The older woman bustled away to the kitchen to deal with orders—the place was surprisingly busy—and Kody sank down onto the other end of the love seat.

Fuck. Did he just triple in size? I didn't care what anyone said, there was not enough space on this little sofa for both of us.

I shifted uncomfortably, looking around for a spare chair I could drag over.

"Chill the fuck out, Madison Kate," he drawled, stretching an arm along the back of the seat and almost spreading out even more. Our legs were touching, and there was barely even a few inches between our upper bodies. As it was, his arm almost draped around me…like we were on a real date or something.

"What the hell was that all about?" I demanded in an angry hiss. "I thought our deal was for coffee, not to be your fake girlfriend."

His lips twitched so minutely I probably would have missed it if I weren't practically in his lap. "Our deal is for coffee. I just ordered it. Stop being so paranoid."

"Paranoid?" I exclaimed. "What? You just told—"

"Uh-uh," he cut me off, shaking his head. "I didn't tell anyone anything that wasn't true."

I glowered. "You let Nadia *assume* I was your girlfriend. That's lying by omission."

He tilted his head slightly to the side. "Is it, though? You know what they say about assuming."

My hand curled into a fist at my side, and I seriously thought about punching him in the throat. He'd deserve it.

"Now now," he murmured with an edge of amusement in his voice. His hand closed over mine and uncurled my fist. "None of that. Nadia is like a grandmother to me, and I won't have you starting shit in her place of business."

Anger and adrenaline and, okay, a bit of lust burned through me. "Kody, quit playing games. Why are we really here?"

"I told you," he said, voice soft and teasing. "For coffee." His fingers tangled with mine in my lap, and I stupidly didn't pull away and immediately bleach my skin. Instead, I found myself a little bit lost in the rich emerald of his gaze, my breath hitching when his thumb stroked lazy circles on the back of my hand.

"Seriously?" someone exclaimed, and it was the bucket of ice water I needed to snap the fuck out of it. "*This* bitch?"

I tried to pull away from Kody, but his grip tightened. The arm that had been resting on the back of the love seat was suddenly wrapped around me, and our entwined fingers sat in full view between us.

"Drew," he drawled, eyeing the brunette standing over us. "What are you doing here?"

"Me?" the girl—Drew—damn near shrieked. "What am *I* doing here? What are *you* doing here, Kody? And with the goat? What the hell?"

My eyebrows shot up. *Goat? What the fuck was that supposed to mean?*

"I'm here having coffee with a friend," Kody replied in a voice like an arctic breeze, "and we'd really love to be left alone, if you don't mind?"

The way Drew's face was turning an unpleasant shade of purplish red, I'd hazard a guess and say she definitely did mind. Safe to say this was a lover's quarrel that I had zero interest in becoming involved with, so I carefully untangled my hand from Kody's and sat forward.

"Listen," I said, piling on the sweetness, "it seems like you two have history. I'm just going to—"

I'd been standing up as I spoke, ready to walk outside and leave them to air their dirty laundry without involving me. Apparently, Drew had other ideas.

Her hand cracked across my face so quickly I gasped. Not because it hurt—which it really did—but because I straight up hadn't seen that coming.

"You homewrecking bitch!" she howled at me, jabbing me in the chest with a long acrylic nail. "I bet those were your trashy-ass pink panties in his bed last week! How long has this been going on, Kody? How long have you been screwing the goat behind my back?"

I was fucking frozen with shock. So much that it took a second to register why she hadn't hit me again.

"Back the fuck off, Drusilla," Kody growled at her in a voice like murder. His huge hand encircled her wrist just inches from my stinging cheek, and his whole body radiated danger and violence. "If you so much as breathe on her, I will destroy you."

The girl sneered, but it quickly turned to a yelp of pain as Kody's grip on her tightened.

"Don't fucking push me," he warned her, then leaned closer to whisper something in her ear. Whatever it was, she turned an ashen gray and took a big step backward, yanking her wrist free of Kody's hold—something I was pretty confident she couldn't have done if he hadn't let her.

For a moment, she just stared up at the beautiful, green-eyed man. Her gaze was full of hurt, betrayal, disbelief, and there, under it all—though mainly when her attention flickered to me—an emotion I knew all too well: hate.

"You're fucking dead, goat," she whispered, her voice shaking with fear as she threw that one last threat in my direction and damn near ran out of the coffeehouse.

The door slammed closed after her, and Kody released a heavy sigh, his shoulders sagging with relief.

"Sorry," he murmured, turning to me with concern etched across his face. "I didn't think she'd hit you."

He raised a hand to touch my cheek, and I winced. Drusilla—whoever the fuck she was—had one hell of a slap on her. I could practically feel every finger of the handprint throbbing and burning with all the blood rushing to the surface.

"Yeah, but you knew she'd be here," I accused, shrugging off his touch. "And you let her think we were together. What the fuck was that all about, Kodiak Jones?"

His lips twitched with a barely concealed smile when I said his full name, and he gave a small shrug. "Prove it. I just came here for the coffee and cake." He sat back down on the faded floral sofa and nodded to my seat.

My jaw dropped. "You must be kidding me. I'm not—"

"Here we are," Nadia announced, delivering a tray onto the low table in front of our seat. It was loaded with several different types of cake and two of the best-looking coffees I'd seen in ages. She'd even nailed the heart-shaped latte art. Huh. "You two enjoy," she told us with a warm smile. "It's so, so good to see you happy, boy-o." She pressed a quick kiss to Kody's forehead, then hurried back to her kitchen before I could correct her. Again.

I was still standing, arms folded, so it didn't take much to glare down at him. "Explain this or I'm leaving."

He didn't reply for a moment, just peering up at me with thoughtful eyes, like he was trying to decide if I was full of shit or not. I wasn't. If I had to walk the entire way home just to prove a point, I damn well would.

"Sit down, Madison Kate," he finally said. "The cake really is good. It'll take a little sting out of that cheek."

I wanted to show *him* a fucking sting. But I was kinda hungry and more than a little curious—again—so I huffed an annoyed sigh and perched back on the edge of the sofa. Carefully, I reached out and selected the slice of dessert that seemed to have my name all fucking over it. Strawberry and white chocolate cheesecake. Yum.

"Happy?" I demanded, taking a huge forkful and stuffing it into my mouth. Oh, wow. Kody hadn't been joking. Nadia's cakes were downright... "Fucking hell," I groaned, licking the sticky cream cheese from my fork. "Maybe the cake is worth getting slapped."

Kody's eyes were hot as he watched me eat, full of hunger for something somewhat less sweet than cake. "I'm inclined to agree," he murmured, shifting in his seat and not tearing his gaze from my mouth to even blink.

Desire flushed hot through me, and I swallowed several times to get myself in check. "Stop eye-fucking my mouth and start explaining yourself," I ordered him, but my voice came out huskier than intended.

His nostrils flared, and he seemed to need a whole lot of effort to tear his focus away from my face. "What do you want to know?"

I frowned. The obvious answer was *everything*. But I got the feeling Kodiak Jones had no intention of just sitting here and spilling his guts for free. No, he'd require tit for tat, and I was no longer in the mood for games. Or not that type of game anyway.

My revenge was a whole other game to play.

"Why'd she call me *goat*?" I asked, deciding that was the one thing I cared most about. All the other shit—Kody's history with Drusilla, whoever owned the panties I'd just taken the fall for, even Nadia's behavior...it was none of my business. But she'd called me a name that sounded a whole lot like a slur, and I wanted to know what the fuck was up with that.

He sighed, sitting back with his coffee in hand. Considering how friendly he was with Nadia, it occurred to me that his shitty attitude about my coffee over breakfast was all an act. A purposeful insult to try to rile me up. Fucker.

On the other hand, at least he *did* in fact appreciate good coffee.

"Goat," he repeated, crinkling his nose in a grimace. "Short for scapegoat. It's what everyone started calling you during the trial. Everyone knew you weren't the one responsible. Anyone with even a quarter of a brain could have told the prosecutor that pretty little Princess Danvers hadn't orchestrated an event like Riot Night."

Shock held me immobile, and I barely breathed. I needed to hear this. Bree hadn't mentioned *any* of this to me.

"But your father let them charge you anyway. He stood by while they put you on trial, never lifted a finger to close the court and protect your identity...then stood up for the mayor during the elections and preached to the people of Shadow Grove how he loved this town so much not even his own blood would be given a *free pass*. That's what he called it. A *free pass* to...what? Be released of charges for crimes you *didn't* commit?" He gave me a look that was way, way too freaking close to pity for my liking. "It was so painfully obvious what it all was—a publicity stunt. Riot Night needed a scapegoat, and you were it."

The cake sat in my stomach like a lump of clay, and I gave a short, jerking nod. "I see."

Kody sighed again and let out a small groan. "Madison Kate, I didn't—"

"No," I cut him off. "No, you're right. That's exactly what I was. But what I want to know now is why you did nothing about it."

His brows shot up. "What?"

"If it was all so obvious I'd been used as a scapegoat, why the hell didn't you speak up? You knew. You *knew* I was just in the wrong place at the wrong time. So why the hell didn't you come forward and set the story straight?" I was shaking with anger now, my fists clenched in tight balls in my lap.

Kody stared back at me, his eyes wide with shocked panic, like he was desperately searching for something, *anything* that might explain his own inaction. But I was way past listening to bullshit.

Shoving to my feet, I scowled down at him. "Yeah, that's what I thought. Too busy building your superstar career to do the right thing for the girl whose life you ruined. You're just as bad as my father."

The bitter sting of tears threatened, so I hauled ass out of the shop as quick as I could. I had no car of my own and no idea where the fuck I was, but I didn't care. I'd figure it out on my own, just like I'd been doing every damn day since my mother died and left me alone.

"Madison Kate," Kody called out from behind me as I stalked down the street, but I didn't pause. My long, pink hair flapped behind me, I was walking so briskly, but of course that was no match for a six-foot-fuck-knows-what fitness trainer. I only made it past two more shops before he grabbed my arm and yanked me around to face him.

"I'm sorry," he snapped, sounding anything but. "There was more going on that you don't know."

"Oh yeah?" I replied, jerking my arm free of his grip and folding my arms. "Enlighten me."

His brow dropped over those jewel-green eyes, and the tight set to his jaw said more than his words ever would. He wasn't going to tell me *shit*. Not now, probably not ever. And why the hell should he? I was just some poor, little, rich girl scapegoat.

"Go fuck yourself, Kody," I said in a quiet, angry voice. "Take your pathetic friends and get the hell out of my dad's house. I can't stand having you all under the same roof as me."

His jaw clenched tighter—if that was even possible—and his eyes hardened. "Sometimes, Princess Danvers, we don't get what we want." He flicked his eyes to the shiny blue Maserati and clicked the key fob in his hand. "Get in the car. We can go back to hating each other at home."

Unfolding my arms long enough to flip him off, I smiled a nasty smile. "Bite me."

I started down the street again, only to find myself airborne, then thrown over a wide, muscular shoulder.

"Wha—" I shouted, shocked beyond belief. "Put me down, Kody. Put. Me. Down! I can find my own way home!"

He didn't reply, just manhandled my struggling ass into the passenger seat of his car and even buckled my seat belt up. If it hadn't been for the way he pinned my wrists with one of his hands while strapping me in, I'd have punched him in the junk. As it was, he moved so quickly we were already back on the highway before I could fully fight back...and then I had too much sense to risk a car accident.

"I fucking hate you, Kodiak Jones," I told him in a cold, detached voice when we eventually pulled into the driveway of Danvers Mansion.

He released a long breath, his knuckles white on the steering wheel. "At least you're alive to feel that hate, Madison Kate."

CHAPTER 10

Monday morning rolled around way too fast. I'd spent the remainder of the weekend holed up in my room, plotting my revenge. While I had a handful of promising plans for both Archer and Kody, Steele was proving a harder target. Not just because his whole social media platform seemed totally false and impersonal—all professional modeling shots that he seemed to have been roped into thanks to Archer's massive MMA sponsors—but because out of the three of them, I hated him the least.

Since I'd arrived back in Shadow Grove, he'd been nothing but nice, and on Riot Night his only part had been to send Bree home when she was supposed to drive me.

Still, Kody's confession about how *everyone knew* just ripped the scabs clean off my wounds. Everyone knew, yet no one came forward? No one had spoken up on my behalf, and certainly the real guilty parties had never stepped up to accept responsibility.

So yeah, guilty by association or just straight-up guilty, all three of these guys were going to feel my wrath before I'd be satisfied.

A sharp knock on my door made me jump slightly, and I scowled at my reflection. I'd been standing there in front of the mirror for ages, lost in thought, but it was game time.

"Madison Kate?" Steele called through the door. At least he didn't just let himself in like Archer had done on my first day here. "We need to leave now if you're going to make it to your first lecture."

I rolled my eyes at myself in the mirror. As if I needed these big, bad boys escorting me to my first day of university. But much to my dismay, when I'd finally gotten ahold of my father over the phone on Saturday night, things had seriously spiraled. Now not only had the guys been instructed to drive me to and from campus every day, but my father had given me very stern, no bullshit instructions to *behave*. Like I was some kind of unruly puppy.

"I'll catch a lift with Bree!" I yelled back, not bothering to open the door and speak to him like an adult. My father wanted to treat me like a child? I'd damn well act like one.

Apparently that was as far as Steele's patience went because the next second my bedroom door opened and he scowled at me with folded arms. "Quit making shit harder than it needs to be, Madison Kate. Just march downstairs, park your cute ass in my car, close your eyes, and pretend you're back in Cambodia until we get to campus."

I ignored the flicker of excitement that him calling my ass *cute* stirred. "Or what?" I shot back. "You going to force me into the car like Kody did on Saturday?"

Steele winced but then shrugged. "If I have to, sure."

I seethed, but where the fuck did that leave me? I was counting on Steele being their softest link, the least likely to manhandle a woman against her will. Apparently, I was wrong. Or they were *all* epic pricks with no sense of personal space and appropriate conduct.

"Fine," I hissed, stalking past him and stomping down the grand staircase.

"That's a shame," he murmured from way too close behind me. "I was kind of hoping you'd give me an excuse to smack that ass."

Shock made me stumble, and if Steele hadn't been so close on my heels—close enough to catch me with a strong hand under my elbow—I'd have tumbled the rest of the way down the stairs.

He gave me a knowing wink, then carried on ahead of me with his hands in his trouser pockets and a smirk on his face.

Yep. Definitely misread that one.

So why were my cheeks flushed and my panties damp?

_____

The drive to Shadow Grove University was tense but quick and mercifully silent. Neither Kody nor Archer was anywhere to be seen, and when Steele pulled into a reserved parking space close to the main entryway, I bolted.

Okay, so it wasn't totally silent. Steele had offered to help me find my way, seeing as I'd missed orientation, and I'd politely declined. By politely, I did mean with just a smattering of insults rather than a plethora.

I didn't need to be shown around. Just like I hadn't needed orientation. The "new" Shadow Grove University was a combination of the old East Shadow Grove Country Club and the West Shadow Grove High School. While I'd never really spent a whole lot of time in West SG before, I was plenty familiar with the country club.

It was a tiny campus compared to most universities but big enough to serve the purpose, I supposed.

Thanks to Steele's somewhat above speed limit driving, I'd arrived in plenty of time to find my first class and choose a seat near the middle of the room. Scrawled across the brand-new whiteboard in dry erase marker: CRIM 100—Introduction to Criminology.

Excitement and nervous energy tingled in my veins as I read those words and pulled my laptop out. My arrest might have fucked up my path to becoming a prosecutor—because I was under no illusions that my *very* public trial wouldn't work against me in that respect, whether the charges had been dismissed or not—but I still wanted to pursue a career in criminology. Somehow. The end goal was murky for now, but I'd enrolled in all the classes that struck an interest in me and I'd work out the rest later.

"Wow, I thought the whole Madison Kate trend died out a few months ago," someone said from behind me, flipping a piece of my dusky-rose hair over my shoulder.

"Excuse me?" I frowned up at the rude-as-fuck dude who clearly had no concept of personal space. He was cute, in that preppy, football-player sort of way—the kind of guy I used to date and the kind of guy that used to bore the pants off of me. Literally, in some cases. Sex generally made them stop rattling on about sports shit.

"You know," he carried on with a teasing laugh. "The whole pink-hair thing. You must be a hardcore Madison Kate groupie to still be rocking that color a year later, huh?"

My frown deepened into a scowl. "What the fuck are you talking about?" I demanded. What the hell did this asshole mean, calling me a groupie of…me? It wasn't like I was some kind of musician. Legit, I couldn't sing for shit…but I wasn't terrible on piano.

His grin grew a little less natural. A little more uncertain. "Uh, you know…those chicks who became all obsessed with Madison Kate while she was on trial? And…like…wore 'freedom for innocents' T-shirts and…shit?" He'd totally lost the smile by the time he finished stuttering his explanation out and was looking *really* uncomfortable. His attention drifted over me again, probably taking in my pretty awesome resting bitch face, then dropped to my bag, slung over the back of my chair. On the leather flap, gold-stitched embroidery read MKD. A gift from my father.

"Oh shit," the guy whispered when I said nothing back. "You're actually *her*. Aren't you?"

"If you mean, am I the infamous Madison Kate who got falsely accused of a list of bullshit offenses that I had exactly *nothing* to do with? Yeah. I am. But I'm seriously starting to regret dying my hair back to pink." I released a heavy sigh and returned my attention to my laptop. I figured the guy would walk away, but he kept hovering.

"Is there something else?" I snapped, not altogether kindly. Okay fine, not at all kindly. But in my own defense, I'd been walking the tightrope over a full rage breakdown for days. All it would take was one misstep from any of my three new housemates, and I would start cutting heads off. And I didn't mean the ones above their shoulders.

The guy grinned, and it was one of those arrogant playboy grins. Ugh, I hadn't missed those in Cambodia, that's for sure.

"Yeah, wow. Sorry. I'm just super surprised to see you. Here. Wow. Cool. Madison Kate Danvers in the flesh." He had a funny kind of stunned look on his face, and I was pretty confident he hadn't blinked since realizing I was me.

Giving him a tight smile and feeling the eyes of other students on us, I shrugged. "Yep. I don't think I caught your name?" I arched a brow, silently urging him to quit with the freak-out and advance like a normal human being meeting another normal human being.

"Oh shit," he blurted out, blinking a couple of times to break the weird trance he'd fallen into. "Yeah, sorry, where are my manners, right? I'm Rhett, but my friends call me Bark." He stuck a huge hand out for me to shake, and I took it gingerly.

"Nice to meet you, Bark?" I ended that like a question because who the fuck called themselves Bark?

He nodded, giving me a small grin as he hitched his bag a bit higher on his shoulder. "Yeah, it's a carryover from high school football 'cause—"

"Mr. Barker," an authoritative voice came from the front of the room. Somehow, our professor had walked in and started setting up without me even noticing. How? Probably because the huge dude standing in front of me was effectively blocking my view of, well, everything. "Please take your seat. We're about to begin."

Football dude—*Bark*—flashed me another winning grin, then slid into the empty seat beside me. Of course the seat beside me was empty. I was starting to think I'd just woken up in a clichéd teen movie or some shit.

"Welcome to CRIM 100," the professor continued, picking up a fresh dry erase marker and turning to the whiteboard as he spoke. "I'm Professor Barker, and before anyone asks, yes, that Neanderthal trying to chat up the prettiest girl in the room is my son, Rhett." The professor spoke in the kind of way that suggested he had zero intention of making this class easy on his son. In fact, I almost felt sorry for *Bark*. I'd rather run twenty miles over broken glass than have my father as a professor.

The lecture period flew by so fast I was actually shocked when Professor Barker declared the end and started packing up his things. My laptop was full of notes, and for the first time since stepping foot back into Shadow Grove, I was excited to be home.

CHAPTER 11

After Intro to Criminology, I rode an excited high all the way through my next class—Intro to Psychology—and by the time I made my way to the cafeteria for lunch, I was damn near smiling.

I hadn't seen Bree yet—our class choices were pretty polar opposite—but on the upside, I also hadn't seen Steele, Kody, or Archer either.

"You know, for a girl the entire freaking campus is gossiping about, you're surprisingly hard to track down." It was Bark again, stepping up beside me as I browsed the lunch options. There were all kinds of salads, some freshly made roast meats, and there were even some shellfish options. Dad had really gone all out on this university... Made me wonder where all the money had come from. Not that Samuel Danvers couldn't afford to fund something like a brand-new, top-tier university...just that he *wouldn't*.

"I wasn't aware anyone had been gossiping about me," I replied, a blatant lie. The whispers had followed me all morning, but I was pretty good at tuning it all out. Let them talk; it didn't affect me.

Bark laughed, flashing that winning smile at me again and making me want to roll my eyes. I had exactly zero interest in flirting with him, but apparently my resting bitch face was having very little success in dissuading his attention.

"Sure you weren't," he said, grinning like we were sharing some kind of joke. We weren't.

I opened my mouth to tell him as much, but he planted a hand on the counter in front of me, stopping me from walking any farther down the buffet.

"What are you doing Friday night, Madison Kate?" he asked, dropping the joking tone but laying the flirting on a whole lot thicker. If that was possible.

I blinked at him a few times, trying to comprehend the fact that he was trying to ask me out. Or that's what I was assuming. I'd barely actually spoken ten words to this guy, but apparently my reputation preceded me.

Ugh. Crap. My *reputation*.

I'd be willing to bet money that he wasn't asking me out based on my reputation as the Riot Night scapegoat and exiled heiress. Nope, that leering twinkle in his almond-brown eyes said it was all about my reputation as a cheap drunk and easy lay. Damn my past promiscuous self.

It was right there on the tip of my tongue to decline. I had no attraction to Bark and even less inclination to revisit old, slutty-drunk Madison Kate of a year ago. But then someone caught my attention, storming across the cafeteria like a thundercloud.

Deep sigh. *Here it goes.*

"What the fuck are you wearing?" Archer snarled, shoving Bark aside and getting all up in my personal space like he had *no* right to do.

Admittedly, I'd kind of known my outfit would set one of them off in some way…except my money had been on Kody trying to get into my pants. Then again, Archer being pissed off and all alpha male might be better.

"Clothes," I replied, my voice dripping in sass and my hands propped on my hips. "Clothes that *your* lovely mother left for me, I might add. Is that a problem for you?"

I mean, I was still surprised Steele hadn't said anything on the drive to school. Then again, Archer definitely had the worst case of BDE—Big Dick Energy—so I should have known it'd be him that had an aneurysm over my *tiny* pleated skirt, tight white T-shirt, and thigh-high socks worn with high-heeled Mary Janes. I looked like—

"You look like you just stepped out of a schoolgirl porn video," Archer growled, his blue eyes flashing with so much disdain that it almost made me laugh—okay, fine, I chuckled out loud. "Go home and change. Now."

Shrugging, I stepped away from him and flipped my long, rose-colored hair like a pro. "Take it up with Cherry if you don't like her taste in women's clothes. In the meantime, I don't take orders from you. So, you know, fuck right off."

Brushing him off like he wasn't still hovering right there, glaring like he could set my clothes on fire with the power of his mind, I grabbed a few items of food and added them to my plate. In fairness, I had no idea what I'd just grabbed because every one of my senses was focused on Archer.

"Madison Kate," Archer snapped again as I paid for my food at the self-service machine. I continued pretending he wasn't there and turned back to Bark, who was shockingly still standing there with his jaw gaping.

"So sorry, Bark, that was really rude of my new stepbrother. You were saying?" I smiled sweetly, indicating he should join me as I made my way to a vacant table and placed my tray down.

He hesitated a moment, shooting his gaze between Archer and me several times before scanning my outfit and clearly deciding I was worth the effort. "Yeah, I was, uh, I was asking you..." He trailed off, glancing over his shoulder nervously. Archer was just a few yards away, glaring at Bark now, and it was making my potential suitor all kinds of uncomfortable.

"You were asking me out, right?" I prompted him, trying to pull his attention back to me. I was going off plan with this, but anything that made the vein in Archer's temple throb like his head was at risk of exploding seemed like a good tactic.

"You're acting like a brat, Madison Kate," Archer informed me—like I wasn't aware. His fist was clenched at his side, and I smiled sweetly at him.

"Which is it, Archer? A brat or a porn star?"

His gaze darkened with something that spoke to a dark, depraved corner of my soul. "Both."

Unnerved by the way my heart raced when he said this, I pasted my best forced smile back on my face and batted my lashes at Bark once more. "I'd love to go out on Friday night, Bark."

"Fuck off, Bark," Archer snarled.

The preppy footballer looked between us again, then backed away a step. "I'll, uh, I'll see you in class, Madison Kate."

He beat a hasty retreat, and I glared at Archer. Not that I particularly gave a shit about him running Bark off—I would have found some excuse not to turn up on Friday anyway—but he was acting like he had some claim on me.

"Go home and change, Madison Kate," he ordered me, folding his impressively tattooed arms over his chest, his muscles shifting in a way that would normally make my panties wet.

"With what transportation, D'Ath? I don't have a car, remember?"

His eyes narrowed dangerously. "I'll loan you mine."

Ignoring his suggestion, I ate a forkful of my lunch—ew, oh so gross chicken pot pie—and chewed very slowly before replying to him.

"Bite me, Archer. Oh hey, Bree!" I waved at my friend who'd just entered the cafeteria, then gave Archer a quick up and down. "You can go now, unless you have anything more interesting to say? No? Didn't think so." I shifted my chair to give him my back, then greeted my friend enthusiastically when she sat down opposite me.

Archer said nothing more, and soon I saw him take a seat across the room, where Steele already sat with several girls. Kody was nowhere to be seen, so I guessed it must have just been my bad luck to share a lunch break with both Archer and Steele.

"What…was that all about?" Bree asked with raised brows, casting a quick look over her shoulder at where the guys sat. "And what's with the outfit? I thought you were all jeans and sneakers these days and the primped Barbie-doll look was a thing of the past? Not that you don't look great—you do. I'm just… confused."

I gave a small shrug. "Spur-of-the-moment idea to piss my new housemates off. I think subconsciously I could smell the alpha-male BS on those three and wanted to poke it with a stick."

Bree snorted a laugh and grabbed the slice of cake from my tray. "Well, be careful. It might be *your* first day, but those three have already built an entire army of enamored followers." She darted another quick look, and I couldn't help but follow her line of sight. Steele was chatting to a pretty blond who looked a couple of years older than me, and Archer…hmm. Archer had a brunette in his lap and was whispering something in her ear that she seemed to find *hysterical*.

Ugh. I knew her type. I used to *be* her type. If that was the kind of girl my new housemates were into, then we definitely wouldn't be forming that reverse harem Bree kept teasing me about.

"Anyway, I'll deal with them later. After we get through at least a few days of this…unconventional university." I wrinkled my nose, looking around the cafeteria. It used to be the main restaurant of the country club, so it was actually really nice. Just strange, considering my last class had been in a building so hastily painted you could still make out the graffiti on the walls. On the other hand, the food—for the most part—was restaurant-quality good so there was no need to leave campus to get decent lunches Assuming one made better choices than I had with the chicken pot pie, of course.

Bree nodded, waving a fork covered in cake crumbs. "You're telling me. Girl, we were supposed to be at Stanford this year."

I sighed and glowered across the room again. Not that it was Archer, Kody, and Steele's fault so many students in Shadow Grove had suddenly been denied entry into their college of choice…but they damn well knew more than they were letting on. It wasn't a coincidence the stolen Laughing Clown key had been in Kody's pocket that night. It also hadn't been a coincidence that Zane had been exchanging a big old bag of cash with some creepy dude dressed as Beetlejuice.

"Quit staring at them," Bree teased, kicking me under the table. "Anyone would think you've got a crush…or two."

"Ha!" I scoffed. "Hardly. I'm just thinking through my plan. I'll start small, I think. Only escalate if and when more drastic measures are called for." I drummed my fingertips on the table thoughtfully, observing my prey. Steele was laughing at something Archer had just said, and damn, he was pretty when he laughed. The brunette had disappeared from Archer's lap, but a strawberry-blond was glued to his side like…uh…like glue.

"Typical man-whore behavior," I commented with a disappointed sigh. "Acting all caveman because I dressed a little provocatively, then letting a revolving door of women paw all over him. Double standards in action."

Bree nodded and shrugged like this wasn't anything new. She was right, it wasn't, but damn that trope was getting exhausted.

My friend started to say something; then her attention shifted over my head and she gasped. "Watch out!" she exclaimed, but it was too late.

Sticky, orange liquid drenched me, soaking my entire T-shirt and puddling in my lap.

"Oops," a girl said from behind me. "Sorry, I guess I tripped." This bitch sounded *anything* but sorry.

Furious, I shoved my seat back and turned to confront the

clumsy juice owner. Then I laughed. "I guess I should have seen this coming a mile away," I commented, eyeing the pretty brunette with disdain as Archer, Steele, and their posse wandered over to us. "Stupid me for thinking crap like this belonged in high school."

The brunette—the same girl who'd just been giggling in Archer's lap—just smirked and flipped her hair, sauntering out of the dining hall and leaving me standing there in my sticky puddle of orange juice. Steele sighed and shook his head at me, then followed her, but Archer? Yeah, he lingered a moment.

Textbook bully behavior right there.

"Wait," I said, holding my hand up when he parted his lips to deliver what I was sure would be a truly devastating zinger. "Let me guess. *Now you have to change, Madison Kate.*" I adopted a deeper voice to say this, mocking him. "Or maybe you were going to go with the whole fake-concern angle? *You should have listened to me, Madison Kate.*"

Archer tilted his head to the side, running his thumb across his lower lip and shrugging. "Take your pick, gorgeous; sounds like you got the message."

My eyes narrowed, seeing victory all over his face.

Fuck. That.

"Um, sure," I replied, nodding. "If your message was that you time-traveled straight out of the fifties when it was socially accept-able for men to shame women for dressing in a way that flaunts their sexuality? Was that the message you were aiming for? If so, I got it...but I respectfully decline to accept it." Grasping the hem of my orange juice–soaked T-shirt, I peeled it up and off, tossing it onto the floor at Archer's feet. My miniskirt followed, hitting the floor with an audible *splat*, as every student had their eyes on us, rather than conversing.

"What the fuck are you doing?" Archer demanded when I met his gaze unflinchingly.

With what was no doubt a feral kind of smile, I propped my

hands on my hips. It wasn't like I was stark fucking naked or anything; I still had my bra and panties on, despite the fact that my bra
was soggy with juice too. It was no more revealing than a bikini,
so where was the embarrassment?

"Bree, babe, you don't mind if I borrow your cardigan, do
you?" I asked my friend, nodding to the thin, baby-pink garment
draped over the back of her chair. She obliged, handing it over
while she turned red from holding back her laughter.

I slipped it over my arms, then tied the loose belt around my
waist to hold it closed. Sort of. The fabric was long enough that it
covered my ass—just—but the crossed-over front showed a whole
lot more bra than I'd thought it would.

Fuck it. I was only proving a damn point, so long as no admin-
istrators saw me before I could find an actual change of clothes…

"Try harder next time, Archer," I advised him, bending over to
pick up my backpack and flashing my ass to anyone who cared to
look. "Oh, and those clothes are dry-clean only."

Yep, there it was. That little vein pulsing over his temple like a
ticking time bomb.

"MK: one; shady fucker: nil," Bree snickered under her breath
as we left the cafeteria with our heads held high. "This is going to
be so fun."

CHAPTER 12

Somehow I managed to make it through the next few days without running into the guys at all. After the showdown between Archer and me in the cafeteria on Monday, people had been giving me a wide berth, which I was more than okay about. It gave me a chance to actually settle into my classes, get a handle on the course load, and find a bit of normalcy in this strange new school.

Bree had taken to picking me up a full hour earlier than I'd have liked, but it served a double purpose. It got me out of the house before the guys had finished their gym workouts—yeah, that was a thing they did—and it gave me some time to reconnect with my old bestie. The fact that we also had time to pick up coffee from the one moderately decent coffee shop near SGU was an added bonus.

"All right, spill," she said as we collected our orders in the cute unicorn reusable cups she'd bought for us both a couple of days ago.

I thanked the barista, then arched a brow at her. "Spill what?"

Bree narrowed her eyes at me. "Don't play innocent with me, MK. I know you. It's been four days since that scene with Archer in the dining room, and I *know* you have something planned in retaliation."

I couldn't stop the grin curving my lips. "You don't think it was enough to strip down to my underwear in front of the entire dining hall?"

Bree snickered but shook her head. "Not by half. He orchestrated a *Mean Girls* moment, and there's no way in hell you'll let him get away with that shit so easily."

I smirked, sipping my coffee as we made our way across the park to the SGU campus. "I don't know what you're talking about, Bree," I said rather unconvincingly, checking my watch for the time. "But I'd really love to swing past the student parking lot before we head to lectures."

She gave me a curious—okay, suspicious—look but followed as I detoured from our usual shortcut. We arrived with perfect timing, which was no shock considering I'd been stealthily tracking Archer's schedule all week. He was punctual to the point of anal, and that predictability was what let me be in the right place at the right time.

His midnight-black Corvette Stingray careened into the parking lot and stopped in one of the few reserved spaces right near the main entrance to the university. I knew from Monday's drive to school that Steele would take the next space over when he arrived in about half an hour, but he wasn't my target today. Archer was.

"Okay, what are we here for?" Bree asked after a few moments when no one exited the car. I laughed to myself, imagining Archer sitting there fuming and working up the balls to show his face.

"You'll see," I murmured back, unable to wipe the grin from my face. The driver's door popped open, and I bit the inside of my cheek to contain my anticipation. It was a simple plan, but—

"Ah shit," I cursed, seeing Archer's perfectly handsome face as he stepped out. Had he seriously changed his routine on the same day as I'd hatched a revenge tactic? Then again, I had to cut myself some slack; it could have just been a coincidence that his routine hadn't deviated in the short time I'd monitored it.

Then Kody stepped out of the passenger side, and Bree sucked in a sharp gasp.

"MK!" she exclaimed in a hushed scream. "Did you do that?"

Laughter bubbled up in my chest as Kody turned his face in my direction. His bright purple face. "Oops, that was a misfire. Oh, well, means to an end, I guess." I shrugged and gave my two nemeses a little wave when they both glared daggers at me.

Archer took a few steps forward, like he wanted to confront me over the childish prank, but Kody grabbed his arm, halting him. A few quiet words passed between them, and then Archer wrenched his arm free and stomped off toward the sports center.

Kody and his pretty purple face sauntered over to where I stood with Bree. A huge crowd of snickering students stood around, pointing and laughing and making jokes, but he seemed totally oblivious to them all.

"Let me guess," he drawled as he stopped a few feet away, indicating his purple face. "Payback for Kalley's juice on Monday?"

I shrugged, still smirking. I wasn't admitting to *shit*.

Kody shook his head, looking torn between anger and amusement. "I had nothing to do with that, you know. I don't even have the same scheduled break as you all."

I nodded. "I know. But all's fair in hate and war, Kodiak. Sometimes there's collateral damage."

He gave me a knowing smile. "I figured as much. What was it? Powdered dye on our sweat towels?"

I gave him a brow quirk. "I'll admit to nothing. But *if* I were the responsible party, yeah, that's how I might do it. Sweaty face after a workout wiped with a towel coated in powdered purple food dye..." I shrugged again. "But that's childish and so very high school. We're better than silly pranks and bullying tactics, aren't we?"

Kody threw his head back and laughed. "Oh, babe. No. We're really, really not. You're so lucky purple suits me, but my PR manager might have a few words for you if this doesn't wash off in time for Sunday's photo shoot."

I batted my lashes, pulling on the fakest innocent act imaginable. "Well, in that case? Maybe avoid the body wash in the shared bathroom."

His eyes narrowed briefly, and he shook his head with a laugh. "Game on, gorgeous."

When he brushed past me, swaggering into the university halls with total confidence, like it had been his *choice* to dye his face purple, I let out a long breath. Every time I spoke to him, it was like I only breathed half as much as I needed to. I always seemed to walk away light-headed and weak.

"Damn, girl," Bree whispered, linking her arm with mine as we wandered in the direction of my first lecture. She didn't have anything until later in the day but insisted it was good for her to be up so early so she could study. "Remind me never to piss you off again. What did you do to the body wash?"

I chuckled. "Nothing. I just like making him paranoid."

Bree screamed with laughter and was wiping her eyes as she left me to make her way to the library. Me, though? I was already plotting my next strike.

My day went much like the rest of the week had—lots of gossiping and whispering going on around me but no one brave enough to speak directly to me. Not that I gave two craps, though. So long as they stayed out of my war with Archer and his boys, we'd be fine.

Surprisingly, though, at the end of the day when I headed out to the back lot, I found a broad-shouldered guy wearing an SGU football hoodie waiting for me.

"Bark?" I asked, recognizing his messy brown hair from behind.

He turned around, revealing a petite blond that he'd been chatting with. But they were standing right beside Bree's car, so I had to assume he was waiting for me. Or maybe I was being self-important?

"Hey, Madison Kate," he greeted me with a way too enthusiastic smile. "I was waiting for you."

I grinned, laughing at myself silently. "Cool. Uh, hi." I waved to the girl, who was still standing there and staring at me. Like, hardcore staring. She hadn't blinked once, I didn't think.

"Madison Kate, this is Ella. She wanted to…meet you." The odd hesitation in his phrasing made me pause, and I quirked a brow at him. He just gave me a sheepish smile, though, and rubbed the back of his neck.

Totally confused, I gave the girl a smile. "Hi, Ella."

Her eyes grew wider, if that was even possible, making her look younger. Too young to be a student at SGU, at any rate. Her bleached-blond hair was cut in a messy bob with a heavy fringe touching her mascara-coated lashes, and there was something vaguely familiar about her face.

"H-hi. Oh my gosh," Ella gasped like she was meeting a celebrity or some shit. "Wow. It's really you. When Bark said he knew you, I was like, nuh-uh, no way, but then Dad said Bark wasn't lying, and I figured if I came by here, maybe I'd see you for myself and oh my god. You're so pretty in person. So much prettier than when you were on TV. For the record, I never believed those charges against you, Madison Kate. Never. I can't believe it ever went to trial." She was verbal vomiting, but I wouldn't have known what to say even if she had stopped for a breath.

As it was, her stream of babble cut off when Bark clapped a hand over her mouth and gave me an apologetic grimace.

"Sorry about her," he said, ignoring Ella's muffled protests from behind his huge hand. "You met her, okay? Now go home. Mom will be worried."

The vague familiarity of her face clicked into place. She looked like Bark and Professor Barker. She must be his little sister.

"It was so, so nice meeting you," Ella gushed when Bark

released her mouth once more. "Oh my god, wait till my friends hear about this." She let out a little squeal of excitement, then—after a pointed glare from her brother—rushed across the lot to where a little white convertible was parked.

"Sorry about her," Bark apologized when she drove away with a huge wave.

"Little sister?" I asked, and he nodded. "And I'm guessing those girls you were talking about when we met the other day..."

He grimaced and nodded again. "Yeah. Sorry. Ella was one of your biggest supporters during the trial. Our mom only just convinced her to dye her hair back to blond a couple of months ago."

I frowned, biting my lip while I thought. It was a bit flattering, I guessed? I'd had no idea that *anyone* was on my side during the trial, and I'd left for Cambodia almost the second I'd been released. Then again, Kody's girlfriend calling me *goat* the other day had implied everyone believed in my innocence...just in a less flattering way.

"Don't worry about it," I told Bark. "I'm just glad she didn't have a phone to take selfies like I'm some kind of pop star."

He cracked an amused smile, agreeing. The university's no-phones rule had actually worked in my favor this week. It meant no one had photographic evidence of my little juice-covered strip tease; otherwise, I had no doubt that shit would have been all over the damn internet by now.

Instead, it was good, old-fashioned gossip and rumor mill until we collected our phones at the gate on our way home each day.

"Well, anyway," Bark said, turning the full force of his flirtatious charm back up, "I wanted to see if we were still on for tonight? I didn't manage to get your number the other day, and you ran out of Crim too fast for me to grab you yesterday."

We only had that class twice a week, and apparently it was the only one Bark and I shared. I'd bolted as soon as the lecture was over because I wanted to avoid having this exact conversation with him.

"Tonight?" I repeated. "Uh, I kinda figured you'd changed your mind on that." *Or Archer had scared you off with his macho bullshit the other day.*

Bark flashed a cocky, self-assured grin. "No way, babe. I was just biding my time."

Something about the way he called me *babe* made my skin crawl. Strange how the same word sounded so very different coming from Kody.

"I guessed if I chased you too hard around campus, I'd be risking Archer giving me a more physical incentive to steer clear. You know that guy is a professional MMA fighter? No offense, Madison Kate, but I don't want to get in a fight with him."

I stifled a sigh. "Yeah, I'd heard."

"So, tonight?" Bark pushed, and I found myself nodding. It wasn't like I had anything else to do, so why not? Bree had mandatory family dinners with her grandmother on Fridays, so unless I suddenly made other friends at SGU, I'd be stuck at home all night. The risk that one of the three guys would be there? Too high. Suffering through a shitty movie with Bark was far more appealing.

"Cool." He grinned. "I'll pick you up around eight?"

I gave another nod, seeing Bree coming from across the lot. "Sure. You need my address?"

Bark laughed. "You're funny, Madison Kate. Catch you later."

He walked away, still chuckling, and I wrinkled my nose at his back.

"Weird," I muttered, shaking it off as Bree clicked the doors to her car unlocked, and I slid into the passenger seat a beat ahead of her on the driver's side.

She arched a brow at me and looked pointedly at Bark's retreating back. "Did I just see the SGU Ghosts quarterback chatting you up, MK?"

I smirked. "Maybe. Got time to help me pick a date outfit before you're due at Nanna Grave's?"

Bree's jaw dropped, and then she squealed with excitement as we peeled out of the parking lot.

CHAPTER 13

At about ten to eight, after ignoring Steele knocking on my door to say dinner was ready, I made my way downstairs to wait for Bark. It wasn't exactly a date that I was getting butterflies over, but it'd be nice to do something normal. It'd just been so long since I'd been out with a guy who was even remotely interested in me as a woman, seeing as Aunt Marie had lived in an all-female community.

"Is there a party we weren't invited to?" Steele seemed to pop out of freaking nowhere, making me stumble on the last step of the staircase.

"Fuck!" I shrieked as my ankle rolled in the high-heeled pumps I'd put on, but of freaking course, someone caught me. I was seriously starting to wonder if I'd hit my head and woken up in a new adult romance novel.

"Careful, baby girl," Kody warned me, carefully setting me back on my feet but not removing his hands from my waist. "No matter how much I love seeing you fall for me, I'd rather you didn't mess up that pretty face in the process." He shot me a flirtatious wink, and I scoffed.

"The whole knight-in-shining-armor image is a bit ruined by

the fact that you still look like an overgrown Smurf, Kody." Ugh. Lies. He was still as gorgeous as ever. How unfair was that?

"Smurfs are blue, not purple," Steele commented, folding his arms. He was sweaty and streaked with dark grease, and I locked my jaw to prevent any involuntary drooling.

Really, how fair was it that the three guys who'd ruined my life all looked like they'd stepped straight out of my sex dreams?

"Whatever," I muttered. "Get out of my way, Kody. I'm going out."

"Out with who?" the green-eyed devil demanded, folding his own muscular arms in a mirror of Steele's pose. "I thought Bree had a standing family engagement on Friday nights."

I scowled. "How do you even know that?"

Kody smirked, superior as fuck, and I resisted the urge to smack him in the face.

"Whatever," I snapped again, feeling like a sullen thirteen-year-old. "I have other friends."

Steele snorted a quick laugh. "No, you don't. The only other person you've said more than three words to this whole week was..." I looked over at him just in time to see the realization dawn on his face. "You're going out with that meathead quarterback? No way."

"Fuck you," I spat. "I'm a grown-ass woman; you don't get to dictate who I spend my time with. And what the hell, have you three been stalking me or something? How the fuck would you know who I've been talking to on campus?"

Steele just shrugged, leveling a flat, uncompromising stare at me. Kody smirked. Again.

"What's going on here?" Archer asked, stepping out of the den and eyeing the three of us suspiciously.

I threw my hands up. "Oh, the whole gang is here! Fantastic. I can tell you all to fuck off at the same time. Here it goes. Fuck. Right. Off. You don't own me, so stop playing this bad-boy, bully crap. It's a tired, overdone trope."

Pushing past Kody, I tried to exit the house, but Archer's hand shot out and grabbed my wrist in a bruising grip.

"Where do you think you're going, Princess?" he asked me with utter piles of condescension. "We had plans tonight."

I scoffed. "*We* did not have any plans. Nor will we ever in the future. You're a minor inconvenience that I intend to be rid of sooner rather than later. Now, let go of me before you make me late for my date."

Yeah, I laid that on thicker than I really needed to, given how seriously unexcited I was for this date with Bark. Hell, I'd barely even dressed up for it. The heels had been a last-minute plea from Bree after she realized I couldn't be swayed from my black skinny jeans and soft gray camisole.

"She's going out with the Ghosts QB," Steele informed Archer, and I shot him a dagger glare.

A dangerous look passed over Archer's face, and I noted the puffy swelling below his right eye. He must have been fighting. Practice or for real? I hated that I was so fucking intrigued.

"Cancel it," he ordered me, his hold on my wrist not easing even a fraction.

I sneered. "No."

His left eye twitched, and it was like a thundercloud just formed over the two of us. "Cancel the fucking date, Madison Kate, or you'll regret it."

My jaw dropped at the clear threat. "Are you fucking serious right now? You're telling me if I don't cancel my date, you'll what? Beat Bark up?"

Archer smiled then, but it was a cold, unpleasant expression. "I'd never do something like that, Princess." He released my wrist abruptly, and I stumbled a couple of steps back as he disappeared back into the den.

"What the hell?" I muttered, staring after him and rubbing my aching wrist.

Steele sighed and shook his head, drawing my attention. "Arch would never beat up some sleazeball for trying to date rape you, gorgeous, because if he hit someone, he could be charged with attempted murder. As a professional fighter, his fists are considered lethal weapons."

I gaped at this information. That was a pretty serious accusation to just throw out there about someone. Did Bark have a reputation? The part about Archer's fists I filed away for use at a later stage. Steele wasn't finished, though.

"So…Arch would never beat up some idiot to warn him away from you…" He cocked his head to Kody, who was grinning like an escaped mental patient.

"But we would," Kody finished the sentence, cracking his knuckles menacingly.

I shivered, and *damn*, I wished I could say it was from fear.

"You're messing with me," I whispered, not even believing those words myself. I knew who these three were, and I didn't mean whatever their fucking PR manager was putting out on Instagram. I meant I knew who they *really* were. Gang members. Criminals. Thugs. Yeah, I didn't think Kody would even think twice about breaking some bones in Bark's body just to prove a point.

"I'll go tell your date you changed your mind," Steele generously offered, then disappeared out the front door, leaving the echo of his laughter in his wake.

Kody slung his arm over my shoulders and tried to steer me into the den, where Archer had disappeared a moment ago. "Come on, babe. It's not as bad as you think. We're just looking out for your well-being, like your dad asked us to."

I shrugged out of his arm and retreated toward the stairs. "Fuck you, Kody. That's not how this is going to work. You won this round, but you know I'll just hit back harder."

He laughed, and I flipped him off, stomping back up to my bedroom with hate searing through my veins.

CHAPTER 14

The guys only allowed me about half an hour to stew in my foul mood before Kody busted into my room without even knocking.

"Rude, much?" I snapped, glaring at him with raw fury. "Get the fuck out of my room, Kodiak."

He flashed me an unrepentant smile, flopping down on my bed like he belonged there. His cheeks were pink where he'd been scrubbing at the food dye, and—much to my disappointment—he'd managed to get most of it off.

"You know it's kind of a turn-on when you use my full name like that, Madison Kate?" His gaze ducked away from me as he said that, and I sensed the lie. It's a common misconception that lies can be detected based on the direction a person looks while speaking, but I'd found, more often than not, people will break eye contact for fear of their lie being detected.

I snorted a bitter laugh. "Sure it is. What do you want?"

I folded my arms, glaring at him from across the room, where I leaned against my dresser.

He arched a brow, then did a long look around him. "Well, first of all…this room is fucking disgusting. No one likes pink this much, not even you."

"No shit," I replied with a scowl. "But you didn't come here to criticize Cherry's decorating skills. I'll ask again, what the hell do you want?"

He tucked his toned arms behind his head, looking way too damn comfortable in my princess-pink bed. "We're going out."

"Okay. So go. This didn't require a face-to-face meeting to discuss."

Kody grinned, shaking his head, then stood from my bed and prowled toward me like a predator. "Let me clarify, Princess. *We*"— he indicated between him and me—"are going out. All of us. So put those sexy-ass shoes back on and let's go. We're already late."

I tilted my head back to look up at him, seeing as he was standing way too close and without my heels he was way too tall. Intimidating tall. Sexy tall. Dammit.

"No."

Kody smiled again, but it wasn't a nice smile. "Put your shoes on and come of your own free will, or I'll throw you over my shoulder and carry you out of here. If my hand happens to slip and smack your ass on the way, well, what was it you said? All's fair in love and war?"

I glowered. "I said *hate* and war."

He shrugged. "It's a fine line. So? What's it going to be? We're not leaving you here alone tonight, and we can't miss this fight, so decide quickly."

I wanted to dig my heels in and refuse. I kinda wanted to see if he was serious in his threat. But I couldn't fight the spark of excitement that flared to life inside me at the mention of a fight. I used to be obsessed with MMA and UFC. Not that I'd ever trained myself, but I'd been a huge fan of the sport...until last Halloween. Riot Night had soured my interest in the whole damn thing. Until now.

"Who's fighting?" I asked against my better judgement.

Damn it, Kody knew he had me. His cocky fucking grin said it all. "Guess you'll have to come along and find out."

I bit my lip, debating my options, but when Kody's eyes dropped to my mouth and his gaze turned hot, I knew my time to decide was running short. "Fine," I said finally, ducking under his arm and swiping my shoes from where I'd kicked them off. "But don't expect me to be pleasant company. I'd still rather trek across the Sahara naked than socialize with you three."

Kody laughed, watching as I stepped into my heels and tugged open my bedroom door. "Ah, that's a shame," he murmured, stepping past me into the hallway. "I was hoping you'd make me do things the hard way."

I ignored him but couldn't help remembering Steele say something similar on Monday morning when he was offering me a ride to school. Something told me these boys liked it rough.

Stop it, MK. Stop thinking about how they'd fuck.

"Let's go!" Kody bellowed as we reached the bottom of the stairs, then slung his arm over my shoulders like we were on a fucking date. "You can ride shotgun if you want, babe."

"Fuck no she can't," Archer snapped, brushing past us on the way to the garage. He stomped over to an army-green G Wagen and sat his ass down in the passenger seat. "Hurry up. We're late."

My eyes narrowed, his surly attitude prickling at my skin. I didn't even want to go out with them in the first place, and now he wanted to be a brat?

Two could play at that game.

Bypassing the back door, I reached out and opened the passenger door again. Archer scowled at me in confusion, his hand on the seat belt.

"What the fuck are you doing, Princess Danvers?" he sneered at me. "I'm not getting out so your prissy ass can ride up front."

I gave him a nonchalant shrug. "Suit yourself."

Using the doorframe and running bar, I hoisted myself up into the SUV and sat my ass directly in his lap. I was small enough that it was possible without embarrassing myself by getting stuck, but fucking hell…it was a tight squeeze. Archer was freaking huge, and I doubted any vehicles would comfortably fit him alone, let alone with a girl in his lap.

Maybe I hadn't thought this through.

"What *the fuck* are you doing?" he demanded with a throaty growl of anger and outrage underscoring his words.

Losing my damn mind, apparently.

Screw it. *Own your actions, MK.*

"Riding shotgun, like Kody told me I could before your bratty ass pushed ahead," I replied with sheer sass. I didn't even give a crap about sitting in the front, really, but the fact that Archer had said I couldn't? Well, it was time to get a few things straight. Namely, that I didn't take shit from anyone. Least of all these three bastards.

"Get out," Archer snarled. "You're acting ridiculous."

"No," I replied, "you get out." I twisted in his lap, sitting sideways so I could meet his blue eyes with a clear challenge in my glare. "Better start getting used to your supreme authority being challenged, sunshine."

Fury washed over his handsome face, and he leaned out of the car. For a moment, I thought I'd won that standoff, but then he yanked the door shut. He made no move to fasten the safety belt, and a jolt of apprehension shot through me.

"Stubborn prick," I muttered but folded my arms and refused to move myself, even if my palms were sweating now.

Archer's chest rumbled with a small laugh. "Takes one to know one."

Kody cleared his throat, turning on the ignition and arching one eyebrow at me. "Well, this is going to be a fun night," he muttered under his breath, reversing the G Wagen out of the garage. "I can already tell."

Steele, in the backseat all alone with enough space to spread out comfortably, just yawned and propped his head against the window with his eyes closed. Apparently wherever we were going, it was far enough to warrant a nap, but his fingers drummed on the leather seat beside him in some complicated pattern, like he was playing an imaginary piano.

Archer circled my waist with his arms, pulling me closer against him, and I stifled a gasp of shock.

"What are you doing?" I growled, desperately praying my cheeks weren't as flushed as they felt. As much as I hated this asshole, my body couldn't deny the attraction.

He gave me a sly half smile in return. "Getting comfortable, Princess. It's a long drive to the Rainybanks showgrounds, and I don't need your bony ass digging into my leg the whole way."

My eyes widened before I could catch myself, and a flash of satisfaction lit Archer's eyes. Fucking hell. Rainybanks was the next town over from us in Shadow Grove—a full forty-five-minute drive away.

The only saving grace to this failed plan? Archer would be just as uncomfortable as me in such close contact for so long. Based on the way his jaw was clenched and his brow furrowed, I was probably on the money there.

CHAPTER 15

For the longest forty-five minutes of my freaking life, we drove mostly in silence. Kody attempted conversation a couple of times, but with Steele asleep, Archer replying in grunted, one-word responses, and me just glaring at him to shut the fuck up, he didn't try for long.

Eventually, we turned down the street marked with Rainybanks Showgrounds, and I breathed a sigh of relief—just in time for Kody to slam on the brakes and damn near send me hurtling through the windshield.

I didn't, of course, but only thanks to the way Archer's arms tightened around me like a racing harness and crushed me to his chest.

"Kody!" Archer roared while I frantically chased my lost breath.

My heart was thundering, and adrenaline washed through me with enough potency to make me tremble.

"I'm sorry!" Kody shouted back, sweeping a hand over his bleached hair and shooting me an apologetic look. "A dog ran out in front of us. I didn't want to hit him."

"What's going on?" Steele asked from the backseat, his voice thick with sleep. "You almost tossed me off the seat, dude."

Kody scowled, turning his attention back to the road ahead of us and continuing at a *much* slower speed. "I said sorry, fuck. Just didn't think you guys wanted to be cleaning chunks of dog off the car."

He said that, but the way his eyes darted around suggested he was looking for the renegade mutt to make sure it had gotten away unharmed. He also shot a couple of worried glances in my direction. Checking if I was okay? Or embarrassed?

"It's fine," I found myself saying, reassuring him. "We're all okay, right, Steele?" I shot a hard look at the grumbling, sleepy guy in the backseat.

He scowled back at me but mumbled an agreement that he was, in fact, unhurt.

Archer hadn't said anything else after yelling at Kody, and his grip on me hadn't relaxed even a fraction. The way my back was plastered to his chest, I could feel his heart racing almost as fast as my own, and it softened something in my hatred toward him.

But then...

"Just get us there without fucking killing anyone, Kody," Archer snapped, a thread of fury woven into his voice. "The sooner I get this spoiled brat off my lap, the better."

"Maybe you should have thought about that forty-five minutes ago when you had the chance to move," I replied with heavy snark. Kody pulled into a parking space in a lot where dozens of cars were already parked, though, and effectively ended our stupid, childish argument.

I squirmed in Archer's hold, popping our safety belt and reaching for the door handle, pausing only when I heard him suck in a sharp breath.

An evil smile curved my lips as I realized I'd just effectively ground my ass against his crotch, and I made a deliberate point of doing it again before hopping out of the SUV.

"You need a minute, sunshine?" I asked sweetly, batting my lashes at him when he didn't shift from his seat.

He snorted a sarcastic laugh. "You wish, Princess."

I needed to take a couple of quick steps backward to avoid getting knocked over, but instead of passing me and stalking off into the night—like I'd expected—he grabbed my arm and yanked me closer.

"Don't fuck around tonight, Madison Kate," he ordered. "Don't wander off, don't get drunk, don't talk to strangers, and for the love of all things holy, *don't* tell anyone who you are. Got it?"

My brows shot up, and I instantly wanted to disobey every single one of his orders simply because he'd ordered me. "News flash, Archer," I replied, curling my lip at him, "I'm kinda famous, thanks to *you*. People might just recognize me from the news." I flipped my pink hair over my shoulder, demonstrating what I meant. I wasn't exactly inconspicuous.

He shook his head, unconcerned. "Didn't you know? You're a trendsetter. I guarantee you won't be the only dumb bitch here who's dyed her hair pink."

Irritation simmered within me at his description of me, but it wasn't worth the effort. I'd already decided to make his whole evening as infuriating as possible, and I took a gamble on where to start.

Jerking my arm out of his grip, I said nothing, just walked away to where Kody and Steele were waiting farther down the parking lot.

"Madison Kate," Archer barked after me, and the gravel crunched under his boots as he followed. He caught up to me just as I reached the other guys and, once again, grabbed my arm like some kind of fucking Neanderthal. "Did you hear me? This is important."

Keeping my calm, I peeled his fingers off my arm one at a time, then shoved his hand away before tilting my chin up and meeting his eyes.

"For starters, of course I *heard* you, Archer. I'm not deaf. Secondly, if I wanted to be told what to do with my life, I'd call my father. Lastly, if you're concerned with people knowing who I am, I'd probably recommend *not* yelling my name across the parking lot. Just a thought." With another hair flip, I strutted my shit away. Where the fuck I was going, I had no idea. I just headed in the same direction Kody and Steele had generally been heading, knowing that one of them would catch up before I got lost.

Boots crunched gravel again, and I sighed at the predictability.

Except this time instead of Archer grabbing me like I was a disobedient dog, it was Steele who caught up and walked beside me.

"Drew the short straw?" I asked in a voice as dry as the desert. I'd give him shit, but of the three of them, Steele was easily the most tolerable. Even after that stunt earlier with my failed date.

He shot me a lopsided smile. "Taking one for the team."

The other two passed us, their long legs eating the distance twice as fast as I could walk in my high heels, but Kody tossed a wink over his shoulder at me like we were in on some kind of joke together.

"They've got work to do," Steele explained when I said nothing more. "I'm just here for the entertainment. So I get to babysit our new troublemaker all night."

I rolled my eyes but followed along anyway. What else was I going to do? Walk my ass back to Shadow Grove? Also, the mention that there would be a fight tonight had sparked my excitement and curiosity. Was Archer fighting? He hadn't really dressed for it, wearing dark denim jeans, leather boots, and a black T-shirt, but he could be getting changed.

Questions sat on the tip of my tongue, but to ask Steele everything I wanted to know would be to engage him in an actual conversation. My skin prickled at the idea of being friendly to someone I hated so much, so I kept my mouth shut and just used my own powers of observation to figure shit out.

The event, so to speak, was held within one of the few buildings on the showgrounds. Most of it was just flat, open grass, and

I silently thanked all that was holy for the fact that it was, in fact, empty grass. I didn't think my brain could have handled more abandoned amusement park rides like at The Laughing Clown.

"You want a drink?" Steele asked me as we entered the clubhouse and made our way through throngs of people. They were all dressed pretty casually—ripped jeans, flannel shirts, a handful of miniskirts and heels. Surprisingly, Archer had been right about my hair not giving me away; I spotted at least two other girls rocking different shades of pink, along with a few purple and even one blue. The colors were on both guys and girls, and it gave me warm fuzzies to see. Maybe their hair choices had absolutely nothing to do with me, but it went a long way toward making me feel less conspicuous.

"I thought I wasn't *allowed* to drink?" I replied with a sarcastic eye roll, following him through the crowd to the makeshift bar. It was essentially just a couple of iceboxes full of cans and a couple of kegs, but despite what Archer thought, I wasn't fussy. Beer was never going to be my first choice, but if that's all there was, I'd take it.

Steele handed me an ice-cold can—unopened—then grabbed one for himself before straightening up. "No, Arch told you not to get *drunk*. Big gap between *a drink* and *drunk*, is there not?"

I grinned and cracked the top of my drink. Quietly, I appreciated that he'd given me an unopened can and not poured me one from the keg. You could never be too careful in the modern age of drink spiking and date rape. What a depressing thought.

"Come on," Steele said, taking my hand in his and leading me back through the crowd of party people. "Let's grab a seat with a view."

Tingling sparks of thrill zapped through me, and I didn't pull my hand away. I let Steele guide me with those long, strong fingers of his intertwined with mine, and I told myself over and over that I was just excited to see this fight…whoever it was. That the way my pulse sped up had nothing to do with Steele holding my hand, because his actions were just sensible in a crowded room.

"Here," Steele said when we reached the next room. It was a much larger area, one that was used for placing bets, if the shoulder-height, windowed counters labeled "betting" were any indication.

He set his drink down on one of the betting window counter-tops, then wrapped his hands around my waist to boost me up to sit beside his beer. When I was seated, he did a stupidly hot push-up thing to get himself up beside me, and I had a hard time tearing my eyes away from his arms.

"Hey, Madison Kate," he said, a teasing smile pulling at his lips, "quit looking at me like a piece of meat and hand me my drink, would you?"

Heat flooded my face, and I quickly passed over his beer, wiping the condensation off my hands on my jeans while searching my suddenly blank brain for a change of subject.

"So, who's fighting tonight?" I finally asked, sipping my beer and peering out across the room. A very crude octagon had been laid out not far from us, and our elevated position gave us a prime view. One thing was for fucking sure: this was no official UFC-sanctioned event.

Right as that thought passed through my mind, a rat scurried across the floor, weaving between people's feet, and I choked on my beer as I laughed.

"Not the worst venue we've been to," Steele commented with a grin, watching the rat disappear out the door. "And to answer the question you're *really* asking, it's not Arch. We're just here for research."

I huffed but didn't bother trying to deny it. That was what I'd really wanted to know. I just took a long gulp of my beer instead, cringing at the watery-yeast taste.

"So we're just going to sit here in silence all night?" Steele asked, bumping me with his shoulder. "That's cool if we are. Just checking so I can stop wasting my breath making conversation."

I turned my face to give him a *look*—one that said, yeah man,

I don't want to be your friend—but he wasn't getting the message. Or he was choosing not to get it. I suspected option two.

"I just thought you might have things you want to know, you know? Now's a great time to ask." He shot me a winning grin. "Promise not to tell anyone that you willingly conversed for something other than threats and insults. I wouldn't risk your tough-girl image like that."

His gray eyes were twinkling with mischief, and I wanted to hit him. Or…something. The warmth inside me was just from the beer, I was pretty sure.

Denial was also not just a river in Egypt.

I drained the rest of my can and placed the empty beside me on the countertop, the side that didn't have a tall, toned, gray-eyed mystery sitting on it.

"I need another drink," I muttered, mostly to myself. Also sort of praying some magical drink fairy would deliver something to my hand so we didn't have to give up our prime position for the fight. More and more people had filtered through from the other room, and I spotted Archer and Kody standing near the doorway, chatting with a guy in a ball cap.

"Here." Steele bumped me with his elbow, holding out a flask. "I brought backup. Don't tell, okay?"

Unable to help myself, I grinned. "Thanks."

I raised the flask to my lips and took a long sip, not even checking what was in it first. It didn't matter, so long as it was stronger than beer. Fire burned a path down my throat, pooling in my belly, and I licked my lips to savor the rich, caramel taste of rum.

"That's good," I commented, handing the flask back to Steele, only to find his hooded gaze locked on my mouth. His eyes were heated and hungry, and I was by no means unaffected. But still… "Hey, Steele?" His stare skipped up to meet my eyes, and I smirked. "Quit looking at me like I'm a piece of meat."

He snorted a laugh, looking away from me as he took his own

sip from the flask. His pierced tongue clicked against the metal, making me all kinds of squirmy. Even without his eyes on me, I could still feel the heat. The intensity. Some crazy part of me wanted to toss all my hatred aside and give in to that feeling. Kiss him. Or…more.

Clearing my throat, I took the flask back and gulped another mouthful of rum.

Across the room, two tough-looking guys stripped down to their shorts and started taping their knuckles up.

"Oh good," I murmured. "They're starting."

Steele chuckled, and it was one of the hottest fucking things I'd ever heard.

Damn hormones.

CHAPTER 16

The fighters were good, I'd give them that. Evenly matched and well trained, it seemed like they might go the full five rounds. Steele and I watched in silence for the first round, with Kody drifting over to hand us more beers during the one-minute rest period.

He lingered for part of the next round, leaning his back against the counter beside me, but at a nod from Archer across the room, he left us alone again.

"So you're in the mood to answer some questions, huh?" I finally broke the silence with Steele when the tension between us got too much for me to handle. He hadn't done anything, but I could fucking *feel* his eyes on me while I watched the fight. It was dizzying, and the rum only contributed to part of it.

Our fingers brushed when I handed the flask back, and I desperately tried to ignore how badly I wanted to touch him more than that. Apparently almost a year of celibacy had broken something in my brain.

Steele shrugged, screwing the cap back on the flask and returning it to his jacket pocket. "Maybe. Depends what your questions are."

Typical. I tucked some hair behind my ear and opened the fresh beer Kody had brought over.

"Okay…" I took a sip, thinking. "Why did you run off my date tonight? Honestly."

Steele made a thoughtful noise himself, and I couldn't help looking over at him. I *should* have been watching the fight, but despite how good the combatants were…they weren't Archer. And that prick had ruined MMA for me now.

"Your date?" Steele replied, arching a brow at me over those beautiful gray eyes of his. "Bark…he was overheard saying some less than flattering things in the SGU locker room earlier today. It might have seemed like a douchey controlling move, but it was for your own good."

I snorted a bitter laugh and rolled my eyes. "For my own good," I repeated. "That's such a fucking cop-out. You have no clue how capable I am of protecting myself."

Steele gave a small nod of acknowledgment. "That's true." He didn't push the subject any further, not even to defend his own actions. "What else have you got, MK?"

My shoulders tightened at his use of my nickname. "Don't call me that," I snapped. "Only my friends call me that."

"Which we are not," he murmured, blowing out a breath.

"Why are you guys living in my father's house?" I asked, changing the subject.

The corner of his mouth tilted up in a half smile, and my pulse raced. Fuck.

"Because it's convenient," he replied. "Because Cherry wanted her son close by and the three of us have lived together since high school, so it wasn't even a question for all of us to move in. Because we heard that the princess of the household was coming home and *some* of us let our curiosity win over logic and reason. Pick your answer, gorgeous. They're all true in some way."

I had nothing to say to that, and I was too tipsy already to dissect his games. So I turned my attention back to the fight and let myself get sucked back into the action until the bell rang again for the end of the round.

Steele seemed totally comfortable sitting in silence, but his fingers tapped the countertop beside him in that same complicated rhythm as he'd done in the car.

It reminded me of another question. "Why weren't you allowed to play video games the other night?"

"Oh, so you actually want to know something about me?" He was teasing. I thought.

I shot him a glare that clearly said I wasn't going to stroke his ego, and he grinned. Damn, he had a nice smile.

"So, I take it you never tried to look any deeper into my social media profiles, then?" He didn't look too concerned...just curious.

I'd actually totally forgotten about that discussion we'd had. Between starting university in my hometown, dealing with all the whispers and gossip behind my back, and plotting my revenge on Archer for the juice incident... "Uh, no. I haven't. You said they're all bullshit anyway, didn't you?"

"True," he agreed. "But it would have given you a hint."

Steele pulled his phone from his pocket and used his thumb to unlock it and open Instagram. Once on his own profile, he scrolled the whole way down the feed until he reached some of the very first images posted, then handed the phone to me.

I frowned at the image he'd selected. It was an artistic sort of black-and-white image of Steele's hands—I knew they were his, don't ask me how—lying gently on...

"A piano?" I asked, uncertain if that's what the image was actually of. It had sharp shadows and highlights, but the more I looked, the more certain I became. "You're a pianist?"

He gave a rolling shrug, like it made him a bit uncomfortable. "I was. Am. I dunno. My parents had plans to make me into a concert pianist, but it doesn't really gel with...me. I guess." He sort of mumbled his answer, then took a long gulp of his beer.

I frowned. "But wait. Why are video games banned but working on cars is okay? I doubt you're constantly covered in grease just 'cause it makes you look hot."

He gave me a sly grin. "You think I'm hot, Hellcat?"

I rolled my eyes. "You know you are."

He barked a laugh. "Yeah, I do." Reaching over, he swiped the screen so it scrolled up to more recent images. Modeling shots of him, Kody, and Archer in nothing but jeans and a whole lot of sweat. Sweet. Baby. Jesus. "Part-time male model, remember? But I'm just verifying the fact that *you* think I'm hot. Totally different thing."

"Shut up and answer the question, Max." I deliberately used his first name and was rewarded with his slight cringe.

"Which is it, Hellcat? Shut up or answer the question?" He raised his brows at me, taking another sip of his drink without breaking eye contact. Fucking *hell*. Ugh, I'd be lucky to make it back to the house with my dignity intact if he kept that up.

I narrowed my eyes, and he smirked.

"Working on cars is not *okay*, exactly. Neither is sparring with Kody and Arch. But Jase—our manager—has given up trying to stop me from doing shit that I love. The video games, though?" He wrinkled his nose, looking a bit ashamed. "Four years ago we had a hardcore gaming session for an entire weekend when a new game got released. Somehow, uh, I broke a bone in here." He extended his left hand to me, pointing at a small scar at the base of his thumb, near his wrist. "Then a couple of weeks later, while I was in a cast, the expansion pack got released. So we had another gaming session, and I rebroke the same healing bone."

I winced sympathetically, and he laughed.

"It wasn't that bad, really. Except I missed my audition for Julliard and my parents threatened to sue the console manufacturers. After that, video games were banned." He sighed wistfully, and I almost wanted to smile. Almost.

"How is that still a thing?" I asked instead. "You're, what, twenty-one? Who gives a shit about what your parents say?"

"Uh, yeah. They can take a flying leap off a tall building for all I care. But until I decide whether I'm actually done with piano or not, the guys and Jase are holding me to it." He finished his beer, then pulled out the flask again.

I nodded, having nothing more to say about his situation. It was interesting, though, and totally unexpected from this tattooed, grease-covered bad boy. Oh fuck, fine, who was I kidding? It was sexy as hell, and I couldn't stop my mind from whirling on how good he must be with his fingers...

I switched my attention to the fight once more, having totally lost track of what round they were on. Four? Five? Why was it suddenly so fucking hard to focus?

My beer was gone, but Steele handed me the flask of rum again. Like more alcohol would help me keep my sanity. Ha.

"Can I ask you a question, Hellcat?" he asked after a moment of tense silence between us. The crowd was loud, roaring and cheering for the fighters in the ring, but I barely even noticed. It was like the two of us existed inside a bubble.

I gulped rum again, shuddering as it scorched my throat. "Sure."

He shuffled closer to me on the countertop, his leg brushing mine as he leaned in close. "Watching MMA fights turns you on, doesn't it?"

I sucked in a sharp breath, my shoulders tense. It was an observation that I couldn't deny for the most part, except tonight. Tonight...my dizzy state of arousal had nothing to do with the fighters grappling in the octagon and everything to do with my drinking buddy.

Raising the flask back to my lips to buy a moment, I risked a quick glance at Steele. Or it was meant to be a quick glance, had his gaze not captured and held mine.

"I don't know what you're talking about," I lied, my voice

husky and low. I took a sip of rum, and he broke eye contact to watch my lips on the flask. Against my better judgment, after I lowered the flask, my tongue swiped the excess spirit from my lips.

Steele's eyes flashed with unmistakable desire, and he raised his hand to my face. His thumb swiped over my lower lip, then he placed it in his own mouth, sucking the flavor from it.

"I think I found my new favorite drink," he commented in a rough, lust-filled voice.

Fuck. Me.

My whole being was aware of his nearness, and all it'd take was a couple of inches to close the gap between us. It'd be so easy... so fucking easy to just give in to desire and forget all the ill will between us. But then where did that leave me? Without my hatred and resentment toward the three boys I'd met on Riot Night, I didn't even know who I'd be. I'd totally lost myself in the past year, and it scared me too much to just *let it go*.

So I did what any girl in my situation would do. I wrenched my gaze away and scanned the room for an escape route.

"I've got to pee," I announced, slipping down off the countertop and damn near running in the direction of the ladies' room I'd just spotted.

The second I created some distance between Steele and me, it was like I could breathe again. Maybe if I splashed some cold water on my face, I could snap the hell out of it. Except Archer had given an order, hadn't he? Don't wander off alone. Silly me for thinking he hadn't also impressed this upon his boys.

Long, tanned fingers circled my wrist as I ducked into the corridor leading to the restrooms, and Steele jerked me around to face him.

The raw, desperate desire on his face was all it took to snap my already shaky control.

I was so utterly *screwed*.

CHAPTER 17

Kissing Steele was *nothing* like I'd imagined it would be. And I wasn't even trying to deny I'd imagined it multiple times over the past week, if not just in the past twenty minutes.

No. It was about sixteen thousand times *better.*

His fingers twisted in my hair, yanking my head back and as he kissed me like he was drowning. It was frantic and wild, our teeth clashing and our tongues wrestling as I explored that piercing that'd teased me all week. My arms locked around his neck, clinging and pulling him closer even as he pushed against me, walking me backward into the nearest restroom.

Neither of us spoke. We didn't need to when our bodies were doing all the talking for us. Steele's lips left mine, trailing across my jaw and down my neck as I boosted my ass up on the vanity and yanked him closer. But I needed more. I needed him closer still.

I shoved his jacket off his shoulders, then slid my hands across his flat, hard stomach, searching for the hem of his shirt. He was so fucking hot, I felt like I was literally playing with fire. But then I was way past the point of caution. I stripped his T-shirt off, letting it drop to the dirty floor with his jacket, then sucked in a sharp breath of appreciation.

Steele was fine as *fuck*. Not as heavily built as Archer or as sharply defined as Kody, but holy hot damn, I could see why he'd been included in those shirtless modeling shoots. No retouching needed.

Tilting my head back, I caught his lips once more, kissing him to stop myself from babbling incoherently and totally losing all my chill. Steele grabbed me by my hips, jerking me forward to the edge of the vanity and grinding his hardness against me. Silently I cursed my decision to wear jeans, but on the flip side, the dark denim was the only thing preventing him from seeing how soaked I was already.

I sucked his lower lip into my mouth, nipping him a bit harder than necessary, but the groan he let out was all hunger and lust. His hands skated up to my waist, sliding under my top and shoving it up over my boobs, baring my black bra.

Breaking our kiss, he breathed a curse, then dropped his head to my chest. He yanked the soft cups of my bra down, then latched his mouth on to one of my rock-hard, aching nipples, flicking them with his piercing. I moaned as he sucked and nipped, the throbbing need in my core growing hotter by the second. It was an itch that so damn badly needed to be scratched. Hard.

I reached for Steele's belt, unbuckling the supple leather from the warm metal of his buckle. My hands were steady and sure as I flicked his button open and dragged his zipper down. I gave myself a quick mental high five that the screaming need to feel him inside me hadn't made me shake like a cold Chihuahua.

To my surprise, though, Steele wasn't wearing any underwear, and in an instant his bare, scorching flesh was in my palm. There was something *crazy* hot about a guy going commando.

He hissed at that first contact, his tongue stud clicking against his teeth, and I allowed a feral smirk to cross my lips. His mouth was quickly back on my breast, though, and when my grip tightened, stroking him, he bit down hard enough to make me cry out.

His warm breath feathered my skin as he chuckled that same dark and dirty laugh from earlier. The one that did all kinds of delicious things to my throbbing cunt.

Still, we didn't speak as he tugged me off the vanity and spun me around so that his tall, toned figure was draped all over me. He made quick work of my fly, peeling my tight jeans down just enough that he could fit his hand inside.

A desperate, whimpering moan escaped me when he stroked my clit through my lace panties, and I grabbed on to the edges of the sink for stability. Steele teased me through the thin fabric only a few moments before tugging them aside and driving two fingers deep inside me.

A groaned string of curses fell from my lips, and I tipped my head forward for a moment, my legs shaking as my core clenched around his long fingers. He used his free hand to sweep the rest of my hair over my shoulder, baring my neck for his lips. Shuddering waves of ecstasy skated over my skin as he sucked and kissed the sensitive skin of my throat and neck, but my focus was entirely on the hand buried between my legs.

I arched my back, pressing into him and feeling every hard inch of his body against mine. He held all the power, though, and for once I didn't care. I wanted him to take control. I loved that he'd put himself in a position of dominance, and even though I'd hate myself for it later...I wanted nothing more than to be shoved to my knees and his cock forced into my mouth.

Our heavy, gasping breathing was the only sound in the dirty restroom as Steele proved to me just how strong and skillful his fingers were, bringing me to the edge of orgasm in mere moments. My face felt all kinds of flushed, and I was eternally grateful some-one had already broken or stolen the mirror so I didn't have to watch myself come. Because when I did...

"Holy fuck," Steele groaned as my teeth sank into the hand he'd hastily clapped over my mouth, stifling my scream so we didn't end up with an audience, no doubt. I had no apologies for him, though; he'd brought it on himself. His own breathing was just as rough and ragged as mine, and it took me a moment to realize he'd come too.

Good thing my tank top had been pushed up over my breasts because all it took was a quick swipe with a paper towel to clean off the small of my back. My panties were a whole other fucking issue. They were drenched.

"Fuck," I muttered, cringing as I buttoned my jeans. "That's unpleasant."

Steele snickered one of those satisfied masculine sounds as he pulled his T-shirt back on. "Underwear is overrated, Hellcat. Just take them off."

His abs flexed as he rolled the fabric down, and I tried really, *really* hard not to ogle him like I wanted to lick him all over. I failed. He noticed.

"I'm not taking my panties off, Steele," I grumbled, running my hands through my hair in an attempt to calm down what was undoubtedly some pretty wicked sex hair. Two steps across the dirty bathroom, though, and I cringed at the moisture between my legs. "Fuck it." Steele smirked, and I glared at him. "Wait outside. I'm not taking my panties off while you're staring at me like that."

His grin was pure evil. "Staring at you like what, Hellcat?"

My eyes narrowed farther. "Like I'm a piece of meat." I bit back the smile threatening to kill my serious, threatening image. "Go!"

He rolled his eyes and turned to face the door. "Better? Just hurry up. The fight is probably over."

Shit. The fight was *definitely* over by now. It'd been practically over when we'd started. The last thing I needed was Archer and Kody knowing what we'd just done.

I quickly stepped out of my heels, stripped off my jeans and sodden panties, then put the jeans back on—sans underwear.

The rough seams of my tight jeans rubbed me in all the wrong ways—or right ways, depending on perspective—and I uttered a small groan of frustration.

"I don't know which is worse," I admitted under my breath, stuffing my feet back into my shoes. I brushed past Steele and shoved the restroom door open with him hot on my heels.

The room where the fight had just been held was rapidly emptying out of people—which explained why no one had busted in on us in the accessible bathroom—but standing in front of the betting windows were two very irate-looking guys. Kody had his phone out, texting, and Archer looked like he wanted to kill something or someone. With his fists.

There was no time to escape, though, because a second after I'd spotted them, Archer's furious glare met my eyes across the room.

Fuck.

I still had my damp panties balled in my fist, but as Archer stomped over to us, Steele slipped them out of my hand and into his pocket. Small mercies, I guessed.

"Where the fuck have you two been?" the big, tattooed dickhead demanded, getting all up in my personal space in a way that made me want to junk punch him.

I sneered up at him, refusing to be cowed. "None of your fucking business, Archer. Back off before I intimately introduce your balls to my knee."

His brows shot up, and he scanned my face with eyes far too damn intuitive for my own good. Then cursed. "Steele, what the *fuck*? This is your idea of keeping her out of trouble?" For a moment I thought he was referring to what we'd just done in the bathroom, but then he continued his rant and the anxiety in my stomach eased. "You're both drunk. How? How the fuck do you get this drunk on that piss-weak beer they had here?"

Steele snorted a laugh, shrugging off his friend's ire like he'd gone through it a thousand times before. "Because I came prepared, bro." He pulled his flask from his pocket—admittedly almost empty now—and tossed it into Archer's hands. "Maybe take a shot and lighten the fuck up."

Steele brushed past Archer, making his way out of the building—but not without shooting me an evil wink over his shoulder...like he was nowhere near done with me yet.

Shit. What have I started?

"I told you not to get drunk," Archer snapped at me, shifting his anger back in my direction now that Steele was gone.

I smiled as sweetly as I could. "And I told you where to shove your orders, sunshine. I'll give you a hint, in case you missed the subtext. It's where the sun *doesn't* shine." I gave him a highly condescending pat on the chest, then followed Steele out to the parking lot. Of the three devils I'd been saddled with for the near future, he was easily the least hateful.

Kody and Archer followed like dark clouds, and when Kody unlocked the G Wagen, I slid straight into the backseat with Steele.

"Huh," Kody murmured, taking the driver's seat. "Note to self: drunk Madison Kate is less combative than sober Madison Kate."

Archer paused outside the car, scowling at me in the backseat; then he looked at the empty shotgun position like he was confused as hell. But, shit, dude. I'd made my point on the way over. No sense in being uncomfortable as fuck the whole way home too.

After a moment, he sat his ass down in the vacant seat and shut the door with a heavy thunk. Typical fucking Archer, though, couldn't just leave it at that. He simply *had* to have the last word. Or try to.

"Nice to see you're capable of being trained after all, Princess Danvers." The scorn in his voice made it sound like he was talking about a dog.

Oh. Hell no.

Alcohol and adrenaline still coursed through my veins, mixing with the lingering endorphins from my recent orgasm—a potent mix at the best of times. And this? Well.

Sliding across the back seat, I swung a leg over Steele's lap, straddling him and bringing my lips to his for a bruising kiss. Shock only froze him for a fraction of a second before his hands grabbed my ass, grinding me down onto his already hardening cock and kissing me back with scary-level intensity.

So much so that I needed to seriously force myself to stop kissing him before tossing my hair and giving Archer a feral smile. "Or maybe I just prefer the company back here."

It took *every* ounce of my willpower to slide off Steele's lap and sit back in my seat, but the murderous look on Archer's face made it totally worthwhile.

Kody exhaled heavily, turned the ignition on, and reversed out of the space we were in. "I take that statement back," he murmured. "Drunk Madison Kate is six million times *more* combative. Good to freaking know."

I bit my lip to keep from laughing, but Kody caught my eye in the rearview mirror. The raw lust in his eyes was enough to make me second-guess my actions. These three were dangerous, unrepentant bastards, and I needed to remember that when I was dealing with them. They weren't just some cute—okay, fine, gorgeous—guys from my university. The three of them had made me into the Riot Night scapegoat and never looked back once.

I hated them, and I needed to stop forgetting that fact.

Messing around with Steele had been a huge step in the wrong direction, and it was one I needed to rectify. Tomorrow.

CHAPTER 18

Sunlight streaming into my bedroom made everything…pinker. Sparklier. Maybe I shouldn't have turned down Steele's offer to repaint my room after all. If nothing else, I needed proper blackout curtains to block the light better.

Fuck. Thinking about him made me think about the night before. How we'd sat together, sharing drinks and talking like, well, like two people who didn't have the baggage we carried.

I groaned into my pillow, cringing at my own behavior. I had no idea what had gotten into me—other than Steele's way too talented fingers—and I couldn't even really blame the alcohol. Sure, we'd been a bit drunk, but I barely even had a hint of a hangover to justify my dumbass decisions.

"Dammit, MK," I whispered aloud, flipping onto my back and staring up at the ceiling. "Idiot."

Still, I was having a hard time getting him out of my head. The way his lips tasted or how he bit my breast or…shit, or the way Kody had looked at me with naked hunger in his gaze and Archer had glowered like I'd kicked a puppy.

Those three pricks were in my head and under my skin, and it was all getting too much to handle. I needed to step up my plan, starting today. I'd had too many misfires already, so to fix that? A three-way attack.

I rolled over in my huge bed, hunting for my phone, and finally found it tangled up in my sheets. I would need help for what I had in mind, and I knew just who could help me.

"Good morning, gorgeous," Bree drawled when she answered my call. "Have you called to tell me all about your date with the quarterback? I hear he has a massive cock. Verify."

I cringed. "Not exactly." My voice was a bit rough from raising it while talking to Steele over the crowd at the fight. "Long story. Come over? I've got a plan."

Bree laughed. "You have me intrigued. Anything I need to bring?"

"Yeah," I replied, grinning to myself. "Does Dallas still live in Shadow Grove?"

There was a pause on Bree's end; then she whistled. "I'm *very* intrigued now. I haven't heard from him in a couple of months, but yeah, last I knew he was. Want me to pick him up?"

A small sigh of relief rushed out of me, quickly replaced by a buttload of anxiety. "Could you? I need his expertise for this one."

"Your wish is my command, Princess Danvers," she replied with a laugh.

"Ugh," I grimaced. "Don't call me that, girl. That's what Archer calls me, and I want to punch his teeth in every time he does it."

Bree howled with laughter down the phone. "No shit, babe; that's exactly why he's doing it. It's also super catchy."

"Fuck you, Brianna," I growled back, and she hissed a fake noise of pain before hanging up.

I tossed my phone onto the bedside table and started getting ready for the day with a hell of a lot more pep in my step than I'd woken up with. The sketchy plan I'd been thinking on all week was going to have to work, and Dallas was my best chance of that happening.

Better yet? His mere presence in the house would infuriate the guys to no end.

A fraction more effort went into my hair and makeup for the day, and I spent about an extra fifteen minutes deciding what to wear before finally settling on ripped jeans and a cropped tank that showed off my toned stomach, still golden brown from the Cambodian sun.

I tried to tell myself the extra attention to my appearance was for Dallas's benefit, but deep down I was also conscious of running into Steele downstairs.

When I'd wasted every possible extra minute I could, I finally hunted out my big-girl panties and made my way down to the kitchen for breakfast. It'd be at least an hour before Bree and Dallas arrived, seeing as she'd need to drive all the way to the far side of what *used* to be West Shadow Grove to pick him up. My rumbling stomach wasn't going to wait that long, and besides, I wouldn't want the guys thinking I was hiding.

To my relief—and slight disappointment—the kitchen was empty when I got there. Based on the time, though, I'd guess they were in the gym. Yep, every damn morning, the three of them spent two full hours in the gym...if not more. Steele was usually the first to bow out, though, so it was no huge surprise when a single set of footsteps padded into the kitchen about fifteen minutes later. Steele's unmistakable fingers stroked the hair back from my brow, his fingers lingering on my skin, and for a moment I leaned into him where he stood behind me.

But it was just a moment, and a weak one at that.

I pulled away, grabbing my freshly made coffee and taking it back to the island where I'd put my bowl of cereal.

Steele released a frustrated sort of sigh, his toned shoulders deflating somewhat as I created physical distance between us without a word of explanation. He knew, though. He knew it hadn't changed the way I felt about them. They'd still fucked me over, and I still needed to make them pay.

"Don't suppose you made any more of that special coffee, did you?" he asked hopefully, arching a brow at me over his shoulder while grabbing a mug from the cupboard.

I just took a spoonful of my cereal and shook my head. Let them suffer with that awful drip shit they all drank.

Steele went to work setting up their machine, dropping in the filter and probably stale-as-fuck pre-ground beans. Gross. Still, it allowed me a couple of moments to admire the huge angel tattoo spread across his bare back. The fact that he was dressed in nothing but low-slung sweatpants was pushing my self-control, that was for freaking sure.

I ate my breakfast in silence, watching Steele from under my lashes as he moved around the kitchen. By the time he dropped his plate and mug on the counter beside me, I'd given myself a sufficient mental pep talk, reminding myself that no matter how badly my body craved his…it didn't change the past.

"So, it's like that, huh?" he asked after sitting on the stool beside me. He didn't sound annoyed or pissed off, just resigned. It tweaked something painful inside me, but I ignored that weird reaction and gave him an impassive shrug.

"We all make mistakes, Steele," I replied in a cool tone.

He stiffened, finally showing an edge of anger through that calm, unruffled exterior. "Yeah, Hellcat, we do. You'd do well to remember that."

I sucked a breath in, grinding my teeth together in irritation. He wasn't even remotely subtle, implying that their framing me was a *mistake*. If it was such a fucking mistake, why had none of them come forward to clear my name?

I shoved back from my seat, grabbing my dishes and taking them over to the enormous sink. "Maybe we do," I said softly, not looking at him while I rinsed my bowl and cup out, "but it's how we deal with those mistakes after the fact that defines us."

A frustrated sound came from Steele, but before he could say anything more, the doorbell rang.

Thank the gods of good coffee, Bree and Dallas were early.

"Madison Kate," Steele called after me as I hurried out of the kitchen and went to answer the door. "Wait, don't just walk away like that."

"Sorry, Steele," I replied over my shoulder, sounding anything but. "Would love to stay and chat, but I have plans today."

I reached the front door before the butler—a mostly silent, rarely seen older gentleman named Steinwick—and swung it open, ignoring the sudden rush of butterflies in my belly.

"You made it," I exhaled, my eyes taking in the blast from the past standing on my doorstep beside Bree.

My bestie smacked a kiss on my cheek, then breezed past me into the house. "I love when you're excited to see me, MK," she teased.

I rolled my eyes and couldn't fight the grin spreading over my face. "Hey, Dallas. Long time no see."

The huge guy still standing on my doorstep gave me a lopsided smile, stuffing his tattooed hands into his pockets. "When Breezie told me you were back, I had to see it for myself. Damn, Kate. You look great."

I couldn't hold myself back any longer, launching myself at my old friend and wrapping my arms around his neck in a tight hug. When he hugged me back, he lifted me off the ground, thanks to the almost foot difference in our heights. He'd definitely gotten bigger since the last time I'd seen him, and I'd bet he would give Archer a run for his money in the tall, dark, and strong-as-shit department.

"Fuck, Dallas," I laughed. "You got huge. When the hell did that happen?"

His body rumbled under me, but he didn't put me back on the ground. "Probably sometime in the four years since you last saw me?"

"Uhh, has it been that long?" I did the math in my head, but

144

he was right. The last time we'd seen each other had been the Christmas before I'd turned fifteen. After that, I'd become busy with my life as the perfect little private-school girl, and Dallas had gone to prison. He'd been released almost two years earlier, but I'd never worked up the courage to contact him again before the events of Riot Night, then Cambodia...

Dallas carried me into the house because I was still hugging him like I was a hungry squid, then set me back on my feet in the foyer.

"Oh, hey, man," he said, doing one of those tough-dude head nods, and I peered over my shoulder to see Steele standing there with his arms folded and a face like thunder. "I'm Dallas. I didn't know Katie had a new boyfriend." He gave me a side-eye and I whacked him in the seriously hard abs.

"I don't," I snapped, giving Steele a glare. "Why are you still lurking?"

He glowered back at me, ignoring Dallas's introduction. "Because we were in the middle of a conversation, Madison Kate."

"No we weren't," I replied, my tone hard and final.

Bree let out a low whistle, looking between Steele and me with raised brows. "Well, I for one can smell the sexual tension from here."

I scowled at my friend, then spotted the tray of coffees in her hand and smiled once more. "Oh, you angel. Come on, let's go up to my room."

Just my fucking luck, before we could escape the foyer, the echo of footsteps and male voices came from the direction of the gym, and I groaned inwardly. I'd hoped to get a moment alone with my friends before dealing with Archer and Kody as well, but it wasn't to be.

The two of them emerged from the hallway behind the staircase and paused when they saw the four of us all standing there.

Dallas noticeably tensed beside me, and his eyes narrowed on the biggest, blue-eyed fuckwad of the house.

"Archer D'Ath," he ground out from clenched teeth, then shot a sneering look at Steele. "I knew you looked familiar."

Crap. I'd known Dallas being here would piss the guys off—Archer in particular—but I hadn't banked on them having crossed paths already.

"Okay, cool, we've all met. See ya." I gave Dallas a shove to get him moving and tried to escape up the stairs to my room. Kody grabbed my hand as I passed him, though, and held me back.

"Madison Kate," he said quietly, "can we talk a minute?" He gave a pointed look at Bree and Dallas. "Alone?"

I wanted to jerk my hand free and tell him to stay out of my damn face. But there was something in his tone…

"Please?" he added, and I exhaled heavily.

"Go on up to my room," I said to Bree and Dallas. "I'll be two seconds."

Dallas looked like he wanted to argue, but Bree slapped him on the ass and hustled him up the stairs with her tray of coffees balanced on one hand.

When they were out of sight, I yanked my hand out of Kody's grip and folded my arms under my breasts. "What?"

He glanced over at his friends and nodded toward the kitchen. "Give us a moment."

Archer looked like he wanted to crush someone's skull between his hands but stomped off anyway. Steele was considerably more reluctant to leave. His clenched jaw and folded arms radiated stubborn anger, and his gray eyes burned into me like lasers.

"Steele," Kody barked, his voice brokering no arguments. "Go away."

I half expected him to refuse, but after a tense moment, he stalked off in the direction Archer had gone, cursing under his breath.

I waited as Kody turned his attention back to me, curious to see what was so important he needed to send the other two stooges away before telling me.

He sucked in a deep breath, studying my face as he released it. Sweat still glistened on his muscles, and there was a towel tossed over his shoulders like he'd been on his way to the shower. Not that I was looking.

"Madison Kate, how…" He trailed off, shaking his head like he was trying to rearrange his thoughts. "That shit with Steele last night—"

"Was nothing," I interrupted before he could, I don't even know, warn me off his friend or something? "I just wanted to piss Archer off for that bullshit comment about *training* me. That's all."

Kody arched a brow, his gaze dropping to my neck and pausing there. Shit. I'd thought I'd done a good enough job of hiding the marks Steele had left. Apparently not.

"Uh-huh. Sure. How the hell do you know Dallas Moore? And why is he in your bedroom right now? Is this today's plan to piss us all off enough that we move out? Because you'll need to try a hell of a lot harder to make that happen."

A flicker of satisfaction warmed my belly. "Dallas and I are old friends," I told him with total honesty. "He's here to help me on a project. Not everything has to do with you three assholes, you know?" Okay, that part wasn't so true. Whatever.

Kody's brow dropped, and he ran a hand over his damp blond hair. Fuck, even with his hair all messed up, he was still heart-stopping-level gorgeous. Those green eyes that had haunted my dreams for eleven months were almost too much in real life. Too freaking observant.

"Madison Kate, you don't get it. Dallas is—"

"A gangster? Yeah, I'm aware. I'm also aware that the tattoo you, Archer, and Steele all share isn't just 'cause you're BFFs. Those in glass houses shouldn't throw stones, Kodiak Jones." I mean, not that I was admitting to having spent *way* too long checking out their ink when they didn't think I was looking. But *if* I had, I might have noticed all three of them had matching grim reaper tattoos woven into their other ink. I'd lived in Shadow Grove all my life and wasn't ignorant enough not to recognize that as the symbol of Zane's gang—the Shadow Grove Reapers.

Kody's nostrils flared as his green gaze hardened. "Then you damn well know you just invited a fox into the henhouse. What the *fuck* were you thinking?" He stepped closer, invading my personal space as he towered over me, and his hand grabbed my upper arm like he wanted to shake some sense into me and barely suppressed the urge.

I refused to step back, though. I refused to give ground and let Kody think he intimidated me, because he *didn't*. At least…not in the traditional sense.

"I was thinking that I just got back from a year in exile, and I'd love to catch up with an old friend," I half lied, tilting my head back to meet his furious gaze. "And I was thinking that I don't give two shits whether you three have a problem with it. Better yet, if it bothers you that much…leave."

I wasn't actually as reckless as I was making out. The reaper tattoos on their skin had all been modified in some way—something that Zane would never allow if they were actually still part of the Shadow Grove Reapers. Not that I'd ever heard of anyone *leaving* a Shadow Grove gang before, but there were exceptions for everything and I was hardly the expert authority.

Kody's jaw clenched so hard I could almost hear his teeth creaking. "The more you try to make us leave, the longer we're going to stay."

I scoffed. "Don't be childish, Kody. If that's all you had to say, I think I'll go and join my friends now."

His grip on my arm tightened, and my breath hitched as he leaned down and hovered his lips near my ear. "Don't push us, Madison Kate. You won't like it if we retaliate."

It was a threat, and it should have pissed me off. Or worried me. It definitely shouldn't have excited me, but there it was, that spark of exhilaration burning inside my chest.

I really should have taken Aunt Marie's offer of professional therapy.

Oh well.

"Do your worst, Kody," I whispered in response before brushing a featherlight kiss over his cheek. "I know I will."

I stepped away and he released my arm, but I could feel the weight of his stare on me the whole way up the stairs. It wasn't until I reached my bedroom door that I let out a breath and scrubbed my hands over my face.

Everything was getting tangled and distorted. It should have been a clear-cut war on my enemies, merciless and brutal. Instead there was all this tension and hurt all mixed up into the cold hate, and it was starting to mess with my head.

Maybe it was because they *hadn't* really retaliated yet? Aside from Archer's stupid stunt with the juice on Monday, they'd not given me anything to work with. All I had was the lingering resentment from a year ago, and even that was starting to fade with every sexually charged interaction.

It was time to force their hands. Once they fought back, things would be clearer again.

Surely.

Resolute, I opened my bedroom door and grinned at my two friends waiting on my bed. "I hope you brought your A game, Dallas. We've got some work to do."

CHAPTER 19

Hours later, within which time Bree and I mostly lay on my bed talking shit and catching up on gossip while Dallas sat in front of my computer, the job was done.

"I'll leave this in your hands, Kate," he announced, spinning around in my desk chair and stretching those massive arms over his head. To anyone who didn't know Dallas, all they'd see was a thug. He was covered in ink all the way up to his jawline and down to his fingertips and held the physique of someone who spent half his life lifting weights. They wouldn't see what was under the surface: a full-fledged tech geek and digital artist. I'd never met anyone quite so talented at photo manipulation.

"It's all queued up from an untraceable email; just hit send if you decide to go ahead." He raised his brows at me like he was advising me against that move.

"Thanks, Dallas," I replied with a wide grin. "You rock, you know that?"

He smiled back at me, standing up to accept my appreciative hug. "I do know that. Now, I better go or I'll be late for work. Breezie, we good?"

Bree yawned and clambered off my bed, where she'd made

herself cozy with a book about an hour ago. "Yep, let's roll. You going to be okay here if you hit send?" She gave me a concerned frown, and I waved her off.

"Of course," I replied with a casual laugh, ignoring the anxiety building in my gut. "This is just the first in what I expect to be many blows traded. It'll take more than this to send them packing."

Dallas sighed, sharing a look with Bree before turning back to me. "I'm worried about you now, Katie. If I'd known who you were mixed up with..." He shook his head. "Girl, those boys are dangerous as fuck. Even I'd be cautious messing with them, and you know I've got no sense of self-preservation."

My smile dropped. "Yeah, well, they didn't try to frame you. They thought I was an easy mark that night, some prissy rich girl to take the fall for the whole Laughing Clown event." The familiar acid of hate and resentment burned through me, and I welcomed it with open arms. "I probably could have let it go—eventually—but then I come home and find them living in my house? Acting like they have some right to control my life? Nope. No way. Nobody tells me what to do."

Dallas sighed and tugged me into another tight hug. "Ain't that the truth, girl."

"Come on, lovebird," Bree said, poking Dallas in the side and heading out of my bedroom. "Work waits for no man. Especially an ex-con."

I followed them downstairs to see them out and was all too aware of Archer, Kody, and Steele playing video games in the den...in full view of the foyer.

Apparently Dallas noticed them too, because the hug he gave me at the front door lingered and his hands caressed my back in a less than platonic kind of way. His chest vibrated with a dark chuckle, and I knew he was messing with our audience. Or I thought that was what he was doing.

"It was good catching up, Kate," he told me when he put me

back on the floor. "Let's hang out this week. Just like old times." The wink he gave me was evil as fuck, and I didn't hold back my answering chuckle.

Dallas headed out of the house, swaggering his fine ass toward Bree's convertible while she air-kissed my cheeks and said goodbye.

"What *old times* is Moore referring to, Princess Danvers?" Archer demanded, tossing his PlayStation controller on the couch and stalking over to where I stood in the foyer. "Sure as shit sounded like you have history there."

Bree, bless her heart, had paused in the doorway at the sound of his voice and whipped around with her blond hair flying. "Oh, Archer, honey," she answered for me, laughing a throaty sound, "I'm sure Dallas just meant how the three of us used to hang out and get milkshakes while MK was supposed to be at vocal lessons."

I breathed a small sigh of relief that was all she said.

Too soon, though.

"Then again, maybe he's talking about the times he climbed through MK's window and, you know, spent the night." She waggled her brows suggestively. "You're capable of reading between the lines there, right?"

I'm going to kill her.

Then again, based on the way Archer's vein over his temple was throbbing again, maybe I'd give her a high-five instead.

"'Kay, cool, I'll leave you to play that scenario out inside your head." Her smile at Archer was wicked as sin, and I snorted a laugh. "Bye, babe. Let me know if you go through with the thing." She gave me a pointed stare, and I nodded.

"Oh, Bree babe, you'll know." I closed the door after her, then turned to race back upstairs, only to find my path blocked by a bad-tempered douchecanoe. "Oh, what *now*?" I drawled. "The whole big-man intimidation bullshit is getting tired, Archer; pick a new tactic."

I stepped around him, making it up two steps before he replied.

"Have you fucked him?"

Turning slowly, I glared pure death at him. "Excuse me?"

Archer's eyes sparked with something frightening. Disgust, maybe? "You heard me, Princess. Bree just implied you and Moore have sexual history, so is she stirring shit or *have you fucked him?*" His question was dark and threaded with warning. Every instinct screamed at me not to poke the bear...but what the fuck did they know?

"Not that it's any of your business, Archer, but *yes*. Multiple times. And I'm really looking forward to catching up on *old times* with him again soon. I hope you sleep deeply 'cause I'm a screamer." I smirked pure smug satisfaction and left him standing there with a dumbstruck look on his face as I scurried up the stairs.

I paused when I turned the corner, out of sight, and took a moment to catch my breath. My heart was thumping wildly from the confrontation and from my half-truth, but it was thanks to that momentary pause that I heard the solid *thump* and cursed shout of Archer punching a wall.

The rush of emotions that flooded through me was too complex to even try to unpack, so I rushed into my bedroom and slammed the door behind me. My fingers trembled as I clicked send on my computer, but I knew it needed to be done. I needed to hit them harder, if only to make them hit me back. Make it easier for me to hold on to all my hate.

Somehow I managed to avoid all three guys all weekend, choosing to eat in my room for dinner—thank goodness for my father's household staff—and duck out early to hang with Bree all Sunday. Not that I would have run into the guys, anyway, seeing as they'd left before dawn for some photo shoot.

By Monday morning, the pictures I'd emailed out to the entire SGU mailing list had gone damn near viral.

"Madison Kate!" The enraged roar echoed down the corridor as I made my way to class, and I flinched. Fuck.

I'd known it was coming, obviously. I was actually shocked they hadn't seen it sooner. Then again, I'd sent the blast to everyone's student address, and I guessed not many people used that email over the weekend.

Spinning on my heel, I pasted an innocent expression on my face. "Yes, Archer?"

The fact that he'd actually used my name and not "Princess Danvers" should have been my first clue about how pissed off he was. Then again, I didn't give a crap.

"Spare me the bullshit; I know this was you," he snarled, holding his phone up for me to see.

Faking confusion, I took the device from him and peered at the screen, then let out a low whistle. "Wow, Arch. I knew you three were close but not *this* close. No judgments here, though. Why are you showing me your home porn?" I held his phone back out to him, and he snatched it back. "Also, I should probably point out that it's against SGU policy to have mobile phones on campus. You could get in trouble for that, you know?"

"I'm through playing nice, Madison Kate," he hissed, pointing a menacing finger at me. "You'll pay for this." He started to turn away, then swung back around and stepped in close enough that our chests touched. "And we both know I'd be on top."

Laughter bubbled up in my throat as he stomped away like a bear with a bee sting, and I only just swallowed it before Kody and Steele appeared from around the corner.

"Look, if you've come to tell me about your ménage relationship with Archer, he's already filled me in. I think it's so great you're all exploring your sexuality like this, but it's a bit in bad taste to share the pictures around campus, you know?" I kept my face as straight as I possibly could, but a hint of laughter wove into my voice.

Steele just shook his head, looking...*disappointed* as he walked away, following in the direction Archer had gone.

Kody, though, he was eyeing me up with those intuitive eyes of his.

"How'd you do it?" he asked, looking considerably less annoyed than I'd really hoped. "I mean, it's obviously a good photo manipulation, but shit, babe, you even got our tats right. How'd you manage that?"

A surge of satisfaction zapped through me. That'd been the best part of my plan, and the part that made the images so *very* convincing. When I'd told Dallas what I wanted him to do, he couldn't decide whether it was hilarious or diabolical. I think both.

"Well, if you're trying to tell me it's a prank and not something leaked from your personal archives, I'm not so sure I believe you. Nor will lots of people. But if such a prank were to be executed so beautifully...I might question just how many nearly nude images there are of you floating around the internet." I shrugged, grinning. "But hey, at least now I know why Archer is so threatened by me. You really should stop flirting with me in front of your boyfriend."

Kody gave a small laugh, eyeing me shrewdly. "That's cute, Princess. But I've barely even *started* flirting with you yet. Guess I need to step up my game."

My brows shot up, and he stepped forward, backing me into the wall between a portrait of Thomas Edison and the door to a classroom.

"Kodiak," I growled with warning, "what are you doing?"

His body pressed against mine, and I bit back a pathetic moan that wanted to escape my throat. "Turning up the heat," he whispered back, then captured my earlobe between his lips and sucked on it. This time I barely managed to clamp my mouth shut when a shudder of arousal ripped through me, and Kody's dark chuckle told me he'd noticed. Damn him.

"Cute touch putting Archer as a bottom, babe. I'm pretty sure that's the part he's most pissed about. But hey, at least you got my favorite position right." He smacked a quick kiss against my shell-shocked lips, then swaggered away with a mocking "See you at home, Princess!" tossed over his shoulder.

After he was gone, the uncomfortable realization that I was far from alone came flooding back to me, and I pulled my barriers back up. Other students were whispering and staring, so I dished out a heaping of death glares and hurried my ass into my first class of the day.

Kody was proving to be a harder target than I'd anticipated. If a very convincingly Photoshopped image of him and Steele spit-roasting Archer wasn't going to push his buttons…maybe I was approaching him the wrong way.

I needed to rethink my plans for him.

Dropping my bag next to a vacant space in the lecture hall, I dropped into the seat and glanced up at the board, reminding myself what class I'd just walked into.

CRIM-100

Ah shit.

I looked around until I spotted Bark sitting two rows away, the hood of his SGU Ghosts sweatshirt pulled up and his face ducked low over his books. Almost like he could feel me staring, though, he looked up, and I gasped.

The side of his face was a puffy, mottled purple, like he'd run into something hard. Repeatedly.

It could have been a football injury, but based on the way he glared at me, then skipped his gaze away again…yeah, I doubted it.

Fucking Steele.

CHAPTER 20

Considering the guys were three years above me at SGU—they'd transferred from elsewhere and I hadn't cared to ask where—it was no shocker that I didn't see them again throughout the day. Bree and I left campus for lunch—she had her period and was craving Mexican—so I didn't get a chance to confront Steele until I got home at the end of the day.

Even then, I needed to hunt him out.

"Steele!" I called out, entering the enormous garage and making my way through the line of stupidly expensive cars and motorbikes. Most of them were my father's—I recognized them from before Cambodia—but some were new to me, like the G Wagen and Steele's silver muscle car…whatever that was. "Are you in here?"

I reached the workshop area just as he slid out from under a jacked-up car, lying flat on his back with one of those rolling things mechanics use.

"Hey," he greeted me, sitting up with a delicious ab flex. "How are you?"

My lips had been parted to go off on him, blast him about beating up my date on Friday night rather than just sending him home, but his question confused me. Even more so, the genuine look of concern on his face as he asked.

"How are—huh? Shouldn't I be asking *you* that? I'm not the one who just had his home porn blasted to the entire university campus." I frowned in confusion, and a brief flash of irritation passed over his face.

"Yeah, well, as flattering as it was that you'd start a rumor I was gay *after* what we did on Friday night…it could have been worse." He shrugged and gave me a lopsided smile. Damn him. Why was it *so freaking hard* to hate Max Steele?

"Oh yeah?" I found myself asking, playing along. "How's that?"

His grin spread wider. "I could have been in Arch's position." He winced, and I laughed before catching myself.

"Yeah, well. It's always the big ones who like to be dominated in the bedroom. Or so I hear. Anyway, I came here to yell at you, and you've just taken the wind out of my sails." I scowled, but it totally lacked the heat of a few minutes ago.

Steele stood up and pulled a rag from his back pocket, using it to wipe a streak of grease off his face. All he managed to do, though, was smear it further, and my nipples hardened at the sexy image he portrayed. Why, *why* had he suddenly stopped wearing shirts around the house? It wasn't fair.

"Shall I give you a minute?" he suggested, teasing. "Maybe you can find that outraged anger again."

"Fuck you," I replied, but it was totally without conviction.

His grin turned wicked, and he came closer to me, crowding my air space in that infuriating, intoxicating way all three of them seemed to love to do. "That's what I'm hoping you'll do," he murmured, dragging a grease-darkened finger from my throat to belly, then grabbing me by my jeans to yank me closer still. "Just say the word, Hellcat."

I needed to swallow several times before I could force the right words off my tongue.

"Never going to happen, Steele."

He studied my face for a second, no doubt reading the lie all over me, but released my jeans and took a step away. "So, what did you come to yell at me about?"

I cleared my throat and frantically searched for my invisible shields. The pesky ones that seemed to turn into mist whenever I was around Steele…or Kody for that matter. Okay fine, Archer too, not that I'd *ever* admit it to anyone.

"I saw Bark today in class," I told him, folding my arms over my chest. "He looked like he'd run afoul of something hard. Maybe, say, someone's fist? You wouldn't know anything about that, would you?"

A smug smile crossed his lush lips, and he tucked the greasy rag back in his jeans, then reached for the open beer on the floor. "Now then, beautiful, you know my dirty little secret. Do you think I'd risk my hands just to punch some meathead jock over comments that seriously walked the line toward a rape threat?" He held up his right hand, showing me all the smudges of grease… and totally undamaged knuckles. What little anger I had left in me deflated, and I felt a bit guilty for assuming the worst.

Steele snickered, heading out of the workshop with me following. "His car door, though, might have a few face-shaped dents in it."

I gasped. "Steele!"

He shot me an unrepentant smirk over his shoulder. "Anyway, how are you dealing with the whole stalker situation? You okay?"

I stopped dead in my tracks.

"With the *what* situation?"

Steele paused too, turning back to face me with a stunned look on his face. "Oh shit," he murmured. "Arch hasn't talked to you yet? That prick."

Fury was building inside me with speed. "Talked to me about *what*?" I demanded, my fists balling at my sides. Steele hesitated, looking pained, and I lost it. "Tell me, Steele!"

He blew out a heavy breath, his gorgeous gray eyes sympathetic. "You've got a stalker, Hellcat. And they don't seem content to watch from a distance anymore."

My stomach churned, and acid rose in my throat.

Dizziness swept through me like a wave, and everything became hot. It was hard to breathe.

Fuck. *Fuck.* I was having a panic attack.

"Madison Kate," Steele's voice was muffled and echoey, like he was underwater. Or I was. "You're okay. Hey, come on." His voice was coaxing as he guided me to the floor, encouraging me to sit with my head between my knees.

He rubbed circles on my back with a firm hand while whispering reassurances to me, and ever so slowly, the blackness receded.

"What's going on?" I heard Kody ask moments before his feet appeared in my limited field of vision. He crouched down. Gentle hands stroked my hair, and the two of them spoke to each other in hushed voices. But my ears were ringing, and I couldn't be bothered to work out what they were saying.

For several moments, I just focused on not passing out. Whoever was stroking their fingers through my hair was seriously helping in that regard, and I leaned into the touch.

"You okay, babe?" Kody's soft voice was right beside my ear, and I slowly raised my head to meet his eyes just inches away. I nodded the tiniest of nods, not totally believing myself.

He gave me a small smile, then scooped me up in his arms and stood. "You need a drink and some food."

I wanted to protest. I wanted to tell him to put me down because I could walk myself, dammit. But then...I also didn't want to. There was something so incredibly comforting about being in Kody's arms that I just bit my tongue and relaxed into him. Maybe it was just that he'd been there during my last panic attack. When he'd held me immobile in that tight, dark space while Archer headed off Zane, he'd distracted me so thoroughly away from the fear... Maybe my brain was remembering that incident.

He carried me through to the kitchen, but instead of putting me down on one of the stools against the island, he sat down himself and held me in his lap.

Steele grabbed a glass from the cabinets, filled it with water, and placed it on the counter beside me, but Kody scoffed.

"I meant a real drink, dickhead."

Steele didn't seem to take any offense, instead just disappearing into the den, presumably to raid my father's fully stocked bar.

"Why am I in your lap, Kodiak Jones?" I asked, yet didn't make any moves to get off him.

His arms tightened around me. "Because you love it," he replied with that typical Kody arrogance. "Besides, you're still really pale, and I don't want you to pass out and whack your head or something."

"Sound medical logic," I mumbled, resting my head on his chest and closing my eyes for a second. That panic attack had just hit me like a ton of bricks. Not that I was any stranger to them. After witnessing my mother's murder, I'd had them routinely over the tiniest of things. I'd thought I'd left them in my past, though. These days the only time I spiraled like that was when I got trapped in a small space.

A soft touch on my arm made my eyes open once more, and I took the offered drink from Steele. I took a sip and found myself pleasantly surprised by the sharp tang of ginger and lime.

"Thanks," I said with sincerity. "This is really good."

He arched a half smile at me. "Spiced rum with ginger beer and lime. Seemed like your kind of drink." The shine to his eyes suggested I wasn't the only one who now associated rum with public bathroom make-out sessions.

"What's going on in here?" Archer's unmistakable, grumpy rumble saw me tensing in Kody's lap. He was permanently angry, I was pretty sure, so fuck it. I'd stay right where I was.

More to the point… "Did you forget to tell me something, Archer?" I placed my drink down and leveled him with the most venomous glare I could, given I was literally using his friend as an armchair.

The big guy just met my glare without the slightest flinch.

"Nope. I think the less we speak to each other, the better off we'll both be." He rubbed a hand over a dark, stubble-covered cheek. "Wasn't your whole mission to get rid of us?"

I frowned slightly. "Still is."

A mean smile touched his lips. "Sitting in Kody's lap like you're about to ride his dick probably sends the wrong kind of message, then. Come to think of it, so would letting Steele finger fuck you over the sink in a dirty public bathroom."

I wasn't quick enough to catch my own gasp as my accusing gaze snapped to Steele. He didn't look apologetic in the least, though. Just…impassive.

Kody's fingertips seemed to tighten on my waist, but that could have been my imagination considering how much fury and betrayal had flooded through me.

"Tell me, Princess Danvers," Archer continued, sneering with an edge of disgust. "Did you ever get those black lace panties back?"

My stomach bottomed out. For a hot second I'd started thinking I was wrong about Steele, that my hatred toward him was misplaced. But he'd been playing me all along. For what? Bragging rights with his buddies? I should have done worse than that Photoshopped image.

I would do worse.

Swallowing past the bitter hurt in my throat, I refused to look at Steele. It was so much easier to focus on Archer. Fucking Archer. Ugh, I needed to destroy him.

"So, you had no intention of telling me about my stalker?" I curled my lip at him in disgust, even as I casually slid off Kody's lap. He tried to tighten his hold on me, but I was determined and it would have been all kinds of obvious if he'd forced the issue. "That's a whole new level of low, D'Ath." I deliberately used his surname, the same way Dallas had. It pissed him off; I could see it in the tightness of his jaw.

Never one to back down, he just folded those huge arms and gave me a *so what* kind of shrug.

I stared back at him for a long moment, studying his ice-blue eyes for any scrap of apology. *Any* morsel of human decency. I found fucking nothing.

"You really want to step it up like that?" I gave a cruel chuckle, like some kind of deranged book villain. "So be it. You'll regret ever messing with me, Archer D'Ath. Trust me on that."

Casting a disappointed look over Kody—because I hadn't heard a single squeak from him since Archer had walked in—I left the room, heading straight up to my bedroom. I didn't look at Steele before I went. I couldn't. That apathetic, blank face he'd worn as Archer revealed intimate knowledge of what'd passed between us? That had broken me more than I cared to admit.

I needed to step up my game. Forget waiting for retaliation; this was war and there were no fucking rules. No polite etiquette. Only the brutal and bloodthirsty survived.

CHAPTER 21

I couldn't sleep that night. How could I, knowing someone was stalking me? The worst part was not having any more detailed information than that. Steele could have meant someone leaving anonymous love notes in the mailbox…or he might have meant they'd taken photos through my window. Or worse. What was worse? The mind boggled.

I was desperate to know, but to hell with asking those three. They could go take a flying leap off a cliff.

No, I needed to aim higher.

Lying in bed as the sun rose, I stared at the screen of my phone for *ages* before finally finding the courage to press call.

The ring echoed through my room, and with every extra trill, my stomach sank. He wasn't answering. Of course not. He was having too much fun with Cherry the gold digger to answer a call from his only child.

Bitterness swirled in my gut, and I tossed my phone aside to get ready for the day. I had classes to attend and three stupidly attractive guys to destroy. There was no time for me to feel sorry for myself that Daddy didn't love me. That was nothing new.

I rushed my shower and threw on some clothes. I hadn't slept and was ready almost a full hour earlier than usual, so it'd be just my luck to run into the guys in the kitchen. Hopefully, though, they'd already be in the gym for their grueling daily workout. No wonder they were all cut from marble.

I breathed a sigh of relief walking into the kitchen to find it empty of toned, tattooed twat-buckets. Just Karen, our weekday cook, who was wiping down the benches with a microfiber cloth.

"Good morning, Miss Danvers." She greeted me in a soft, hushed tone, the same one she used in any of the rare moments I happened to run into her. My father's staff were all the never-seen-or-heard type. Always had been, so I was used to it.

I smiled at her, not fully awake yet, and headed over to the espresso machine to make my coffee.

She disappeared somewhere between me grinding fresh beans and steaming my milk to velvety consistency, but she'd left me a bowl of Bircher muesli with fresh fruit and Greek yogurt on the counter—somewhat healthier than my usual choice of Lucky Charms, but it was a kind gesture.

I hummed under my breath to a song that was stuck in my head while pouring two shots of espresso, then swirled my steamed milk to mix it before pouring it ever so carefully into my mug. Just as I was jiggling the milk jug to create the perfect fern leaf in the crema, a sharp crack made me jump, and milk sloshed onto the counter.

"Mother*fucker*," I snarled, wiping off my hand and turning to glare at whatever had just frightened the ever-loving shit out of me.

Then my mood soured further.

"The fuck do you want?" I snapped at Archer, channeling *all* of my shitty mood into my glare. "Shouldn't you be in the gym admiring your flex in the mirror?"

He gave me a sarcastic laugh. "Funny. Here." He slid a manila folder across the island where he'd just dropped it. The sound that had startled me must have been him whacking it down on the marble surface. Prick.

I eyed the folder with supreme suspicion. "What's this?"

He arched a brow—damn, that was sexy—and tilted his head to the side. "You wanted to know about your stalker? Well, that's everything. Happy reading."

I stared down at the folder like it was poisoned, but Archer leaving the kitchen jolted me out of my trance.

"Wait!" I blurted out, making him pause in the doorway. "Why did you give this to me? Is there something, like, really awful in here that you think will make me run screaming or something?" I was scared. I was also woman enough to admit that, if only inside my own head.

Archer didn't reply for a long, tense moment. He didn't even turn back around.

"Knowledge is power, Princess Danvers," he said eventually, his voice rough with some undecipherable emotion, "but ignorance is bliss. You decide for yourself which one you prefer."

———————————

The packet of documents sat on the counter in front of me as I ate my breakfast, then drank my coffee ever so slowly. It just…sat there. Staring at me. Daring me to open it.

"Shit's sake," I breathed, reaching the end of my coffee and shaking my head at my own crippling paranoia. Chances were, there was nothing bad even in there. It was probably another stupid Archer flex. Messing with my mind.

I glanced at the time on my phone. Bree would arrive to pick me up soon, so I needed to get it over with.

Open the damn envelope, MK.

Biting down on my lip, I shoved my empty dishes aside and slid the envelope closer. Before I could talk myself out of it, I flipped the flap open and tipped the contents out onto the marble countertop.

Instantly, I regretted that choice.

They were all photographs—some blown up to full A4 size, some smaller, from a Polaroid camera. All of them were of me. Some were through my bedroom window. None of them were with my consent.

The most recent picture, taken on the weekend when I was hugging Dallas on the doorstep, explained Steele's comment about my stalker not being content to "just watch" anymore. Not that that would have been okay either, but this sent chills down my spine.

I'll cut his touch from your skin, then clean the wounds with my tongue.

It was scrawled over the back of the photo in jagged, black-inked letters. I dropped it like it'd stung my fingers and clasped my hands to my mouth.

A million things ran through my mind. Questions, concerns, what-ifs.

Then a thought occurred to me.

Could Archer and the guys have made this up? Was this their payback for my little pranks on them? There were no photos of me with any of them…no photos from the fight on Friday night or of our run-ins on SGU campus. Was that simply because my stalker wasn't around at those times? Or because they'd orchestrated it themselves?

My mind latched on to that idea, and I scooped all the images up into a pile. If they thought they could intimidate me with a fake stalker, they were sorely mistaken.

Anger and outrage built within me as I stomped down to the home gym and slammed the door open. Then almost swallowed my tongue.

But I wasn't here to drool over sweaty, tattooed, male perfection. I was here to prove that their stupid plan had failed.

"Madison Kate," Kody greeted me, setting down the weights he'd been using and snatching up a sweat towel to mop his face. "What are you doing here? Is everything okay?"

Archer folded his arms, watching me, and Steele barely even spared me a glance. He just continued punching the heavy punching bag in the same steady rhythm as when I'd walked in.

Fucking prick. I'd definitely had him all wrong.

I threw the stack of photos down on the gym floor, scattering them. "You three must think I'm some kind of stupid. You can save your money and call your photographer off because I'm not buying the fake stalker story."

Steele finally stopped punching the bag, shooting an incredulous look at me, but I'd said all I needed to say. Bree would be here any minute anyway.

"Wait, Madison Kate!" Kody shouted as I left the gym. I half expected him to come running after me and deny that they'd made the whole thing up, but Archer's voice stopped him. And me. But they couldn't see me, paused in the corridor outside the gym.

"Leave it, Kody," he barked, his voice radiating authority.

There was a pause, and I almost walked away before Kody replied.

"Archer, this is getting out of control. Fix it." He sounded deadly serious. It was a side of him that I'd only ever glimpsed before.

Archer scoffed. "Fix *what*? I gave her the photos. What more do you want me to do?"

Surprisingly, it was Steele who answered. "Tell her the truth," he said so quietly I almost didn't hear him. "The whole truth."

The sound of a fist hitting leather—probably the punching bag—echoed down the hall.

"No."

That was it. Archer always had the final word.

I didn't hang around to hear any more, instead racing out of the house and meeting Bree at the bottom of the driveway.

"You okay?" she asked when I slid into her car.

I nodded, pulling my phone out of my pocket and opening the contacts screen.

"Super," I replied. "Just need to fight fire with fire."

I found Dallas's number and hit call before giving Bree a grin. "Nothing I can't handle."

I hoped.

CHAPTER 22

I was sure the whole stalker thing was Archer and his boys' lame attempt at getting me back over the Photoshopped spit-roast. Pretty sure, anyway.

But no matter how many times I told myself that, I couldn't get away from the feeling of someone watching me.

It didn't help that even two weeks into classes, people were still staring and whispering when I walked down the halls. I'd have thought the whole thing might have blown over, but with the anniversary of Riot Night in just a couple of weeks, it looked like I'd be the center of attention awhile longer.

Even after Bree dropped me home after classes, the tension didn't ease from my shoulders. So many of those images had been taken *through* the windows of my father's mansion. If this stalker was real—not that I believed that—but *if*...then nowhere was safe.

Just in case, I drew the sparkly pink curtains in my bedroom before changing into comfy sweatpants and a tank top. I was expecting Dallas to come by, but despite what I'd insinuated to Archer, I had no desire to seduce my old friend. Sure, we'd slept together before—that part had been true—but only once. And we were much better off as friends.

On a whim I tried calling my father again, but it went straight to his voicemail. I didn't bother leaving a message. If he wanted to speak to me, he'd have called back by now.

Trying to swallow past the bitter disappointment I felt toward the last remaining parent I had, I tucked my phone into my pocket and headed downstairs. After the stress of feeling constantly watched all day, I needed snacks.

Just as I reached the bottom of the stairs, a familiar voice in the den made me stop in my tracks. Was that...my father?

Curious and confused, I took two steps closer to the den and paused just outside, shielding myself behind a huge, antique vase full of lilies while I eavesdropped.

His voice was muffled, on speakerphone by the sound of it, but I'd bet my left tit it was Samuel Danvers speaking—something that was confirmed moments later when his words became clearer.

"...thought I'd handled that situation four fucking years ago," he snapped, the sound of seagulls and crashing waves in the background. "Last time that little shit put his hands on my daughter, I had him sent to Mantworth for two years. You're not seriously telling me he hasn't learned his lesson?"

My blood turned to ice. He was talking about Dallas. *My father* was responsible for Dallas going to jail? How? Why? Dallas had been arrested in a stupid gang crime and taken the fall for whoever he was with at the time. His whole involvement in the Shadow Grove Wraiths was a major reason we'd fallen out in the first place...but could my father have had a hand in all of that?

Outraged and blinded by anger, I stormed into the den to confront the guys—and my father—over what I'd just heard. But before I made it three steps into the room, Kody shot out of his seat on the couch and grabbed me, clapping a hand over my mouth to prevent me from saying anything—no sounds that would make my father aware I was listening.

I thrashed in Kody's hold, but I was no match for Captain

Fitness. He held me easily, lifting my feet from the ground and carrying me back to the sofa to sit down.

Archer held the phone—of course—flat in his palm with the speaker cranked up loud for them all to hear. And for *me* to hear? Call me paranoid, but I was starting to see ghosts in every shadow.

Steele had his elbows resting on his knees, and when I flicked a furious glance over him, his gaze ducked away. Feeling guilty? Probably. He had every reason to feel that way.

Archer, though, met my gaze steadily and totally unflinchingly. He almost looked gleeful as he spoke to my father. *My father.* He'd been too busy to take my calls, too busy to even shoot me a message to say "Will call you later," but not too busy to speak with Archer?

"It certainly seems like he requires more incentive to stay away," Archer was saying, not giving even a hint that I was listening. "It's a shame; Madison Kate is having such a hard time readjusting to Shadow Grove. She could do with friends. We're just terribly concerned Dallas Moore is going to get her into trouble. You're aware, I'm sure, that he's a member of the Wraiths."

"Of course I'm aware," my father spat, his voice like acid. "It's how I managed to get him locked up in the first place." He grunted an annoyed noise, and I swallowed to hold back the stinging tears of betrayal. Kody's arm around my waist wasn't as tight anymore, but he still wasn't letting me go. He wanted me to hear this. *They* wanted me to hear this and know what my father had done.

"Leave it to me; I'll get him removed from Shadow Grove by the end of the week."

My eyes widened, and I desperately tried to wrench myself out of Kody's grip. He held me firmly though—not for the first time, come to think of it—and all that could be heard of my protests were small, muffled squeaks. Nothing that my father would hear down the phone at any rate.

Archer held a single finger up in the air, warning me, telling me to calm the fuck down. It was scary how well I could read his intentions.

"That won't be necessary, Samuel," Archer said after a moment's pause. His cold blue gaze held my eyes as he spoke, and the threat was crystal-clear. "I'm sure we can talk sense into Madison Kate. Dallas won't be hanging around anymore."

My father gave a disbelieving grunt. Archer's lips curved in a cruel smile, and he didn't break eye contact with me for even a second.

"Good luck with that," my father scoffed. "That girl is just like her useless fucking mother. All looks and no brains. Wouldn't know common sense if it came up and bit her right on the ass."

This time I couldn't hold the burning pain inside. It spilled out in hot tears rolling down my cheeks. Not for myself—I couldn't care less what he thought of me—but hearing him speak of my mother like that... *Shocked* didn't even begin to cover where I was at.

Archer, though, didn't flinch, didn't look even a bit remorseful at what he'd drawn out of my father while I sat there listening and unable to retaliate.

"Regardless, I think we have it handled," Archer reinforced, and I suppose he expected me to be grateful to him? Fucking bastard. I was going to destroy him.

"I'm sure you do," my father laughed. "If that's everything, I have better things to be doing right now."

"Not quite, Samuel," Steele said, and I jolted in Kody's grip. What fresh fuckery did they have now? Nothing good, judging by the regret in Steele's gaze as he looked at me. "Madison Kate has a stalker."

I rolled my eyes. They were really pushing their fake-stalker story, even after I'd called them out on it? My father didn't appreciate dramatics or hysteria, so they were probably going to get a solid "don't be stupid," followed by him hanging up.

But instead, there was a long pause.

"And?" My father's gruff voice finally cracked the silence.

Steele's brows arched, and Kody breathed a hushed curse. Fuck, even Archer showed a flicker of surprise at that response.

"This is old news, gentlemen. Just file the details in my office filing cabinet. There's a folder marked with her name." He sounded as casual as if he were giving a weather report. *Oh, tomorrow looks like it might be sunny with intermittent showers of deranged stalker.*

Steele made a small sound of shock, his brow furrowing as he stared at the phone. "Samuel, are you saying we *shouldn't* report this to the police?" His voice held genuine disbelief, and suddenly I believed them. This wasn't a hoax.

"Absolutely not!" my father barked. "It's some harmless crazy. He's been sending shit to the house for years; nothing ever comes of it. Just file the details and forget about it."

Holy shit. *Holy shit.* This creep had been stalking me for *years* and my father knew about it? He knew and never said anything?

"Hey, Princess." Kody's low tones in my ear shifted my attention. "You're freaking out. Deep breaths, okay?"

Real fucking stellar advice when your hand is over my mouth, you donkey-fucking piece of shit.

He must have realized what I was thinking too, because he somehow adjusted his grip on me in a way that let him easily carry me out of the room. He didn't take his hand off my mouth until we reached his bedroom.

Not that I would have made a noise. I was too busy freaking right the fuck out.

He sat me down on the end of his bed and crouched in front of me, murmuring soothing words to help me calm down. I didn't need it, though. The second he got me out of the room—away from my father's voice—I was able to get a grip and calm myself down.

I let him comfort me while mentally running myself through the meditation techniques Aunt Marie had tried to teach me. When I was sure I'd dragged myself out of the depths of panic once more, I batted his hand away from my hair.

"I take it you're okay now?" Kody sat back on his heels and arched a brow at me. "More's the pity; I was hoping I'd have the perfect moment to kiss you this time."

I scoffed, rolling my eyes. "Like you ever wait for the perfect moment to kiss a girl." I was thinking about that first day when I'd arrived back and was blindsided by my three new housemates. I'd almost fallen on my face and Kody had stolen a quick kiss after saving my ass.

He cocked his head to the side, running his fingers through that bleached-blond hair of his. I usually hated guys who put so much obvious effort into their appearance, but there was something so totally *Kody* about that hair.

"Yeah, you know what? You might have a point." As if to deliberately prove me right, he sat forward, cupping a hand to the back of my neck and crushing his lips against mine.

A startled squeak of surprise escaped me, but I was a slave to my baser desires. When Kody's mouth moved, his tongue parting my lips, I didn't stop him. Hell, I kissed him right back. For a moment, I shoved all the bullshit aside and let myself bask in the intoxicating warmth of desire and attraction.

Then I slapped him.

He touched his fingertips to his cheek, but the look in his eyes was all primal hunger. It spoke to some deep, dark slice of my soul, and that scared the crap out of me.

"Guess I asked for that," he murmured before he dragged his tongue across his lower lip. A shudder ran through me as I imagined he was still tasting my kiss.

I shot up off his bed—because that suddenly seemed way too tempting—and folded my arms. "You did that deliberately," I accused.

"Kissing you?" he replied with a sly grin. "You fucking bet I did. I'd do it again too, if I didn't think you'd knee me in the balls."

I glowered back and tried to ignore the flutter of excitement at his words.

"I'm talking about that phone call. You knew I'd overhear. You wanted me to hear all of that shit. My—" My voice failed over the word *father*. How the fuck could my own father have said and *done* all those things? I felt like Dorothy when the curtain got ripped away. Except instead of a well-meaning scientist, I had a manipulative, bullying thug for a father.

Kody nodded, at least having the grace not to try to deny it. "Yeah, we knew you'd hear some of that. Call it payback for the sausage-fest porn. It's lucky chicks dig a bit of MM, or that could have really damaged my sex life."

The idea that Kody still had a sex life turned my stomach, and I wasn't naive enough to think that wasn't jealousy talking.

"You went too far," I replied and flinched at the raw vulnerability in my voice. I hadn't intended to let that out, but considering he'd just seen me almost melt down over my father's truth bombs, it was just…whatever.

Kody gave a small nod, stuffing his hands into the pockets of his sweatpants. He constantly looked like he'd just stepped out of an athletic-wear commercial. It was hot as hell and infuriating for the fact that I found it hot.

"We didn't force your dad to say that shit, MK," he said softly. I wanted to object to his use of my nickname, but it was so much better than the condescending way they always said *Madison Kate*. As fragile as my emotions were…I let it slide. Just once. "To be honest, there was no way we could have known *that* was what he'd say. Or what you'd hear."

I tucked my arms tighter around me, like I was giving myself a supportive hug. "So what was your whole plan, then? Just call him and tattle about Dallas being back in my life?"

Damn it all to hell, I wanted to believe Kody. He just had one of those faces…those sincere green eyes… Fuck. I never should have kissed him back.

"Arch…" Kody started to explain, then trailed off, biting his lower lip. He shook his head, blowing out a heavy breath. "It doesn't matter what we planned. What matters here is what he said."

I nodded, bitterness rising up in my throat again. "Yeah. That he thinks I'm a vapid bitch, that he somehow arranged a two-year prison sentence for the guy I lost my virginity to, and that he's known about my stalker for *years* and doesn't care enough to do anything about it. God forbid he even make me *aware* of it."

Dark emotions were crowding my brain again, and my skin itched with the need to get them out. Kody's brow had furrowed, but the way he was staring at me seemed at odds with the utter, heart-wrenching betrayal I was experiencing.

"What?" I snapped.

"You lost your virginity to that asshole? He's old enough to be your dad." Kody said it like he was making a joke, but there was an edge of anger in his voice that confused me.

"Very funny, asshole," I replied with a growl. "He's not that much older than *you*."

Based on what Bree had told me, Kody was twenty-one. Dallas was twenty-three now, but at the time... Yeah, it had crossed a few lines back then. Part of the reason we had agreed to keep it a one-time thing and just stay friends.

Of course, then things had gotten weird and we'd drifted apart. Next thing I knew, he'd been arrested and sent to Mantworth. My father's doing, apparently.

I shook my head, trying to rearrange all the jumbled thoughts. "I need to get out of here," I muttered, reaching for his door handle. "This whole situation is getting more fucked up by the second, and I'm just about done with it all."

I yanked Kody's bedroom door open, only to find Steele right there on the other side. His hand was raised, like he'd been about to knock, but who knows how long he'd been standing there. I sure as shit wasn't sticking around to find out, so I shoved him aside and started down the hall.

"MK, wait!" Kody shouted, chasing after me and grabbing my arm. "Where are you going?"

"Literally *none* of your business. Like I told you the day I got back, stay out of my fucking way, or you'll regret it." My death stare encompassed both Kody and Steele, and when I whirled around to leave, I found Archer standing there with his arms folded over his broad chest. "Move it, D'Ath."

"Go to your room, Princess Danvers," he ordered me, his bored glare pure ice.

It just enraged me further. "How does *get fucked* sound, dickhead?"

"Sounds like a spoiled brat throwing a temper tantrum because Daddy doesn't love her," he replied, his voice totally flat. "Now you go to your fucking room, do some fucking homework, and stop acting like such a fucking brat."

He turned as if to leave, as if that was the end of conversation and I'd scurry back to my princess-pink room with my tail between my legs. Clearly, he'd forgotten who he was dealing with.

"No, I don't think I'm going to dance to your tune today, Archer D'Ath," I mused aloud and somewhat caustically. "Not today or ever. What are you actually going to do? Force me to stay?"

Archer turned back to me ever so slowly, and his eyes held a distinctive, wicked gleam. That vein throbbed over his temple, and I looked at him with pure contempt.

He took two steps toward me, and I tilted my chin, challenging him. Part of me was pretty confident he was all talk and threats, hoping to intimidate me into falling in line. The other part of me? Yeah…I had a feeling he actually would force me to stay.

Crap.

His huge hands clamped down on my upper arms, and he gave me a mean smile. Suddenly *all* parts of me were sure. He one hundred percent intended to physically force me into my room, then probably lock the door.

Nope. Not happening. No way, no how.

As he applied pressure, pushing me backward, I did the only thing any self-respecting woman in my position could do.

I slammed my knee into his nuts.

Then ran like hell.

CHAPTER 23

I should have just taken one of my father's cars. Maybe then I wouldn't have found myself walking down the street in *pouring* rain with no shoes and no coat.

Hindsight is a beautiful thing. And really, it'd have taken me so long to mentally talk myself into *actually* driving that the guys would have caught up and dragged me back—probably—kicking and screaming.

Thankfully, though, I was only out in the rain for five minutes before Dallas drove past, braked, then reversed to stop in front of me.

"Katie? What the hell are you doing?"

He was so concerned that I just ended up a sobbing mess in his passenger seat. I asked him to take me to Bree's place because, as badly as I wanted to spend time with Dallas…I couldn't get my father's voice out of my head.

"Are you ready to tell me what's going on?" Dallas asked as we pulled into Bree's parents' mansion. She'd moved into the pool house, so we bypassed the main entrance and let ourselves through the gate hidden by hedges. We'd spent enough time there in the past, and nothing had changed.

"Can you tell me about what happened to you?" I asked him,

leading the way through the garden path. "When you got arrested? I thought it was a robbery charge, but the more I think about it, the less I can remember." Actually, the more I thought about it, the more sure I was that Dallas hadn't been the one robbing that pharmacy at all.

"Uh, it's in the past, Katie. I did my time, and now I'm all reformed and shit." He scratched uncomfortably at his new neck tattoo, a geometric wolf.

I snorted a soft laugh. "Reformed my ass, you big liar. I know you're still in the Wraiths."

Dallas shot me a wicked grin, then knocked on Bree's patio door before giving me a small frown. "Why do you ask?"

I bit my lip, then shook my head. "No reason," I lied. "Just thinking about how we lost touch. We used to be so close."

He arched a lopsided smile at me right as Bree opened the door. "Hey, guys, what's up?" She raised a brow at my soaked-through, barefoot outfit. "Okay...pretty confident this will be a good story. Come on in..."

I ducked past Dallas and into the warmth of Bree's home, but Dallas paused, checking his phone.

"Ah, sorry, ladies. Someone called in sick at work. I've got to go back and cover their shift." He looked annoyed but not necessarily surprised. He was a floor supervisor in some kind of warehouse, which I was pretty sure the Wraiths owned and operated some dodgy shit out of. Not my circus, not my monkeys. "Sorry, girls. Another night?"

"You bet, babe," Bree replied with a sassy wink, and I did a quick double take between them. Dallas shot her a small smile back, and I started wondering if there was something going on between the two of them.

"Oh, wait," I gasped as Dallas made to leave. "Did you manage to get the stuff I was after?"

He nodded, his brow furrowed, and pulled a plastic bottle of white powder out of his pocket. "You sure you know what you're doing with this, Kate? Feels like you're getting in deep here."

I scowled and took the bottle from his outstretched hand. "I know *exactly* what I'm doing. That fucker will regret the day he ever messed with Madison Kate Danvers, that's a certainty."

Dallas just sighed and tucked his hands back into his pockets. "All right, just…be careful. Okay?"

"I will." I gave him a reassuring nod. "What do I owe you for this?" I inspected the drug in my hand. There was a lot. More than I'd expected…but then how the hell would I know what was normal?

Dallas just waved me off, stepping back out into the rain. "On the house, gorgeous. Just be safe."

When he was gone, Bree closed the door and leaned her back against it, her eyes sparkling mischief. "You're actually going to do it, then?"

I placed the bottle down on her low coffee table, then cringed at the sopping fabric of my sweatpants against my legs. "I'm *definitely* doing it. Archer D'Ath is going down."

She smirked. "What a shame you don't mean that in the fun way. I bet he'd be a freaking beast in bed."

I rolled my eyes. "I can safely say I will *never* find out for myself. Now, can I borrow some clothes? I'm freezing here."

My friend laughed like I was being all kinds of dense but went to fetch me dry clothes anyway.

By the time I'd finished filling her in on everything that had happened, we'd finished a full bottle of her mom's fancy chilled champagne and eaten three blocks of imported Whittaker's chocolate from New Zealand. If it hadn't been for all the heavy shit I had to tell her, it would've been a damn perfect evening.

"Holy shit, MK," Bree finally said when I'd fully caught her up. "That's a lot. A lot, a lot."

I nodded, taking the last sip from my glass. "Yup."

We sat there in silence for a few moments, just listening to the rain falling outside.

"So..." I yawned. "Can I stay here tonight?"

"Of course, girl. *Mi casa es*...blah, blah. You know what I mean." Her words were slightly slurred, and I snickered. She was such a lightweight. "Stay as long as you need. I won't even tell Carol and Greg you're here, okay?"

I wrinkled my nose at the mention of her parents. "Yeah, that's probably best. Last thing I need is for my dad to call and scream at me. Not now."

"You got it," Bree agreed, then within moments started snoring.

I stifled a laugh but tucked a pillow under her head and a blanket over her body before crawling under the covers of her bed. If she wasn't going to use it, I might as well.

Despite how exhausted I was and how soothing the sound of rain and Bree's snores was, sleep totally eluded me. I probably dozed off lightly sometime after four in the morning, but when Bree's alarm clock went off, I felt like warmed-up dog shit.

My best friend—still asleep on the floor where she'd passed out—startled awake and sat up with some epic haystack hair. "It's morning?" she asked, bleary with sleep.

"Unfortunately," I replied with a yawn. "Thanks for letting me crash."

Bree got up off the floor and stretched her arms over her head with a loud groan. "No worries, babe. Seriously, stay forever if you want."

As tempting as that offer was, I shook my head. "Nah, I can't let them think they've got me running scared from my own home. Besides, I've got Archer's hopes and dreams to crush under my boot."

Bree snickered a laugh on her way to the bathroom. "You're fucking vicious, MK," she called back to me. "I love it."

I grinned as she turned the shower on but left the door partly open so we could still talk. I'd still had my phone in the pocket of my sweatpants when I'd escaped the Danvers mansion last night, so I rolled over in Bree's big bed to check if Dallas had messaged. After all, only he, Bree, and my father had my number, so I couldn't see anyone else contacting me.

How wrong I was.

"Twelve missed calls and twenty-seven messages?" I yelled aloud, double-checking the notification display. "What the shit?"

Swiping my screen unlocked, I groaned.

"Bree! Did you give the guys my number?" Because I seriously doubted Dallas had handed it over... Maybe my father had? Then again, he didn't seem to care much about what I was doing, and I couldn't see Archer asking him for help.

Bree didn't reply, and I narrowed my eyes at the cracked bathroom door.

"Bree..." I repeated, my tone low and warning.

The shower shut off, and a moment later, her face popped around the door—guilt painted all over it. "It was last week," she explained, cringing at whatever was playing out on my face. "Like, before shit got bad. Before the juice incident. Kody asked, and he was all shirtless and sweaty and..." She trailed off with a helpless shrug.

I guessed I couldn't blame her. I'd lost my brain plenty of times thanks to those boys being shirtless and sweaty, and if he'd asked before we started classes, it wouldn't have seemed like such a crazy request. We *did* live together.

"It's fine." I waved off her concern and sighed. I clicked into the messages to scan the content. It was all fairly unsurprising shit. *Where are you?* and the like.

There were three different numbers, and there was one message from each that helped me identify who each number belonged to.

Max Steele: Come home, hellcat.

Anger flared, and I deleted the rest of his messages without opening them. Fuck that. He'd told his friends *everything* that we'd done, right down to the fact that he had my panties. Had he shown them or something? Ugh. So gross. Talk about drunken mistakes.

The next one I kept. Don't ask me why; I'll blame it on my stupid, girly hormones.

Kodiak Jones: I'm not sorry for kissing you. I'd do it again, if you didn't slap so hard.

Charming bastard.

The last one made me want to throw my phone across the room and only solidified my determination to fuck shit up.

Archer D'Ath: Typical princess behavior. We'll be discussing some ground rules when your tantrum is over.

I couldn't help myself. I tapped on *reply* and typed out a quick message, sending it in a flurry of irritation.

Madison Kate: Take your ground rules and shove them straight up your ass, you micropenis, dirty douchebucket.

Then because I was still frothing with anger, I sent another.

Madison Kate: Quit the domineering act too. You're no Christian Gray.

His reply was almost instant, and I jumped when my phone vibrated in my hand.

Archer D'Ath: No. I'm worse.

A shiver ran through me, and I decided against continuing the asinine conversation with him, instead tossing my phone back onto the bed and going for a shower now that Bree was out.

"Hey, you want to cut classes today?" I asked her while lathering shampoo into my long, pink locks. My walk in the rain the night before had made it all tangled and gross, so it needed the freshen-up.

"Cut classes?" Bree replied, sounding surprised. "It's only the second week, girl."

She had a point, even if it did feel like I'd been back in Shadow Grove for months already. "So, no?"

"I didn't say no." She appeared in the doorway of the bathroom, holding up two dresses. "Which one?"

I swiped water out of my eyes and considered both outfits. "Black one." I picked. "With those cute thigh-high flat boots you've got."

She nodded. "Yep, that'll look cute on you." She hung the sweater dress I'd chosen on the door handle, then disappeared back into her bedroom.

I smiled and rinsed out my hair. I'd thought she meant for her, but of course she was making sure I didn't go home in my sweatpants from last night. Typical Bree, she was already thinking about how to make me look amazing, just in case we ran into the guys.

Not because I felt any need to be primped and made up for them, fuck no. But because when we felt good about our appearances, it acted like armor. It boosted our confidence, and I could do with every ounce of that I could find today.

Sometime later we were both dressed, makeup on, and hair done. I had to hand it to her, too; I felt ready to tackle whatever the day wanted to throw my way.

There was just one thing missing.

"So," Bree said, propping her hands on her hips. "Coffee, then…a movie?"

It was raining again, and to me that was perfect weather for daytime cinema visits. So I happily agreed to her plan. "I know the perfect place for coffee," I told her, "and zero chance of running into anyone we know."

"Sounds good to me," Bree replied, grabbing her car keys and leading the way out of her villa. "So, where are we heading?"

I grinned. "West Shadow Grove. Nadia's Cakes."

CHAPTER 24

Walking into the coffee shop, a flutter of anxiety hit me. Last time I'd been here, some chick had assumed I was Kody's new girlfriend and slapped me for exactly no good reason.

To my relief, the shop was fairly quiet, and the bitchy brunette, Drew, was nowhere to be seen.

"Okay, you're right," Bree declared after we'd finished our coffee and two servings of cake each. It was never too early for cake.

I grinned, licking my fork. "Good, right?"

She nodded, groaning and rubbing her stomach. "So good. How'd you find this place? You've been back in town for, like, three seconds."

I grimaced, remembering my coffee date with Kody. "Long story." Thankfully Nadia wasn't there, so I didn't have to field any awkward questions about my "boyfriend" in front of Bree. The old woman was too sweet for me to correct her.

We left the coffee shop in a great mood, huddling under a shared umbrella as we made our way back to Bree's car.

"You want to drive?" she asked, looking over at me through her lashes and holding out her keys.

I bit my lip and shook my head. She knew my hang-ups but

never pushed me too hard. I had my license, but driving wasn't something I *enjoyed*, thanks to past trauma.

"Nah," I replied, trying to keep my tone light. "You'd kill me if I scratched your rims or something."

"Probably," she agreed, clicking the key fob to unlock her car when we came around the corner. Across the street, a couple stood under a wide black umbrella, locked in an intense kiss. There was something strangely familiar about the girl...

"Oh shit," I breathed, stopping dead in my tracks beside Bree's car.

It was Drew, the girl who'd slapped me. But that wasn't what had just made the bottom fall out of my stomach. She'd just shifted the umbrella, revealing the guy's bleached-blond hair and broad, muscular frame.

Bree gasped. "Is that—?"

"Yep." I bit the word off, feeling bitter disappointment churn in my stomach. "Come on; let's go before he sees us."

Not waiting for her reply, I yanked the door open and slid into the safety of her car. Thank god it was raining and her roof was up.

She opened her door, tossing the umbrella into the backseat, before getting in and slamming the door shut.

"Well shit," she commented, turning the car on and not even subtly looking over her shoulder to where they'd been standing. "I didn't know Kody had a girlfriend."

I drummed my fingertips on the armrest, doing my absolute best to ignore the sour emotions swirling within me. "Me neither."

For small mercies, I hadn't told Bree that he'd kissed me last night. If I had, then I'd really be feeling stupid now.

"So, movies?" she asked in a weak attempt to change the subject.

I started to nod, then paused. "Can we swing past my dad's place first? If Kody is here, hopefully the other two are at SGU and the house will be empty."

"You got it," she agreed, navigating the streets back to the neighborhood we both lived in. Despite the integration projects, there was still a clear demarcation when we reached East Shadow Grove once more—houses were bigger, gardens were more pristine, cars were more expensive.

Bree parked directly in front of the main entrance, and I grabbed my pile of clothes before leading the way into the house.

"I'll be quick," I told her. "Then maybe we can catch that new thriller that just came out?"

My best friend wrinkled her nose, not being a huge fan of thrillers. "Or a rom-com. Same difference."

I rolled my eyes, dropping my pile of clothes onto the floor of the kitchen and heading straight for the pantry. It took me all of thirty seconds to locate the big black tubs of protein powder I'd seen Archer filling his shaker with, and an additional ten seconds to dump the contents of my brown medicine bottle into it and stir.

It might have been more effective if I'd dosed each of his shakes individually rather than diluting it in the whole tub of powder... but I figured this should do the trick.

After all, I was trying to get revenge, not kill him.

Yet.

Leaving the walk-in pantry, I waved the empty powder bottle at Bree and grinned over my impending victory.

"You're diabolical," she muttered with an edge of admiration. "I also don't think we're alone, so maybe dispose of the evidence?"

I frowned, then heard what she was talking about—the low, thumping bass of music coming from somewhere deeper into the house. I'd been so excited about my plan that I hadn't even noticed it until she pointed it out.

"Good thinking," I murmured. I rinsed the bottle out, then dropped it into the recycling bin, being sure to bury it under several empty beer bottles. "Let's get out of here."

We made it within three feet of the front door—so freaking close—when my name reverberated down the hall like a gunshot.

My shoulders bunched, and I turned around slowly to confront the dark cloud storming toward us.

"Archer, I'm not deaf. You don't need to bellow." I arched a brow at him and flipped one of my loose twin braids over my shoulder.

He got all up in my personal space—classic big-man intimidation bullshit, right there—and glowered glacial fury down on me. "Where the fuck were you all night, Princess? You take off with that criminal, Moore, then just drop off the damn radar? You didn't show up for classes this morning either. Explain yourself."

Narrowing my eyes, I drew a deep breath that was *meant* to be calming. It wasn't.

"Maybe I spent the night with Dallas," I told him flippantly. "Catching up on *old times*. Maybe it was all so very exhausting I overslept and missed my morning classes. Who knows? More to the point, who cares? You keeping tabs on me, D'Ath? I wasn't aware that was your job." The vein over his temple throbbed, and I sneered.

"Well, now you know," he snarked back. "And you didn't stay with Dallas all night. He got called into work awfully suddenly." His gaze flickered to Bree. "I guess I know where you were now. I thought Bree had vocal coaching in Southbridge on Monday nights."

"Uh, you know my schedule?" Bree wrinkled her nose. "Not creepy at all. Besides, neither of us have actually gone to that class in years, not since Mrs. Turner *died*. We just never told our dads so we had a plausible excuse to be out of the house."

Archer barely even acknowledged her words, his cold gaze locked on my face.

"Cute hair," he commented, his words twisting with a distinct cruelty even as he stroked his fingertips down one of my braids and looped the loose end around his hand. It was only then that I realized his knuckles were wrapped in tape and his T-shirt clung to his chest with the dampness of sweat.

"How come *you* aren't in class?" I countered, ignoring his fingers teasing the end of my braid. He was doing it to unnerve me, and I wasn't letting it show. "Pot calling the kettle black, perhaps?" I folded my arms under my breasts and could have sworn his attention flickered over my cleavage for a moment.

"I only take three subjects," he informed me, "and right now, I'm in training. Or I would be if my trainer hadn't gone out looking for your vapid ass."

It didn't take a genius to figure out his trainer was Kody. Except he'd seemed far more interested in finding the back of Drew's throat, so maybe I wasn't the only one he'd lied to.

"Okay, cool chat," I remarked, turning to leave. Archer had other plans, though, yanking me to a halt with his grip on my braid. "Ow!" I protested as he wound my braid around his fist, pulling me close enough that his hot, hard body pressed into my back.

"Don't," he growled in my ear, "push me, Princess Danvers. You won't like the consequences."

I scoffed. "Yeah? How'd you like my knee slamming into your balls, big man? Or are they so shriveled from all the steroid use that it barely tickled?"

His chest rumbled, and I couldn't tell if it was a laugh or a growl. "So interested in my balls, Princess. If you want to see them up close and personal, all you've gotta do is ask." He tugged me closer still, demonstrating how very wrong I was about his shriveled genitals, and that's where my bravado broke.

Twisting in his grip, I smacked his wrist to make him release my hair. "It's not cute when boys pull girls' pigtails because they like them. It speaks to some serious mommy issues. Maybe you should look into that." I batted my lashes sweetly, then dropped my smile to glare. "Come on, Bree. The air in here is a bit thick on testosterone for my liking."

I stalked out of the house with Bree close behind me, and shockingly, Archer didn't follow. I paused a moment, trying to catch my breath as the door slammed behind us, and Bree let out a low whistle.

"Girl," she said with a laugh, "the sexual tension between you two just made *me* wet. Please tell me you're planning on riding him like your personal pony. Soon."

I rolled my eyes at her but couldn't find the words to deny that I'd thought about it. Just once or twice.

"Stop it," I murmured without conviction. "Let's go before the other two stooges get home. I don't think I can handle them right now. At least Archer is easy to be mean to."

My friend snickered and muttered something under her breath about how she'd like Archer to be mean to her. Naked. But I ignored her and popped the passenger door open. I paused a moment, looking back up at the house and second-guessing my plan for Archer. Was I going too far?

But then again, he'd hand-delivered me to the police with evidence of a crime literally in my pocket. Even more unforgivable was his total lack of remorse for derailing my life. So no. Fuck him. He deserved everything he got.

Resolute, I started to get into the car, only to spot something on the seat.

"What the—" I broke off with a small scream when I reached out to move the item. "Bree!"

"What's up?" she replied, sliding into the driver's seat. "Suddenly realized you'd prefer a hot and dirty hate-fuck with Archer D'Ath over a movie with me? I'm shocked."

I shook my head, my hand pressed to my own mouth as I stared down at my seat.

Bree followed my line of sight and froze.

"What…the fuck…is that?" she breathed, sounding just as terrified as me.

I shook my head, crouching beside the car to take a closer look without touching it.

"It's…" My voice was hoarse, and I licked my lips before trying again. "It's a doll."

A Barbie, to be more specific. Or something of that style. Hard plastic, about twelve inches tall…that in itself was enough to spark fear in someone with mild pedophobia—a fear of dolls—but that wasn't the part that made me want to scream.

Her long hair was pink, and she wore a doll-sized version of sweatpants and a tank top. The leather seat was soaked, a pool of water spread around the doll, and she was totally drenched. Just like I had been last night when Dallas picked me up on the street.

Cold fear washed through me, but it was quickly chased away by blinding fury.

"MK?" Bree asked, her voice quivering. "What are you thinking?"

"I'm wondering whether I can get away with murder," I snarled, snatching up the offensive little doll. "Because I'm going to *fucking kill him*."

I didn't need to elaborate. It was pretty obvious which *him* I was talking about as I stormed back into the house. The thumping bass of music provided an angry soundtrack for my steps as I made my way through to the home gym and slammed the door open dramatically.

The smirk on Archer's face when he saw me there was pure satisfaction, and I wanted to claw his damn eyes out.

"I knew you'd be back," he admitted with a smug laugh. He'd been working the heavy sandbag, but as I stalked into the gym, he ripped his gloves off and tossed them down on the mat.

So much adrenaline coursed through my veins that I trembled as I tilted my chin up to meet his eyes. There wasn't even a single scrap of remorse, as per usual, and it only drove the inferno of my hate higher.

"You're fucking sick," I spat, throwing the Barbie at his chest. It bounced off his shirt, dropping to the crash mat with a soft sound, and Archer frowned down at it in confusion. "You think this whole stalker thing is *funny*?" I demanded. "What the hell is your endgame here, Archer? What did I ever do to *you*?"

He gave me an incredulous look, then stooped and picked up the doll. His brows hitched, and my heart seemed to pause. Either he was a really good actor or...

"Madison Kate, this wasn't me," he said with total sincerity. Or so it seemed. That was exactly what he'd say if he was guilty, wasn't it? Fuck, I didn't know what to believe anymore.

I scoffed. "Bullshit, Archer. Just leave me the hell *alone*. I'm done. I'm fucking done, do you hear me?" I was screaming by the end of this, but I was past caring. I'd had enough of their games when I didn't even know *why* they were doing it. At least I'd been clear from day one why I hated the three of them. They deserved my anger, and they damn well knew it.

Archer grabbed hold of me before I could leave again, his huge hands clamped over my upper arms like I'd been caught in a vise. "Madison Kate, I *didn't do this*." His eyes held mine, searching for something. "You have to believe me."

I just shook my head. I didn't *want* to believe him, because the alternative was so much worse than a stupid prank from my future stepbrother.

"Bree?" Archer pushed, not letting me go as he turned his slightly frantic stare to my friend. "You believe that this wasn't me, don't you?"

I shot my gaze over at her, and she gave me a helpless sort of shrug. She was pale, and her eyes were wide with shock. "I kinda do," she said in a small voice, looking at me, not Archer. "I'm sorry, MK. I don't think this was him... It's too creepy. Way too creepy. Didn't your dad confirm that this stalker is real?"

I shook my head again, wanting to deny all of it. Denial was my safe place.

"They could have made him say that," I said with weak conviction. Not even I believed me. "They could have…" I shrugged, tipping my head back to look at the ceiling while desperately fighting back the panic. Because, really, honestly? I knew better. I knew there was no freaking way Archer and his boys were behind *this* prank. They couldn't be…because they couldn't have known what significance dolls like that had to me.

They didn't know that one had been left on my mother's grave a year after her death. It had been a replica of her looking exactly as she had when I was released from that closet the night she was murdered. Bloody and beaten, her lilac-blue eyes lifeless and flat.

Tremors shook my limbs, and I slipped free of Archer's hold, crumpling to the floor in a puddle of fear and dread.

Archer barked orders at Bree, telling her to stay with me while he called the guys. But what help could they possibly be? This creep had been *right here.* He'd been inside the property gates, he'd placed that doll in Bree's car just minutes ago.

Holy fuck, he could still be here.

This was real.

I had a stalker.

I could only pray I didn't end up like my mother.

CHAPTER 25

Hours later, after giving police statements and repeating my limited knowledge of the whole situation numerous times, I sank down on the couch. I was mentally and emotionally exhausted, and all I wanted to do was curl up in a ball and sleep. Except...I couldn't sleep in my room. Not when I knew this creep had been able to take pictures through my window.

He'd been inside the house.

When the police had asked for a copy of the file from my father's office, it was nowhere to be found—just a blank space in the filing cabinet where Archer swore the file had been not twenty-four hours earlier.

He'd immediately called in a security company, and I watched silently from the couch as the uniformed guy talked Archer and Steele through the new system. Bree had gone home, albeit reluctantly, and that left me with Kody.

"Here, I made you cocoa," the buff, blond god said softly, sitting down beside me on the couch and handing me a steaming mug. I took it because no one in their right mind—or otherwise, as the case may be—would decline fresh cocoa while it was storming outside and they were experiencing any level of shock.

But that was the *only* thing I wanted from him.

"Don't you have somewhere better to be?" I asked him, my tone caustic. It was a poor coping mechanism, transferring my emotions into being a bitch, but whatever. I've never claimed to be perfect.

Kody gave me a small frown of confusion, and from the corner of my eye, I noticed the security guys had finished up and were leaving.

"Uh, no? I cancelled my PT clients for the day when Arch called earlier." He sounded genuinely confused by my snarky remark.

I rolled my eyes. "You sure Drew isn't waiting for you somewhere? You two sure looked like you made up from last weekend's fight."

Kody's lips parted, and he seemed a bit stunned. Too bad for him that the other guys had heard what I'd said.

"What's this about?" Archer asked, folding his arms. "I thought you took care of Drew."

"I did," Kody replied, his tone sharp. "I can only assume Madison Kate happened to see me today at the exact moment *Drew* kissed *me*. Which, I might add, is terribly coincidental timing, Princess. Were you following me?"

I barked a laugh. "Like hell. I went to Nadia's for coffee and cake. And it didn't look much like you were pushing her away."

Kody stared at me for a tense moment, and then his lips curled up in a grin. "Damn, MK. Green is a good color on you."

"Oh fuck off," I sneered. "I'm not jealous, just wondering what the hell I got slapped for if you were still hooking up with her anyway."

"Hold up," Archer interjected. "You got slapped? When? How?"

I broke eye contact with the green-eyed playboy beside me and peered up at Archer, who still stood there with his huge-ass arms folded. At least Steele had sat down on the armchair opposite us.

"Last weekend when Kody took me to Nadia's. His *girlfriend*—"

"Not my girlfriend," he butted in.

"—assumed I was the latest victim in the revolving door of his bedroom and slapped me for the fun of it. I guess. Isn't that kind of fucked up, though? Blaming the other woman for a man's infidelity?" I crinkled my nose, still annoyed about being caught in the crossfire on that one.

"Nice one, dickhead," Steele murmured while drumming his fingertips on the arm of his chair and staring at me way too hard.

Archer just shook his head and sighed. "You're an idiot, bro."

Kody shrugged but didn't say anything to the contrary.

"Okay, new security system is all set up. No one is getting in without half of Shadow Grove hearing about it." Archer checked the time on his phone. "Dinner will be ready in about an hour and a half. Kody, we got time to do a quick session?"

"You bet," Kody replied, ruffling his hair with his fingers. "I'll get changed and meet you in the gym." He gave me a weighted look, like he was trying to silently communicate something to me, but I was drawing a blank. When I just blinked back at him like a damn owl, he sighed, then stood up and left the room.

Steele laughed quietly, shaking his head.

"What?" I asked, confused as all hell.

His lips arched up in a smile, and it transfixed me for a moment as I remembered how intoxicating it felt to kiss him. But it was only a moment; then I remembered Archer's sneering disgust as he demonstrated thorough knowledge of that intimate moment.

"Nothing, Hellcat," he replied with a chuckle. "Nothing at all."

Liar.

I decided not to reply. Instead, I tucked my knees up tighter to my chest and sipped my warm cocoa. It was really good...*really* good. What the hell did Kody make it with to create such an intense flavor?

"Careful," Archer murmured, "Kody spikes his cocoa with liquor."

I nodded. "It's delicious."

The corner of his mouth tugged into what he might consider a smile. To everyone else, it would just be an involuntary facial twitch.

Steele wandered out of the room, mumbling something about having work to do—I guessed he was heading to the workshop—but Archer paused halfway out of the living room.

"What now?" I asked him in a flat tone. "Just thought of a cutting barb you needed to deliver before it got stale? Want to call me an idiot for not believing you about the stalker in the first place? Just spit it out and go pump some iron or whatever. Literally nothing you can say will touch me right now, so do your worst."

He rubbed his palm across the dark stubble on his jaw, giving me a look that walked the line way too close to pity. "I was just going to say you're welcome to come mope about your shit decisions in the gym. You know, if you don't want to be alone right now."

Just like that, Archer D'Ath proved me wrong again. His words touched my soul, all right. Just not in any way I'd been prepared for.

―――――――――

I lasted about half an hour in the gym, sitting on the floor and watching Kody put Archer through the paces of what, to me, seemed to be the workout from hell.

Don't get me wrong; despite having avoided the gym since arriving home, I was no slouch in the fitness department. The difference was, though, that I worked out to stay fit and healthy so I could run away from someone chasing me. Riot Night had proven the necessity of that. Archer and Kody seemed to relish the sheer pain of pushing their bodies to the absolute limits. It was scary hot, but soon the novelty wore off.

I yawned and stood up from the floor right when Kody was making Archer do this weird thing with two huge-ass ropes that stretched half the length of the room.

"I'm bored," I admitted after Kody barked at Archer not to stop, then came over to check on me. "I'm going to go see what Steele is working on in the garage."

Kody grabbed a small towel and wiped the sweat off his face. Despite his role as Archer's trainer, he wasn't exactly sitting back and watching the whole time.

"I thought you were pretty pissed off at him," he said, watching Archer as he continued making waves with the heavy-ass ropes. The big guy then dropped the ropes and did some stupidly impressive push-ups with one hand, then some jumping things, then back to the ropes.

I cleared my throat, realizing I'd just gotten distracted. "Uh, yeah. I am. But I'm also shit-scared some psycho will jump out from behind a hat stand and, like…make a human skin suit out of me. So I'll make lemonade for now."

Kody gave me a half smile. "Babe, life gave you more than lemons. You got, like…I don't even know. Tomatoes. When you ordered strawberries."

I wrinkled my nose and sighed. "True that."

He reached out and touched my face gently, stroking his finger down my cheek, then raising my chin up so I'd meet his eyes. "Don't even worry, MK. You can just make Bloody Marys instead."

Kody shot me a teasing wink, then turned back to his training session with Archer.

I shook my head, confused as hell with his behavior, then left the gym with the intense sensation of eyes on my back. Except these eyes didn't make my skin crawl and my anxiety spike. They just made me feel…seen.

Not wanting to be alone for any longer than necessary, I hurried through to the garage. All the lights were off inside, though, and I seriously doubted Steele worked on cars in the dark.

"Crap," I muttered to myself. He'd said he had work to do… maybe coursework? I didn't even know what the guys were studying at SGU. Shows how much attention I paid to anything that didn't further my revenge plans.

Not wanting to return to the gym so soon, I made my way upstairs and knocked on Steele's bedroom door. He didn't answer immediately, and I started to walk away just before the door opened.

"Madison Kate?" he called out, his words shadowed with surprise.

I turned back around to face him, feeling uncomfortable all of a sudden. He had headphones looped around his neck, and his hair was mussed up. Had he been watching porn or something?

"Hey, uh, I was just…" I trailed off, biting my lip and feeling like a *total* idiot. I was still angry as hell at him for playing me at the fight and for telling his stupid friends all about it afterward. But…I'd enjoyed the time we'd spent together before making out in the bathroom. Okay, fine, that part too.

He arched a lopsided, understanding smile at me. "You got bored as hell watching those dickheads work out, huh?" I nodded sheepishly. "Well, you can come hang out in here, but I can't promise you'll be any less bored."

His cheeks tinted slightly as he said this, and my curiosity got the better of me.

"Why? What are you doing?" I stepped into his room as he held the door open, then realized I hadn't actually seen the inside of his bedroom before. "Ohhh, I see."

Against one wall he had a large desk with an expensive-looking keyboard sitting on top. Based on the sheets and sheets of music pages scattered across the rest of the desk, the floor, even on the bed, I could guess what he'd been doing.

"Make yourself at home," he invited me, waving to the bed. It was really the only place for me to sit, seeing as his desk chair was clearly where he'd been sitting. "I was just…messing around."

I shrugged, sitting awkwardly on the edge of his bed and trying really hard not to snoop around with my gaze. It was a pretty simple room, masculine in the use of dark wood and cool gray-blue tones. The walls just held a few framed pieces of ancient-looking sheet music, but that was it. No photos or awards or trophies or…really anything personal. But maybe that in itself spoke more truthfully to Steele's personality.

"How come you're not using the music room?" I asked him after I'd gawked at everything I could see. "There's a full-size grand piano down there."

He sat back down on his desk chair, rearranging some of the scattered papers and setting them aside. "Yeah, I know. But…here I can connect my headphones to the keyboard so that no one else hears me play."

That explained the wireless headphones around his neck. I was suddenly so damn curious to hear him play, though. He'd said his parents wanted him to become a concert pianist, so he had to be good.

"Can I?" I asked, blurting the question out without thinking it over first. "Hear you play, I mean."

He seemed startled, and I sort of expected him to say no. But then he gave a small nod and set his headphones aside. "Just…stay super quiet, okay? So I can pretend you're not there."

It was an interesting request for someone considering a career that depended on huge halls of people watching and listening. But what did I know? Maybe that was a normal thing for musicians.

Steele arched a brow at me, and I mimed zipping my lips. That seemed to satisfy him, because he turned back to the keyboard and rested his fingers ever so softly on the keys.

He paused like that long enough that I worried he'd changed his mind about playing for me. But I was wrong.

From the very first notes he played, I was lost to his music.

He poured his entire fucking soul into the piece he played for me. All his emotions, his hopes and fears and *desires*. It was utterly spellbinding.

At some point I found myself shuffling up his bed and lying down with my head on his pillow, closing my eyes, and just letting the raw energy of his song wash over me.

CHAPTER 26

I don't know how long Steele played his keyboard for, but it felt like all night. I drifted in and out of sleep, but the soothing sound of his music lulled me. When morning came, all was quiet.

Quiet and warm.

I breathed a deep sigh, my nostrils filling with the scent of clean soap and underlying grease and gasoline. Steele.

"I didn't mean to fall asleep here," I whispered, knowing he was there by the radiating warmth beside me. I didn't open my eyes or raise my voice above that soft whisper because I loved that moment suspended between sleep and waking. I never wanted to rush it.

Steele shifted, the sheets rustling. "I'm glad you did," he whispered back, his voice rough with sleep.

Neither one of us spoke again for an indefinite amount of time, just lying there dozing. We weren't touching, but our bodies were close enough that it was strangely intimate.

Sounds of people awake in the house, footsteps in the hallway and doors opening and closing, finally broke our bubble, and I flipped onto my back.

"What time is it?" I asked, turning my head to the side just enough to look at him through my lashes. My mascara was probably halfway down my face, and I was still in Bree's black sweater dress from yesterday, but at least I'd taken the boots off.

His gray eyes found mine, and a soft smile touched his lips. "Time to get up if you're planning on attending classes today."

I wrinkled my nose but scrubbed a hand over my face and nodded. "Yep. Classes." I sat up with a mammoth effort and cringed when I felt the bird's nest that my loose braids had turned into. "Don't you usually wake up at the crack of dawn to work out with the other two stooges?" I arched a brow at him, but my insult held no heat.

After tugging the hair ties from my braids, I ran my fingers through to loosen the strands out.

Tucking his arms under his head, he just gave me a slow grin. "Usually. But then I'd have missed seeing you like this."

I frowned. "Like what?"

Steele shook his head. "Never mind." He yawned, then climbed out of his bed. "Hey, seeing as I let you sleep in my awesome bed all night..." He trailed off, pausing near the door and shooting me an over-the-top pleading look.

"Yes...?"

"Will you make my coffee this morning? You don't understand how bad that shit Archer makes is." He looked pained at the thought of it, so I snickered and agreed as we both left his bedroom—him, to the bathroom the three guys shared, and me, back to my own room. The fact that I had the only en suite bathroom in this section of the house hadn't escaped my notice.

I hurried through my morning routine, feeling the prickling sensation of paranoia the whole time I was in my room alone. What if there were hidden cameras?

Just in case, I dressed inside my closet—a navy-blue, lace-detailed top; black skinny jeans; and knee-high leather boots—then opted to leave my braid-kinked hair loose and messy.

After a lightning-fast swipe of makeup, I grabbed a leather

jacket from my closet—because the weather had definitely taken a cold turn in the last few days—and headed downstairs.

It only took me a few minutes to make coffee for both Steele and myself; then on a whim I made two extras. Clearly my brain hadn't fully woken up yet, because I didn't even bat an eyelash when Kody came in from the gym and took one with an appreciative groan.

I did, however, experience a flash of guilt as Archer walked in drinking the last of his protein shake out of his plastic shaker. But I easily pushed the guilt aside. Regardless of his rare display of kindness around my stalker, he was still an unrepentant prick who needed to be punished for framing me.

"You made coffee for everyone?" he asked me, frowning down at the mug with a perfect fern leaf created out of crema and milk foam.

I shrugged. "Not a big deal."

He kept frowning at the coffee like he was confused, but Kody smacked him on the arm.

"Shut up and drink the damn coffee, dickhead," he muttered. "You've got a one-hour rest, and then you're back in the gym. Got it?"

Archer grunted a sound of understanding, then gulped his whole coffee in one hit. He set the empty cup into the sink, then stalked out of the kitchen without another word.

"What got his panties in a wad this morning?" I muttered under my breath, pouring sugary cereal into a big bowl and filling it up with milk. "There's such a thing as too much time working out, you know."

Steele chuckled into his coffee, and Kody looked horrified. He reached over me and grabbed the box of novelty cereal, pouring his own big bowl.

"Wash your mouth out," he scolded me teasingly. "Besides, Arch is training for a big fight coming up."

Excitement flared inside me, and I frowned like I'd totally forgotten about his televised UFC debut scheduled for just a week after Halloween. "Oh yeah, I forgot."

"Uh-huh." Kody squinted at me like he didn't believe that for a fucking second. "Anyway, you're welcome to come and work out with us some time. I wouldn't mind showing you some grappling techniques." His wink was all sex, and I needed to bite my lip to remind myself *not* to get turned on. Damn it.

"Thanks but no thanks," I forced myself to say, then raised my brows at his choice of breakfast food. "Uh, aren't fitness dicks supposed to be all clean-eating and shit? Lucky Charms probably don't even feature on your food pyramid at all."

Kody just shoveled a huge scoop of cereal into his mouth and chewed before giving me a grin. "Don't be a hater, MK."

I rolled my eyes but had no comebacks. Whatever he was doing, it was clearly working. He was just in a pair of loose shorts—no shirt—and every damn muscle was defined. Every. Single. One.

Catching myself drooling, I cleared my throat and searched for a change of subject.

"What was the song you were playing last night, Steele?" I asked, genuinely interested. "It's been on loop in my brain all morning."

Kody's spoon paused halfway to his mouth, milk dripping back into his bowl as he stared at me...then at Steele.

The gray-eyed guy gave me a deer-in-the-headlights kind of look, and I got the distinct impression I'd said the wrong thing. Did this have something to do with him using headphones rather than playing in the music room?

"Um," he finally replied, ducking his eyes away from mine. "Just something new I was working on." He checked his phone for the time, then quickly stacked up his plates. "We should probably go. I'll get the car out of the garage."

"Wait, what?" I shook my head. "I don't need a lift. Bree picks me up for class, remember?"

Kody and Steele exchanged a look, and I narrowed my eyes at the two of them.

"What?" I snapped, folding my arms.

"Nothing," Steele replied, giving Kody another quick look. "We'd just feel better if we could keep an eye on you for a couple of days. Is that okay?"

It was a good thing Steele said that and not Kody, because he somehow managed to make it sound like a caring request and not a macho-man power trip. But still…were they implying Bree could have had something to do with the stalker?

"Archer already told Bree you had a ride anyway," Kody added. "So you'll be late if you wait for her to drive over now."

Stifling another eye roll, I didn't protest any further as Steele left the kitchen to grab his car. It was just a ride to class, and if I was totally honest with myself, I felt safer with the three of them around anyway.

How fucked up was that, that the three guys responsible for derailing my life were now the ones I leaned on?

I cleaned up my mess, then grabbed my jacket and bag before realizing Kody was staring at me thoughtfully.

"Something else to say, Kodiak Jones?" I prompted, pulling my jacket on and sweeping my wavy hair out of it.

He ran the pad of his thumb over his lower lip like he was debating how much to say to me. Something was clearly on his mind.

"Steele played piano for you?" He hesitated slightly as he asked this, his gaze darting in the direction his friend had just gone.

I nodded, frowning. It was all too obvious I was missing something to do with Steele and his music. "Yeah. Didn't you hear him? He played for ages. I sort of fell asleep."

Kody shook his head. "Nah, Arch and I only stopped briefly for dinner, then headed out the back to swim." His smile turned cruel. "Or Arch did. I stood on the side and yelled, uh, encouragement."

"Sounds fun," I replied, my tone loaded with sarcasm. I started to leave, but he spoke again and made me pause.

"We haven't heard him play in over a year," he said in a quiet voice. "I had no idea he'd started writing again."

Yep, I'd definitely waded into something I knew *nothing* about. So instead of pressing Kody for more information, I just shrugged and headed out of the house to find Steele.

If anyone was going to tell me that story, it'd be him.

"Uh...really?" I asked, eyeing his vehicle of choice parked in front of the main entrance to the house.

Steele flashed me a devilish smile and tossed a black helmet at me. I fumbled but managed to catch it. "Live a little, Hellcat," he teased. "You're too pretty for frown lines."

I wanted to tell him where to shove his shallow comment, but it was all too obvious he was running from his demons this morning. There was a tightness to his jaw that hadn't been present when we woke up, and I felt partly responsible. It had been me mentioning his music in front of Kody that shifted his mood, so I kinda owed it to him not to argue this small thing.

That, and I badly wanted to ride his motorcycle.

Hell yeah.

CHAPTER 27

Over the next week and a half, I found that without Bree driving me to and from SGU every day, it was increasingly difficult to see her. First it was late tutorials that prevented us from hanging out in the evenings, and then she had to spend the weekend with Granny Graves. I was starting to feel a bit like she was deliberately avoiding me.

Dallas was just as absent, but in his case I was the one finding excuses not to hang out. My father's threats were all too fresh in my mind, and I'd never forgive myself if Dallas was sent back to jail again. Worse than that, the threat on my stalker mail was haunting me every time I saw Dallas's name pop up on my phone. What if some sicko hurt him because they thought he and I were together? Nope. I wasn't going there.

By the end of the next week, I'd pretty much decided Bree was being a bitch. So of course, that's when I found her waiting for me after my psychology lab.

"Well, fancy seeing you, stranger," I muttered, brushing past her and continuing down the hallway. Steele was still driving me to and from SGU and hadn't once asked why I wasn't driving myself, which I appreciated. But he started getting irritated if I made him wait too long—he had an admirer on campus who saw it as her opportunity to flirt shamelessly—so I tried to be considerate.

Bree laughed like I was joking. I wasn't.

"Sorry I've been so busy lately, MK. I feel like such a shitty friend, considering everything that happened last week." She bit her lip, her eyes shifty as I scowled at her. "Anyway, I want to make it up to you."

"Oh yeah?" I asked, not touching her comment about being a shitty friend. "How so?"

She beamed a little too brightly as I pushed the doors open to the back parking lot, where Steele had taken to parking on the days Archer and Kody weren't in class.

"I'm throwing a party," she announced. "Tonight. My place. I've invited a bunch of the old Shadow Prep crew too. It's about time you expanded your social horizons, you know, *outside* of Danvers Mansion."

I gave her a knowing smile but shook my head. "As much as I'd love to come to one of your parties, it seems like a really dumb idea considering...my situation."

Her smile slipped slightly, but then she raised her brows. "Didn't your dad basically say that you've had this stalker for years?"

I frowned in confusion. "Yeah, so?"

She shrugged. "Well...what needs to change? You went to parties before you knew, and nothing happened. You shouldn't have to live in fear, MK. You're tougher than that."

Bree was trying to manipulate me and doing a pretty crappy job of it. "There were no creepy dolls left before."

"How do you know?" she challenged. And damn, she had a point. My father hadn't found it necessary to tell me about my stalker or even report it to the police. So how the hell *would* I know if any other dolls had been left? They had. I knew they had. The one on my mother's grave had been too similar for this to be all a big coincidence.

Even so, a party still felt like a bad idea, one of those too-stupid-to-live decisions that movie heroines made.

I glanced around the parking lot while considering how to decline Bree's invitation, then realized something. Steele wasn't waiting for me.

A moment later, I realized why.

A familiar midnight-black Corvette Stingray zipped into the parking lot and screeched to a halt beside Bree and me.

"Get in, Princess," Archer barked, not even bothering to get out of the car.

I bent down to peer through the open window and found Kody grinning at me from the passenger seat. Of Archer's *two-seater* car.

"Doesn't look like there's any space," I replied.

Archer tilted his sunglasses down, looking up at me with those ice-blue eyes of his. "Never stopped you before."

Bree laughed, even if she didn't get the joke. "Okay, there's an inside joke going on there. So, I'll see you tonight, MK. Dress sexy; Leon will be there."

I groaned, shaking my head. The fact that my ex-boyfriend was going to be there was *not* a selling point for me. Then again, Bree never had understood why I'd broken up with that two-pump chump in the first place.

"What's tonight?" Archer asked before I could make my excuses to Bree.

She beamed at him. "A party at my place," she announced. "You guys can come too, if you want."

My head whipped around, and I glared death at her. Her eyes widened like she'd just realized what she'd said, but the damage was done.

"We love parties!" Kody yelled from the passenger seat with a whoop. "Count us in."

Bree gave me an apologetic grimace, then hurried over to her car and left me to deal with two of the three pains in my ass.

"Get in, Princess Danvers," Archer repeated. "Steele got held up working on the Cobra."

I could only imagine that was one of his project cars. Given that I had no desire to walk the whole way home and Bree had just left, I rounded the hood of the car and popped Kody's door open.

"Shift over," I told him, but he just laughed and hauled me onto his lap.

It was safe to say sitting on Kody's lap in a two-seater Corvette was vastly different from sitting on Archer's in the G Wagen. For one thing, the G Wagen had *considerably* more space inside. For another, Archer hadn't *wanted* me in his lap. Kody definitely did.

"If I have to slap your hands away from my tits or cunt one more time, Kodiak Jones…" I scolded him with only lukewarm heat after removing his hand from my inner thigh for maybe the fourth time.

He snickered under me, and Archer shot us both a dark look from the side of his sunglasses.

It didn't take us long to get home, though, and I practically jumped out of the car when it stopped. Not because I hated sitting in such tight confines with Kody underneath me…but because I liked it a little *too* much.

"Princess Danvers," Archer called out after me as I ran up the front steps to the house. "Who's Leon?"

"Why do you care, sunshine?" I replied. But then, because I didn't care to keep it a secret, I added, "He's my ex. But don't stress yourselves; I'm not looking to reconcile with any guy who declares the female orgasm a myth perpetuated by feminazis."

That really had been the last nail in our relationship coffin a few months before Riot Night. It didn't help that I'd also overheard him bragging to his stupid friends about everything he'd do with *my* trust fund once he married me. Yeah, never happening, bud.

When neither of the guys seemed to have anything more to say, I carried on into the house and went straight up to my room.

Closing the door behind me, I chucked my bag down on the floor and cringed at all the sparkly pink.

"I need to paint this fucking room," I murmured to myself. I'd thought I could handle it. It was just a bit of pink glitter, right? Who cared?

I did. It made me physically nauseated.

I made a mental note to talk to Steele about a trip to the hardware store over the weekend, then started to get ready for Bree's party.

Sometime later, I headed back downstairs to get some dinner before we left. Bree's parties were typically heavy on the alcohol and light on the food—not a great combination under the best of circumstances, and these were *far* from that.

"Damn, MK." Kody let out a low whistle as I wandered over to where they sat in the den. The huge flat-screen was on, and Archer was playing some sort of first-person shooter. Steaming pizza boxes sat on the table unopened, like they'd just arrived.

Fridays were our cook's day off, so I was quietly glad they'd taken the initiative to order in.

"Damn, good? Or damn, bad?" I squinted at him but flopped down onto the couch beside Archer. It was the only free space, seeing as Kody and Steele were fully kicked back in the matching recliner chairs.

Kody's grin was sly, and his mischievous green-eyed gaze ran all over me before he replied. "Both. You're going to cause trouble tonight, I can tell."

I smirked back at him, quietly pleased by his reaction. My dusky-rose hair was pin straight, falling around my bare shoulders like a silken cape, and my mascara was heavy. My black dress wasn't anything too fancy, but it fitted my curves to perfection and had a fun fringe around the short hem, which tickled my thighs as I walked.

"A girl can hope," I replied, biting the inside of my cheek when

I heard the clear flirtation in my tone. Apparently I needed to have a stern word with myself because last I'd seen, Kody had a girlfriend. Or at least a girl he felt comfortable kissing in public.

Archer paused his game, turning his head to take in my party appearance, then tightened his jaw. "This is a bad idea," he muttered.

I tucked my feet up on the couch and reached for a slice of pizza. "You don't have to come, sunshine. You can stay here and glower at yourself in the mirror while lifting weights or some shit."

Archer just glared at me, then continued playing his game, leaving a bloody trail of bodies on the screen as he picked enemies off with practiced ease. His temper had been getting steadily shorter by the day—with every protein shake he drank—and I was starting to feel more than a bit guilty. But it was only a few weeks until his UFC debut now, so the damage was already done.

Fuck it. He still deserved it.

"This is going to be all kinds of fun tonight," Steele commented, then drained the rest of his drink and stood up. "I'll grab you a drink, Hellcat. Then we can take bets on which one of these dickheads will piss you off enough to get slapped first tonight."

Kody snorted a laugh. "No bet, bro. We all know Arch is coming home with MK's palm print on him *somewhere*."

Now was it just me, or did that have a dangerously sexual hint to it?

A girl could dream.

CHAPTER 28

Some things never changed. The sun rising each day. The rotation of the earth. Gravity. And of course, Bree's ability to throw one hell of a party.

"How does she even know this many people?" Steele muttered as we parked down the street and walked the rest of the way.

I snickered. "Bree's a social butterfly. You just haven't seen this side of her...yet."

She really was too. When we'd been at Shadow Prep, it had always been her dragging me out to parties and daring me into pushing boundaries. With the exception of Riot Night, of course. That one had been all me, desperate to see that mysterious up-and-coming MMA fighter.

Glancing over at him now, I could hardly reconcile the two versions of Archer.

This one seemed determined to rule my life like he had some kind of ownership over my actions and choices. Deluded prick. He'd already tried to give me a lecture on the drive over about being "responsible" and "safe" while we were at Bree's.

Such a downer.

"Madison Kate, for the love of god, *don't* get drunk tonight," he ordered me as I opened Bree's front door, and I gave him an eye roll.

"Okay, Dad," I scoffed, then immediately ditched all three of them.

It wasn't as reckless as it sounded. I'd spotted Bree across the room chatting to some girls we used to go to school with, and I knew perfectly well at least one of them followed me like a bad smell.

"You made it!" Bree squealed, throwing her arms around my neck and damn near knocking me on my ass with the strength of her alcohol breath. "I'm so happy you made it," she cooed, oblivious to the fumes rolling off her. "Your stupid guard dog can suck it. He can't keep us apart forever."

I laughed at her drunkenness but shot a dark look over my shoulder at the *guard dog* I had no doubt she was talking about. He just stared back at me, impassive as he sipped a bottle of water.

Ugh. Straitlaced prick. Of course he wasn't drinking tonight. Wouldn't want to risk some innocent booze showing up on any random drug screening between now and his big fight.

The girls Bree had been talking to greeted me and made small talk. But their smiles were forced and I could tell they were uncomfortable. As soon as I could, I made some weak excuse and walked away. On my way through the kitchen, I snagged a still-sealed premixed vodka drink, then made my way out to the pool area.

It was cold out—way too cold for the skimpy dress and heels I wore, but I preferred the freezing temperature to the whispers and side-eyes I was getting inside. Why the fuck Bree had thought this was a good idea for me, I had no idea.

I'd just hang out long enough to piss Archer off and be done with it.

"Kate," a familiar voice called out from the house, and I spun around with a smile for Dallas. "I was starting to think you were avoiding me, gorgeous."

He was teasing, I could tell. He knew full well I was avoiding him, but he didn't know why.

"Never," I lied, twisting the top off my bottle, then taking a sip. It was some sugary, watermelon-flavored crap, but it'd do. "You here officially?" I nodded to his white bandanna, tied loosely around his tattooed neck. It was printed all over with the black symbol of the Shadow Grove Wraiths, and it was the first time I'd seen him wearing it since I was fourteen, the night we'd argued about him joining the gang in the first place.

He gave a half shrug. "Sort of. Couple of the boys heard about a party in rich-ville, so I figured I should come along and keep an eye on *things.*"

I nodded my understanding, knowing he really meant he'd come to make sure his friends didn't destroy Bree's parents' house. If he could help it.

"You coming back in?" he asked me, pointing back to the party humming inside. I was the only one dumb enough to be out in the cold near the pool, so far. Once people got a bit more liquor in their bloodstreams, the frosty air wouldn't bother them so much.

I shook my head. "Nah, just hanging here for a bit. I have exactly zero desire to reconnect with my old Shadow Prep friends. You know, some of them actually go to SGU and I never noticed?"

Dallas laughed. "Real observant, Katie. I guess your attention has been a bit dominated by your *new* friends."

He followed me as I wandered over to one of the lounge chairs beside the pool and sat down. Dallas perched on the next one over, pulled a packet of cigarettes from his pocket, and lit one up.

"Hardly my friends," I muttered, but I couldn't deny that Archer, Kody, and Steele had taken up a serious amount of real estate in my brain. I held my hand out, and he passed me his cigarette. I took a drag, my pink lipstick leaving a smear on the paper, then handed it back. "But yeah." I blew out the smoke with a long exhale. "There's...so much shit going on."

We sat there in silence for a while, passing the same cigarette back and forth. I didn't smoke and wouldn't have one of my own, but I wasn't averse to a few puffs on Dallas's. Like I said, some things never changed.

"Want to talk about it?" he asked me eventually, and I shook my head.

"Nah. Ignorance is bliss, babe." I winked at him, teasing, and he grinned.

He stabbed the butt out in a potted plant behind us, then stood up and held his hand out to me. "Come on; let's find something better to drink than whatever that crap is." He nudged my full bottle with his toe, and I laughed. I'd barely taken one sip out of it, but I felt strangely dizzy.

Oh shit.

"Dallas? Was there weed in that cig?"

His grin was lazy. "Of course there was. You know I've been cutting my tobacco with weed for fucking years, Katie."

I ran a hand through my hair, laughing lightly. I did know that. I'd also forgotten. Whoops.

"It's just a light buzz," he said with a shrug. "Nothing too serious."

"True," I agreed, leaning into his tall frame as he slung an arm over my shoulders. We rejoined the party but lingered near the edge until a couple of vaguely familiar guys came over to us. They both wore the Wraiths bandannas; one had it tucked in his back pocket and the other had it tied around his wrist.

"Madison Kate." The smaller of the two leered at me. "The scapegoat herself. Ho-*ly* shit. D, man, you've been keeping secrets. Boss won't like that." He ran his tongue over the front of his teeth, and I cringed when I saw a gold tooth.

"Benjamin," I greeted the punk-ass kid, "nice to see you made something of yourself."

His smile dropped, and his glare turned menacing. "It's Viper, you mouthy bitch."

I wanted to make fun of him for playing at this tough gangster bullshit. But I wasn't dumb enough to think things hadn't changed in the four years since I'd seen this kid. Back then, he really had been just some scrawny brat playing tough...but you didn't survive long in the Wraiths *or* the Reapers if you couldn't walk the walk.

"Well, this was fun," I muttered with extreme sarcasm. "That's my cue to leave. Peace out." Ducking out from under Dallas's heavy arm, I jumped out of the frying pan and into the fire.

A strong hand gripped my upper arm as I ducked into the hallway, yanking me into the formal dining room. The sliding double doors slammed shut behind us with a sharp bang, and I stifled my reaction. Fuck this prick for trying to scare me.

"What the hell are you thinking, Madison Kate?" Archer demanded, his voice a low, dangerous growl as he crowded my space. Instinctively, I backed up a couple of steps until my thighs hit the edge of the long, polished oak dining table. "Are you drunk? I *specifically* told you not to get drunk! Do I just talk for the sake of hearing my own voice?"

I shrugged and set my hands on the table behind me, affecting a supremely casual kind of stance. "Probably. I can't imagine you actually think I listen to your bullshit."

That vein in his temple pulsed, and I smiled. One of these days I'd possibly make his head explode out of sheer irritation.

"Madison Kate," he snapped, like my name was a curse word, "you're just standing around getting drunk with known gang members. Are you actually as airheaded as your father seems to think you are?"

I arched a brow and tilted my chin up defiantly. "I'm not drunk, Archer."

His eyes narrowed so hard I wondered if he could still see me. And just to get a stronger reaction out of him, I elaborated.

"I am, however, a little bit stoned."

Boom. There it went. Little bits of Archer's beautiful head

221

splattered all around the room, painting it red and leaving nothing but a bloody stump where his neck used to be.

Metaphorically speaking, of course. That was what happened inside my imagination, and it was oh so satisfying. In reality, his eye just started to twitch.

"Princess," he breathed out. It wasn't a nice sound, though. It was more like the kind of noise a dragon might make when it'd just spotted a virgin damsel ripe for barbecuing and eating.

I grinned, all teeth. "Yes, sunshine?"

The nickname made me smile even wider because Archer D'Ath was the antithesis of sunshine in every possible way.

He was so close to me now. When had that happened? The rough fabric of his jeans brushed my bare legs, and he towered over me in a classic Archer-intimidation tactic. When was he going to learn that he didn't scare me? Not like that, anyway.

His cold blue eyes were locked with mine, and I tilted my chin back farther, refusing to break first.

"Fuck," he cursed, then slammed his mouth against mine.

There was zero hesitation on my part as I kissed him back with equal intensity and hunger. Anger. Hate.

His huge hand tangled in my hair, pulling it as he tried to control our kiss, but I wasn't having a bar of that shit. Bracing my hands against his chest, I shoved him back a couple of steps, breaking our lips apart.

Archer looked dumbstruck. Confused as hell and *mad*.

Not that I gave him long to stand there and weigh the pros and cons of what was undoubtedly a *terrible* idea on both our parts. I launched myself at him, our lips meeting once more in a bruising clash of breath as I hoisted myself up his body, my legs wrapping around his waist as *I* took what I wanted from him.

A surge of satisfaction flared within me, gloating at having the upper hand, but it was short-lived. He spun us around and crushed me to the door, grinding his hard length against my core in a way that made me cry out in agonizing need.

No words passed between us as our teeth clashed and our tongues fought. His rough beard scratched my face like sandpaper, but fuck it. That was what concealer was made for, wasn't it? That and covering hickies.

His hands shoved the short skirt of my dress up, finding the micro thong I had on and tearing it off me like it was made of paper. His fingers found my wet heat, and I groaned with encouragement.

Bang!

The door at the far end of the dining room slammed open, spilling two giggling drunk girls in as they clutched red Solo cups of alcohol.

Archer growled a scary noise but quickly released me, and I tugged my dress back down over my bare ass. Talk about timing.

"Come on," he snapped, shooting the drunk girls a death glare and grabbing me by the hand.

I stumbled only a little bit as he yanked me out of the dining room again, and I wanted to state for the record that it was due to my thin stiletto heels and not because my knees were like jelly and my pussy throbbed with indignation.

I was also very big on lying to myself.

Archer hadn't let go of my hand, and I was pretty confident I knew where his head was. He wanted an empty room, any room, just somewhere we could hate-fuck the hell out of each other so we could break the choking tension.

"Upstairs," I suggested. He paused, glancing over his shoulder at me with a curious frown, so I just shrugged and held his eyes confidently. "Guest rooms are upstairs."

He stared at me a second longer, then seemed to double his speed, practically dragging me through the party on his mission to reach the stairs.

Just as we reached the foyer, he stopped so abruptly I almost ran into the back of him.

"Uh, yo, Terminator," I joked, poking him in the back, "you just forget what we were about to do?"

He turned and gave me an almost *amused* look. Maybe I'd smoked more weed than I'd realized, because that seemed totally out of character for Archer D'Ath.

"I doubt I could ever forget," he said, mostly under his breath, then gave a frustrated sigh. "But I just spotted someone who shouldn't be here. I need to find Kody and Steele to warn them."

I was annoyed, no question, but the tight set to Archer's shoulders gave me a clue that this *someone* could cause big trouble. So I tried *really* hard not to pout as I shrugged and separated my hand from his. "No worries; go do your thing. Bree is right there anyway."

He scowled, looking like he wanted to argue, but I was already weaving my way through the tightly packed dance floor—also known as Bree's parents' living room—to where my fun-loving friend was writhing to the music. I grabbed her hands, dancing with her a moment before she spun around and grabbed my face between her hands.

"MK, you minx," she purred, her eyes glazed with alcohol. "You've been making out with someone."

I cringed, touching my fingertips to my swollen lips. "That obvious?"

She cracked up, then nodded and gave me a knowing smile. "Come on; I've got some seriously kick-ass concealer in my room."

We pushed our way back through the people, then ducked across the silent pool area to Bree's room. It dimly occurred to me that Archer was busy looking for Steele and Kody, so no one was watching me. If my stalker was at the party looking for an opportunity...I'd just handed it to him on a platter.

Maybe I was as stupid as my father thought after all.

CHAPTER 29

To my intense relief, Bree made quick work of fixing my face, totally erasing the evidence of my heated, frantic make-out with Archer, and we made it safely back into the main house without anyone turning me into a skin suit.

Small wins.

We found all three guys in the kitchen, talking in low voices with their serious faces on. If anything, those faces only got more serious when I joined them.

"Wow, you guys sure look like you're having fun," Bree commented, the sarcasm piled on thick. "I'm going back to dance. You coming, MK?" She held a hand out to me in invitation. But I was getting a seriously weird vibe from the guys, so I shook my head.

"Nah, you go," I told her. "I'll be in soon."

She shrugged and disappeared back into the crowd of party people. I folded my arms and eyed all three of the guys suspiciously.

"What's going on?" I looked to Archer first, but his gaze was cold and flat. Unemotional. It was almost a shock to see that expression back on his face so soon, as if *nothing* had just happened between us.

Bitter disappointment curdled all the fuzzy, sexed-up feelings inside me like sour milk, and I hardened my own eyes.

No one answered me.

"Of course, silly me for expecting to be kept in the loop when *I'm* the one with a deranged stalker." Anger colored my words, and Steele gave me a concerned look, reaching out to touch my arm. I flinched away before his hand made contact with my skin, though. These three assholes totally short-circuited my better judgment, and I'd just about had enough.

He frowned, seeming hurt at my flinch, but tucked his hands in the back pockets of his jeans. "This has nothing to do with your stalker, Madison Kate."

It was stupid and petty, but hearing him call me by my name instead of "Hellcat" made my heart hurt. Not in a good way.

I jerked my attention across to Kody, who was giving exactly nothing away as he stared at me with unnerving intensity. Archer... well, I wasn't wasting my time or my pride by paying him any attention.

"Fine. Suit yourselves. I might go find Dallas and his little friends. They seem like fun boys to party with." I started to leave the kitchen, but Archer grabbed my wrist in his viselike grip.

"Don't fucking test me right now, Princess Danvers. You have no idea what's going on here." His voice was low and menacing, but there was a note I hadn't heard before. Deep, buried under layers of irritation, he was almost pleading.

"Incoming," Steele announced, and Archer's attention shifted past me.

He cursed under his breath and dropped my wrist. That in itself made me curious enough to see who, exactly, was "incoming."

I turned my head to look in the direction of Archer's stare and groaned.

"Great, Kody's girlfriend is here," I muttered, sounding a whole lot more nasty than I'd meant to...out loud anyway.

Archer gave me a sharp look. "Jealous?" he whispered, his lips barely moving. Before I could deny it, though, he turned his furious glare on his blond friend. "Get rid of her, bro. You know the score."

Kody just gave a pained grimace, taking a gulp of his drink. "What do you want me to do? Drag her out of here by her hair?"

Archer rumbled, and even I knew he was practically at breaking point. "I don't fucking care what you do, Kody. Just get rid of her. Now. Before I'm forced to do something we'll all regret in the morning." He stepped back, leaning his bulk against the cabinets. Apparently he was content to let Kody handle this on his own, but something about that whole exchange sat strangely with me.

"Better think fast, dude," Steele murmured. He was sitting on the island, his long fingers looped casually around the neck of a glass beer bottle. "She's spotted you."

Kody cursed, then held a hand out to me. "MK, I need your help."

My brows shot up. "Fuck no. Last time I helped you, that bitch slapped me."

Steele covered a laugh with his beer bottle, but I shot him a quick glare anyway. Kody just gave an exasperated sigh, wriggling his fingers to try to hurry me up.

"I promise she won't slap you this time," he said in a rush, his eyes darting past me—tracking Drew's progress across the party, no doubt.

I folded my arms. "What's in it for me?"

This time, I could have sworn Archer cracked a grin, but he rubbed a palm over his lower face so I couldn't know for sure.

"Anything," Kody replied quickly. "Seriously. Anything you want. No parameters."

Well, that was a deal just too good to pass up. I placed my hand in his, accepting the offer, and his fingers closed around mine.

"Thank you," he whispered, then tugged me hard enough that I stumbled into his chest. His arms slipped around me just a fraction of a second before I heard an outraged female shriek.

"What the actual fuck, Kody?" Drew snarled. I couldn't see her face—my back was to her thanks to my front being pressed to Kody's body—but I could imagine the bratty-girl, hands-on-hips stance. "You're with the goat again? I thought you were done with her. Did last week mean nothing to you?"

There was a malicious edge in her voice, like she was trying to hurt *me* by implying a whole lot more had happened between them. She had no idea I'd seen them kissing near Nadia's Cakes but clearly wanted me to know.

"Drew," Kody replied, his voice bored. He took one hand from my waist to grab his drink from the counter. It allowed me enough space to turn slightly and see the girl's reaction. "You're talking about last Tuesday when *you* kissed *me* in the street, and I pushed you away?" His remaining hand tightened on my hip, making it clear he was reinforcing these details for my benefit. "I told you then, plain as day, I'm not interested. Go home before you get yourself in deeper trouble than you counted on tonight." I caught a small, pointed head dip in Archer's direction, and Drew's eyes widened a bit. She seemed...scared of Archer. Why? He'd already told me he wouldn't beat anyone up just for the sake of it. He wouldn't risk his MMA career like that.

But if his power didn't come from physical violence...what else did he have going on? I seriously doubted he was one to use his brother's position as leader of the Reapers to his advantage. They hardly seemed close.

Still, Drew was a sassy thing and forged ahead. "You're just play-ing hard to get," she told Kody, like she really believed that herself. "I bet you're not even fucking the goat. She's just here for show."

Now she was just pissing me off. I couldn't quite work out if it was the implication that Kody and I *wouldn't* sleep together or the consistent use of "goat" or just the fact that she was talking about me like I wasn't standing right freaking there, but regardless, I was getting annoyed.

Reaching up, I stroked my hand down the side of Kody's face. My fingers applied a bit of pressure to his chin, tilting his face down to me. I'd intended to just get his attention so I could say something, tell him the air in here was getting too desperate and we should leave. Maybe cap it off with a cutesy nickname, then leave the kitchen holding hands.

That's what I'd intended to do.

That's not what happened.

Kody's green gaze caught mine, and the next thing I knew our lips were locked together in a passionate, starving kiss. I gasped against his mouth, my lips parting, and he pressed the advantage to deepen our kiss. Or maybe I did that.

My hands slid up his body, grasping the back of his strong neck and holding tightly, demanding more.

Glass clunked against the countertop—Kody dropping his beer, I guessed—then his arms were banding around my waist. He spun us around, then hoisted me up to sit on the edge of the counter. Not that it was such a stretch to kiss me standing up, thanks to my four-inch heels, but there was something insanely sexy about this dynamic shift. It allowed him to crush in tight to my body, forcing my knees apart so that his hard length, encased in denim jeans, could grind against my core. My—oh shit—totally naked core, thanks to my missing thong.

Drew was railing on about something, but her shrill voice faded to a blur of noise as Kody kissed me like I was the last woman on earth.

This kiss. This was the kiss I'd been craving from him since the night we'd met almost a year ago—since he'd teased my neck with those featherlight kisses in the dark of the fun house.

My breath hitched in a small moan as his hands ran all over my body, and it took every ounce of willpower I had to remember we were still in public. We were on Bree's parents' kitchen counter, for fuck's sake. People were watching.

People like…

My eyes shot open, looking past Kody and catching straight on Archer's *furious* glare. Beside him Steele's brow was furrowed and his jaw clenched tightly in anger.

Fuck. What had I gotten myself into?

"Fuck this!" Drew snarled—finally. She grabbed a Solo cup full of beer, then chucked it at Kody's back.

The cold splash of beer made him pull away from me, but only an inch. His shoulders tightened, and his eyes—so close to mine—glittered with fury, but he didn't pay her any attention.

Me? I was just glad it was Kody who wore the beer and not me.

"She's gone," I told him in a soft voice as Drew stormed out of the kitchen. A teasing smile played over my lips, and nothing I could do would make it go away.

The tension dropped from Kody's body in perceptible waves, and he gave me a mischievous grin. "Thanks, MK. I owe you one."

"Literally," I replied, then swiped my tongue across my lower lip. My mouth was tingling and hot, and I was going to have one hell of a time trying to forget the feeling of kissing Kody. Or Archer, for that matter.

Steele's kiss had been firmly placed in a lockbox inside my mind labeled "betrayals, never to be forgotten."

"What makes you think she'll actually leave?" I asked, clearing my throat as I peeled my beer-splashed hands away from Kody's neck. I really badly didn't want to let him go. I wanted him to pick me up and carry me to a guest room so he could follow through on the promises his body had just been making. But logically I understood he'd just been getting rid of a clingy ex. Or that's what it'd seemed.

Kody took a beat to reply, his gaze caught on my mouth for a moment, like he was considering kissing me again. He still hadn't stepped away, remaining situated between my spread thighs, and thank fuck too or everyone would get one hell of a view of my laser hair removal.

"She will." Steele was the one who replied, but he still looked all kinds of pissed off and tense. "Drew's pride won't let her hang around to watch you and Kody basically fuck on the kitchen counter all night."

Kody's fingers tightened on my hips, hard enough to probably leave bruises tomorrow, and his chuckle was pure evil. "Doesn't have to be just on the kitchen counter. I'm adept at fucking on all kinds of surfaces."

I snorted a laugh, pushing him away and quickly yanking my skirt down to cover my cunt. "I'm sure you are, man-whore. Excuse me for not wanting to be the next notch in your bedpost."

I don't know why I had such an unflattering opinion of Kody. Aside from Drew, I hadn't seen him with any girls in the three weeks I'd cohabited with him. Come to think of it, I hadn't seen any of the guys with women. Aside from that first day at SGU when Archer made a show of flirting with juice-girl, none of them seemed to whore around much at all.

Then again, three weeks wasn't long, and boys that attractive with that much arrogance and charisma? Yeah, something told me they weren't exactly saints.

"Can we go home now?" I asked as I slid down off the counter. Kudos to me that my knees didn't wobble as my high-heeled shoes touched down on the floor.

Archer looked annoyed—or frustrated—and shook his head. "Not quite yet." He rubbed his palm across the dark stubble on his chin. "We have something to deal with first."

Steele's brows shot up. "We're bringing Madison Kate with us?"

It was pretty clear that wherever they were going, Archer did *not* want to take me along. But he gave me a considering look and sighed heavily before turning back to Steele. "You got any better ideas?"

Steele grimaced, running a hand over his short hair. "Not really."

"No, that's cool, guys," I commented with supreme sarcasm. "Just talk about me like I'm not here. Seriously, keep going. I love it. It's my favorite thing in the whole world."

Stupid me, I should have known Archer of all fucking people would conveniently miss the sarcasm and take me at my word.

"Hey, what do you guys think about giving Princess Danvers a curfew from now on?" he asked his friends, totally deadpan. "Or maybe a tracking device?"

Scowling, I stalked over to him. "Don't you fucking dare, Archer D'Ath." I punched him solidly in the upper arm, but he just grabbed my fist and pulled me closer to him.

He bent down until his lips brushed my ear. "Don't push me, Madison Kate," he replied in a husky whisper. "You have no idea what I'm capable of."

When he released my hand and stepped away, his eyes were as glacial and intense as ever, but there was something more there. Something fucking terrifying.

He stalked away, and I rolled my shoulders, shaking off the heady mixture of fear and arousal that marched across my skin like a thousand army ants.

"Come on, gorgeous." Kody draped his arm around my shoulders, aiming for casual nonchalance and falling just a fraction short. "This is turning out to be a hell of a night."

Steele sighed and followed along behind us as we headed in the direction Archer had gone. "Just don't hate us for what happens next," he said so quietly I wasn't totally sure I was meant to hear. I did, though, and so did Kody, if the stiffness in his body was anything to go by.

The question was, though…what the fuck were they about to do?

And why was I so damn excited to find out?

CHAPTER 30

Lots of partygoers had spilled out into the front yard of Bree's mansion, standing around drinking and laughing. Some girls danced to the loud music pouring from the open windows, and several couples were making out in the grass.

That's where we found our target.

Archer made a beeline for a couple making out under one of the big willow trees, and Steele grabbed hold of my hand, holding me back.

"Trust us, okay, Hellcat?" he said quickly, quiet enough for only me to hear. "Don't freak out."

I startled, giving him a double take, but there was no time for me to question his strange comment. Archer reached down and grabbed the guy by the back of his neck, forcefully lifting him off the moaning girl and throwing him across the lawn.

That's when I realized I'd been a little off the mark assuming they'd just been making out. His dick was out, and the girl screamed as she covered herself up with her short dress.

"Take him," Archer ordered, and both Kody and Steele stepped toward the tattooed guy who was trying to stuff his cock away again. When he saw the boys descending on him, his eyes widened, and he took off running.

He didn't make it far, though, with Kody catching him easily and locking him in a painful-looking arm bar to frog-march him back across the grass to where I stood near Archer.

The girl grabbed her shit and took off too, but no one even spared her a glance, let alone dragged her back kicking and screaming like her boyfriend. Or…random hookup as the case may be. She sure as shit wasn't hanging around to involve herself in his drama.

"Let's go," Archer said in a voice like ice, turning to leave and just *expecting* everyone to follow him, I guessed. The commanding tone rubbed my combative personality the wrong way, but for once in my life, I bit my tongue. There was so much more going on with these guys, and this was my opportunity to find out what.

Silently, I followed Archer back to our car, where Kody and Steele manhandled the random dude into the trunk and slammed it closed.

"Now what?" I asked as Archer pulled the keys from his pocket and spun them around his index finger. He didn't reply but gave Kody—who stood closest to me—a pointed look.

Kody gave a short nod in reply, then swept my hair over my shoulder and brought his lips close to my ear. They loved doing that to me, and I was starting to question if these things really did need to be secrets or if they'd just worked out that it was one of those nonsexual turn-ons that made my knees weak and my nipples hard.

"Stay silent, MK," he urged me. "Anything you say can and will be repeated back to Zane. Better to give this prick nothing to work with, yeah?"

Chills raised the hair on the back of my neck at Zane's name. Whatever the fuck these guys were involved with, I wanted *no* part of it.

But then…was I ready to walk away? Would my curiosity let me just close my eyes and play ignorant to what was about to happen? Those weren't even serious questions, because I already knew the answers.

No. No way in hell.

So I gave Kody a small nod of agreement and silently slid into the backseat with Steele beside me.

Someone called out to Archer, pausing him before he got into the driver's seat. I couldn't hear what was said, but Archer's response was clear.

"Allowances were made for *you*, Moore. Not your boys. Next time you forget that, the message will be sent to Ferryman." The threat was evident in his voice, and I strained my ears to hear Dallas's response.

There was a short pause, then, "Understood. It won't happen again. Can I have a minute to speak with Katie?"

Archer didn't hesitate for even a second. "No."

He slid into his seat and slammed the door, starting the engine and pulling out of park before Kody had even buckled his seat belt. Archer didn't make any move to put his belt on, and my anxiety spiked.

After a minute of driving, I cracked.

"Put your seat belt on," I snapped, biting my lip as soon as the words left my mouth. But for fuck's sake, it was the law for a *reason*.

Archer peered a quick look at me over his shoulder, and that only ratcheted my anxiety up higher. Thankfully, though, he must have seen how serious I was and smoothly clicked the buckle home a second later.

I forced myself to release a breath, letting go of the slight panic. Steele silently reached across the seat and snagged my hand in his. I tried to pull away, hating that they'd just seen that, but he held firm, lacing our fingers together.

As much as I still wanted to hold my grudge against him, he

was fast wearing me down. His grip on my hand was reassuring and grounding. I kind of loved it.

———————

Archer didn't drive us home. Not that I'd really expected him to take a kidnapped gangster—because I was going out on a limb and guessing he was a Reaper—back to our home, but I hadn't expected the destination we'd ended up at.

"Here?" I asked, stunned and full of dread as I peered up at the giant, dilapidated clown face. Apparently The Laughing Clown hadn't been one of my father's integration projects, or he hadn't made it this far yet, because it looked just as run-down and shitty as the last time I'd been there.

Archer flashed me a warning look as we got out of his car, and I mimed zipping my lips shut. Kody and Steele hauled the guy out of the trunk and threw him on the gravel of the parking lot.

"You don't want to do this," the guy yelled at them—us—as he rolled to his feet. "You're making a big mistake. Zane told me to go to that party. I was on orders."

Archer—so very clearly the one in charge here—folded his arms and sneered at the tattooed gangster. Now that I was taking a better look at him, I spotted the prominent reaper tattoo on the side of his neck and the black bandanna with white reaper logos tied to his belt loops.

"That's exactly why you're here, Skunk," Archer commented, his voice hard and resigned. "Zane threw you to the wolves. Be sure to let him know how much I appreciate him testing the limits."

He nodded to Kody and Steele, both of whom wore the hardened expressions of practiced killers. Steele was taping his hands to protect them against whatever they were about to do. It didn't take a genius to work that one out.

What the fuck have I walked into?

The guy—Skunk—babbled pleas for mercy, but they fell on

deaf ears. He howled with pain as the first strike of Kody's fist landed across his face, and I flinched.

"Princess," Archer rumbled, turning his back on the scene and stroking a long lock of pink hair away from my face. His index finger tipped my chin up, bringing my eyes in line with his as his huge body blocked everything behind him. "Look at me. Not them."

The heavy sound of fists hitting flesh, accompanied by the cries of pain from Skunk, made me want to look. I started to turn my face, but Archer shifted his grip and held my chin firm.

"I said, *look at me.*" His tone was sharp and unyielding. It did all kinds of confusing things to my fucked-up emotions, but regardless of whether I was scared or turned on or both...I did what he said.

For what felt like an eternity, Kody and Steele beat the shit out of Skunk until no more noises came.

I breathed a small breath of relief when the sounds stopped, but I relaxed too soon.

"Break his legs," Archer ordered, not losing eye contact with me for even a second. His fingers still gripped my chin tight enough to hurt, but I let him. Maybe it was weak of me, but I didn't *want* to see. It was enough that I heard and knew.

Seconds later, the sickening crush of breaking bones echoed through the still night, and my stomach rolled dangerously.

"Turn around," Archer ordered me in a quiet, no-arguments voice. "Go back to the car and get in. Do *not* turn back. Understood?"

Fear and anxiety choked me, but I didn't argue. I tried to nod, but he hadn't let go of my chin, and a fucked-up part of me didn't want him to.

"Tell me," he ordered, his voice rough.

I licked my lips, wetting them before replying. "I understand."

Archer gave me a tight nod, then fucking *kissed me.*

It was a quick kiss, almost like a reflex gesture, but the sheer dominance and possession in that one kiss made my heart damn near fucking stop beating.

"Go," he told me when he released me, and I stumbled over to his car, feeling like I'd just taken a shot of pure adrenaline.

I popped the door handle of the passenger side, sliding into the front seat without a second glance over my shoulder. But after I closed the door, my curiosity won. I looked in the side mirror.

It was dark, the only light coming from the bright moon, but I was still able to see enough. I watched as Archer walked over to Kody and Steele, peering down at the crumpled heap of unconscious gangster on the gravel at their feet. He crouched down, pulling a butterfly knife from his back pocket and flicking it open with *way* too much ease. The blade glinted a vibrant, bloody red in the moonlight; then he leaned over Skunk to do…something. His broad body blocked Skunk from my view, but when he stood up again, the tip of his blade dripped crimson onto the gravel.

Holy shit. Did he just stab him? Am I an accessory to murder?

Cold shock washed over me, and I swallowed a couple of times, my gaze locked on the mirror as Archer wiped his knife off with Skunk's bandana and tucked the blade back in his pocket. He stood there a moment, talking to Kody and Steele and I just…watched.

Shouldn't I have been more worried? More disgusted and horrified and…scared?

But I wasn't. The fear was there, no doubt about it, but stronger than any other emotion in me…I was fucking excited.

Adrenaline burned through my veins in the same way my hatred used to. These boys were turning out to be much, *much* more than I'd given them credit for, and I was craving the depths of their darkness like a drug.

It was a shame they'd tried to screw me so hard a year ago, because I might have just found my soul mates.

CHAPTER 31

No one spoke the whole way home. Steele and Kody were coated in blood, and Archer's right hand, resting on the steering wheel, held unmistakable rust-brown marks.

When we pulled into the garage, I made no moves to get out of the car straightaway. I had so many questions I couldn't even think where to begin.

"Go and wash up," Archer told the other two, looking at them in the rearview mirror. His voice still held that cutting edge of authority, and it wasn't one that encouraged arguments or disagreement.

Kody let out a long sigh, then hopped out of the back seat and slammed the door behind him, no doubt hurrying to get to their shared bathroom first—such a brat.

Steele popped his door open, and I spoke before he got out.

"You can use my shower," I said in a soft voice. "If you don't want to wait." I turned my head to look at him over my shoulder and internalized my flinch at just how much blood coated him. His hands and arms were the worst, but spatters coated his face and neck too. His dark T-shirt hid any blood there, but it was a safe bet to say it was probably messy. "We both know Kody will need to shampoo his hair about sixteen times to stop it from staining pink."

I was joking—blood didn't stain hair that quickly—but he'd want to get onto it soon, considering he'd bleached it and opened the hair cuticle up.

Steele shot me a quick grin. "Thanks, Hellcat." He climbed out of the car and closed the door somewhat softer than Kody had before heading into the house.

And that left me and Archer alone in the silent car.

"You handled that well, Princess Danvers," he said after a long, tense silence. He wasn't looking at me but at his hands on the steering wheel.

I made an annoyed grunt in my throat. "You can stop calling me that any day now."

A half smile tugged at his lips, and he shifted his gaze toward me. "Never."

I rolled my eyes. "Okay, so…am I allowed to ask questions now?"

He turned slightly in his seat, facing more toward me and bracing his elbow on the steering wheel. "You can ask anything you want, Princess."

I narrowed my eyes in a glare. "Subtext being that I can ask, but you won't necessarily answer. Prick."

A brief, amused look flashed across his face, and he inclined his head in agreement. Secretive fucking bastard. I quickly wondered if I might have an easier time getting answers from Steele or Kody but quickly dismissed the idea. Archer was the one in charge, and if he wasn't talking, no one was.

I considered everything that had happened that night, from Dallas's guys showing up, all the way to Kody, Steele, and Archer coming home coated in blood.

"Who was he?" I asked, referring to Skunk.

Archer's eyes didn't change. No remorse or guilt even flickered, and I bit my lip. Something about that hard-ass attitude drove me wild. It spoke to a seriously damaged history, and it drew me in like a magnetic field.

"No one," he replied, cold and detached. "He was a means to an end. Nothing more."

I nodded slowly, having sort of drawn that conclusion already myself. "He was a message," I clarified. "To your brother?"

"He was a *warning*," Archer corrected, "to the leader of the Shadow Grove Reapers."

"And what were you warning him about?" I was burning with curiosity, and it was all I could do to keep my tone calm, my voice even. Archer wasn't going to respond to screaming, hysterical demands for answers.

He tilted his head to the side, his gaze assessing as he answered me. "To respect the terms of our agreement," he responded cryptically. "He broke the rules by sending Skunk to Bree's party tonight."

Interesting.

"And Drew? How does she factor into this?"

A small smile played at his lips again. "She's a Reaper."

My brows shot up. I hadn't expected *that* answer.

"She's also a loose end that Kody has been needing to cut off for far too long, so thank you for helping in that regard tonight." Something flashed in his eyes, and an arrogant part of me imagined it to be jealousy.

I couldn't help myself.

"My pleasure," I replied, with a self-satisfied smirk.

His gaze darkened to dangerous depths, and I quickly moved on.

"What's your agreement with Zane?" His name burned my tongue like acid, and I swallowed heavily after saying it. That deranged piece of shit had murdered my mom, and the dirty cops of Shadow Grove had let him get away with it.

Archer gave me a small head shake. "Try again, Princess Danvers."

I sighed in frustration, not wasting my breath on any other pointless questions. He wasn't going to tell me anything useful.

"Can I see your knife?" I have no idea why I asked that, except that I wanted to see why it'd looked red in the moonlight. It was one of those odd details that my brain was tripping on. A glitch in the matrix.

One brow arched, and he gave me a curious look. "You weren't supposed to look back, Madison Kate."

I smiled, smug. "I didn't. But you see, cars have these really cool things attached to the sides, and they've got this reflective stuff that shows you what's behind the car."

His eyes narrowed. "Semantics."

I shrugged, unrepentant. "Learn to be more specific in your orders, D'Ath. So, can I see it?"

He watched me a moment longer, face impassive, before leaning forward and taking the butterfly knife from his back pocket.

"Happy?" he asked, holding it out in his flat palm for me to see. It was still folded, but I could tell I hadn't imagined things. The blade itself was a lush, deep copper red and the handle a brushed charcoal gray. I'd never seen a knife quite like it in my life...not that I made a habit of looking at tattooed thugs' weapons.

I reached out to touch it, but Archer whipped it out of my reach and pocketed it again.

"Not a chance, Princess," he murmured. "Is that all? I really need to wash the stink of pathetic gangster off my skin."

I sighed. "For now, I suppose."

We exited the car, then walked through the garage to the house in strangely companionable silence. Something had shifted between us, and it wasn't totally because of that quick make-out session at Bree's party.

"You know Steele is probably jerking off in your shower, right?" Archer commented as we flipped the lights to the garage off and set the perimeter alarms.

I spluttered and laughed. "What? Why would you say that?"

He just shrugged, totally serious. "Because it's true. He will have used your shampoo or something. Then started picturing you

242

in the shower washing your hair, then he'd be thinking about you wet and naked, covered in soap…" He arched a brow at me as he headed for the stairs. "I don't blame him; I would too."

With that fucking *grenade* tossed, he jogged up the stairs and left me standing there with my mouth hanging open. It was a sexy look, I was sure. Thankfully, no one was around to witness it, though, because it took me way longer than I'd have liked to find my brain again.

"What the fuck?" I whispered to myself, dumbfounded, as I slowly made my way up the stairs. I was exhausted, confused, and still had no panties on. I badly needed some pajamas and my bed.

I pushed my bedroom door open, then froze two steps into the room. Steam billowed out of my attached bathroom, thanks to the half-open door. Steele was apparently still showering and hadn't bothered closing the door properly before he got in.

Or had that been intentional?

Archer's words played in my mind, taunting me as I quietly moved across to my dresser and opened my pajama drawer. I snatched out a comfy pair of sweats and a T-shirt, then moved up to the top drawer to grab some panties. When I straightened up, my gaze snagged on movement in my mirror.

Fucking hell.

My mirror was positioned in such a way that it reflected the bathroom mirror when the door was open. *That* mirror? That one showed the tall, tanned, tattooed man in my shower.

My breath caught in my throat, and I goddamn *knew* I needed to look away. I knew it…but I didn't do it. I couldn't. His back was to the mirror, and I simply couldn't tear my eyes from the slick planes of his muscles. A tattoo of an angel covered his whole upper back, and it sparked questions in me. He didn't strike me as the religious type, so what did the angel represent? Who?

He shifted then, turning his body into the spray and giving me an uninterrupted view of his thick, straight shaft firmly grasped in his soapy fist. His eyes were closed, and I felt like the worst kind of pervert, but I didn't look away. I watched, unblinking, as his hand worked up and down his cock. His pace increased until he braced himself against the tiles with his free hand and came with a low groan. Semen erupted from his engorged cock, mixing with the running water and disappearing instantly.

My mouth watered, and my cunt clenched with desire, but still I couldn't look away. His inked chest was rising and falling heavily, and I watched while he rinsed himself off again—using my body wash—then ducked his head under the spray.

That should have been my cue to leave, but I was damn near rooted to the spot, frozen there with crippling arousal. Maybe I was scared that if I moved, I'd come from the friction of walking. Who knew? Regardless, a second later, his eyes flickered open and met mine dead-on in the mirror—like he knew I'd been there all along.

"Fuck!" In my haste to pretend I *hadn't* just watched him jerking off in the shower, I slammed my underwear drawer shut and caught my finger in it. I stuck my finger in my mouth to dull the pain, cursing myself out mentally in a million different ways.

The shower shut off, and my heart kicked into overdrive. I needed to get out of there before Steele left the bathroom; otherwise things were going to be supremely—

"Where do you think you're going?" he asked as my hand reached the door handle, and I froze.

"Uh…" I didn't turn around. I couldn't. My face was probably pinker than my hair, and I felt like *such* a creeper. Then again, he should have closed the damn door! It was my bedroom, after all. I had every reason to be in there. "I was just going to grab a glass of water," I lied. *Lame.*

"Madison Kate," he said, and he was so close I almost jumped out of my skin. How'd he get so close? Damn soft carpet. "Turn around."

Nope. No way.

"Um…" I couldn't think of a damn thing. Certainly not a good reason why I couldn't turn around and face him. All I could think about was the sight of his fist working over his hard cock and how badly I wanted it to be mine.

Fuck me.

"Turn around, Hellcat," he murmured, stroking his fingers through my hair and tugging teasingly on the ends. "Or are you afraid?"

Yes! I am!

But also, damn him. He knew I'd never admit that, certainly not to one of them.

Gritting my teeth and mentally reminding myself that I was a grown-ass woman and not a slave to my hormones, I turned around to face him.

He was still dripping wet, like he'd just stepped straight out of the shower and simply tucked one of my glittery pink towels around his waist. Good *lord*, it was a good look on him. Not the pink sparkles—those wouldn't suit *anyone*—but the whole naked and wet thing? Yep, Steele was rocking that.

A slow smile curved his lips, and I snapped my gaze up to his face. I'd been blatantly checking him out, and he knew it.

"Were you running away from me, Hellcat?" he teased, leaning in close and bracing his hands on the door to either side of my head. My pink towel was tucked so loosely around his slim waist it surely wasn't going to hold much longer. Surely.

I licked my lips and forced a bit of iron into my voice. "I don't run from anyone, Max Steele. Certainly not you."

His smile turned to a smirk, and he leaned closer still, pausing only when his lips were a bare inch from mine. "Prove it."

Oh, for all the coffee-loving gods. I groaned inwardly. He was waving a red flag at a bull, and I was powerless to resist the urge. I closed the gap between us.

CHAPTER 32

Steele's towel dropped about three seconds after I started kissing him. It was a satisfying sound, hearing that heavy fabric hit the floor, and I grinned into his kiss with satisfaction.

"Did you enjoy watching me?" he asked when our kiss broke off. He trailed hot, open-mouthed kisses along my jaw, then dragged the metal of his tongue stud down my neck. I gasped as he found my sensitive point, right at the back of my neck. His mouth sealed to my skin, and he sucked that patch, probably marking me. Not that I cared. After what seemed like an entire night of teasing, I was—regardless of what I'd just told myself—most definitely a slave to my desires.

It took me a second to remember his question; then I groaned. "Yes," I admitted, my mind flashing those images at me again. But I didn't need the mental replay; I had the real thing right there in front of me. "But if you didn't want me to watch, you really should have closed the door."

I ran my hands over his body, sliding my fingers into his short, wet hair. He smelled like me. Like my shampoo and my body wash. It was kinda crazy hot.

"Who says I didn't want you to watch?" Steele countered,

moving back just enough that he could meet my gaze. His eyes were bright with desire and excitement, probably reflecting my own, and his lips were lush and swollen—begging to be kissed. So I did.

I could probably be happy for the rest of my life just kissing Steele. He had the kind of kiss that met me, challenged me, and demanded more but didn't take anything I wasn't already giving.

His hands found my waist, and he lifted me, carrying me easily across the room and depositing me down on my floral-pink bed—all without taking his mouth from mine.

I still had my black high heels on, but as they had an ankle strap, there was no way I was stopping Steele so I could fuck around with the fiddly buckles. Nope, they could stay on for all I cared. Besides, I was already sans underwear, so what did they matter?

Steele moved his hand to my thigh as he settled his weight between my legs, sliding up and under my short dress.

His hand paused, and he let out a small groan, breaking his lips away from mine. "Do I even want to know what happened to your panties tonight, Hellcat?"

I bit my lip, guilt washing through me. "I don't know. Do you?"

He seemed to think about it for a moment, then shook his head. "Nope. All I want to know..." He trailed off as his lips found mine again, kissing me with renewed intensity as he pushed my dress up. I raised my hips so he could get it up over my ass, then wriggled it over my head and tossed it aside.

"What do you want to know, Steele?" I asked, breathless as he unhooked my bra and peeled the lace cups away from my body. His breathing was ragged, and he was more than ready to go again, despite having just come in the shower.

He didn't answer immediately, taking his time to kiss my breasts. His lips closed over my sensitive peaks, sucking and biting playfully until I was thrashing and panting beneath him. The hardness of his tongue piercing teased me in ways I'd never even imagined.

"All I want to know *right now*, Madison Kate"—he finally continued, releasing my breast and sliding his hand across my flat stomach, then lower—"is whether you have any condoms in this little girl's room. Because I need to fuck you more than I need to breathe right now."

His fingers found my clit, circling it teasingly before sliding lower to my soaking core. My breath hitched, and my hips pushed forward, silently begging him to enter me, but he continued to tease.

I wracked my brain, desperately trying to remember if I had any condoms stashed somewhere in my room. I hadn't had sex in over a year, but it was simply a good habit to always have protection available. Just in case one of your drop-dead gorgeous, male-model housemates wanted to fuck you stupid, obviously.

"Yes," I replied on a groan. "I think so, anyway." *God, I hope so.* "Hang on a sec."

I wriggled out from under him, rolling over onto my stomach, and reaching for my bedside drawer. I yanked it open—a little wider than I'd intended—and fished around for the handful of condoms I vaguely recalled tossing in there while unpacking all my things a few weeks earlier.

Steele's hands clasped my naked butt cheeks, squeezing them and making me groan as my fingers frantically searched the seemingly endless drawer. It didn't help that Steele hitched my hips slightly off the bed, then slid one long finger into my cunt from behind.

Yep. Pretty sure my brain short-circuited for a moment there.

"Any luck?" he asked with a small chuckle, and I mentally slapped myself to stay on task, a job made so much harder as he added a second finger inside me and stroked them in and out.

My fingers touched a squishy foil packet, and I exhaled in relief.

"Found one?" he asked, but I wanted more of what he was

doing. I wriggled my hips, backing up onto his hand desperately. His lips kissed my back, and I felt his weight shifting on the bed as he made his way up to the back of my neck. Still, his fingers lazily stroked my inner walls, and I writhed under his touch, my breath coming in short, sharp gasps.

Steele made a small sound of surprise as he settled against the pillows beside me. His fingers withdrew from my throbbing cunt—dammit—to take the condom from me, but it was the contents of my open drawer that had his attention.

"Madison Kate, what have you got there?"

I propped my head up on my hand, giving him an exaggerated eye roll. "Clearly, my vibrators. Don't act like you've never seen sex toys before, Steele."

His grin was broad as he ripped the condom wrapper open and rolled the rubber down his shaft. "I have," he admitted, his own voice a little breathless as he closed his hand around his erection. "I'm just curious—why so many?"

I smiled back at him, sitting up and pushing him back into the pillows so I could straddle him. "Variety is the spice of life, Steele. Why choose?"

Reaching down, I grasped his hot length and lined him up to my desperate, pulsing cunt. He didn't wait for me to sink down onto him slowly, though. He grabbed my hips and pulled me down onto him, thrusting up to meet me and fully seating himself in my pussy with that one stroke.

A cry escaped my throat, but he swallowed the sound a second later as his mouth found mine for a hot, open-mouthed kiss. Our tongues met and slid together in an echo of the way we fucked, meeting halfway and matching each other's desire equally.

"Fuck, you're incredible," Steele muttered some moments later when my mouth moved to his neck, nipping with teeth and sucking dark marks as I went—repaying the favor.

Seconds later, he let out a low growl and flipped us over.

My back met the mattress, and Steele slammed back into me, forcing the air from my lungs for a second before I sucked in another deep breath and cursed.

He just chuckled, though, one of those deliciously masculine sounds that made my toes curl.

"You have *no* idea how many times I've jerked off over you, Hellcat," he murmured, kissing me lightly. "But the reality is a million times better."

I groaned, remembering him in the shower again. "That's..." I kissed him back, then held his eyes with mine. "Kind of creepy. But also insanely hot."

He laughed, bracing his hand on the bed beside my head and pumping his thick cock into me at an unhurried pace. My orgasm teased me, fluttering around in the shadows but dancing just out of reach every time I thought I had it. It was utterly infuriating, but at the same time I never wanted it to end.

Steele hitched one of my knees up, pinning it to the bed with his weight and increasing the depth of his cock inside me.

"Ah, fuck" I cried out as his broad tip rubbed over my G-spot and my whole body quaked. "Yes, fuck yes, Steele, don't stop." He listened, thank all the gods, he listened, repeating that same movement over and over until I shuddered and screamed into his kiss. My back arched and my cunt tightened with the intense orgasm, forcing him to slow his thrusts until my climax passed enough for him to move freely once more.

"Fuck me, Hellcat," he groaned as my legs trembled with after-shocks and my arms looped around his neck. "That was the hottest thing I think I've ever seen in my life." He kissed me again, his cock still pumping into me slowly, lazily, giving me a minute to come back to earth. "I want to see it again," he declared, his voice a little savage as he withdrew completely, then flipped me onto my stomach.

There was no way in hell my arms *or* legs were holding me up yet, but he seemed to understand that. He swiped two pillows from the head of my bed and tucked them under my belly, propping my ass up in the air.

A low groan came from him, and he positioned himself behind me on his knees, then grabbed two handfuls of my ass. He spread me wide, then drove back into my cunt with a grunt, making me whimper. I was still throbbing and sensitive from my intense orgasm, but he was determined to make me come again.

He'd get no objections from me.

Curses fell from his lips like a whispered prayer as he fucked me hard. I tangled my hands in the stupid floral comforter, holding on for dear life as he quickly brought me back to the edge of orgasm.

"Hold on, baby," he whispered to me, his voice husky and hot with arousal. He slipped a hand around in front of me, wiggling it between the pillows and my body until he found my clit.

That's when the fireworks detonated.

His long, talented-as-hell fingers worked me like I was his own miniature piano, and I came harder than I thought I'd ever come in my life. Sparks erupted behind my eyelids, and my throat hurt from moaning. My legs trembled uncontrollably, but now I had just one thing on my mind.

Steele's hands shifted to my hips, his pace increasing, and I knew he was close. I needed to move quickly.

"Wait," I panted out, licking my lips and trying to pull all the scattered pieces of my soul back together. "Wait, don't come yet."

He made a pained sound, but his thrusts slowed and his fingers flexed on my hips. "Madison Kate…" It was a desperate plea, and I snickered, wriggling out from under him and sitting up.

"Shut up, Steele," I teased, pushing him with a hand on his lower abdomen until he climbed off the bed. I scooted forward and sank to my knees on the carpet in front of him, then peeled the condom off his shaft and tossed it aside. "You're gonna complain about coming in my mouth?"

His jaw was slightly unhinged, his eyes hooded as he gazed down at me. "Fuck no," he muttered. He stroked his hand through my hair, then tangled it around his fingers as my mouth closed over his tip and my hand came up to circle his shaft.

Steele groaned low in his throat as I took him deeper, sucking and licking his thick cock exactly the way I'd pictured it when I'd seen him in the shower. He didn't let me play for long, though. Within moments, he took control, using his tight grip on my hair to hold my head so he could fuck my mouth. With every thrust, he pushed harder, deeper, testing my limits and choking me with his dick until eventually, he pushed in as far as he could possibly fit and his hot cum pulsed down my throat. I swallowed greedily, taking it all and licking his entire length as he released my hair and eased out of my mouth.

For a moment, we just stayed like that, me on my knees in front of him, looking up with teary eyes as he stroked my hair. No doubt my mascara had run black streaks down my cheeks—being face-fucked tended to do that to a girl's makeup—but the look of utter worship on his face made it all so fucking worthwhile.

"Holy shit, Hellcat," he finally breathed out, tugging me to my feet and kissing me long and hard. I still wore my high heels, and it put me close enough to his height that I could reach him with my head tilted back. "That was intense."

I had nothing to say in response because he was dead right.

That was one for the ages.

CHAPTER 33

My dreams that night were filled with blood and violence, scenes of a tattooed gang member on his knees while someone pressed a gun to his head and pulled the trigger. Blood and gore spattered the ground; then it was my mother lying dead on the ground in a spreading pool of blood. Her violet-blue eyes stared at me, lifeless, and dark bruises marred her perfect face and neck.

I woke up at some stage, my heart pounding and sweat coating my skin, but seconds later a set of strong, warm arms circled me. He pulled me in tight to his hot, hard body, and the tension melted out of me instantly.

My thundering pulse slowed, and my breathing evened out as my face pressed to his chest, letting the rhythmic thump of his heart lull me back to sleep.

When I woke again sometime later, those nightmares were just shadowy remnants haunting my mind and setting my nerves ever so slightly on edge.

I stretched out my body, feeling the delicious ache of some seriously good sex, then snuggled back into the warm body embracing me. Reality was slowly creeping back in, regret over everything that'd happened the night before starting to tighten my stomach, but I wasn't ready to face it yet. Maybe if we stayed in bed just a little longer...

Devilish plan in mind, my eyelids flickered open and I pressed a kiss to inked swallows and roses on his chest.

Wait.

Jerking back a couple of inches, I blinked the sleep from my eyes.

"Kody?" My voice was rough and my throat scratchy. "What...?"

I frowned, blinking again a couple of times and trying to remember when the hell Kody had switched places with Steele. Last I remembered, I'd fallen asleep in Steele's tight embrace with the aching glow of incredible sex still rolling through my body.

"Go back to sleep, MK," Kody mumbled, not bothering to open his eyes as he tugged me back down to his chest and lazily stroked my tangled hair. "It's too early."

But my room was bright with sunlight, so I doubted it was all *that* early.

"Kodiak Jones," I murmured sternly, not bothering to move from his chest. He was comfy as hell to sleep on. "You've got three seconds to explain why you're in my bed."

I was still naked, I could feel that much, but the rough brush of fabric against my thighs said Kody at least had some underwear on.

"You were screaming," he mumbled, raising a hand to rub at his face, then ruffle his platinum hair into some seriously sexy bedhead. "I came in thinking you were in trouble, but you were still asleep and thrashing around. So I figured I'd just lie down with you for a bit, until you went back to sleep properly."

Unease pricked at my skin, ghostly flashes of those nightmares coming back to me. The scenes had felt so incredibly real, so much more detailed than my dreams usually were...more like memories than figments of my imagination.

"But you're still here," I commented. I wasn't mad—far from

it. He was the one who'd chased my demons away and allowed me to sleep dreamlessly the rest of the night, and I couldn't be angry about that. Even if I was still naked.

Kody mumbled something, then yawned. "You wouldn't let go of me. But also, show me a man who'd willingly leave your bed, and I'll show you a damn fool."

I laughed softly, and then a wave of disappointment ran through me. "Where's Steele?"

Kody's arm around my waist tightened, and he pressed a kiss to the top of my head. "I said *willingly*, Madison Kate. Steele wasn't given much choice."

He traced gentle patterns down my bare arm, making my skin tingle, and when he reached my hand, I linked our fingers together on his chest. "You gonna explain that, Kodiak?"

"Zane received our message," he told me in a grim tone.

I sucked in a deep breath, releasing it slowly as my thumb stroked over his bruised and scraped knuckles. The violence of what they'd done to that Reaper should have me running for the hills. It should repulse me to touch hands capable of inflicting such brutality.

It didn't.

"So what happens now?" My voice was soft. Mostly I was intrigued but also scared as hell—not of what Kody and the guys could do…but of what Zane might do to them.

Kody shifted farther down the bed, rearranging us so we shared a pillow and could look each other in the eyes. Our hands remained linked together, though, and I was in no hurry to let go.

"Nothing," he told me, his expression open and honest. "Zane requested a meeting with Arch when he got the, uh, message. Steele went as backup, just in case."

My brows hitched. "Backup…in case Zane tried to hurt Archer?"

Kody gave a small nod. "Wouldn't be the first time."

That enraged me, and I swallowed past the dark emotions clawing at my throat. "Why didn't you go too?"

A small smile pulled at his lips. "And leave you here alone, asleep, and *naked* with a crazy stalker out there somewhere? You're kidding, right?"

I bit my lip, a frown pulling at my brows. I didn't want to say what I was thinking. I didn't want to let that vulnerable, pathetic, needy question pass my lips, no matter how hard my mind was demanding to know.

But I didn't need to. Kody had a knack for reading me, of knowing exactly what I was thinking without me needing to voice it out loud.

"Steele was better backup than me for a meeting like this," he explained, his voice soft and low. "He's an incredible sharpshooter, specializing in long-range weapons. Ever since the first time Zane tried to ambush Arch, we've taken precautions. Although it might seem like Arch is arriving alone—per their agreement—Steele is set up with a rifle trained on Zane's chest. He even leaves the laser sight on."

My jaw had fallen open as he spoke; then when he was done, I blinked a couple of times and licked my lips. "Well, shit," I murmured. "I didn't expect that."

Kody laughed. "We do rock the mysterious angle."

I rolled my eyes. "That's for fucking sure." My thumb rubbed over his damaged knuckle again. "Did you even ice these last night? They look fucking painful."

He arched a cocky grin at me. "You should see the other guy."

My jaw dropped again, and I shook my head as he cracked up. "You're unbelievable, Kodiak Jones."

His fingers untangled from mine, and he stroked my hair back from my face, tucking it behind my ear. "Unbelievable in a good way, right? Because, the way you kissed me last night made me think you're softening on that mountain-sized grudge you're holding."

We were so close, our heads sharing a pillow. It'd be so easy to close the gap between us and...

"Answer a question for me," I demanded, holding his green gaze steadily. "Did you deliberately plant that key on me?"

His eyes widened. "Is that what you think I did?"

I nodded, biting the inside of my cheek to keep my nerve in pursuing this conversation. It was long overdue, and now that things were growing increasingly complicated between us all...

"Fuck, MK, no wonder you've been so angry. You think I purposely planted evidence on you, then..." He trailed off looking up at the ceiling and scrubbing a hand over his messy, blond hair. "And then Archer left you on the side of the road where you got arrested."

For the first time in almost a year, the weight of my anger and hate decreased.

"That's not what happened?" I asked, hopeful despite all my best instincts telling me not to be such a damn fool.

Kody turned back to me, his hand cupping the side of my face with almost gut-wrenching tenderness. "Madison Kate, I swear to you, that's *not* what happened. That wasn't even my hoodie that I gave you that night. I'd just grabbed it when shit started going down between the Reapers and Wraiths because it was cold as shit that night."

He could have been lying—of course he could have. But there was such open sincerity in his green gaze... Yeah, maybe it made me a gullible idiot, but I believed him.

It felt *good* to believe him, like a six-ton weight had been lifted off my back and I could suddenly just fucking breathe again.

"What about the cops picking me up like that?" I asked. "Archer had said someone would be there to collect me, and the next thing I knew I was in handcuffs being tossed into a holding cell."

Kody's face tightened, and he grimaced. "You'll have to ask him, babe. I can't speak for him."

My stomach rolled, but I nodded. That was fair. I had no qualms confronting Archer, anyway. In fact, I'd almost started to look forward to my verbal sparring matches with him. It made my blood pump in just the most delicious way.

Kody's hand still cupped my face, and his thumb brushed over my lower lip, teasing. "So, we're good now? Truce?"

My breath caught at the heat in his heavy-lidded eyes, but I gave a small nod. "Truce," I agreed.

A small frown pulled at his brow. "Actually, I think I might still owe you some payback, MK. You dyed my face purple. And you Photoshopped porn with me fucking Archer from behind."

I bit my lip to try to hide my smile but failed miserably. "Yeah, uh, chalk it up to friendly fire?" He scowled, and I swallowed the laughter bubbling up in me. "Okay, fine, you can have one free shot. What's it gonna be? Hair dye in my shampoo? Cling wrap over the toilet seat? Paint my bedroom glittery pink so it hurts my eyes every time I wake up? Oh wait." I rolled my eyes, and he gave me a sly half smile back.

"Nothing so juvenile," he murmured. "One free shot, huh?" I nodded. "Then I'll take this." He closed the gap between us, pressing his lips to mine. I sucked in a quick gasp against his mouth, my lips parting as I kissed him back. He gently bit my lower lip, sucking on it before meeting my tongue with intensity.

Sparks erupted in my belly, my pussy heating and my nipples hardening, reminding me that I was totally naked under the sheets and he was probably just in boxers… It'd be so easy to take things further, except—

"Kody," I gasped, pushing away from him and shaking my head. "I fucked Steele last night."

He cringed. "I know. We heard. Not to mention the fact that he was naked and asleep tangled up against your body when Arch needed to wake him up."

My face flushed with embarrassment, and I pulled away farther.

"Right. So I can't just…" I shook my head, scrubbing my palm over my face. "It doesn't bother you? That I fucked your friend last night?"

Kody sat up slightly, propping himself up on his elbow to look at me with total seriousness. "It does," he admitted. "It bothers me more than I really thought it would. When I heard you guys last night…" He trailed off, his gaze ducking away from me and his jaw tense. "I've never been so jealous of Steele in my life. He's like a brother to me, but I could have happily knocked him out last night."

I blinked a couple of times, taken aback by this response. It was so much more emotional and possessive than I'd expected.

"Right," I said softly. "So, I should go shower."

I started to slide out of the bed, but he leaned over and grabbed my wrist. He pulled me back underneath him as he supported his weight with one thickly corded arm planted on the bed beside my head.

"I'm jealous as hell," he reiterated, "but that only showed me how much I want you. There's no way I'm walking away and bowing out gracefully. Not when you want me too."

This time when he kissed me, his pure, possessive dominance left me panting and frazzled. My pussy throbbed with need, and I could feel my own arousal slick on my thighs.

"I need a day," I said in a husky whisper as he peered down at me with his far too intuitive gaze. "A day to sort out my brain and think about…everything. I never should have slept with Steele in the first place. I'm *still* pissed off at him."

Kody didn't push this advantage, simply nodded and rolled to the side to let me escape. At the last second, I dragged the sheet with me, clutching it to my chest as I made a quick dash to the bathroom.

"A day," Kody repeated from my bed, and I risked a glance back at him.

That was a mistake. Thanks to me stealing the sheet, he was just lying there in the middle of my pink floral bed in nothing but a pair of tight red boxer briefs. Safe to say, underwear like that did *nothing* to hide what he was packing. Or how hard he was.

His smile turned sly. "One day. I can't promise you any more than that, baby."

My stomach flipped and my pulse raced, but I just nodded and closed the bathroom door between us.

Taking a few deep, calming breaths, I dropped the sheet, then cranked my shower on. Cold. Ice-cold. Lord knew I needed a dip in the damn Arctic to cool myself off.

My teeth chattered as I soaped myself up, groaning when the scent of my own body wash just brought images of Steele stroking himself back to my mind.

Some moments later, Kody knocked on the door, then cracked it open.

"You want to go to Nadia's? We probably have a few hours until the guys get back."

My stomach rumbled hard, and I groaned. "Fuck yes! But no ex-girlfriends slapping me this time, right?"

Kody's laugh echoed through the bathroom. "I promise."

He closed the door again, and I hurried through the rest of my ice-cold shower. Now that he'd put the idea in my head, I was goddamn starving.

My bedroom was empty when I emerged wrapped in a towel, so I quickly dressed in skinny jeans, a ribbed, black V-neck sweater that did all kinds of great things for my tits, and my favorite knee-high, black leather, flat boots. After spending most of the night freezing my ass off in that minidress, I was definitely opting for comfort and warmth today.

"MK, babe!" Kody called up the stairs. "You ready to go?"

I hurried down to meet him, tucking my phone into my back pocket. "I'm right here; what's the rush?"

"Arch just texted to say he's been called in to our manager's office for his prelim weigh-in. He'll want to work out when he gets back, so I need to load up on cake and caffeine before then." He led the way through to the garage and clicked the key fob for his blue Maserati.

He slid into the driver's seat as the garage door slowly rolled open, and I buckled my seat belt while waves of nervousness rolled through me. "Prelim weigh-in?" I asked, wetting my lips. "What's involved in that?"

Kody shot me a curious look. "Pretty much what it sounds like. The official weigh-in is a couple of hours prior to the fight itself, and if a fighter falls outside their weight class—"

"Yeah, I know the rules." I cut him off impatiently. "Big MMA fan, remember? I just meant...he has to go in to your manager's office just to record his weight? Seems like a pointless trip when you've got scales here."

Kody shrugged. "Yeah, but they'll often have an official there to do a random drug screening too. That's not the sort of thing you can choose to do whenever you want, you know?"

Oh shit.

I must have looked as panicked as I felt because Kody gave me a confused frown when we paused at the main gates of the mansion. They were electronic but took a moment to open.

"Why so interested, babe?"

I rolled my window down, suddenly super interested in the landscaping around the main gates. "No reason," I lied. Then I spotted something. "Hey, what's that?"

To the side of the main gates, below the keypad that allowed us to come and go without getting out of the car, was an elaborately wrapped present box.

Kody froze, staring at where I was pointing. He shifted the Maserati into park, then climbed out.

I hurried to follow, stopping only when he held a hand up at me.

"Just stay back, MK," he ordered. "It could be anything."

My brows shot up. "Well, no shit. That's sort of why we need to look."

Kody shot me a flat glare, then turned back to the gift box and nudged the lid off with his toe.

"What is it?" I asked, craning my neck from where I'd stopped on his command. "Is it...a bomb or something?"

The way Kody's head snapped back to me and his brow furrowed made me pause.

"Fucking hell, MK. That hadn't even crossed my mind. If it had been, we'd both probably be dead now." He let out a heavy sigh and stooped to pick the box up in his fingers. "No, it's...another one of these." He tilted the package in my direction, and I shuddered when the pink-haired doll stared back at me.

This time she was naked, red flecks of something distinctly bloodlike splattered over her body and coating her hands. On her feet were a miniature pair of black high heels, complete with their red soles and ankle straps.

Bile rose in my throat, and I swallowed it back down, fighting for strength in my voice. "Is that... Are those photos?" I indicated to the envelope underneath the doll.

Kody tossed the box and the creepy fucking doll down on the grass and ripped the envelope open. He flicked through the images quickly, his face set in an impassive mask, before handing them to me.

"Oh fuck," I gasped, clapping a hand over my mouth as I stared at the first image. I'd suspected this when I saw the doll's "outfit," but this was... Holy fuck.

Taking a steadying breath, I flipped through the images. There I was, stretched out naked on my bed, facedown with my heels still on as I reached into my bedside drawer. Steele was behind me, the angle wrong to show his finger buried in my pussy, but the expression on my face kind of made it clear.

In the next one, I was straddling him. The next, he fucked me from behind, his fingers biting into the flesh of my ass and my hands twisted in the sheets. In the last image, I was on my knees in front of him. My back was to the camera, but his fingers were tangled in my hair and his head tipped back with ecstasy.

"He must have used a telephoto lens," Kody told me, taking the images from my hand. "There's no other way he could have managed this. None." He started to tuck them back into the envelope before I stopped him.

"Wait," I said, my voice croaking. "Give them to me."

He did as I asked, and I flipped them over. Sure enough, on the last image were those same jagged, red letters delivering another threat.

No one touches what's mine. I'll remove every part of his body that touched yours, then take pleasure in punishing you for this betrayal.

Nausea washed over me, and I thrust the photos back to Kody.

"I'm going to be sick," I announced, rushing back through the gates and crouching on the grass beside the car.

I heaved and gagged, but nothing came up.

Kody sat in the grass beside me, stroking my hair with soothing strokes and holding it back as I dry retched. He didn't talk, and I didn't blame him. What could he say that would possibly make this better?

"He's going to come after you guys," I finally croaked when I was sure no vomit would actually come up.

Kody grunted a sound. "Let him try."

I shook my head, terror flooding through me anew. "No. No way. I'm not dragging you all down with me. It's bad enough he already threatened Dallas..." I trailed off, feeling the guilt of avoiding my old friend so much.

"That's why you stopped hanging out with him?" Kody's voice was thoughtful, but his fingers still rubbed gentle circles on my back. On a whim, I leaned into his body, and he tucked his arm around me.

"It sure as fuck wasn't because Archer threw his big dick energy around, if that's what you thought." I muttered the words into his T-shirt, soaking in his solid presence.

For a while we just sat like that—fuck anyone watching—but eventually I sighed and peeled myself out of his embrace.

"I need to stay away from you all," I announced, my voice holding more resolution than shock. "Until this stalker shit is worked out, I can't go painting targets on your backs too."

Kody shook his head, a frown creasing his brow. "No. Not a chance. You can't get rid of us that easily, babe. Besides, we will keep you safe from this freak, I swear to you."

He couldn't change my mind, though. Not when it was all so raw on my frayed nerves. I didn't argue, but the way he sighed and scrubbed a hand through his platinum hair made me think he knew. He knew I was going to distance myself, and he wasn't going to force the issue.

Yet.

CHAPTER 34

I barely left the house for the better part of two weeks. Not because I was scared—even though that played a huge factor—but because I'd developed a nasty cold, probably from running around in the freezing night air with no coat and no panties after Bree's party.

One of the guys, I wasn't sure who, had arranged for all my lectures and classes to be streamed for me. It was a sweet gesture and meant that I wasn't falling behind before we'd even been at SGU for two months.

But there was another reason I was becoming increasingly withdrawn.

"Your father said he tried to call you last weekend," Archer commented as I shuffled into the kitchen wearing plaid flannel pajamas, a thin tank top with no bra, and my dirty hair up in a sloppy bun.

I shrugged, pulling the fridge open to search for…something. Anything. I wasn't even hungry. Just bored. "I have nothing to say to him," I replied, my tone flat and cold. I'd seen his call come in and thrown my phone across the room. It'd cracked the screen *and* dented the wall, but I didn't much care.

"Fair enough," Archer accepted. He was sitting at one of the stools with his laptop open in front of him. It dimly occurred to me that I still had no clue what the guys were studying at SGU. Then I dismissed the thought again.

He let out a sigh, closing the lid on his computer and setting it aside. He was staring at me, and I was doing my best to ignore him while staring aimlessly into the fridge.

"The meaning of life won't magically appear between the beer and cheese, Princess Danvers," he muttered sarcastically. "Grab something and close the damn door. We need to talk."

That piqued my curiosity. Archer D'Ath wanted to *talk* to me? Not argue or mock or tease? Ah, then again, that remained to be seen.

"What about?" I took the bait anyway.

He leveled me with one of those cool, blue-eyed stares. "Tonight."

Ice formed in my stomach.

"What about tonight?" Playing dumb seemed like my best option here.

Archer let out a frustrated sigh. "You know what tonight is. It's why you've been moping around the house for the last two weeks."

I folded my arms over my chest, indignant. "Excuse me? I'm sick."

"You're not. You *had* a cold. Colds don't last two weeks, Princess. You've been perfectly healthy all week, but now you're sulking because the anniversary of Riot Night is here and you still haven't resolved all your issues with us over what happened." His voice was flat, unemotional, uncaring. It made me want to punch him in the dick. With my boot. Repeatedly.

He was sort of right, though. Okay. He was a lot right.

After recovering from my very real cold, I'd realized how far through October we were. The anniversary of Riot Night had been coming up, and I already knew I'd be the center of attention around campus. So I saw no harm in milking my cold a bit longer.

And sure, maybe I'd been avoiding dealing with the guys for

a similar reason. Kody and I had talked and resolved things about my arrest. But there was the lingering question of our crazy-hot attraction to each other.

Steele and I had spent that incredible night together but resolved nothing outside of how electric we were in bed.

As for Archer?

"Go and get yourself cleaned up," he ordered me, like I was a dog and he was my master. "We're going to a party."

My brows shot up. "What? No. No way."

Archer just gave me a bored look. "This isn't up for negotiation, Madison Kate. Go upstairs, shower, and get dressed. We leave at eight."

I slammed my can of soda down on the counter. "No."

His brows raised. "No?"

Curling my lip, I gave him a poisonous glare. "I understand this isn't a word you hear often, Archer, but it means the opposite of yes. Here—let me put it in a sentence for you. No, I'm not going to a party with you on the anniversary of the second-worst night of my life. Understood?" I made to stomp out of the kitchen, but he shot out of his seat and blocked my exit with his huge body.

"We're going. You can either get showered and changed or you can go like this." He flickered a disgusted look over my outfit. "But I wouldn't advise it. You'll stand out a bit."

Fury built inside me again, burning away some of the sulking haze that'd settled over me since discovering the stalker's pictures of Steele and me fucking.

"Listen, you overgrown bully," I snarled, poking Archer in his chest and kinda hurting my index finger. "You don't fucking *own* me; I'm my own damn person. You *can't tell me what to do*." I punctuated those last words with more chest jabs, regardless of the pain in my finger for it.

A cruel sort of smile curved Archer's lips. "That's not entirely true."

"Arch!" Steele snapped from somewhere behind me. "Go away. I'll talk to Madison Kate."

I glared Archer down, but the look he gave me in return sent jagged spikes of fear skittering down my spine.

"Arch," Steele said again, his voice like thunder. "Fuck off."

When the bad-tempered, ink-covered bastard left the kitchen, I whirled around to glare at Steele. "What the hell was that all about?"

He scrubbed a hand over his chin, his eyes betraying some level of tension that I hadn't noticed there before. "We—as in Arch, Kody, and I—need to go to this party tonight. It's a...business matter. But because *we* have to go, so do you."

I frowned and folded my arms. I felt considerably less combative with Steele than Archer, but I still wasn't backing down.

"Steele," I sighed, "why are you guys finding it so hard to understand that I don't *want* to go out tonight? Riot Night was a fucking nightmare for me, and I sure as hell don't want to be reminded of it all night. Just go to your party. I'm not leaving the house, so I'll be totally safe here alone."

Steele's shoulders tensed, and he ducked his eyes away from mine.

Shit.

"Steele," I growled, my tone warning. "Why won't I be safe here? If the perimeter alarms are all on, no one is getting in without triggering them."

Steele's jaw clenched, and his lips twisted in a grimace. "Another letter was sent, implying...that something might happen tonight. Arch—no, *we all* would feel a hell of a lot better if we could keep eyes on you."

A flash of fear choked me for a second, but a couple of calming breaths helped me shift it again so that I could speak. "Why do you even care?"

Steele stepped closer to me, brushing a greasy strand of my

pink hair away from my face and stroking his index finger down my cheek. For a tense moment, I thought he was going to tell me something profound and life-altering. Some dark secret that they'd all been hiding, something that would explain *why* they'd become so interwoven in my life.

But he just dropped his hand away again. "Go and get changed, Hellcat. And don't forget, it's Halloween." He gave me a pointed look, then left me alone with my jumbled thoughts and emotions.

I abandoned my soda and made my way back to my bedroom in a bit of a daze. As badly as I wanted to kick back against their orders and tell them to go shove their authoritarian bullshit straight up their asses...Steele had struck a nerve.

They'd received something else from my stalker? When? Why hadn't they told me?

Frustrated, I put myself through a thorough wash in the shower—holy crap, my hair needed it—then tucked a towel around myself while I went through the time-intensive process of drying and straightening it. The rose tone had been fading a bit, but thanks to my color-depositing conditioner, it was back to lush and pink again.

When my hair was done, I went to work on my makeup, laying it on thick and dark. After all, it wasn't just the anniversary of Riot Night. It was also Halloween.

I couldn't imagine Steele had meant for me to wear a costume when he pointed that out, and he'd be shit out of luck if he did. But I did err on the dramatic side with my makeup.

Emerging from my bathroom still wrapped in my pink towel, I found a gift on my bed.

"What are you doing here?" I asked Kody, biting back the smile that wanted to play across my lips. The whole process of showering, doing my hair, putting on makeup...it had grounded me, cleared my head, and helped me gain a bit of clarity on the situation. If they truly felt I was unsafe here at the house alone, then I wasn't going to be a dumb shit and force the issue. That's the kind of crap those too-stupid-to-live heroines of slasher flicks tended to do.

"Came to check on you," he replied, rolling onto his side and propping his head up on his hand. He'd done that a lot in the last two weeks. Checked in on me. It was sweet as hell, but I could tell from the hungry way he watched me that he was biding his time to finish our...*conversation.*

I gave him a knowing grin. "Uh-huh. And you just happened to lose your shirt on the way to my room?" He was all stretched out on my floral-pink comforter in nothing but a pair of dark denim jeans, slung low on his hips as if to deliberately highlight that delicious V that ripped men had.

Kody's smile was all male satisfaction, and my lower belly fluttered in response. "Is the sight of me shirtless distracting for you, MK?"

I narrowed my eyes at him, then continued across the room to my walk-in closet. I needed to find something...*Halloween-y.*

"This isn't a costume party or anything, right?" I called out to Kody while I flipped through the clothes hanging on my racks. Ninety percent of them I hadn't purchased, so I wasn't even totally sure what options I had to pick from.

"Not really," he called back. "Only loosely. Arch has some masks for us to wear, and that's about as much as we'll ever dress up."

Okay, so no need to aim for a specific *look* then. Just something...comfortable? Or...sexy?

I ducked back into the bedroom and grabbed my phone off the end of the bed, pretending to ignore the way Kody's heavy-lidded eyes followed me. I pulled up Bree's number and hit the button for video chat.

"Hey, girl," she greeted me when she answered, then did a double take. "Damn, you look gorgeous! What's the occasion? I thought you were still sick." There was an edge of hurt in her tone, and a stab of guilt hit me.

"Uh, yeah, I'm feeling better," I hedged, taking her with me to the closet. "The guys are making me go to some shitty party with them tonight. Will you help me pick an outfit?"

"Oh!" Her brows shot up, and she looked a bit taken aback. "You're going to a party? That's... I'd sort of assumed you would be at home tonight. You know...*tonight.*" She was glammed up herself, and I remembered we usually went to our old friend Veronica's annual Halloween party.

I laughed. "I'm all too aware of what tonight is, Bree. But the guys aren't taking no for an answer." I rolled my eyes, and she gave a weak laugh in response, then frowned.

"Well, tell them to fuck off. You're a strong, independent woman. You'll be totally fine at home on your own. You've got that fancy security system all set up." There was something off about her voice, but I chalked it up to her being annoyed at me for not inviting her to the party with us.

I just gave her a shrug. "It's not so bad. I need to get out anyway. So, help me pick something to wear?"

A small line creased her brow, but she nodded in agreement.

Some minutes later, after she'd made me virtually walk through all the options I'd been considering, she pulled together an admittedly pretty cute outfit. The look was a bit darker and more punk rock than my usual style, but it was Halloween after all.

"Thanks, Bree; you're the best," I told her, walking back out into the bedroom with my outfit in my other hand. I dropped it on the end of my bed, then turned to grab some underwear from my dresser.

Bree let out a screech from my phone, and I looked down at the screen in a panic.

"What?" I asked, worried something bad had happened.

Instead she was gaping at me, her mouth open. "Um, MK, did you forget to mention the half-naked Adonis lying in your bed?"

I shot a look at Kody, and he just grinned like a smug fucking cat. "No, I didn't forget. He just lost his shirt and wanted to borrow one of mine. I think he wants that baby-blue lace crop top."

Bree just erupted into giggles, shaking her head. "Gossip," she ordered me. "Tomorrow over coffee. No excuses."

"Yes, ma'am," I replied with a grumble, then ended the call as she continued to cackle on the other end.

"That's interesting," Kody murmured as I tossed my phone onto the dresser and gathered the appropriate underwear for my outfit. "You don't gossip about your love life with your bestie? I thought that's what all chicks did."

I snorted a laugh. "No, Kodiak Jones, that's apparently what *boys* do. Otherwise, how the hell did Archer find out those dirty details about what happened with Steele at the fight?"

Yeah, I was still salty on that. There wasn't even a question of him kissing and telling about our sexcapade after Bree's party. For one thing, we'd been loud enough to give the entire house a front row seat. For another, my stalker's telephoto-lens pictures did the deed for us.

Kody gave me a nod of acknowledgment. "Don't hold that one too hard against him, babe. His loyalty to Arch runs deeper than blood, and back then we didn't know you like we do now."

I huffed, folding my arms across my towel and making sure it was firmly tucked in place. "It was only a month ago, Kody."

His brows lifted. "A lot has changed in a month."

A door slammed somewhere in the house, and Kody glanced at the time on his chunky black watch. "I better go try on that lace crop top of yours," he said, sitting up with a delicious crunch of his abs. "See you downstairs, gorgeous." Casual as fucking anything, he smacked a quick kiss on my mouth, then left the room.

I pressed my fingers to my lips, feeling the print of his touch there like a ghost kiss for way too long after he was gone.

Eventually, I gave myself a mental shake and quickly got dressed—after triple-checking that the blackout blind was still firmly in place over my window. I hadn't opened it once since getting those telephoto-lens pictures. I'd rather live in the dark, thank you.

Bree's choice of a black pleated miniskirt, black scoop-neck, form-fitting top, and a belt made of loose, interlinked chains really worked out well. The whole thing was topped off with some black high heels that almost looked like they had laces up the front of the foot. All in all, I looked like some kind of gothic, sexy school-girl—a win-win because it echoed the slutty outfit I'd worn on my first day at SGU. The one Archer had felt so inclined to douse in orange juice.

Giving myself a quick once-over in the mirror, I smiled. Bree had good taste.

I hoped the guys thought so too.

Not that it should matter what they thought of my outfit, of course, but also…I couldn't push it out of my mind. Damn it.

CHAPTER 35

The mask Archer handed me before we got out of the G Wagen was made of red leather with small devil horns attached. Kody and Steele both slipped identical masks over their own faces, while Archer's was black.

I smiled, wondering if this was just a coincidence or...

"Cute," I commented as we got out of the car. "These remind me of Bree's favorite book."

Steele and Kody didn't react at all, but Archer—the one who'd chosen the masks and kept the black one for himself—allowed the corner of his lips to pull up in a sly half grin.

"I find time loops fascinating," he murmured, confirming my suspicions about the masks being a deliberate nod to a romance novel. He brushed past me without another word on the subject and led the way toward the old warehouse, where lights and music indicated the party was happening.

I bit back my own smile, having no clue what to make of that statement. For one, I'd never even seen Archer crack so much as a magazine, let alone a chunky-ass book. For another, the book in question was a reverse harem romance. Meaning the main character—Karma—had more than one love interest and they never made her choose.

Did that mean Archer would be okay with that lifestyle?

Ugh. Come on, MK. Hell didn't just freeze over.

"You going to stand there all night?" Steele asked me, grinning. "Or are we going to have some fun?"

The way his mask hid the top half of his face made his smile so much more alluring, so much sexier. Not that he needed any help in that department.

With a sigh, I slipped my own mask on and took his outstretched hand. I laughed as he pulled me along faster, running a bit in my high heels to catch up with Kody and Archer.

The four of us entered the party together, as a unit. Damn, if that didn't feel kind of awesome. There was heavy security at the main door, checking names off a list and stamping everyone's wrists as they entered, but they just waved us through. Clearly Archer was recognizable.

At the far end of the warehouse, a raised booth had been erected, and an alien-costumed DJ was rocking out to his own tunes while people went nuts below him. The track was familiar, and my brow creased while I tried to place it.

"Wait, isn't that guy kinda famous right now?" I asked Kody, pointing to the bouncing alien. Then again, he was in a full costume, so it could just be some punk-ass kid hitting Play on his laptop.

Kody nodded. "Probably. The girl throwing this gig is a bit of a snob, so she'd have happily thrown a stack of cash around to get the real deal."

That sparked my curiosity. We were over on the poorer side of Shadow Grove, in the industrial area that had been abandoned for probably fifty years or more. So who was this girl throwing a Halloween Party with a Ministry of Sound DJ in attendance? And more to the point...why did the guys *need* to attend?

"I suppose it'd be a waste of breath to ask what business you're doing here tonight," I commented, folding my arms under my breasts. It was cold as shit, and while I'd thrown a leather jacket on before leaving the house, my legs were bare. My tiny skirt didn't exactly cover much.

"Pretty much," Archer replied, his eyes hard and cold behind that black leather mask. "Kody, you got this?"

"*This?*" I repeated in a snarl, knowing perfectly well he was referring to me. Despite how much calmer I'd felt since showering, I was still a bit prickly, and if Archer wanted a fight, I was all too happy to provide one.

The big guy clearly had better things to do, though, as he just gave Kody a meaningful look before disappearing into the crowd.

"Don't worry, Hellcat," Steele said to me with a smirk. "When we're done here, I'll hold him so you can get a free punch in."

I snorted a laugh, and his gray eyes twinkled behind his mask. With a small nod to Kody, he followed in the direction Archer had gone.

"Stuck on babysitter duty again, huh?" I teased Kody as we made our way through the crowded warehouse to find the bar. "Don't tell me Archer needs Steele's particular *skills* again tonight?"

Kody shrugged. "Ideally not. But you never know how these things will go." He guided me ahead of him with a hand on the small of my back. It wasn't a sexual thing, but there was something about that gesture that sent girly flutters through me.

"For the record, though," he continued as we found the bar— which was a seriously professional setup. This chick hadn't cut corners, other than her location. "I didn't get *stuck* babysitting. I volunteered to stay with you."

I gave him a considering stare as we waited to be served. "Why?"

Kody shook his head, his green eyes amused behind his red mask. "Because it seems like a really dumb idea to leave you alone at a warehouse party full of drunk dickheads in costumes, especially as you have an increasingly threatening stalker out there somewhere."

I grimaced, waiting while Kody ordered us drinks. "Well yeah, sure," I agreed. "You could've just left me at home. No one is getting in there."

He just shrugged and handed me one of the plastic cups the bartender had set down in front of us. "I don't think any of us really wanted to run that risk tonight, MK. Did you?"

Now that he put it that way...yeah, the idea of being all alone in my father's eerie mansion would have given me the creeps in a big way. For all my determination to get rid of the guys, I'd grown accustomed to them always being around. Being alone, on Halloween no less, probably would have seen me jumping at every shadow.

"Besides," Kody carried on with a small smile, "I like hanging out with you. And we left a conversation unfinished the other weekend..." His green eyes flashed, and I took a huge gulp of my drink to give myself a moment.

"Shit," I commented, peering into the plastic cup. "This is really good."

He nodded. "It'd wanna be." When I gave him a confused look, he just waved it off. "Story for another day."

There had to be hundreds of people on the heaving dance floor, all in some degree of costume, and with the flashing strobe lights, it created a hell of an image.

"I hate costume parties," I muttered, flinching as a macabre clown brushed past us. "Especially ones with clowns." I shuddered and Kody laughed.

"Let's find somewhere less intense." He took my hand, linking our fingers together and leading the way as we wove through the costumed partygoers once more. He glanced back at me a couple of times as we crossed the room, the flashing strobes catching on his devil mask and sending spikes of irrational fear shooting through me.

It was like I was seeing his real face. Like all the time I'd known him—all six weeks—he was really a demon in disguise. I'd believe it, silver-tongued devil that he was.

Kody shoved a rusty old door open with his shoulder, then released my hand so he could hold it open for me. He kicked an old brick into the opening so it wouldn't shut and lock us out, then reclaimed my hand again.

I kinda loved that.

"Oh, I know where we are," I commented, peering into the moonlit darkness. I'd known we were in the abandoned industrial area, but that was a huge area. "Isn't the old East-West boundary just past that tree line?" I pointed to the hill in the near distance, and Kody nodded.

What I really meant was that the East-West boundary was just past that tree line where The Laughing Clown amusement park was located. Not that the boundary line was a thing anymore, not in the new, "gang-free" Shadow Grove. Yeah right.

Kody and I sat on the hood of an old car—all its tires long gone and the interior totally gutted. Still, it made a good enough seat, even if the metal was freezing against my bare legs.

"I know you won't tell me anything important," I started to say, and Kody shot me a suspicious look. I think. It was hard to read facial expressions when someone wore a mask that covered half their face. "But can you tell me *anything*?"

He didn't immediately deny my request, which was a step in the right direction. "I shouldn't," he said slowly, "but..."

When he didn't immediately complete his statement, I took a sip of my drink. The alcohol warmed my stomach, but I had no intention of getting drunk. So I'd take it slow.

"But what?"

"I could play you for answers," he suggested, sipping his own drink, then setting it down on the hood beside him. "Truth or dare? Seems like the perfect night for it." He leaned back on the rusty car, looking up at the full moon.

I snickered a short laugh. "Truth or dare? What are we, thirteen? No."

He tucked his arms behind his head, drawing way too much attention to those impressive biceps of his. He'd put on a black long-sleeved T-shirt, but it was tight enough around the arms that it wasn't hiding *shit*.

"You scared, MK?"

"Not even close," I replied, lying my ass off. "I've just read enough romance novels to know how this scenario goes. You give me some half-assed, cryptic answers to my questions, then dare me to do something sexual in return. Talk about predictable."

He pouted, and I laughed.

"Well, shit, babe, give me a better idea. Arch could be a while yet, and you don't really look like you want to go dance with the creepy clowns in there." He nodded back to the party, and I cringed.

"Can you at least tell me why we're here tonight?" I'd run a bunch of possibilities through my head, but it was like trying to do a jigsaw puzzle with only a quarter of the pieces. And no fucking corners.

Kody seemed to consider this for a moment before replying, probably vetting his response to remove any real information.

"How much do you know about Archer's old man?" he asked me eventually. It wasn't at all the change of subject I'd expected, and I blinked in confusion.

"Um, not much. Just that he was the founder of the Shadow Grove Reapers and must have been one hell of a scary bastard to create such a brutal gang." And really, a huge amount of what I knew of the Reapers was just what rumors had told me. The Reapers and the Wraiths were the boogeymen that privileged children of Shadow Grove were terrified of but most never actually crossed paths with.

Kody ruffled his hair with a hand through it, then rested his arm across his stomach. His fingers were close enough that I could have shifted an inch and touched him. "Right, so now, what do you know about Ferryman?"

I frowned behind my oppressive mask. "The leader of the Wraiths? Nothing, really. I only know what I do about Damien D'Ath because of Zane." Because when Zane D'Ath killed my mother, I'd developed a small obsession...until he was released from charges a few weeks later, that was. And then I was too scared to pursue my vendetta against him. I didn't want to become his next victim when he so clearly had the cops on his payroll.

Kody sighed, looking back up at the sky. "This is going to take too long to explain, I think. So, to answer your question, we're here to meet with a business contact."

"What? No way. That's not... You can't just backtrack like that." I parked my drink on the car hood so I could shift around and glare down at him. Hopefully my devil mask intensified that glare and didn't make me look ridiculous as fuck.

"Your turn," he said, ignoring my protest at his shitty answer. "Are you and Steele a thing now?"

My mouth went dry. "A thing?" I repeated, like some kind of pink parrot. "Why would you think that?"

Kody gave a dry laugh. "Maybe because you guys fucked after Bree's party and you've been totally ignoring all of my attempts to flirt with you ever since."

My face heated, and I was suddenly thankful for the mask. "I haven't..." My words trailed off, so I tried again. "I was sick. I've barely even spoken to Steele since that night."

"You had a fucking cold, MK, not exactly the bubonic plague. You were also probably a bit shell-shocked after your stalker's last gift, which is totally understandable. I just wasn't sure if you wanted me to back off." There was an edge of uncertainty in his tone that surprised me. In a good way, I think.

"Would you?" I challenged him, unable to help myself. Not for the first time, I wondered why I insisted on playing with fire. "If I told you to back off, would you actually do it?"

Kody sat up, putting him suddenly face-to-face with me. "No," he admitted, his hand sliding into the back of my hair and pulling my face closer. "Because I'd know you didn't really want me to."

His lips brushed mine, and I slid out of his grip—and off the hood. Taking two steps back toward the party, I gave him a teasing smile. "Maybe I do feel like dancing with the clowns after all. You coming?"

He tipped his head up to the sky, like he was praying for patience or cursing the fates—both equally amusing options—then followed after me.

Back inside the warehouse, there were even more people in both elaborate costumes—like the alien DJ—and half-assed efforts like our own masks with normal clothes. Kody and I bypassed the bar, making our way right into the heaving dance floor. Our fingers tangled together as we wove between dancing people, making sure we didn't get separated, until we found a slightly clear section near the enormous nightclub-quality speakers.

The heavy, thudding dance music was so loud there was no possible way to speak. No way for Kody to ask me questions I didn't know the answers to, like how I felt about Steele now or whether I was still fantasizing about Kody in my bed or...what the hell was going on between me and Archer. I had no idea if Kody or Steele had seen him kiss me that night—the night they'd beat the shit out of Skunk—but it was a conversation I wasn't ready to have.

My curiosity could wait. Eventually, I'd find out about what "business" the three of them had and what agreement Archer had with both the Reapers and the Wraiths.

Right now, I just wanted to dance with a drop-dead-gorgeous guy and forget the facts that I had a stalker, that I was insanely attracted to three different guys, and that my father was a total piece of shit.

The heat from the crowd was intense, so I shed my jacket and tossed it into the shadows under the speaker. That left me in just a thin, tight tank top, but even that was too much for the temperature on the dance floor.

I swayed and moved to the music, letting the pounding bass pull me in as I lost myself to the noise. Kody's body seemed to find mine like Velcro, molding to me and moving in perfect harmony with the way I danced and writhed against him.

When the song blended and shifted into something new, hot sweat dripped down the center of my back, and my mask felt like it'd been glued to my cheeks. I turned in Kody's arms until I faced him. My hips were still swaying as I pushed my mask up to my hair and swiped a bead of sweat from the bridge of my nose.

His hands were on my waist, his own body moving with mine, but there was a hungry, predatory gleam in his eyes that made my whole body tight with excitement. I reached up, pushing his mask off his face to rest on his blond hair, then grinned.

"You're not a bad dancer," I told him, having to yell to be heard over the deafening music. My arms looped around his neck, and he pulled me in closer still until every inch of my front touched some part of him.

He didn't reply, or not anything I could hear at any rate, instead pressing his lips to the bend of my neck as we danced. I groaned. Maybe dancing had been a bad idea.

Kody's lips trailed up my neck; then in the blink of an eye, his lips found mine.

On second thought, dancing had been a *fucking excellent* idea.

He kissed me, hard and demanding, forcing my lips to part so he could devour my mouth like a starving man with his favorite meal. Our bodies still writhed together, grinding in sync to the music, even as I desperately wished our clothes would disappear. Judging by the hard length crushed against my stomach, I figured it was a safe bet to think Kody was on the same wavelength there.

"Fuck," he groaned in my ear as our kiss broke off, and his hands roamed my body. "Can we get out of here? I need to touch you."

My belly fluttered, and I grinned into his sweaty neck. "Where?" We still needed to wait for Archer and Steele to do whatever the fuck they were doing, and I was pretty sure I'd seen porta potties set up in place of actual bathrooms.

Kody released me long enough to reach into his back pocket, then showed me an electronic key fob marked with the Mercedes logo. "Car?"

"Sold," I replied with a wide, excited grin.

Kody linked our fingers together and quickly led the way out of the warehouse. Once we emerged into the frigid night air, we all but ran back to the parking lot. The G Wagen unlocked on proximity, its indicators flashing, but we didn't make it inside. Instead, I found my back pressed against the passenger door while Kody and I damn near mauled one another. His hands were inside my tank top, cupping my breasts and teasing my already hard nipples through my bra. My arms were around his neck, my fingers clawing at the back of his hair as I kissed him with raw hunger.

I needed more. I really, badly, desperately *needed* Kody to scratch the itch deep inside me. Preferably with his cock. So I skated my hands down his hard front and frantically unbuckled his belt.

Kody released my breasts, instead sliding a hand up my bare thigh and under my short skirt. The cool air pebbled my skin, but it only made me so much more aware of how scorching hot my core had grown.

Then all of a sudden, his mouth was wrenched away from mine. His hands left my body, and a cool blast of air took his place.

"What the *fuck*?" Archer bellowed, and I needed to blink about sixteen times to catch the fuck up on what'd just happened. Kody was on his ass in the gravel, a murderous scowl on his face and his belt undone. Archer must have just ripped him off me and tossed him on the ground.

But why?

Steele was still some distance away, only just emerging from the party warehouse as I looked for him, but he was running to catch up with us.

Surely Archer wasn't reacting like this because he was *jealous*.

Then again, he did have that extreme alpha-male bullshit going on. So maybe he was.

Pity I wouldn't stand for being treated like a piece of meat for dogs to chew over.

I'd teach him.

He'd learn.

CHAPTER 36

"What's your fucking damage, D'Ath?" I spat at him, furious as I tugged my bra back into place and tried to calm my raging hormones. Apparently I wasn't getting any D in my V just yet. Fucking cunt-blocker.

"My damage?" he roared, his face a scary shade of red that suggested he really might blow his top any second now. His own mask was pushed up to his hair, like mine, but it still gave him a demonic sort of appearance with the full moon behind him. "You want to know what my fucking *damage* is, Danvers?"

He was next-level pissed, and I was growing more suspicious that this *wasn't* about me making out with Kody.

"Arch," Steele called out, reaching us. "Calm down. We can discuss this at home."

"Discuss *what?*" Kody demanded, picking himself up and buckling his belt, a move that Steele took in with a scowl. "What the hell is going on?"

"No!" Archer barked. His enraged glare didn't shift from me for even a second. "No, I've had enough—we're dealing with this now."

"Dealing with *what?*" I shouted back, sick of his intimidation routine. It was hot when it was likely to turn into sex, but I was getting clear vibes that this was *not* heading in that direction.

The vein in his temple throbbed, and his eye twitched slightly. "Did you fucking drug me, Madison Kate?"

I froze.

Oh shit.

That.

"My manager just called me," Archer continued, his voice threaded with pure violence, and a shiver of fear passed through me. "As a courtesy, to let me know that tomorrow I'd be getting disqualified from my fucking *debut* UFC fight. You want to take a wild stab at why that might be happening, Madison Kate?"

A flicker of guilt lit up inside me, but I smothered it quickly. He deserved it.

Own your choices, MK. Back yourself.

Folding my arms, I tilted my chin up defiantly.

"If I were a betting woman, I'd say you tested positive for anabolic steroid use. Sure does explain your short temper and bulging muscles. Not to mention those shriveled balls I'm sure you're hiding." I gave him an unkind, sarcastic smile. "Sucks to see your goals get flushed down the toilet, doesn't it, D'Ath?"

Rage built within him until he was fucking shaking, his muscles so tense I worried he might tear out of his shirt like the Hulk. His fists were clenched, but I wasn't afraid of him. Not really. Okay, maybe a tiny bit.

"You fucking *bitch!*" he shouted, then slammed his fist through the passenger-side window of the G-Wagen, shattering the safety glass and sending rock-salt-sized chunks scattering everywhere. My skin stung where the exploding pieces hit me, but I knew from experience those scratches would be light. Archer's knuckles would be another matter.

Still, I didn't move. I didn't run screaming in fear, and I sure as shit didn't groveled for forgiveness. Fuck that shit.

I stayed motionless and impassive while Archer howled and cursed and generally threw a rage tantrum. Both Kody and Steele stayed out of it too, which I noted. It wasn't until Archer looked like he might hit the car again that Kody intercepted him and grabbed his fist.

"One punch we can fix before the fight with ice, bandages, and bruise balm. Not two." His tone was low and even, not betraying any emotion, and I couldn't help making the whole situation worse.

"What fight?" I asked, snarky as all hell. "He's getting disqualified tomorrow."

Kody's glare in my direction was a crystal-clear *shut the actual fuck up, MK*, but I just grinned back at him. Yeah, I was smug as hell. Archer *deserved* this.

Archer's ice glare swung back around to me, and I bit my cheek to keep from flinching. But damn, he was one scary fuck. "You little—"

"Stop it," Kody snapped, his voice cracking down like a whip, "You're being fucking dramatic, Arch. You know perfectly well that Jase called you tonight so we could fix it by morning. You'll still fight next week."

My jaw dropped in outrage. "So why the hell is he throwing a goddamn toddler tantrum?" I demanded. Now *I* was pissed. He wasn't actually getting disqualified? How?

"He's angry because you almost ruined his whole fight career before it even got started," Steele told me. His arms were folded over his chest and his glare accusing. "Not to mention what it would've done to Kody's future as a trainer. You had no way to know that we could fix the drug test results. You *wanted* Arch disqualified from the fight."

I tipped my chin up once more, defiant to the end despite the stab of guilt I felt for dragging Kody down too. "You're damn right, I did. Now that I know it hasn't worked, I'll just try harder next time."

Archer's scowl turned venomous. "Why? Why would you do this when I've done nothing but *protect* you since you arrived back into Shadow Grove?" He was furious, no doubt. But there was a thread of something else that tugged uncomfortably at my heart.

"You must be joking," I scoffed, ignoring the twinge of guilt at that other emotion in his voice. "You had some random chick dump juice on me because you didn't like my outfit."

His glare darkened. "How is this remotely on the same scale of seriousness? Juice on your slutty outfit versus the attempted destruction of my entire future?"

My own stare turned acidic. "Oh, you mean like when you *framed* me a year ago? How I was arrested for a crime I had nothing to do with, then charged and sent to goddamn, fucking court to prove my own innocence? Like that? How about how you three came forward to corroborate my story and provide the evidence I needed to get out in maybe three days instead of three *months*? Oh wait. You didn't. You left me there to fucking rot and didn't look back twice."

I was screaming this at him. At all of them. My chest heaved and the familiar burn of hatred seared through my veins. It was about damn time.

"How about the way you deliberately handed me over to the police that night? How about the way every fucking Ivy League university I had early acceptance to withdrew their offers the *same day* my arrest was aired on the news? Or how my job prospects are fucking shot now because all anyone sees when they look at *Madison Kate Danvers* is a criminal? An acquittal doesn't count for shit when you've been publicly branded as guilty."

I was on a roll now. The floodgates had been opened, and this wasn't going to be over until I got it all off my chest. So fuck it. Why not go the whole way?

"Or maybe this was justified payback for the fact that *your brother* stalked and murdered my mom?!" I shoved him in the chest as I said that and must have caught him off guard, because he stumbled back a step. But I wasn't done yet. "Oh, but of course the Reapers have enough cops in their fucking pockets that he was let go after just three weeks in holding. Now my mom's murderer is running around free to do whatever the hell he wants, like, oh I don't know, stalk *me*."

Tears stung my eyes now, and to give myself something to do other than burst out crying, I ripped my mask from my hair and threw it at Archer's chest.

"So, yeah, Archer," I sneered, "you fucking deserved a bit of steroid powder in your protein shakes. Be thankful that's all it was."

I stooped down and swiped the key for the G Wagen where it'd dropped out of Kody's hand earlier. I didn't know what my plan was. I hated driving, but I couldn't stay there.

"Madison Kate," Steele said, his voice shocked, "Zane didn't kill your mom."

His words were like a slap in the face, and I reeled back.

"Excuse me?" Of all of them, I hadn't expected Steele to be the one defending that psychopathic murderer. "What the fuck would you know? I was there. I *saw* it."

"Did you, though?" My attention swung around to Kody, and I glared at him. He looked pained but continued anyway. "I'm just saying, you were wrong about me planting that key on you last Halloween. Isn't it possible you're wrong about this?"

My jaw dropped, betrayals hitting me from every side. "I'm not *wrong*. I saw it. He beat her unconscious, then shot her in the head." My body trembled as my mind dredged up those painful, long-suppressed memories.

"You were locked in the closet, Madison Kate," Archer said, his tone low and cold. "You *didn't* see."

I shook my head, denying what they were saying as the dark memories crashed through my brain. Pain and terror clawed at my throat, as fresh as it had been that night exactly seven years ago. Yet another reason for me to hate this stupid holiday—it was the anniversary of my mother's murder. A fact I'd managed to steadfastly ignore every year since then.

Until now.

"I saw," I insisted, ignoring the dampness on my cheeks as my eyes streamed. I was past the point of holding back the tears anymore. "Through the slats of the closet door, I saw everything he fucking did to her. I heard every scream of pain and plea for mercy. I heard her bones breaking and—" My voice hitched with a sob, and I swallowed past the bitter pain.

Sucking in a deep breath, I gathered my shattered emotions up and wrapped them around me like a poison-dipped blanket. "When the closet was opened again, it was *your* brother standing there looking down at me like I was a fucking complication."

If I could have killed someone with the force of my glare, Archer D'Ath would be a smoking pile of ash. All my pain and anger and *hate* that had been building for years now transferred to this bastard.

Yet he just looked back at me with something dangerously close to pity in his eyes.

"Why do you think that makes him your stalker?" Kody asked, his tone low and calm. It was the same tone he'd used when Archer was throwing his temper tantrum.

I cast a scornful look over at him. He'd taken Archer's side, they both had, and I was fucking done with trusting them. Done.

"Because I'm not fucking stupid, Kodiak. My mom was being stalked too. That day she thought someone was following us, and..." I trailed off as the memories assaulted me, becoming confused as they mixed with the haze of time and the warped way an eleven-year-old's mind processed what had happened. "We were in a car crash. Both of us were knocked out, and when we woke up, taped to the steering wheel was a Polaroid of my mom, unconscious, taken probably only a minute before." I swallowed heavily, lost to the memory. I'd been so scared, my head bleeding and my wrist aching with blinding pain where it'd snapped. Mom had been terrified too; I could tell by the way her voice had shaken as she'd called an ambulance for me. "She refused to go to the hospital with me, and no one could get ahold of my dad. Bree's mom ended up dropping me home hours later, but Mom was in a panic. She kept whispering that *he* was in the house. She shoved me in the closet and locked it from the outside. That's when…" I trailed off, swiping at my cheeks with my palms. "That's when Zane killed her."

None of the three guys spoke, all just staring at me, but I refused to meet their eyes. I wasn't done.

"A year later, I visited her grave and someone had left a *doll*." I spat the word out like it burned my tongue. "A replica of how my mom died, covered in bruises, wrists bound, and a bullet hole through the side of her head." I flicked my gaze up to Archer's face. "So yeah, I'm pretty confident your fucked-up brother is the one stalking me now."

"Madison Kate," he said, his voice rough and low. "Zane didn't kill your mother."

I curled my lip, ready to snarl back at him, but Steele spoke first.

"He's right. Zane didn't do that. He *couldn't*. Madison Kate, your mom was having an affair with Zane. She was—"

"No," I barked. "No. No way. Are you shitting me right now? This isn't a fucking telenovela. My mom wasn't sleeping with a gang member ten years younger than her."

Steele blew out a breath, scrubbing his hands over his face and looking helplessly at Archer.

The big guy just tightened his jaw and folded his arms. He was still pissed. Maybe even more now that I'd accused his brother of stalking and murder. "It's true," he said, biting the words off.

I shook my head, not wanting to believe them on this. It was too insane, like the script of a daytime soap opera. Or a slasher flick. But now that they'd said it, more and more long-forgotten memories crept into my brain. Memories of Zane visiting our house while my father had been away on work trips. Of my mom laughing at something he said while touching his arm. Of her dancing around the house like she was deliriously happy...but only when my father wasn't around.

"That doesn't mean he didn't kill her," I finally said, my teeth grinding together so hard my jaw hurt. "She probably broke it off, and he killed her out of rage. It's typical domestic-abuse escalation."

Kody snorted a bitter laugh, and I shot him a furious glare. "Sorry, babe. If anyone was abusing your mom, I'd look a hell of a lot closer to home. Zane fucking loved Deb."

It jolted me to hear them use my mom's first name, but they were few years older than me. If she really had been having an affair with Zane, they might have spent some time with her.

"Look, Madison Kate," Steele said, his voice coaxing like he was trying to harness a wild horse, "think about it logically. Don't rely on the memories of a messed-up, scared eleven-year-old. Analyze it with detachment. You'd been in a car accident, one that hurt you enough that you'd been knocked unconscious. That's a head injury, babe. You probably had other injuries too?" He paused, and I gave a jerking nod as I thought of my broken wrist. "So they would have given you painkillers at the hospital. When you got home, it would have been late. Your mom was freaked out, and that would have freaked *you* out. She shoved you in a closet and locked you in." He was listing these things, and I could sense he was coming around to a point. I wanted to shut him up. I wanted to stop him from getting to that point, because if he did...

"It was late at night too, right? And the lights were off?" He didn't need my response; he clearly already knew this much. "Did you actually see his face? The man who murdered Deb?"

I couldn't speak to answer him. Cold horror washed over me in waves, and my stomach rolled with bile. Could he be right? Had there been someone *else* in the house that night?

"You were in that closet for hours, MK," Kody told me softly. "We've all seen the police reports. The time of death was some six hours before Zane found you there."

I shook my head over and over, refusing to hear what they were saying. Because if what they were saying was true...if Zane wasn't the one who murdered my mom...then her killer was still out there.

He was still out there and stalking me, and I had no clue who it might be.

"You don't believe any of this, do you?" Archer scoffed at me, his eyes hard and cruel again. "Well, maybe this will help you gain some clarity, *Princess Danvers*." He sneered that nickname at me with something that smacked of hatred. "Deb was pregnant. That car crash you were in? She was running away. She'd just gotten the DNA results proving it was Zane's baby, and she was *scared*."

That was the last straw.

I laughed. It was a cold, bitter sound, but it helped me draw up my defenses again.

"You almost had me," I told them, frigid fury dripping from my words. "You fucking *almost* had me." I shook my head and stalked back to the G Wagen. Fuck this shit; I could push past my dislike of driving if it meant getting me the hell out of there.

I yanked open the driver's-side door before turning my derisive sneer back on the guys. "My mom wasn't pregnant. She *couldn't* get pregnant; she had her tubes tied right after I was born."

"Madison Kate," Archer snapped, taking a few steps toward me, "what are you doing?"

I slid into the driver's seat and slammed the door shut, so instead of replying, I just flipped him off through the windshield and turned the engine on.

Archer rushed to the driver's door and tried to yank it open again, but I'd already hit the automatic locks.

Steele was closest to the other side—the one with a shattered window—but I gunned the accelerator before he could reach in and unlock the door.

Fuck this.

Fuck *all* of this.

They'd tried to gaslight me, and they'd almost succeeded.

Tears clouded my vision, and I frantically scrubbed them away so I could see the road. My whole body was tense, and I nervously buckled my seat belt while clutching the steering wheel for dear life. I knew how to drive; I'd forced myself to get my license so that I'd always have the option should I want to drive. But fucking hell, I was not experienced, and in my current emotional state…

Something flashed in the trees, and I flinched, jerking the wheel, then narrowly managed to straighten out before I crashed into a ditch.

"Slow down, MK," I whispered to myself. "Just slow down. Slow the fuck down."

But as many times as I told myself to *slow down*, I couldn't force my foot to ease up on the accelerator.

Memories and flashes of images kept assaulting me, making me flinch and jump. It was like Pandora's box had been unlocked, and the repressed memories wouldn't go away until they'd all been *seen*.

Flashes of my mother, happier than I'd ever seen her, and a pair of heavily tattooed arms around her waist, his inked hands resting on her belly as I spied on them through the half-open door of her bedroom.

But then darker images too. Her leaving me in the car for *ages* while parked outside a shady bar in West Shadow Grove. Me sneaking around, peeking through the dirty windows, and witnessing a skinny, ink-covered gangbanger on his knees, a gun to his head.

A blue-eyed boy, older than me, yanking me away from the window and yelling at me to get out of there.

Tears clouded my vision again, and my chest ached as I sobbed.

Headlights lit up my car, and fear flooded through me. I was speeding, and the car behind was rapidly gaining on me.

Could it be the guys? Maybe. I could imagine one of them probably had the necessary skills for hot-wiring a car, and there had been plenty to choose from parked outside the warehouse.

Except the car following me had its high beams on, momentarily blinding me when I tried to look in the mirror. The heavy revving of an engine, audible thanks to the smashed-out passenger window of the G Wagen, was the only warning I got before the car behind me hit my bumper.

I screamed as my vehicle lurched forward, knowing I was about to lose control. I clung to the steering wheel, fighting to stay on the road as my back end started to fishtail. Another ram from the other car sealed the deal.

The wheel wrenched out of my stiff fingers as my tires caught on the rough surface of the shoulder; then the car hurtled out of control into the ditch.

A deafening bang sounded, and my whole world went black.

CHAPTER 37

Sound came back to me first. A high-pitched ringing in my ears that made me dizzy and disoriented. I blinked my eyes a couple of times, clearing them of white powder.

What had happened? All I could remember was a loud bang and then...nothing.

"Shit," I groaned, touching a hand to my nose. Blood trickled from my nose and the bridge ached, but amazingly, it didn't seem broken. Pretty lucky, considering how many airbags had gone off inside the G Wagen when I collided with the huge-ass tree directly in my line of vision.

The whole front end of the car was crushed, and if I'd been in a smaller car, I would be dead for sure. As it was, the worst of my injuries had come from the airbags deploying and the seat belt cutting into my chest and waist.

It took four or five solid shoves with my shoulder to open my door, thanks to the buckled metal, but when it finally popped free, I tumbled out into the dirt with a cry of relief.

My ears still rang with a high-pitched whine, and my balance was all over the place. Those were lessening by the minute, so I didn't think I'd ruptured an eardrum. Hopefully. There was blood on my neck and ear, but that could have come from the gash at my hairline.

Pushing my sticky, bloody hair back from my face, I sucked in a few breaths and looked around. The car that had pushed me from the road was nowhere to be seen, and the woods I'd crashed into were dead silent. Of course.

I needed to call for help. I needed...

Fuck.

I *wanted* to call the guys. But I couldn't. Not after how I'd just left things with them. Not after the bullshit they'd just tried to spin with me.

Besides, I didn't have my phone. It had been in the pocket of my jacket, which was probably still under the speaker at the warehouse party.

"Fucking hell, MK," I muttered to myself, watching my breath fog in the cool night air.

Wobbling and stumbling, I made my way back up to the road. I still had my high heels on, but I'd keep them on as long as I could, so I didn't tear my feet up on rocks or gravel. The road looked quiet, and I had no idea how long it might be before someone came along. Hell, I wasn't even sure where I *was*. I hadn't paid attention when I left the warehouse, and now I was paying the price for my own stupid decisions.

One thing was for sure—I couldn't stay there. What if the person who ran me off the road came to finish the job?

Decided, I hurried along the road. Maybe if I got my blood pumping, it'd help me keep warm. Then again, it would also make my head wound bleed harder. Such choices. Die of hypothermia or die of blood loss.

Around the next corner I spotted lights through the trees. I needed to get off the road, because walking along the road was just as bad as staying with my car if someone wanted me dead, so I made a quick decision. I'd head for those lights and pray to all the celestial beings it was a diner or police station or something equally useful.

For the next few minutes, I carefully picked my way through the thick undergrowth, heading for the bright lights ahead. The closer I got, though, the deeper my unease grew. When I finally emerged from the tree line, I just stood there for a long time, hardly comprehending what I was seeing.

It was The Laughing Clown. I was at the goddamn, fucking Laughing Clown. Except instead of the dark, abandoned park we'd seen after Bree's party—when we'd left Skunk beaten and bloody under the clown face—it was fully lit up.

Everything was still shitty and run down, debris and weeds everywhere, but someone had reconnected the electricity, and the enormous clown mouth was fully lit up and flashing. Creepy music tinkled from ancient speakers on tall poles, and a deep shudder ran through me.

I'd just walked straight into a trap, tailor-made for me. There was no doubt in my mind.

"Fuck no," I told the huge clown face over the entrance. "No way in hell."

I turned to retrace my steps, but a dark figure silhouetted on the ridge I'd just come down made me freeze. Terror flooded through me, triggering my fight-or-flight reflex. I was no idiot; I fucking *ran*.

Choosing the lesser of two evils, I kicked off my heels and sprinted barefoot under the psychotic laughing clown face and into the dark park. There had to be hundreds of places to hide within the park itself. Places that didn't involve getting lost in the stupid, fucking fun house again.

Note to self. Don't run into the damn fun house again, MK.

I was so focused on not being an idiot, I did what every slasher flick heroine ought to be slapped for: I looked behind me.

There, in the middle of the clown mouth, backlit by the newly fixed entryway lights, was the same broad, shadowy figure from the trees.

It was surreal in a completely terrifying way. I wasn't sticking around to appreciate the drama of the whole setup, even though this prick had clearly put a lot of effort in. Instead, I bolted for cover, ducked behind a line of sideshow booths, then crouched down to hide my progress as I wove through busted-up old rides until I ducked behind the operation booth for the old Tilt-A-Whirl. If I could wait him out…if I could stay hidden and silent until he passed me by, I could run back to the entrance and…

And then what?

I had no car, no phone, no shoes. I was still bleeding from my head, and I was so cold my teeth had started chattering. I clenched my jaw to prevent the noise but needed to keep a hand in front of my face to stop the puffs of fog from my breath from giving away my location.

A slow scrape of boots on concrete reached my ears, and I tucked into a tighter ball, huddling out of sight and desperately praying he'd pass by. The footsteps drew closer, slow and unhurried, like he was supremely confident I wouldn't get away.

Was that classic bad-guy arrogance? Or had he thought ahead and blocked the exits? Fuck, I hoped it was the former.

His steps slowed, then seemed to stop directly beside my hiding place. My heart thudded so hard I worried I might have a heart attack. But a moment later, the steps started again—slow but steadily moving away from the Tilt-A-Whirl and me.

I let out one long breath, trying to calm my nerves before shifting to my knees and peering over the control booth. I needed to see which direction he'd gone.

For a second, I couldn't see anyone, and the back of my neck prickled like he was going to be standing right behind me. But then I spotted movement over near my favorite attraction—the goddamn fun house.

By my guess, he—and I was pretty sure he was a *he*—was taller than six feet and had a broad, muscular build across the shoulders. He was dressed all in black with a hood pulled up and a full black ski mask over his face. Nothing about him struck me as familiar, but that was hardly surprising given the lengths he'd gone to, to conceal his identity.

When I was sure he'd gone deeper into the park, I made my move.

Clambering back to my feet, I jumped over the operation booth's barrier and sprinted at top speed back to the entrance. I had no plans beyond getting the hell out of the park. Maybe I could go back to the wrecked G Wagen. Surely someone would come along and find it sooner or later. Even if I just stood on the road and flagged someone down, I'd be better off. Anything had to be better than hanging around The Laughing Clown waiting to be made into a skin suit.

Skin suits frequently featured in my nightmares.

The lights came into sight, and hope soared inside me, but something crashed heavily in the direction I'd come from. I startled and whirled around on instinct. My nerves totally frayed as I tried to see what had just happened, but I found nothing amiss. Bats flapped frantically out of the big top, so I could only assume something had fallen over—or been pushed—inside there.

Chest heaving and heart pounding, I started running again.

Right into a black-clad man and a deadly sharp blade.

So sharp, in fact, that I didn't even register the pain until he pulled it out of my stomach and held it up to the light. I gasped, pain rendering me speechless as I clasped my hands to the wound on my abdomen. But my gaze remained glued to the blade. That blade that now dripped with my blood…but would have been a pretty red steel even while clean.

I knew that blade.

It was Archer's.

"No," I whimpered, my heart squeezing painfully as my blood dripped from that distinctive red butterfly blade and onto the dark concrete. "No, no, no, not you."

Not waiting around to check if they were playing a prank—the freely bleeding stab wound in my stomach had cleared that right up—I took off running again.

He grabbed for me but narrowly missed as I ducked under his arm and took off into the darkness of the park once more. Tears stung my eyes again, dissolving my mascara and making it hard to see, but my desire to live was strong. Keeping one hand on my wound, I swiped the other over my face and carried on.

I needed to hide. Hiding was my only chance. There was no way I could outrun him now. Or them? Were they all in on this? It would explain how he'd got in front of me so fast.

My stomach rolled, bile rising in my throat as betrayal burned through me. I wanted to scream. I wanted to break down and cry and feel goddamn sorry for myself and all the crappy breaks I'd been dealt in life. But those were luxuries reserved for the living— something I might not be much longer if I didn't fucking *hide*.

My bare feet pounded the hard ground, but I barely felt it. The wound in my side radiated agonizing pain in a way that made me lightheaded and nauseous, and cold sweat was forming on my skin. I knew the signs of shock all too well, but I couldn't give in. I couldn't give up. I'd fought too damn hard to give in now.

I made a beeline for the pavilion, my pink hair streaming behind me as I ran. There was no time to worry about what a target it made me, though. I was more concerned with the blood trail I was inevitably leaving.

Just as I approached the pavilion, a black-clad figure jumped out from behind a hut full of moldy stuffed animals. He grabbed my arm in a bruising grip, and I shrieked.

I swung at him, using my blood-coated fist to punch him in the face with every ounce of fear and rage boiling inside me.

A masculine shout erupted from him. He dropped my arm to clutch at his face and I was gone. Once inside the pavilion, I slowed my pace. It was a hell of a lot darker inside, and I didn't want to trip over something and break an ankle. Ducking behind a thick black drape, I took a moment to pause and lean against the wall. My chest heaved as my breath came in gasps, and my head was swimming. Fuck hiding, I needed a hospital. I pressed my hand back over the wound in my side and prayed Archer's knife hadn't hit anything important. It couldn't have, right? Otherwise I wouldn't still be functioning.

Medical professional, I was not. I added that to my mental list of useful things to study if I ever made it out of the damn Laughing Clown alive.

When no footsteps followed me inside the pavilion, I silently continued on. I made my way through the stacked-up chairs and tables—this had once served as a dining area—and slipped out the kitchen exit.

From there, I could see the west gate of the park. Maybe if I could make it that far… They surely couldn't have every exit covered. Even if they did, I had to try.

There was no time for me to hesitate. If I stayed put, I'd likely bleed to death before they found me and killed me, so I sucked a deep breath and bolted.

My feet were damn near silent on the hard concrete, and I'd made it halfway to the gate when a shadow moved under the moonlight near the fence. A scream tried to escape, but I clamped my lips shut and pasted myself to the wall of a toilet block. The shadows covered me, for the most part, and I just had to hope it was enough.

I'd barely been there half a minute when a warm hand grabbed my wrist, yanking me backward into the restrooms while another hand sealed over my lips, stifling the noise of my screams.

"Shhh," a familiar voice hissed in my ear. "MK, shush; stop screaming. It's me. It's Kody."

Tension wracked my body and fear clouded my brain. He was in on it.

"I'm going to let you go, okay?" he whispered directly into my ear, his grip on me all too reminiscent of the first time we'd met. What the fuck was he playing at? Was this all one big hilarious game to them? Because I wasn't laughing.

Far from it.

"Holy shit," he exclaimed in a hushed whisper as he let me go, "Baby, you're bleeding. Where are you hurt?"

I shook my head, my own terror holding me speechless. My hand still covered my side, but it was slippery with blood and my head was becoming increasingly hazy. Still, I backed away from Kody, watching him for any sign of a weapon.

"Babe, why are you looking at me like that? You're hurt! We need to get you help." He seemed so genuinely concerned, it fucking broke me. How could he do this? Wasn't it exciting enough to stalk and stab a girl anymore? They needed to play with my emotions too?

"S-stay away," I managed to grit out, holding my free hand out like I could possibly ward off an attack from a guy Kody's size. "Stay away fr-from m-me, Kody."

His eyes widened, and his lips parted in shock. I guess he hadn't realized I was on to them. Stupid Archer should have used a more nondescript blade; then maybe I would have fallen for this innocent, caring act.

"MK, babe, I'm really worried. We need to get you help." He was speaking to me in low, hushed tones, but I wasn't listening. Stumbling over the lip of the restroom, I turned and found Steele standing some thirty feet away. Close to the exit gate where I'd just seen a black-clad killer.

"No," I sobbed, my heart officially in shreds. "No, this can't be happening. This can't..." I broke off with a gut-wrenching sob, falling to my knees as the strength in my legs gave out. The world was spinning faster than if I were on a Tilt-A-Whirl for real, and the last thing I saw as my head hit the concrete was Archer's gorgeous blue eyes as he crouched beside me.

"Don't worry, Princess. We've got you now."

BONUS SCENE
RIOT NIGHT

Kody

Usually when my best friend was in the octagon, his fight held my whole focus. I watched every move, taking mental notes about how the fight was progressing, how Archer's opponent was striking, and formulating the best plan to take them down. Every now and then I barked out strategic changes. We'd worked together long enough that he followed my instructions without question. We were a team, and he trusted my judgment.

Tonight, though, I couldn't concentrate. How could I, when there was a gang war brewing right under our noses and we'd been strong-armed into providing a distraction?

"I've got a bad feeling," Steele muttered beside me, scanning the crowd.

Shouts and jeers went up around us, and from the corner of my eye I caught how Arch slammed his opponent into the mat. He had this handled already without my help.

"No shit," I agreed, running a hand over my hair. "I've had a bad feeling ever since Zane forced the issue in the first place." It didn't help that everyone was dressed for Halloween. Everywhere I looked, there were creepy clowns, zombies, and vampires.

Steele nudged me with his elbow. "There's Cass. Maybe he knows something…"

I grunted, following his line of sight to the Reapers' second in charge. The tall, tattoo-covered gangster—who'd once been like an older brother to us—lifted his chin in our direction. "Of course he knows. He knows everything Zane is up to."

"Still, worth a try," Steele replied with an uneasy shrug, already moving away from our position and toward Cass.

More roaring cheers rose from the crowd, and I glanced into the octagon to find Arch closing in for the win. His opponent was barely hanging in there, and once Arch got his arm under the guy's chin, it'd be done.

"Finally," I muttered to myself, impatient to get the fuck out of the old big top. Circuses were the shit of nightmares. The tension was making my skin crawl, and we'd all been so fucking distracted lately that I had no idea what Zane was planning. Nothing good, though.

The crowd around me screamed, making my ears ring. It was nearly over, and then we could get the fuck out of here and—

Bang!

A gunshot rang out, echoing through the big top. People everywhere ducked, and more than one went for their own gun. Shit. Talk about lighting a match in a gas chamber.

Sure enough, more gunshots followed the first, and I gritted my teeth as I made for the cage.

"Arch! Move your ass!" I roared. My best friend was still punching the shit out of his opponent like he hadn't even noticed the all-out gang war that'd erupted around us. Whatever the bloodied fighter on the mat had said, it'd pissed Archer off something wicked because I needed to bark his name twice more before he shook off the haze of bloodlust.

The utter confusion on his face when he ripped off his Halloween mask and met my gaze was infuriating.

"Get your ass out of the cage, idiot!" I shouted. "Look around!"

The deafening pops of more bullets flying *finally* seemed to register, and he climbed the side of the cage like a scorched monkey to get out in a flash, leaving the other man unconscious on the mat.

"Steele?" he asked, not wasting unnecessary questions.

I shrugged. "He'll be fine. Let's get the fuck out before we get mixed up in Reaper and Wraith bullshit."

Arch just grunted his agreement, leading the way through the complete and utter chaos that was the big top. Everywhere I looked, there was either a pair of brawling gangsters or terrified bystanders desperately trying to get to safety without being shot themselves. It was a fucking mess.

We ignored all of it, stepping over injured people and broken chairs to make our way out, but amidst the screams and gunshots, I overheard something that made my blood run cold. Reacting on instinct, I grabbed Arch's arm to tell him to wait, frowning as I searched for the owner of the voice.

"...I'm not bullshitting," the same voice shouted, edged with near-hysterical laughter. I spotted a skinhead Wraith and redirected closer. "Got her right in the fucking chest, bro. Between those perky, little tits. Pow. Princess Danvers is *dead*, and I pulled the trigger." He barked laughter, and it was the last sound he ever made.

Archer always held back in the octagon. He had to. But not now...not when this prick was bragging about *shooting Madison Kate*. Oh man. That punk was dead before he even hit the ground, but it didn't stop Archer following up with several more vicious blows to appease his own fury.

The dead man's friend drew his gun, but I was quicker. His lifeless body dropped with my bullet in his forehead and Arch scowled in my direction.

"They're lying," he snarled. "She's not here."

I swallowed hard, dread pooling in my belly. "I fucking hope she's not."

Arch lurched to his feet, glancing around us. I tipped my head in the direction I'd seen the Wraiths coming from, setting off that way. Maybe they were full of shit, but there was no way we could leave without knowing for sure.

"Hey!" Steele called out as he jogged over to us from a mess of brawling Reapers and Wraiths. "Exit's that way. Where are we—" He cut off abruptly as he tripped on a body.

"Get up," Arch growled. "We need to—"

"Oh, *fuck*!" Steele yelped. "Arch, get over here!"

Another stride closer and I could see what he was panicked about. The body he'd tripped over was a woman—no, a girl—with a spill of pale hair and a pool of blood spread around her lifeless body. She wore a tiny plaid skirt that was unmistakably the Shadow Grove Prep uniform and ripped fishnet stockings. Either she'd been dressing as a Shadow Prep girl for Halloween, or—

Archer leaned down and gently placed a shaking hand on the dead girl's shoulder, rolling her over.

I'd seen a lot of blood and death in my years, so it didn't often shake me, but this girl…this was different.

"It's not her," Archer announced in a cold voice. "It's not her." He said it twice, like he needed to hear it out loud again. I didn't fucking blame him because the girl *looked* like the princess of Shadow Grove, but he was right that it wasn't her. Just some poor unfortunate girl.

I released my held breath and tapped Arch on the shoulder. "Let's get the fuck out of here, bro. We don't need this shit on our shoulders."

Neither of my friends argued with that sentiment, and we cut a quick path out of the big top. We'd left our bikes on the south side of the park, away from the main parking lots so we wouldn't get caught in the crowds, but now there were panicked, drunk, costumed dickheads all through the old amusement park. Worse still, half of them were armed, and their gang leaders had apparently taken the leash off.

"You little bitch!" a familiar voice bellowed as we started down a mostly empty "street" of the park.

The sound rocked through us all, and Arch—who'd been leading the way—stopped dead in his tracks.

"Zane?" Steele asked quietly. Archer nodded once, his eyes scanning the darkness ahead. "I'll check the next street over." He slipped away from us silently, drawing his gun from the small of his back as he went.

I did the same but stayed with Archer, who was still shirtless and barefoot. The two of us moved forward with caution, searching for the leader of the Reapers…and for who he was screaming at.

"Hold up," I murmured as we approached a small group of guys drunk off their asses beside a sideshow hut. They'd clearly been there awhile, because beer bottles were scattered everywhere and the whole lot of them were so wasted, they probably hadn't noticed the gunshots. None of them even glanced my way when I strode right up and grabbed two of their discarded hoodies. "Thanks," I said with a smirk, slipping one on and flipping up the hood.

The other got tossed to Arch and he followed my example, zipping it up and hiding his face with the hood. The three of us had far too many enemies roaming the park to wander around feeling bulletproof. Better we remain anonymous if we planned to get out with our skin intact.

Zane's enraged shout echoed through the night again, and we hurried in the direction his voice had come from. Something had rattled the Reaper leader badly enough to cause him to lose his cool, and I for one wanted to know what it was… An enemy of my enemy was my friend, after all.

In the distance, a streak of pink hair and long legs sprinted across the cross street. I dismissed it as just another panicked spectator trying to get out of the dark, frankly creepy-as-fuck amusement park. Until we heard Zane again, that was.

"Fuck! Stop running, Madison Kate!"

Archer didn't say a word, but he didn't have to. I was right behind him as he took off sprinting, cutting through the sideshow booths to the next street over just in time to see the pink-haired girl duck into the fun house. Of all the fucking places.

It was a huge building and she'd darted into the far end, so Archer and I busted through one of the service entrances at the back. Hopefully we could catch her before Zane did.

Neither of us spoke, listening to the frantic sound of her high-heeled boots on hollow floors and trying to head her off before she ran in circles right back to Zane. Luckily, we weren't *unfamiliar* with this fun house—having brought Reaper prospects here previously to scare the shit out of them—so we had a rough idea where she was in relation to us. Once we reached the mirror maze, Arch and I split up. He went left, toward the spinning tunnel covered in UV patterns, while I headed right…toward the pop-out clowns. *Fuck.*

Irritation pricked at my skin and my jaw tightened. What the fuck was this girl even *doing* here tonight? She didn't belong on this side of town, and this exact scenario was evidence why.

In a rush of footsteps, the girl in question rounded a corner, narrowly ducked a spring-loaded clown, then practically fell right into my arms. What luck.

She screamed. Loud. Had this chick literally never watched a slasher movie in her entire life? Way to alert the bad guys to your position…dumbass. Annoyed, I clapped my hand over her mouth to muffle the noise, and the little witch elbowed me for my efforts.

Cute. I was used to taking hits from Archer, so that bony, little elbow wasn't going to do *shit* to move me. I grunted slightly as I lifted her, pulling her backward to where I knew there was a hidden compartment behind the mirrors. It was where the actors would hide while the park was operational, and right now, it'd keep us safe until Zane gave up and left. Or it would if she would *stop fucking thrashing.*

"I don't have the time or patience for this, Madison Kate," Zane bellowed from within the fun house.

The girl in my arms stiffened. Shocked. She must have thought I was Zane and just realized I was, in fact, saving her pretty princess ass. Then she tried to stomp on my foot with her spike heels... so I had to assume she wasn't feeling *saved* right now. I was ready for her when she tried to slam her heel into my balls. Predictable.

"What the fuck?" I muttered, seriously questioning my friendships. Still, I tightened my grip, trying to reassure my captive that I wasn't letting her go.

"Shut it," Arch whispered, appearing out of nowhere and silently pulling the mirror door closed behind him. With three of us in the closet, it was a tight squeeze. "Keep her quiet."

"Easier said than done," I snapped back as quietly as I could. "Fucking bitch just tried to nail my balls." Whether she managed to or not, the intent was there. Rude as hell. Then she started thrashing again, and I clenched my teeth to keep from cursing as I restrained the wild creature in my arms.

"Quit it," Archer hissed, leaning down to ensure she heard him. If anything, that enraged her more, and she tried to say something from beneath my hand. Woman had a death wish or something.

"Madison Kate," Zane called out again, clearly not giving up so easily. "I know you're still here. I can practically smell your fear. Where are you hiding, little mouse?"

All the fight drained out of her in a flash, but Archer hadn't noticed. "Gag her or something. Just do whatever it takes to keep her quiet and out of fucking sight." Then he slipped back out of the hiding spot, silently pushing the mirror door closed most of the way. It remained open about an inch or two, letting sound and a tiny sliver of light inside. It seemed to calm the terrified girl down a little, so I released her foot from where I'd held it captive between my knees and relaxed my grip ever so slightly.

"You're not going to scream, right?" I asked, whispering the

311

words directly into her ear. "If you scream, we can't help you. You're on your own." Surely she was smart enough to work that out.

Arch moved somewhere in the mirror room, his shadow darkening the crack of light for a moment, and the girl inhaled like she was about to scream. I tightened my grip over her face, ensuring minimal sound would escape if she did, but she seemed to swallow the noise at the last moment. Her whole body remained coiled like a whip, though.

"Just fucking chill, Madison Kate," I hissed, terrified myself that she'd give us away. We weren't ready to go up against Zane yet, but that's what this would come to if we were found.

Zane had found Archer now, and they were speaking, but I didn't listen to the words. I was too focused on the girl trembling in my arms, literally shaking with fear. How could I help her? How the hell could I reassure her that we'd keep her safe when the big bad wolf was right outside our hiding place? She was too scared and irrational to release, I could tell. She'd do something stupid.

"Whoa, calm the fuck down," I whispered when she jerked violently against me. Something Zane had said, maybe? Her breathing was speeding up, though, her inhales becoming short and sharp through that delicate little nose like she was hyperventilating. Ah crap. She *was* hyperventilating. "Shit. Hey, hey, stop that; you're going to give us away. Seriously, babe, calm the fuck down."

Then again, maybe if she fainted, she'd be easier to deal with…

Nah, Arch would murder me. Better to try and calm her down. Somehow.

She turned her head under my grip, dislodging my hand just enough to whisper, "*I'm claustrophobic.*"

Fuck. *Fuck.* And I'd dragged her into a small, dark space and had my big old paw covering her mouth. No wonder she was freaking out. As quickly as possible, I removed my hand, letting her drag a shuddering breath between her lips. I wanted her calm, but I couldn't risk her bolting out there, so I kept my arm tight around her waist with her thin wrists pinned together in my grip.

"Fuck, I'm sorry. Just stay quiet a few more moments. Just until Zane is gone." I kept my voice low and calm, attempting to soothe the trembling girl. "Trust me, you don't want him catching up with you. Not tonight."

"I know," she whispered, trying to sound tough even as her trembling intensified. "Why do you think I was fucking running?" Her breathing quickened again, and then she swallowed hard. "Um, who are you? Do we know each other?"

I huffed a quiet laugh, realizing I'd used her name. Smart of her to pick up on that even through her panic, but I sure as shit wasn't going to go spilling all our secrets. "Everyone knows *you*, Madison Kate. I like the new hair by the way. Very eye-catching. Edgy." It helped us spot her sprinting through the night, that was for damn sure.

"It's temporary," she murmured.

I hoped not. It was unexpected, and I kind of liked that…but since she was the princess of Shadow Grove, it'd probably be professionally stripped and returned to prissy blond by morning. "Of course it is." Though her panting had slowed and she no longer shook like a chihuahua in the snow, so the distraction was working. "Are you okay now?"

Instantly her body tensed up against my chest, and I mentally kicked myself for reminding her. *Dumbass move, Kody.* The distraction had worked because it had taken her mind *off* her panic, and I'd just slapped it back in her face. She shook her head with a sharp jerk, and I released her wrists. Distraction was key to calming her down, and I was generally pretty good at distracting women.

"It won't be much longer," I reassured her softly, trailing my fingers down her bare upper arm. "Just focus on something else." Her skin pebbled under my touch, and I smirked to myself. *Still got it.* When I reached her wrist, I started again. She shivered, but it was a good kind of shiver. She liked my touch, and I liked that she liked it.

"This is your idea of a distraction?" she whispered back, her voice breathy. Sexy.

I didn't answer her, instead lowering my face to brush an innocent kiss against the side of her neck. I was playing with fire, no question about it, and it was a dumb-fuck move...but I couldn't seem to help myself. Then she gave a tiny moan, and I had to bite my cheek to keep from spinning her around and kissing her properly.

"Shh..." I breathed, desperate to regain some of my control. And yet, I found myself kissing her neck again, even more deliberately than before. Fuck. I was in over my head.

"What the fuck are you doing?" Archer snapped, suddenly filling the doorway.

Whoops, I hadn't even noticed him open the mirror door. "What you told me to, bro. Keeping Princess Danvers from screaming." Holding my friend's furious gaze, I pressed another kiss to Madison Kate's neck. "At least not in fear, anyway."

The look Archer gave me could have killed a lesser man. His jaw tight, he reached out and grabbed Madison Kate's wrist, wrenching her out of my arms.

Message received, Arch...loud and clear. She isn't mine to hold...yet.

READ ON FOR A PEEK AT THE NEXT BOOK IN THE MADISON KATE SERIES

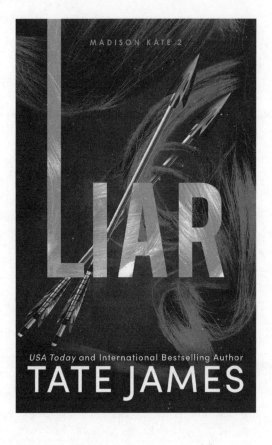

CHAPTER 1

Kody

It'd been two full weeks since Halloween.

Two weeks since I'd finally kissed Madison Kate the way I'd been wanting to for an entire year.

Two weeks since she'd run from us, crashed my car, then suffered a brutal attack at The Laughing Clown.

Two weeks since she'd looked at me with such horror on her face while blood dripped from her fingers. Pure, undiluted terror in her gorgeous violet-blue eyes.

Two weeks since I'd almost lost her forever.

Then again, maybe I had…

"Why isn't she home yet?" I grumbled aloud, looking at the time on my watch for what seemed like the hundredth time in the space of an hour. "You said she was getting discharged at ten, right?" I looked over at Arch, and he just glared back at me. His face was still showing the splotchy purple and green bruises from the ass kicking he'd taken in the octagon last week. Served him fucking right for fighting while distracted.

"You know that's what the hospital said," he replied in a growly, irritated tone. Well, fuck him. It was his fault we weren't there to pick her up ourselves. We should be.

It'd been two weeks since Madison Kate had collapsed at Steele's feet, that gut-wrenching expression of fear on her face. Two weeks since we'd loaded her unconscious body into our stolen vehicle and rushed her to the hospital, covered in blood from her head wound and the deep stab in her abdomen.

It'd been one week since she'd woken up. Since she'd seen Archer sitting beside her bed and *screamed*.

That sound still chilled me when I heard it in my dreams. She'd been hysterical, and the nurses had ended up sedating her again. Arch had left the room and not returned once. Not that he could have... We'd all been stricken from her permitted visitors list and no number of bribes or threats had changed that.

Madison Kate had accused us of attacking her. When the sedatives had worn off, the police had spoken with her. She'd pointed the finger at the three of us. Except, we'd already been questioned and cleared. Par for the course when three guys turn up to a hospital in the middle of the night with a blood-soaked heiress.

The police in charge of her case had assured us that they'd communicated this to her. But as the days had ticked by and the silence stretched, our unease had built.

"She's not coming back here," Steele said in a quiet voice. His fingertips drummed on the arm of the sofa, and I could tell he was itching to play again. To compose. But in some fucked-up self-punishment, he was holding himself back.

"You don't know that," Archer snapped. He was pissed off, and I didn't blame him. "She's stubborn, like a splinter. She'll come back just to be an infuriating bitch and stand her ground here in *her* house."

Steele shook his head, giving Arch the kind of pitying look that was likely to get him punched. "You can only hope, bro. I'm going for a run. All this waiting around is getting me fucking anxious."

He left the room with a heavy, defeated sigh. Neither Arch nor I said anything to stop him either. What the fuck could we even say? Steele was hurting, that much was obvious. He'd given MK space after her stalker had threatened him, but now he was regretting all the unfinished business between them.

So was I, for that matter. I was regretting all kinds of unfinished business with MK, and it was driving me crazy.

Arch? Who the fuck knew what was going on inside his head. He still maintained his delusional opinion that MK was some kind of spoiled brat that deserved a few hard knocks in life. But then... why'd he sit beside her bed around the clock while she was unconscious? Why'd he lose his debut UFC fight after she'd woken up screaming that morning?

"Maybe we should call the hospital again," I suggested, feeling utterly hopeless. She should have been home by now.

Arch rolled his eyes and sighed, like I was being a pest, but he still pulled out his phone and hit redial. He placed the phone to his ear, and I tried really hard not to fidget while waiting. I knew the drill by now. He'd have to speak to the right person to get information, now that we'd been removed from her list. It could take a few moments.

Steele's feet thumped on the stairs as he jogged back down, and I went to intercept him before he left the house.

"Running isn't going to fix it," I told him, leaning on the wall as he sat on the stairs to pull on his sneakers. It'd turned freezing in the past week, so he was dressed for the cold in sweatpants, a hoodie, and a puffer vest.

"Fix what?" he replied, in total denial. His fingers trembled slightly as he tied his laces, and I sighed.

"That." I indicated to his shaking hands. "You need to go and fucking work on whatever tune is rattling around in your brain. I haven't seen you this bad since..." I trailed off because there was a *line* and I'd just come dangerously close to crossing it.

Steele's face hardened, his eyes tightening. "Thanks for the advice, Kody," he muttered, his voice betraying his anger and frustration at my blunder. "I'll be fine. I'm not… I can't…" He shook his head, his hand clenched. "I'll be fine."

I was inclined to disagree but also wasn't in the mood to argue with him.

"I'll spar with you later if you want," he offered, his hand resting on the door handle. "You don't exactly exude calm right now yourself."

I grimaced, but he was right. I was next-level wound up and anxious. Maybe kicking the shit out of one of my best friends would help. Fuck knows I'd stopped winning against Arch about seven years ago, when he started getting massive.

"Sure," I replied with a sigh. "Sounds good. Just keep your wits about you out there, okay?"

Steele flashed me a cocky grin, lifting his sweatshirt to show me his Glock 19 in a concealed holster. "Let them fucking try me, bro. I've got this."

I snorted a laugh, clapping him on the shoulder. He was probably more dangerous than both Arch and me combined. If MK's stalker really did want to follow through on their threats, they'd get a rude awakening.

"Guys," Archer called out, pausing Steele halfway through the front door. As much as he wanted to act unaffected by MK's silence, he cared. "She was discharged early."

Archer's words were like a blow. "What? Like, earlier this morning? Why isn't she home, then?"

He looked at me with a flat, don't-be-fucking-stupid expression. "No, like three days ago."

My heart pounded a bit too fast. "How? How could they discharge her? Was Samuel—"

"No." Archer shook his head. "No, Samuel and my mom are still in Italy on a yacht with their shitty friends. They're due to return in a few days, but last I spoke to them, Sam had no plans to come back early."

"So how was she discharged early?" Steele demanded. "I thought you—"

"She discharged herself." Archer cut him off, his jaw clenched and the vein in his temple throbbing. "She's a legal adult, and there's no reason why she can't."

He was right. She didn't need a direct family member to discharge her if the doctors declared her well enough to make that choice for herself. Stubborn girl.

I asked the question we were all thinking. "Where is she, then?"

Archer's eyes hardened further. "I have no idea."

"How is *that* possible?" Steele challenged him, and Archer's fist clenched at his side. I'd bet money he was thinking about punching Steele right in the face.

Stepping between them, I tried to diffuse the tension. "Back down, dude," I told Steele, giving him a hard glare. He scowled back at me but folded his arms and took a step outside to create a bit of space.

I turned back to Archer. "What *do* we know?"

"Just that she discharged herself and was picked up by an Uber. I'll find her, though. Even if it just helps you two stop sulking around here like your puppy got run over." He cocked a brow at Steele and me like *we* were the ones sulking.

I scoffed a laugh, shaking my head. "Right. You're doing it for us."

Steele muttered something under his breath, then gave us a tight smile. "I'm out. Catch you losers later."

His breath fogged in front of him as he flipped his hood up, then jogged down the front steps and across the fresh dusting of snow on the driveway.

"We need to find MK before Steele slides back into that dark place again," I commented quietly as both Arch and I watched our friend jog down the long driveway.

Archer grunted a noise of agreement, his arms folded over his chest. "I'll find her," he said with total confidence, "but she's not going to willingly stay here."

He went back into the house, leaving me standing there shivering and mentally cursing the infuriating girl who'd walked into our lives a year ago and set off a fucking pipe bomb.

Archer was right. She wasn't coming home. Not if she had any choice in the matter.

So…we'd simply have to take her choice away.

After all, we could do that.

Or Archer could.

CHAPTER 2

Madison Kate

It'd been three days since I'd discharged myself from Shadow Grove General Hospital. Three days since I'd taken Bree's offer of help… and her credit card.

Now I was doing something that could possibly be my stupidest decision to date. Or hell, who knows? Maybe it'd be the best thing I'd ever done for myself.

My Uber pulled away from the curb, leaving me standing out in front of a rough kind of bar, deep within what used to be West Shadow Grove. It looked identical to how I'd seen it just a few weeks earlier, when some deeply repressed memories had resurfaced.

My new phone vibrated in the pocket of my jeans, and I pulled it out to answer, all while stalling what I'd been on my way to do.

"Hey, girl," I said, shivering despite the warmth of my leather jacket. "What's up?"

Bree was the *only* one with my new number. I'd have happily not had a phone at all, but she'd talked me into it from a safety perspective.

"Your boys were just over here," she replied, and my stomach lurched. I'd known they'd work it out sooner or later—that I'd discharged myself and wasn't coming home. But that'd been quicker than I'd given them credit for. "Don't worry," she continued in a rush. "I didn't tell them anything. I didn't even lie because I *don't* know where you are. Why won't you tell me, again?"

I snickered. "For that exact reason. They'd get it out of you somehow. Fuck, they've probably already worked out I'm using your credit card, and I'll find them on my doorstep when I get back."

Bree made a thoughtful sound. "So you have a doorstep, then? Interesting."

I laughed again. "Idiot. You know I'm staying in a hotel, and it wouldn't be hard for you to check your credit card statement."

"I know," she replied, "but I won't. You trusted me when you had no one else to ask, and I won't let you down again, MK. You're my bitch."

"Stop it," I muttered. "You're making me blush with all this emotional crap."

"Jesus, you've got the emotional range of a damn cucumber sometimes, girl. Anyway, I wanted to let you know that they're on your trail. Want me to throw down any false leads?" Bree sounded far too into that idea, and I didn't have the heart to tell her it was pointless.

"Go for it," I replied instead. "I've got to go; I'm about to meet with an old family friend. I'll call you later, okay?"

"You better," she grumbled, "and I want to know which of those three bastards you're fucking, because guys don't act all caveman possessive like they just did when there's no penetration involved. Fact."

I had nothing to say back to that, so I just ended the call and slipped the phone back into my pocket. Her words had stirred up a whole pile of conflicting emotions, though.

I'd slept with Steele, and it had been incredible.

I'd made out with both Kody *and* Archer...

But was that enough for them to go "caveman possessive" like Bree said? She was likely exaggerating.

Then again, why did I care? A week ago, I'd thought they'd tried to kill me.

I still kind of believed they had, despite the evidence to the contrary.

Shoving those thoughts aside, I focused on the task at hand. My freshly colored pink hair was up in a messy bun, but loose tendrils tickled my face as I made my way across the parking lot. Motorcycles dominated the lot, but there were plenty of old beaters there too. I was certainly a long way from home.

I pushed through the main door and hesitated only a second before making my way to the bar. Every damn eye in there seemed to follow me as I picked my way across the room, but I kept my shoulders back and my head high.

"You lost, girl?" the middle-aged woman behind the bar asked me. Her brow held a crease of concern, but I shook my head.

"I'm looking to speak with someone," I told her with iron threaded into my tone. "I was told I might find him here at this time of day."

The bartender cocked a brow at me, clearly curious. "Oh yeah? Who's that, then?"

"Zane D'Ath," I replied. "Tell him Deb's daughter is here."

I waited for only a few minutes before the bartender ushered me through the kitchen and into a large back room filled with rough, tattooed guys and a handful of girls. Apparently the public side of the bar was exactly that: public. This side was all Reapers.

"Your funeral, girlie," the bartender muttered, closing the door again once I was inside. Shutting me in with the hungry wolves.

Shit. Maybe this was dumb.

Still, I couldn't back out now. So I hardened my expression and crossed the room to where a familiar face stared back at me.

"Madison Kate Danvers," Zane purred, raking his gaze over me and making a sound of appreciation. "You grew up."

I tucked my hands into my back pockets and gave him an unimpressed stare. "No shit. That's what time generally does to a person. The last time you saw me when I *wasn't* running away would have been, what, eight years ago? Seven?"

A cold smile curved his lips, tugging at the tattoos below his right eye. "Something like that." He stared back at me for a long, tense moment. There wasn't a lot of familial resemblance between him and Archer. For one thing, Zane was a fraction of Archer's size and all slim, wiry muscles where his little brother was bulk and hardened brawn. But it was there in his eyes, those same ice-blue eyes that seemed to cut like daggers.

"Why'd you come here, Madison Kate?" he asked when it became clear I wasn't going to say anything first. It was his kingdom, after all. "Seems like a real stupid move for a girl with your... connections." His lips twitched over that last word, like he was making fun of something.

I scowled. "If you mean the fact that your brother is living in my house, I have no control over that matter. I tried to get rid of him; he wouldn't go."

"*Your* house?" Zane repeated, that mocking smile pulling at his lips.

My glare flattened. "My father's house. Whatever."

He said nothing, his cold blue eyes not leaving my face for even a second, but then he nodded. "Look, I'm going to cut you the benefit of the doubt here, kid—seeing as you're clearly so deep in the dark you couldn't find your own cunt. Ask whatever burning questions made you put your life on the line, then get the fuck out of my bar."

A vaguely familiar guy with neck tats made a sound of protest,

325

pushing the girl in his lap to the floor and slamming his beer glass down on the table.

"Boss," he started, but Zane shut him up with a sharp look.

"Actually, Skunk," Zane said, and the pieces clicked into place. Skunk. This was the guy Kody and Steele had beaten the shit out of a month ago at Bree's party. "You can serve as a visual example to Madison Kate of what happens when we wander into territory uninvited." Zane got up from his chair, dropping his own beer onto a table, and slouched his way over to Skunk. He kicked the table in front of Skunk out of the way, revealing two long plaster casts covering his legs from knee to ankle.

I gasped. Not out of shock—I already knew what had happened to him—but because I'd somehow managed to forget about that night in all the madness that'd followed.

"Here, little girl. Take a look at this." Zane yanked Skunks T-shirt up, revealing angry, purple-red scarring across his chest. I stared hard at the letters that had been cut into his flesh and made a mental note to stop pissing Archer off.

Strike One.

"This is what happens when my guys accidentally wander into my little brother's territory. So what do you think might happen to you, strutting straight into the Reapers' headquarters?" Zane released Skunk and took a few menacing steps toward me. He casually flipped out a butterfly knife that looked so much like Archer's I did a double take.

"She already knows, boss," Skunk answered for me, his voice a sneering growl of anger and resentment. "She was there when they did this to me."

Zane's brows shot up. "Was she, now?"

"I forgot until just now. Head injuries will do that to ya."

He glared daggers at me, and I skipped my gaze back to Zane.

AUTHOR'S NOTE

Hey reader! If you've made it this far, you probably just finished the first book in Madison Kate's story.

So first, thanks for reading! You rock my world. Seriously.

Second, uh, I feel like it's probably the author's duty of care to do a quick health check here. You okay? That ending was a bit mean, huh? I'd like to take this opportunity to blame that rude cliff-hanger entirely on my co-author who...ah, shit. I didn't have a co-author on this. Well then, ahem, I guess I'm to blame here.

Uh...sorry? If it helps at all, I'm working on a super-strict quick release schedule for this series so you won't have to wait six million years to see what happens next!

Anyway, moving on. *Hate* is my first solo release in almost eight months. That seemed totally insane to me when I worked it out the other day! I asked myself, what the fuck have I been doing in that time? Then a friend gently reminded me that I put out four cowritten books, cohosted BABE (a pretty epic book-signing event in Sydney, if I do say so myself), I kept my babies alive that whole time (winner), but most importantly...my mum died.

It's been six weeks today, as I write this, and it's still at the stage where it doesn't totally seem real. I'm still struggling to fully comprehend the fact that she's not just overseas like she has been most of my adult life. It's no longer a matter of going a few weeks without talking, but always having her *there* when I needed to talk or send pics of my kids or check in and hear about her new hobbies or adventures. She's gone, and I *can't* do any of those things, but I'm still finding it hard to make myself understand that. Except now. Now, as I finish writing my first solo book that she hasn't read… it feels real.

My mum was the first person who ever read my work. She had no idea what "reverse harem" was but went to the internet to educate herself. She never judged me for the messed-up shit I wrote. She never questioned why I felt such a burning need to pour myself into words when I had a four-month-old baby at home. She just avidly supported me, asked questions about plot and characters, gave me subtle reminders not to make everyone too perfect, and quietly chose her favorites in all the countless book boyfriends I've written since that first book.

So, today it hit me. This book is the first book my mum hasn't read. She doesn't know the characters or the world or any of it. And that fucking kills me. I don't know if this would have passed her inspection. I don't know if she would have chosen a favorite or if she might have made me go and change any scenes or interactions. I don't know anything that she might have said in this awkward stage between finishing a book and releasing it into the world. So I'm just crossing my fingers and hoping with my whole broken heart that this book, and these characters, lives up to her standards.

I've always written my books with the goal in mind that I want my mum to love each one more than the last. I wanted her to always see me improving and evolving as an author, and to make her proud of her law school dropout turned bartender daughter. She's not here to offer me that validation anymore, but I've already come so far that now I have you! My readers. So while this new series release is bittersweet for me, I hope you enjoyed it. Madison

Kate and her boys have been consuming my brain lately, and it's a relief to finally be able to share them with you.

I'm leaking profusely from the eyeballs now, so I'm going to go put on an orange dress that I hate but mum loved and get red-wine drunk in the marigold garden.

This book, like all my books past and present, is for you, Mum. I love you and I'll never forget all you've done for me.

ABOUT THE AUTHOR

Tate James is a *USA Today* bestselling author of contemporary romance and romantic suspense, with occasional forays into fantasy, paranormal romance, and urban fantasy. She was born and raised in Aotearoa (New Zealand) but now lives in Australia with her husband and their adorable crotchfruit.

She is a lover of books, booze, cats, and coffee and is most definitely not a morning person. Tate is a bit too sarcastic, swears far too much for polite society, and definitely tells too many dirty jokes.